EIGHT WILL FALL

EIGHT

WILL

FALL

SARAH HARIAN

HENRY HOLT AND COMPANY

NEW YORK

Henry Holt and Company, *Publishers since 1866*
Henry Holt® is a registered trademark of Macmillan Publishing Group, LLC

120 Broadway, New York, NY 10271 • fiercereads.com

Copyright © 2019 by Alloy Entertainment

Library of Congress Cataloging-in-Publication Data is available.

ISBN 978-1-250-19664-4 (hardcover) / ISBN 978-1-250-75036-5 (Fairyloot edition)

Our books may be purchased in bulk for promotional, educational, or business use.
Please contact your local bookseller or the Macmillan Corporate and Premium Sales Department at
(800) 221-7945 ext. 5442 or by email at MacmillanSpecialMarkets@macmillan.com.

FIRST EDITION, 2019 / DESIGNED BY KATIE KLIMOWICZ
Printed in the United States of America

1 2 3 4 5 6 7 8 9 10

For Jesse, my calm in chaos

ONE

Beneath Larkin's glowing lantern, luminite shimmered like fish scales in the darkness of Ethera Mine. Her heart jolted as she unearthed a vein as wide as her thumb. It was the most valuable mineral in all of Demura Isle.

Larkin brushed a few dark curls from her brow and shut her eyes, searching for a shift in emotion within the other miners further down the tunnel. But their pickaxes continued to sing against stone. They weren't close enough for her to sense, which meant they weren't close enough to catch a glimpse of what she'd found.

The sensation of Garran's surprise ignited her spine, and she peeled one eye open to see her little brother lowering his axe and wiping the sweat from his face. "Sweet Ilona."

Larkin pressed a finger to her lips, scowling. Garran knew better than to attract the attention of any greedy thieves. Hells, she'd almost sent a pickaxe through the face of a miner just last week for trying to pinch her ore. She didn't want to fight today. She only wanted to celebrate.

She handed Garran a chisel and wedged her own into the stone crack, striking it with her hammer. The lode crumbled into chunks of hardened clay and mineral.

Larkin grinned at Garran, excitement pulsing through her. They were never this lucky. Too often she left the mine sore, with nothing to prove for her labor. Their mother had used the last of the stone-ground flour this morning. Larkin needed marks, or her family wouldn't eat.

She knelt and reached down. The feeling of Garran's surprise evaporated as her fingers grazed the luminite. She cupped the ore in her hand, the iridescent mineral glimmering. It was as beautiful as it was crippling, suppressing her magic, just as it would suppress the magic of every Empath in the capital.

Hatred for the mineral rose inside her, but Larkin forced herself to remember that she and Garran were fortunate. The presence of luminite should have doused her ability to sense entirely, but the two of them were stronger than the other miners. A *resistance*, her mother called it. Larkin and Garran had inherited the gift from her.

The moment Larkin dropped the ore into her bucket, Garran's amazement came fluttering back. She curled her fingers into her palm and reveled in the thrill as she siphoned his emotion.

Garran grasped her wrist. "Don't you dare." He sounded like their father. Hells, the older he became, the more he looked like their father too, caution ingrained into every one of his soft features. Even his threat was as mild as a lullaby.

"The handle on the bucket is broken." Larkin stole her arm back. "Won't take long to fix it."

"I'll carry it."

"It's my birthday." She smiled defiantly.

"No."

Larkin dropped her hand. Garran was right; magic was as forbidden as luminite was coveted, the mineral drawn from the bowels of the isle to be crushed and smelted and gilded onto every surface in the capital. Protection against the likes of Larkin and her family—Empaths—who could siphon the emotions of others and use them to conjure or destroy.

And yet Garran was also wrong. Larkin knew that no one was watching them, because she was always careful. No miner or guard paced their tunnel.

She could argue this with him a thousand more times and it wouldn't matter, so she chose to change the subject. "Thirty marks?"

Garran dug through the ore. "At least. Canyon rumor has it our benevolent Queen Melay raised the price of luminite today, just for you." He winked at her.

"Just for me?" Larkin clasped her hands.

"She wants you to have a birthday feast."

She gasped dramatically. "Such mercy! What fortune!"

"*Shh*—keep it down." Garran looked over his shoulder. "Next thing I know, you'll be Melay's newest advocate."

Larkin raised an eyebrow. "Never. Cross my heart and spit on Ilona's grave." She pointed at the remainder of the lode. "Shift's about to end. Hurry!"

She and Garran had only gutted half the vein when the bell sounded. Larkin rammed her chisel into the loosened rock and cursed when the falling ore nicked her hand. She examined the wound in the lantern light before wiping her blood-glazed knuckles on her trousers.

Garran tossed the ore into the bucket. "Be careful."

"I'm fine." Larkin grabbed her knapsack and stood. She thought of their sister Vania's glittering joy every time Larkin and Garran brought anything home from the market district. A full bucket was well worth a few cuts and scratches.

Garran covered the bucket with a filthy handkerchief and picked it up, hugging the ore to his chest. Larkin kept an eye on him as they fell in line with the others, worming their way to the mine's main artery. The shallow chambers of Ethera had been picked clean, and miners like Larkin and Garran had been burrowing deeper for years now, the snaking tunnels shored with timber. The line of tired workers stretched endlessly before and behind them. The air stank of salt and sweat. Five years in these mines and the crawl to Ethera's entrance was still as agonizing as the first time. At least Larkin's nightmares of being buried alive had stopped.

To distract herself, Larkin focused on deciphering the swell of emotions surrounding her—the crackling abrasion of Garran's annoyance with the long lines. The miners carrying empty buckets, their disappointment like cold water to glowing steel.

At the conflux of two tunnels, Larkin almost collided with Adina, a girl whose family lived two doors down from them. Dirt and sweat coated Adina's fair skin, clay caked in her feathery hair.

"Any luck?" Adina clutched her own bucket with buoyant delight.

"A bit," said Garran. Larkin sensed his eagerness at seeing Adina and smirked. He jabbed her in the ribs.

"Where are your brothers?" Larkin asked, frowning. Adina was never alone.

Adina's face fell. "They've gone to find Edric."

"Is he well?" Larkin pressed, sensing Adina's worry. Edric was Adina's older brother, who had been reassigned from the mines to one of the farms. Before he left, Edric was a cheerful companion in Ethera, even on days when he found no ore. His smile was a welcome change from the drudgery of the mine.

"Nolaa Farm was destroyed. The cottages are nothing but splinters, like the worst storm you could ever imagine came through. No one can explain it. Most of the harvesters are missing. Edric, and our aunt . . ."

A chill numbed the tips of Larkin's fingers, and she squeezed her hands into fists. Sure, there had been rumors for the past year or so of strange disturbances beyond the city gates—structures crumbling to dust, farmers disappearing. Larkin had heard the stories only through echoing conversation within the mines; workers had picked up word from the farms in the vale. Queen Melay had yet to make an official statement.

But this was real, not a rumor. Edric was someone whom Larkin had shared an axe with. He'd offered her a shoulder when a cart had run over her boot last spring, before he was reassigned.

"I'm so sorry," Larkin whispered. Besides the mines, the farms were the only other place Empaths were sent to toil. Edric could have been someone from her own family. He could have been Garran, or her father.

"My other brothers left this morning to help with the mess and to try to find him," said Adina. "I don't even know if they were able to get a permit to leave the city."

"I'm sure they did." Garran exchanged glances with Larkin. Larkin knew what he was thinking. As soon as Nolaa Farm was repaired, Melay would assign another batch of Empaths to tend the land, as if they were nothing but bodies. None of Larkin's family had been reassigned yet, but the strands of luck she clung to were shredding beneath her fingers.

Garran put his hand on Larkin's shoulder, and she knew he sensed her fury.

Anger changed nothing. Not in this damned gilded city.

The chamber widened. Adina was jostled into another line. Larkin and Garran only had time for a quick farewell before they found their own line to the smelter. She reeled from Adina's story.

Nolaa Farm may have looked like it had been destroyed by a storm, but Larkin knew better. She'd heard about destruction magic of that scale once, several years ago—rumors of a young boy who destroyed an entire village in the foothills. Melay had the boy executed.

If the same thing was happening again, then perhaps an Empath was to blame. But destruction magic wouldn't explain the missing harvesters.

"You think it's magic," Garran said. It wasn't a question.

"I don't *want* to think it's magic," she replied, ignoring the churning in her stomach that told her otherwise.

The cavernous mouth of the mine echoed with the conversations of hundreds of miners. Larkin sensed the usual bubble of anxiety. They were nervous to see how many marks they would be taking home.

She pressed a hand to her belly as it flipped. No, not anxiety. Confusion. Both roiled through her gut, but the confusion made her nauseous.

"Where are the guards?" Garran asked.

The smelters' tables were always accompanied by a handful of city guards, but Larkin didn't spot any today. Normally, she would be grateful for their absence—she hated the way their eyes followed her particularly close—but now it was troubling.

"I'm surprised a riot hasn't broken out," said Garran.

"Don't give anyone ideas," Larkin muttered. When there were riots, Melay's soldiers converged at the capital and Empaths died. The last was a year ago, the memory still fresh and raw, the haunting stench of blood still potent.

Plus, she had no interest in rioting against the smelters. It was the guards who knocked the hilt of their swords against her head when she wasn't walking fast enough, the guards who visited Empath homes to reassign mothers or fathers or children to the farms, tearing families apart with glee. Fantasies ran rampant in her head of what she wanted to do to them—what she *could* do to them—with the magic she possessed.

They approached the smelter's table, and Garran dropped their bucket on the scale. A small man with sizable spectacles glanced inside, raising thick eyebrows. He made some charcoal scratches in his ledger. From his coin purse, he counted out twenty-four marks and placed them in Larkin's cupped hands.

Larkin clenched her soiled fingers around the coins until her fingernails bit into her palms.

"I'm short," she said.

The smelter shrugged and shooed her along with a wave of his hand.

Larkin's pulse beat in her ears. She ached to siphon Garran's disappointment. She needed to break something. Maybe the smelter's spectacles.

Garran muttered a thanks to the smelter, shoving Larkin away and up the steps to the mine entrance.

Larkin took a few deep breaths of the dusty air. *It's not his fault,* she chanted until the beat of her heart slowed. Smelters had no control over the wages. Only Queen Melay did.

"Tomorrow she could drop the price of ore to a quarter-mark an ounce," Larkin said. "The mines would be filled with starved corpses because all of us would have to work until we keeled over—"

"*Stop.*"

Larkin turned to Garran, flustered.

He was smiling. "What's in your hand?"

"Twenty-four marks, Garran. You were standing right there."

"Exactly." He gripped her shoulders. "Flour, meat, salt, oil . . . All of that will be fifteen marks at most. That's nine left over."

"Nine marks left over for what?" His giddiness, as weightless as it was, also annoyed all hells out of her.

He laughed at her. "Don't play daft. For your birthday, or did you forget already?"

She didn't forget. Seventeen felt old. Trees had rings, and she had another layer of soot on her olive skin, now sallow from days spent in darkness. Another hot coil of rage tightening around her heart. Was this what older meant—the same, but filthier and angrier?

She should save any leftover marks. That was the responsible thing to do. But Garran was right. She deserved something nice, and so did he. Vania, her mother, her father. These marks were for them.

Larkin funneled the coins into the purse on her belt. "I guess this could only mean one thing."

Garran followed her up the steps to the entrance, satisfied. "Cake."

TWO

The late sun clung to the sky like an overripe fruit. Soot from nearby smelteries curled up from limestone bricks and disappeared into the bath of light, and as Larkin emerged from the mine, her eyes watered.

It was her favorite time of the year: early summer. The dry city smelled of baked stone and pine. The sun's warmth soaked her face as she lifted her chin. When her eyes adjusted to the still-bright evening, she saw a boy her age watching her from across the cobblestone path.

Larkin stalled. She'd seen him before; the capital was small enough that she recognized most faces, and he had a carefree one that matched the contentment Larkin sensed in him. He was much taller than she was, with bronze skin and eyes like smoked quartz, and he smiled at her like he knew her. Larkin felt herself smile back, her cheeks flushing.

"Ilona's blessings!" he said. "Will I see you at the temple this afternoon?"

She froze. Turning on her heel, she grabbed Garran's arm. "Walk." They sped away from the boy, who still beckoned them toward the Temple of Light.

"Aren't you going to say hello?" Garran teased.

"Sure, and then I'll tell him to shove his goddess's blessings up his—"

"Really, Larkin. He was only being polite."

"Just like how the goddess Ilona wanted to politely smite our kind?"

"He's an Empath, too," argued Garran as they melted into the crowd's current. "Clearly a miner. Did you see his clothes?"

"Then he's a stupid Empath if he believes in the goddess." *All of the pretty ones are stupid*, she thought. If Queen Ilona, the first in the dynasty, truly had been immortalized, surely she made the stupid ones pretty to spite Larkin.

It didn't matter anyway. There was no time to be distracted by pretty Empaths. She had the market to visit and supper to help with.

"You were so captivated for a moment." Garran elbowed her.

She pushed him away, rubbing at her side. "Don't make me cuff you in luminite."

Larkin ignored Garran's smugness as they hiked past mine entrances. Workers poured from them and made their way up the mountain toward the market district.

Demura's capital was etched into the mountain, every shop and building fashioned from granite. Queen Melay's palace was built into the very peak, sculpted towers frosted with luminite balconies. The apex of the entire capital. The rest of the city coated the mountain like snow: the city gates and the gilded Temple of Light below to the east, the mining district down the north slope, and the canyon—her home—slicing through the mountain's base to the west. Everything glistened with luminite, as though ready to melt and collect in the central canal that ran down the face of the alp, drainage and dust and sparkling minerals.

Larkin and Garran followed the canal to the crowded market

stalls nestled in a bowl beneath the palace. Most of those who bartered with the street vendors were miners from the canyon, sifting through barrels of threshed wheat and baskets brimming with shriveled fruit. Their determination bordered on desperation; a successful haggle was the difference between food on the table or another supper of clear broth.

The stalls were surrounded by bronze-doored shops and pillars of granite. Guards normally patrolled the entrances, forcing patrons to display a full coin purse before they could enter. They were absent today, just like in the mines.

They'll be back, she thought, dipping her hand beneath her frayed tunic and grazing her purse. Her father would want her to barter at the stalls instead of entering one of the shops. But that would mean forfeiting . . .

"Cake?" Garran asked encouragingly.

Larkin nodded, knowing he could sense her nerves. "Two of us in the shop will look suspicious. I'll meet you in the canyon."

Garran frowned. "Let me go in."

"You know I'll be fine," Larkin said.

"Then I'll wait for you outside."

"Garran." She stared hard at him. "Go home."

Garran bounced on his toes, uncomfortable, but Larkin would win. She'd die on the steps of this shop before going home first. Most shopkeepers thought Empaths loathsome, and Larkin much preferred to take the brunt of their cruelty rather than subjecting Garran to it.

Garran gave in, his shoulders sagging. "Don't be too long.

I'm starving," he said, casting one final glance at Larkin before crossing the canal bridge home.

Larkin approached the nearest bronze door and ducked into the shop. She blinked as her eyes adjusted to the low light, and she saw a candlelit effigy of Ilona in the center of the room. Larkin almost laughed. The goddess's face was deformed with the help of the artist's poor skill.

As in every shop she'd been in before, small luminite trinkets were strung along the edges of the ceiling. The shopkeeper must have paid a small fortune for them. She thought of the Empath boy who regularly peddled fake luminite trinkets in the market, wondering if these were fake too.

Beneath the trinkets, a woman and a young girl in an embroidered dress browsed shelves stuffed with sugar-glazed pastries and imported candies. The woman's eyes kept darting over her shoulder.

She's used to guards, Larkin thought. How wonderful it must be to find comfort in those polished suits of armor.

Larkin was only able to glimpse at the shelves before the shop owner, dressed in a crisp linen tunic and leather apron, strode over to her. She felt the sensation of mud dribbling down her skin. *Disgust.* Her unkemptness disgusted him. Larkin stared back, forcing herself not to swipe at the dust on her cheeks.

"Can I help you?"

"I have twenty-four marks." She proceeded to rattle off everything she wanted, allowing him to do the math for the cuts of meat and pounds of flour. The man busied himself, scurrying about to fulfill her request.

Larkin stood by the counter and waited, the child behind her chattering with glee as she and her mother made decisions on sweet rolls and toffee. Every so often, the shop owner glanced at Larkin, but his indulgent smile was laced with the kind of suspicion that made the hair on the back of her neck stand on end.

She met his smile, widening her eyes innocently.

The shop owner returned with her requested items. "Twenty-two marks."

Larkin emptied her purse into her palm, counting out coins as he wrapped her cut of salted meat. As she held the marks out, he stalled, studying her hand.

Black clay crusted over the fresh scab on her knuckle, black clay beneath her fingernails. Black clay lined her palms like roads on a map. Only Empath miners burrowed deep enough to hit black clay.

His suspicion intensified, and hate sparked on Larkin's tongue and scorched her throat like molten ore. But the shopkeeper's calm face didn't betray his hatred, which told Larkin one thing: He was used to turning down Empaths like her.

"Take your coin to the shop down the road," he said flatly. "They'll serve you."

Larkin wouldn't beg. She refused to beg. "My marks are as real as any."

Silently, the shopkeeper plucked the items off the counter and placed them all on a shelf behind him. He turned back to her and crossed his arms, waiting for her to do or say something—anything—to cry and scream or shuffle out of the shop.

Larkin wouldn't give him the pleasure.

Slowly, Larkin reopened her purse and funneled the coins

back in. One fell and hit the ground, ringing. She bent down to pick it up, then paused.

Larkin should have been out the door already, the shopkeeper all the wealthier. Yet here she was, crouched beneath an assortment of fake trinkets. She could still sense the man's revulsion.

It was almost too easy.

She closed her eyes and siphoned his scalding emotion, ushering it, her hand curling into a fist. She focused on the shelf near the woman and the young girl, fanning her fingers as her body exhaled his rage.

With a crack, the shelf snapped in half, glass jars smashing against the floor. The girl screamed as the shards shot across the tile. The shopkeeper swore and raced to assess the damage.

In the chaos, Larkin quickly evaluated what was in reach—rounds of aged cheeses, three rabbits, and two unplucked pheasants hanging by their feet. No cake. *Sorry, Garran.* She stuffed it all into her knapsack.

Above her, the delicate trinkets swayed with the commotion, useless.

Larkin punched open the shop door and scrambled down the steps. She ran through the circle of outdoor carts, dodging vendors and patrons, and across the footbridge toward the shelter of the canyon.

She imagined the shopkeeper's face when he realized what she'd stolen and grinned.

He could have had her money but chose her wrath instead.

THREE

The strap of Larkin's bag cut into her shoulder as she rushed toward the canyon. The sun had just dipped beneath the city's mountain, stall vendors filling wagons with leftover wares to cart home.

She scanned for the patrol and found none. The streets were vacant of guards, just like the mines and the shops. Any concern was quickly overwhelmed by her relief. The absence of guards had granted her a satchel full of food and a purse heavy with marks.

She'd gotten away with magic.

Destruction magic.

Loathing like that of the shopkeeper wasn't unfamiliar. The merchants and gentry were saturated with it. But their hatred was always mixed with fear. They knew that were it not for the luminite, she could glean their silent loathing and use it against them.

Her own exhilaration at using magic surprised her, and she quickly sobered. To be caught using magic meant a lifetime in a cell, or worse. Her family couldn't afford to lose her wages.

She couldn't risk it, not again.

Larkin hurried through the canyon, the granite cliffs trapping the stench of garbage. Broken lampposts lined the path, and a luminite cable crisscrossed the high walls like an iridescent web. As Larkin neared the canyon's bottom, she passed a woman sweeping the steps to her home. A dejected man on the next stoop drank from an opaque bottle.

She sensed the same emotion every evening as she walked up

to the door of her home. The same emotion, but not a constant one. Because love wasn't a fine-tuned note that rang without changing pitch. Love was harmonized by worry and trust, bright with joy, and sometimes heartbreaking. There were few emotions like that, ones that took Larkin's breath away every time she felt them. Even as angry and exhausted as she was now.

The door groaned as she pushed against it. Larkin's father sat at the kitchen hearth, preparing dinner as her mother chatted with Garran and Vania at the worn table.

Garran stood and met Larkin at the door, planting a kiss on Larkin's forehead. She sensed his relief that she'd made it home safe. "How was the shop?"

She set her bag down. "No cake, but we'll eat more than broth tonight." She smiled and forced herself to relax so Garran wouldn't sense anything strange.

"Angry?" He raised an eyebrow.

She was angry. *Still* angry. But if she tried explaining this to Garran, he'd be disappointed in her.

"The shopkeeper tried to overcharge me."

He grimaced. "Some shopkeepers think the luminite's gone to our heads."

Thank Ilona, Larkin thought, out of habit.

Vania ran toward them, jumping into Larkin's arms. Larkin groaned, steadying herself to keep from toppling over. "You're almost too big for this."

Vania flashed a grin full of missing teeth, batting away dark, unruly curls. "Maybe."

Larkin released Vania and approached her father, who was slicing bread near the hearth. She glanced inside the pot, the broth no thicker than brackish water. With a flourish, Larkin pulled the pheasants and the rabbits from her bag, and her father paused mid-slice.

"Did you pinch this?" he asked, much too seriously. *Ilona's breath*, everyone was suspicious of her today.

Larkin erupted in laughter. She'd learned from experience that laughter was a good distraction, the easiest way to hide her emotions.

She didn't exactly have the cleanest slate when it came to theft. As a child, she used to steal bits of fruit and dried meat from the stall vendors after her shift. When her mother found the hidden stash beneath Larkin's bed, she made Larkin scrub their entire home with a pig-bristle brush the size of her thumb, hoping that would stanch the bad behavior.

It didn't work.

"She found a luminite vein in the mines," said Garran.

"See?" Larkin knocked her shoulder against her father's. "You have no faith in me."

"It's Ethera Mine he has no faith in," her mother chimed in.

"Perhaps it's less dry than you think." Larkin knelt and hung the rabbit on a skinning hook near the fire. "You should come back. Mine with me and Garran again."

Her father frowned. He'd been working in the Vault, a newly dug shaft. Prone to cave-ins and noxious gas, the mine churned out more casualties than any of the others. But the work paid well.

"We don't need all of this," he said, examining the pheasant. "Did you spend everything?"

"Oh, Jallus." Her mother hobbled over. "A nice meal for once won't kill us. It's Larkin's birthday."

Her father sighed. "Fair enough." Larkin hid a smirk. He knew better than to try to argue with her mother.

"Garran, help Vania wash up," said her mother, easing onto a kitchen stool.

Garran swept the young girl off her feet and rushed her to the kitchen basin, Vania giggling as Garran splashed her. Their joy was warm, and Larkin's muscles relaxed.

"I can heat a blanket for you," Larkin offered as her mother stretched out her bad leg. She had broken it in the mine years ago. When she didn't heal properly, Larkin took her place, Garran following suit soon after.

"Oh no." Her mother lifted Larkin's hand and examined it. "What did you do?"

"It's just a scratch," said Larkin. She felt a flash of disorientation and heaviness, as if she were poisoned. Guilt. "Mum . . ."

"I only wish I could give you a day," her mother murmured. "Take your place so you could have one day from that awful hole in the ground."

"The mines keep me out of trouble." Larkin hugged her. It wasn't fair that her mother felt any guilt. None of this was her fault, and Larkin could remind her of that over and over again, but it didn't matter.

I love you, thought Larkin.

Her mother's arms tightened around her, returning a love warmer and more familiar than any other emotion Larkin knew.

*　*　*

After supper, full and drowsy from pheasant-and-rabbit stew, Larkin took Vania by the hand and led her up the narrow stone staircase to the bedroom they shared with Garran.

Larkin lit a candle and helped Vania into bed. She sat behind her, unwinding a matted ribbon from the girl's dark curls and grabbing a brush from the nightstand.

Vania yawned. "Mum is going to start teaching me how to read tomorrow. Then I can be just like you and Garran."

Larkin smiled. "You'll be reading faster than us in no time." Empaths were banned from formal education, so their mother had taught Larkin and Garran how to read from her small set of heirloom folklore tomes.

Even their mother didn't know how old the tomes were, or whom they belonged to first. There were no names inscribed, no owners or ancestors listed. Empaths weren't allowed to have a surname either, and Larkin had little knowledge of her lineage beyond the mysterious books. Books that hinted at a time when Empaths weren't hated and practiced magic freely. The dynasty erased their names and their stories, stories that had kept her up late, wondering if Empaths once had a goddess of their own. But Larkin knew as little as her mother did, and perhaps as little as her mother's mother. Their history was gone.

And once Vania learned how to read, she would have the same questions. Knowledge of the magic within these books had given Larkin an itch she was always desperate to scratch, like poison beneath her fingernails. And there was no antidote.

Part of Larkin wished that Vania could stay ignorant of such knowledge forever.

"And then, maybe soon, I can start working too," said Vania. "Just like you."

Larkin combed her fingers through Vania's now-silky strands. "You don't need to work, sweet girl."

"But I want to help." Vania craned her neck to blink at Larkin.

Larkin kissed the top of her sister's head. "You can help me by staying home with Mum and keeping her company. You can join me and Garran once you've grown bigger and stronger. How does that sound?"

Vania sighed reluctantly.

After tucking Vania in, Larkin picked up the threadbare ribbon from the nightstand and brought it to the table in the corner, sitting down. Mending it herself would be simple, and in the privacy of her home, where there was no chance of getting caught, the risk was worth it.

Around the same time Larkin had learned how to read, she'd taught herself how to conjure and destroy. When everyone else was asleep, she worked with odds and ends—nothing that would be sorely missed—crushing clay mugs and iron buckles to create tiny figurines she'd kept beneath the floorboard. She made one for each member of her family, imagining them living on a farm surrounded by miles of forest, in a land without a queen.

The figurines were gone now. She'd destroyed them only a year ago, after the riot, severing herself from such a childish hope. She'd needed to grow up.

Now she tried to be practical and cautious with her magic. But it was her birthday.

Larkin concentrated, sensing her father's worry bubbling up through the floorboards. She siphoned and projected onto the fringed ribbon, shredding it into a pile of wispy threads. Destruction was the easy part, but she usually had trouble pulling together enough positive emotion to conjure. Tonight, it would be simple.

Garran laughed from downstairs, and Larkin siphoned his buoyant amusement. Thread rushed back into her palm, a tendril of crimson ribbon spiraling around her fingers.

Tomorrow, Vania would wonder for only a moment why her hair ribbon looked new, and their mother would be too busy to notice.

Larkin looked up as Garran entered the room, the trill of anxiety below growing.

"They're arguing again." Garran joined Larkin at the small table. "Father told me to go to bed."

Their parents' conversation had grown serious upon Garran leaving the kitchen. Larkin could barely hear them.

"The disappearances in the hills are getting worse," said her father. "Heard rumors in the mine this morning. Not only that, but more destruction—homes, crops, wagons—all crumbling to dust."

Larkin met Garran's eyes as they listened intently.

"This has gone on for far too long," said her mother. "What if one of us is reassigned to the farms? What then?"

"Melay has sent her army to investigate. Even the city guards have gone. Something about a scarcity of soldiers."

"A scarcity? Do you know how large the Demuran army is, Jallus? Are they dead?"

"Faie . . ."

"Missing, like the farmers?"

"You know I don't know, Faie. No one does."

"Dead?" whispered Garran.

Larkin knew that Garran was thinking about Adina and Edric. These weren't just rumors; Edric was missing.

Her eyes darted to Vania, but her sister was asleep. Melay's soldiers couldn't be dead. The dynasty had always kept a large army even though Demura rarely faced a real threat. Still, she couldn't help but entertain the thought. Would it be so terrible if the guards never returned?

"Jallus?" her mother asked. "What if it's destruction magic?"

"It's just a rumor, Faie. Who could be powerful enough? Unless the magic is coming from below. From the—"

"*Don't.*" Her mother's voice was sharp. "Myth does not belong entangled in truth." She paused. "And keep your voice down. The children are listening."

Her parents' voices became indecipherable, but the prickle of their anxiety lingered.

"What was Dad going to say before Mum cut him off?" asked Larkin.

"I think he was going to say the Reach."

Larkin barked a quiet laugh. "You can't be serious."

Garran shrugged, his concern a cold, dull chisel grating against her rib cage.

"You heard Mum. It's a fable." Larkin kept her voice light and soothing. The last thing she wanted was Garran's emotion waking up—

"What's a fable?" Vania said quietly from her bed.

Larkin groaned. "Now you've done it."

Garran lifted his hands in mock surrender.

"What's a fable?" Vania repeated, sitting up.

"You'll learn soon enough when you start reading from Mum's books," Larkin said, and waved her hand. "Now to bed."

"I want to know *now*. What's a reach?"

Larkin simpered at Garran. "The honor's all yours." She knew Vania wouldn't rest until she got her answer. Better they tell her now than risk her asking Mum about it in the morning.

Garran scratched his head. "The Reach is a big cave."

"How big?" asked Vania.

"The biggest on the whole isle. And a long time ago, the queen threw *very mean people* inside of it as punishment. But it's just a fable, Vania. People tell it to keep naughty children like you from doing anything bad."

"Then it's a mean story." Vania crossed her arms.

"Indeed it is." Larkin grinned. "A very mean, very *short* story."

Garran matched her smile. "I do my best."

The tale was meant for Empath children: a warning should they ever attempt magic. The bad Empaths in the story were led by the villain Otheil Kyran, who wanted to steal the throne from Queen Leliana Ilona. When Ilona defeated Kyran and his six disciples a thousand years ago, she cast them into the Reach, and magic was forever banned.

The tale's most thrilling moment was when a captured and bound Kyran told Ilona that, though he had fallen, darkness would rise once more.

And Ilona ever famously responded: *Darkness cannot exist where there is Light.*

Ilona had since been revered as Demura's Goddess of Light, Kyran the God of Darkness. Good pitted against evil.

But to Larkin, the story had a much more practical meaning. *Ilona and Kyran were two mortals with too much power. Ilona loathed magic, and Kyran abused it. Nothing more.*

Of course, Melay continued to uphold the legend as truth, graciously allowing Empaths to exist on the isle. Their inherent darkness was ever doused by the dynasty's light, after all.

Fortunately, Larkin didn't have to explain any of this to a satisfied Vania, who had fallen back to sleep. But Garran's concern remained.

"Do you think it's Kyran?" Garran whispered as they slid into their beds.

"There's no such thing as gods," said Larkin. And she believed it. Demurans chose to believe in stories about goddesses and underworlds. Empaths *chose* to worship Ilona, even if it wasn't in their best interest.

Fables, however untrue, were less terrifying than the unknown.

The Reach was not a place of magic ruled by a dark god. There was an explanation for the destruction magic happening now on the farms and the disappearances—there had to be. Larkin knew Queen Melay would find a way to use the rumors of dangerous Empaths to her advantage, so she had to lay the fable's power to rest.

FOUR

What exactly do you plan on doing?" Garran stuffed a canteen into his bag as they readied for work the next morning. "Roam around to different miners and tap them on the shoulder? *Excuse me, ma'am, have you heard of our dark underlord, Otheil Kyran?*"

Larkin watched Vania to make sure she was still asleep. "I was thinking, *On a scale of one to ten, how likely is it that our fabled dark underlord is not an actual underlord?*"

"Good luck with that one."

"They'll talk to me." Larkin shoved her foot into her boot. Miners excelled at stories that could be told within a single whisper, quick enough to share at the tunnel junctions. She knew better than to trust a rumor floating through the darkness, but she trusted Adina, and she trusted her parents' worry. There *was* destruction in the hills, and perhaps an Ethera worker knew where it was stemming from.

A knock sounded at the front door, and Larkin's head snapped up. Their father had already left for work. No one came over unannounced. No one came over at all. Empath congregations were punishable by death.

Larkin sensed a storm, the static before the strike of lightning. She hurried down the stairs, her brother at her heels. Her mother was in shock, her shoulder pressed to the door, a hand over her mouth.

"What is it?" Instinctively, Larkin searched the room for a weapon. She grabbed a fire poker propped against the hearth.

Her mother's hand fell from her lips. "Guards."

Larkin tightened her grip on the fire poker until she couldn't feel her fingers. "No." The word escaped her mouth, an order to the guards to stay away, but her voice trembled. Blinking back hot tears, she swore.

Melay still had capital guards left in her command. And there were only two reasons why guards knocked on Empath doors: to reassign, and to arrest.

Her mother backed away from the door. "They're taking some of us to the farms."

"Larkin?" Garran's voice sounded from the stairs, and she fought through his confusion to find her thoughts. This had nothing to do with the farms. The taste of last night's stew rose in Larkin's throat. She swallowed, running to her mother, still holding the poker. "Mum . . ." How could she explain what she'd done? The shopkeeper had obviously notified the guards of her theft. Perhaps even of her magic.

She'd never see the light of day again.

The handle rattled as someone rammed against the door. Her father had meant to fix the lock . . .

Larkin didn't have time to explain. Forget explaining; she couldn't even apologize. Maybe her family would think that she was being taken to the farms and never know better. "Garran and Dad are going to take care of you, Mum, all right?"

Larkin's mother grabbed her shoulders. "What are you talking about? *What did you do?*"

The lock gave way and the door slammed open, morning light pouring in. Larkin shielded her eyes. The sun reflected off the brightest armor she'd ever seen. Luminite armor.

Luminite was too heavy for battle; only the palace guards wore it. Palace guards didn't march all the way to the canyon to arrest Empaths like her for stealing rabbits, did they?

The tallest, a surly lieutenant, stooped as he stepped into their home. He wasn't wearing a helmet, and somehow that made it worse. More personal. Weathered by age, the man looked as though he'd made these arrests hundreds of times, but Larkin knew this wasn't a normal arrest.

She couldn't sense him—not with his armor—but caught a glimpse of alarm in his eyes as he unclipped the luminite shackles that dangled from his belt. Three other guards swept around the lieutenant and into the house. Startled, Larkin dropped the fire poker, wincing as one yanked her arms behind her back. The lieutenant clamped the luminite shackles around her wrists.

Garran cried her name.

"Stay back!" she shouted, knowing full well what guards did to Empaths who fought arrest. She tasted iron at the memory of sprayed blood, imagining it was Garran's.

No. She couldn't let that happen.

As the luminite metal grazed her skin, her Empath sense extinguished entirely.

"What did you do?" her mother repeated.

Larkin opened her mouth, but the explanation was lodged somewhere deep inside her.

I didn't want us to starve.

I was humiliated.

I wanted to hurt him back.

As she fought to find the right excuse, her mother's confusion sickening her, the lieutenant nodded toward Garran.

A scream tore from Larkin's mouth. "NO!"

Garran flinched, holding his hands up as if to surrender.

"He didn't do anything! He wasn't even with me!" A fierceness rose, something untamed that wanted her to protect what she cared about most. She'd spent her whole life doing just that. She couldn't give up, not now.

Larkin thrashed against her restraints. "Don't touch him!"

The guard holding Larkin threw her at the wall near the hearth, her head slamming against stone. Pain blinded her.

As her mother wept, Larkin homed in on the sound, using it as an anchor to keep from blacking out. Her vision refocused as a guard cast her mother to the kitchen floor. Her mother landed on her bad leg, crying out.

"Mum . . ." Larkin's eyes darted across the room until she saw Garran backed into the corner. Brandishing a knife, the guard grabbed Garran by the collar and shoved him outside.

The lieutenant's fingers closed around a fistful of Larkin's hair, and he yanked her away from the wall. Tears of pain streamed down her face as he pushed her through the open doorway. Larkin stumbled down the steps to the canyon.

Even with her hands behind her back, she whirled to the open doorway and the collapsed form of her broken mother. With all the armor and the shackles, Larkin didn't know how much her mother could sense. She tried anyway. Love was supposed to feel bright and warm, but her own weighed heavier than chains, the agony deeper than any wound.

I love you.

A guard grasped the door handle and swung it shut.

"Wait!" She wasn't ready.

Larkin felt a sharp pain as the lieutenant bumped his fist against the back of her skull.

"No talking."

She stumbled again, the ground spinning beneath her feet, before she was hauled back up. She heard scuffling from somewhere up ahead of them. Her brother. Larkin lifted her head to see Garran attempting to yank away from the guard who held him. "Leave her alone!"

"Garran, don't." Larkin focused on the pain to keep herself distracted, failing. If she were religious, she would've started praying to Ilona. Asking for mercy. *But I don't deserve mercy,* she thought. Not after what she had done to her mother. To Garran.

Larkin heard him whimper in pain. She'd never forgive herself for this.

Several Empaths stopped in their tracks to watch before scurrying away. Larkin didn't need to sense their fear. She saw it in their eyes.

The growl of rock sounded in the distance. Larkin watched two Empaths stumble and cling to each other at the same moment the ground shifted beneath her own feet.

The guard who held Larkin hesitated, tightening his grip on Larkin's arms. "What was that?"

A deafening crack startled Larkin. She jerked her head

toward the city gates just in time to see the Temple of Light collapse. The structure fell all at once, as though crushed by the grip of an invisible giant. The nightmarish sound of crumbling stone sent vibrations deep into her bones.

Destruction magic. More powerful than she could have ever imagined.

Her breath caught as she watched, stunned. For a moment, Larkin wondered if she had done it. But that was impossible. She couldn't sense anything beneath these shackles.

Plumes of dust erupted from the debris. Beneath the echoing rubble, screams reverberated up the mountain.

"Sweet Ilona," Garran said.

Some of the surrounding guards drew their swords, but the lieutenant held his hand out.

As the dust dissipated, the market square dissolved into chaos.

"Do something!" a vendor screamed at the guards. Some were throwing wares into carts before hauling them off, others abandoning their stalls entirely. Folks stampeded past Larkin like the wild rush of a river current. Before her, a man fell and was nearly trampled, and she watched in horror as the guards—her guards—did nothing.

Her luminite shackles bit into her wrists. She was almost grateful for them—the terror of the vendors would have been maddening. Was the canyon safe? The mines?

"Dad!" Larkin cried. She looked to Garran, who stared down at the ruined temple with wild eyes.

The lieutenant dropped his hand. "Continue escorting the prisoners."

"But, sir—"

"Do it now," barked the lieutenant, stepping over the fallen man. "Queen Melay's orders."

Melay? Larkin must have heard wrong. Why would the queen bother to personally give a damn about their arrest?

Larkin's guard steered her north, shielding her from the crush of people. "Out of the way!"

"Where are you taking us?" Larkin pleaded.

Her question soon answered itself. They'd been arrested by order of the queen. And now—amid the crumbling capital— they were headed to the palace.

FIVE

The palace cellblock smelled of old hay and piss.

Larkin was surrounded by three brick walls; in front of her, bars of luminite stretched from the floor to the ceiling. The other cells were full, the prison heavy with misery. She had a bucket to relieve herself and nothing else: no bed or blanket, and no light other than the torches that flickered between the cells. Her pulse sped as if she were trapped in the mines.

But this was worse than being trapped in a cave-in. A cave-in was unavoidable. She'd brought this upon herself. Upon Garran.

Her brother was locked in the cell to her left. With the brick wall between them, Larkin couldn't see him. Her luminite shackles were gone, so she tried sensing him, but it was difficult with her head throbbing like she had every hells' fury trapped inside of it.

Larkin crawled to the corner where the bars met brick. Garran threaded his hand through the bars and reached out into the prison hall, and she did the same, their fingers lacing together beyond their cells.

How could she tell him that she was sorry? It didn't matter. Nothing could fix what she'd done. Larkin had only one option. It wouldn't make things right, but at least Garran would know the truth of why they were here.

"I stole from the shopkeeper yesterday. I distracted him with magic."

Garran's disappointment chilled her. "I knew you weren't telling the truth."

"If I'd known what was going to happen—"

"That's just it, Larkin. We do know what always happens: the worst possible outcome. Every time. You knew what would happen; you just chose not to think."

She said nothing in response. Larkin knew Garran could sense her shame, and it was her only offering to him. She couldn't reverse their fate or the pain she'd inflicted on her mother. It was burned into her mind—the broken heap of her mother on the kitchen floor.

"I didn't think you'd dare to risk something so stupid, not after . . ."

He drifted off, but she knew what he was going to say. Last summer's riot, when the price of luminite plummeted. They'd been caught in the crowd outside the mines. The soldiers had descended, slashing through the chaos with blinding luminite swords. She'd been so close—close enough to witness death, and not just once. There was enough blood to distinguish its sharpness from the scent of iron. The horror had roiled inside her, so violent she thought it would tear her in half.

The same horror she would have sensed today if she hadn't been shackled. There was no such thing as a successful rebellion. Not Kyran's uprising. Not the miners' riot. Not Larkin's brazen destruction and theft.

"I'm going to fix this," she said.

"You can't." Garran's defeat weighed heavy on her. He let go of her hand and pulled it back into his cell, out of reach.

He was wrong. She had no other option *but* to fix this. Propping herself up on her elbows, she glanced around her cell. Thanks to her resistance, the luminite bars weren't close enough to completely inhibit her magic, and the surrounding brick walls looked old with deteriorating mortar. She could destroy a section of the wall, and she and Garran could shimmy between the break in the bars.

And then what? Somehow manage to dodge every guard until they found an exit? Neither of them knew the layout of this place. Not only that, but she didn't know if she could bring herself to kill someone if they were spotted.

Larkin sat back against the brick, catching the eye of the girl in the cell across from hers. She leaned against the luminite bars and grinned at Larkin.

What do you have to be smug about? Larkin wanted to shout. Perhaps the prison had made the girl mad, though she didn't look delusional. She watched Larkin with utter fascination. Her expression was curious, her mouth delicate and cheeks round.

Larkin couldn't take it anymore. "Do you want something?"

The girl shrugged, reaching up to retie her mass of dark, crimped hair. "New visitors are always a refreshing sight, is all."

Larkin stared at her. "*Visitor* implies I'm going to leave soon."

The girl's eyes were so wide that they caught all of the surrounding torchlight. "We're all going to leave this place eventually. We're mortal."

Larkin rolled her eyes. The girl was mad after all. Larkin hoped her lack of a response would shut her up.

In the silence, the girl's words kept churning inside her. They were mortal, and the dynasty's stance on magic was set in stone. She and Garran were going to rot in here.

Larkin knocked the back of her head against the brick wall, the pain a punishing reminder of her stupidity. *You can't cry,* she thought. She didn't deserve to cry.

The girl tapped her fingernails against the bars. "Your crime?"

Larkin thought of Garran, who was surely listening on the other side of the wall. The wound of his disappointment was too fresh. "I'd rather not go into it."

Standing, the girl moved about her cell, kicking moldy hay to the corners until the floor was clear.

"You're an Empath, right?" She laughed as if she'd made another joke. "Obviously. There are only Empaths here. And those shackles they brought you in with! I've never seen anything like them." She flung herself at the bars, beaming at Larkin. "You used magic, didn't you?"

"I'd rather not get into it."

The girl frowned. "Not much of a talker, I see."

Larkin lay back on the grimy floor and folded her arms over her belly.

"That's all right. Talking grows old after a while, even when you have as many great stories as I do. But I don't mind if you're quiet; it's nice to not be alone. Your cell's been empty for so long."

Larkin wondered how long the girl had been in here, and what had happened to whoever had been in the cell before her. But further conversation sounded about as fun as pulling her teeth out one by one.

The girl busied herself eventually, pacing across the now vacant floor and scratching her chin, as if assessing something. Then, she began to dance.

From her precise, delicate movements, it was obvious that the girl was skilled. Strange for an Empath—when did she find the time to learn how to dance?

In the silence of the prison, she danced for the span of what must have been an entire damned mine shift, not even pausing when her hair fell loose. She even managed to work the act of retying her hair gracefully into her routine. Dancer's deep copper skin sheened with sweat, but she didn't stop until a guard stomped over from the cellblock's entrance.

"Quit that!" he bellowed, unsheathing his sword.

As if on cue, Dancer twirled to the back of her cell and pressed herself against the wall. She bowed to the guard, so low her face was hidden. "Why of course, Your Excellency."

The guard grunted, flattered. Something told Larkin that he was new to this post. "Excellency," he muttered. "I'm not even a lieutenant. Just quit with the dancing."

"Most certainly, Your Excellency."

The moment he walked away, Dancer picked up again with twirls and sashays. Larkin sensed the hot anger of the guard as he whirled back toward her, but another guard grabbed his arm. "Just leave her alone. She'll mess with your head, that one."

Dancer stopped mid-twirl to wink at Larkin, and Larkin couldn't help but smile at her defiance. Pointless, perhaps, but amusing.

"You're good," Garran called out to Dancer. His kindness even now made Larkin's heart ache.

"I live to entertain." Dancer bowed in his direction, and then continued.

Larkin grew bored with watching her and rolled to her back, staring at the cracked stone ceiling. The cellblock was maddeningly quiet, filled only with an occasional groan, the shuffling of Dancer's feet, and the chill emanating from Garran.

The silence was broken when a man several cells down loudly uttered a prayer to Ilona.

Larkin groaned; her first instinct was to tell the man to shut up.

Another woman beat her to it. "I can see all that praying is working in your favor. Ilona isn't going to save you, old man."

A few prisoners from the surrounding cells applauded and jeered, but their mockery was half-hearted. Larkin looked over to Dancer, who had stopped dancing and was peering at her again through the bars. She chewed her bottom lip and waited, as if expecting Larkin to offer her spiritual philosophies.

Larkin took the bait. "Don't tell me you're a believer."

Dancer studied her pointed foot as she trailed it across the floor. "If she's watching me, I'm sure she's not all too happy. My troupe's been telling tales of Kyran's revenge for years now."

"You're from a traveling troupe?" Larkin sat up, intrigued. That explained the dancing and the theatrics. She didn't know Empaths were allowed to be in a troupe. She thought they weren't allowed to do anything other than farm or mine.

Dancer nodded eagerly. "How do you think I landed here? Got wrangled into it, if I do say so myself. Mum was transferred to the farm all on her own when she was pregnant with me. Died a few years ago. When you're on your own like that, you start listening to your friends, you know?"

Friends. Larkin wanted to laugh. Once she and Garran finished up at the mines, they were expected at home. Her family members were her friends. Anyone else, like Adina and her brothers, were nothing more than a wish—a cruel reminder of friends she could have if there were more time in the day.

"Wouldn't have done it on my own, but all that space and land gets Empaths dreaming up big ideas." Dancer released a theatrical sigh. "I couldn't exactly say no. There were five of us who got caught sneaking out of the farm one too many times, and the rest is history." She dragged her toe across the dirty floor, pensive. "I think about it a lot. All that space. I dance to make this cell seem bigger than it is. If it were any smaller . . . hells, I'd go mad, I guess."

So the girl wasn't mad yet, just on the brink. In the short span of time, Dancer had already grown on her. Which was good considering how long they might be living across from each other.

"You'll have to tell me one of your tales sometime," Larkin said.

Dancer brightened, opening her mouth.

"Please, Ilona, not again," someone groaned from the cell next to Dancer.

Dancer's mouth snapped shut. She frowned sullenly.

Garran hissed Larkin's name, distracting her.

Larkin crawled back to the edge of her cell. "I'm here."

"There's a farmer in the cell on the other side of me. We got to talking. Remember the people disappearing in the hills? The farmer said they're disappearing into holes."

"Disappearing into holes?"

"Holes in the ground. Out in the harvesting fields."

"Sinkholes? That doesn't make any sense, Garran."

"His daughter . . ." Garran's inhale rattled in his throat. "He heard his daughter screaming in the field and ran toward her. She was clutching onto the edge, and he had almost made it to her when she couldn't hold on anymore."

Holes in the earth—could that be where all the missing harvesters had gone? Had they been swallowed? Larkin had wondered if the farms had been destroyed by magic. But magic didn't come from the ground. It came from Empaths like her.

Who could be powerful enough? Unless the magic is coming from below. From the—

No.

She batted the Reach and Otheil Kyran from her mind. They were corpses now. *He* was a corpse.

Garran interrupted her thoughts. "Can you imagine watching someone you love just slip away like that forever?"

"Mum and Dad and Vania are safe in the city," she reminded him.

"They could be transferred to the farms any day. You know that."

Garran's hand slid beyond the bars, and Larkin reached out from her cell and took it again. She shut her eyes, picturing her mother and father near the hearth. Garran helping Vania wash up for supper. The candle on the table in her bedroom that cast shadows on her hands as she conjured the ribbon. The scent of her sister's hair, her giggle.

Garran squeezed her hand. She knew he could sense her emotions.

Larkin had no hope to give Garran, but she could give him love. Her memories were all she had left. She dwelled within them for what must have been hours, until sleep claimed her.

Larkin jerked awake as a raw jolt ignited her spine. Shock flowed from the opposite end of the prison. She sat up, murmurings spreading like a slowly burning fire. The stone floor vibrated as prisoners surged toward the fronts of their cells.

Larkin pressed herself against the bars and caught Dancer's wide, bleary eyes as the girl woke. "What's going on?"

Dancer crawled toward her. "Something exciting."

Down the corridor, a cell door creaked open.

"Please, my queen," a woman sobbed. "I'm getting married!"

My queen? Surely Melay wouldn't be in the prison. She had guards for her dirty work. Larkin peered through the bars in an attempt to see their newest cellmate, but it was too dark.

Gradually, the sounds of scuffling and the occasional quiet sob grew closer. People were being dragged from their cells.

"Larkin?" Garran called her name quietly.

"It's all right, Garran." She couldn't remember the last time her brother had sounded so small. So terrified. "I'm here." Maybe if she kept talking, he'd feel better, but she couldn't think of what to say. "I'm here," Larkin repeated. "I'm here, I'm here."

"This block is too full." A commanding female voice resonated from the front of the hall. "There are more than twenty prisoners waiting to be assigned."

"The other blocks are at capacity, my—"

"When has that stopped you from making room before, Hathius?"

A cell door creaked open. Larkin strained to see between the bars and glimpsed moving shadows down the hall.

Crushing terror nearly floored her. A wet, viscous noise was followed by a thud, and panic and whimpers rushed through the cellblock. Garran cried her name again, but Larkin couldn't coax forth a soothing remark.

Another cell door opened. She winced with the expectation of sensing another death, but only heard a struggle.

"Devon," the woman boomed.

"You'll burn in Kyran's hell for this," growled a male voice.

Larkin made out the noise of restraint. Devon was being taken, not killed.

The remainder of the cellblock visitors neared, and Larkin caught sight of a white gown skirting the soiled floor. Her eyes followed it upward to a jewel-embroidered bodice.

Please, my queen.

It was a face she'd seen only from a distance—sharp and stoic, with flawless citrine skin and eyes of ice.

Larkin gripped the bars, her pulse thrumming in her fingers. Melay.

She felt her bones lock up. She had never thought she'd be so close. The man named Devon had cursed Melay to Kyran's hell. After what Melay had done to her family, Larkin knew she should want to do the same. Her surprise held her back.

Larkin was certain this wasn't a chance for an audience with the queen. Melay wouldn't have come all the way down here just to help move Empaths to different cellblocks or order killings, especially not when the very capital was crumbling.

Something was terribly wrong.

The lieutenant Hathius walked beside Melay, a fleet of guards close behind. The queen's frown was hard, her eyebrows arched. The moment she halted in front of Larkin's cell, her guards followed suit.

The queen craned her neck to peer at Dancer. "Elfina."

Dancer stumbled backward, all grace and poise gone. Melay's lieutenant unlocked her door. The girl's eyes found Larkin and waited, like she wanted Larkin to say something—a whispered warning or encouragement.

Larkin's lips parted, but she had nothing to offer. She'd known Dancer—Elfina—for a handful of hours at most, the girl's brightness bordering on annoying, but she'd been friendly. Now Larkin didn't know what was going to happen to her.

Elfina hesitated before gliding forward. As soon as she was within reach, the lieutenant grasped her wrists and cuffed them behind her back. He secured a collar with the telltale flash of luminite around her neck before a guard swept her away.

Melay continued onward, not bothering to as much as glance at Larkin. She stopped again, this time in front of Garran's cell.

No.

"Garran." His name rolled off Melay's tongue with familiarity, and hatred awoke inside Larkin.

The queen lifted her hand, her fingers curling inward like spider legs, beckoning Garran forward. A ring gleamed on her finger, the large gem a vivid, unsettling blue.

Larkin knew that color. Hauyne. Beautiful and brittle as all hells.

Do something, you idiot.

Garran's terror erupted inside her. Larkin quickly siphoned his emotion. The hauyne in Melay's ring shattered with a crack, bright flecks tinkling against the floor.

Larkin's heart thudded as Melay slowly lifted her hand, examining the empty ring setting with detached curiosity.

Hathius drew his sword and started for Larkin, but Melay stopped him.

"His sister . . . ," began the lieutenant.

"I know who she is."

Melay's eyes narrowed, and Larkin wondered if the queen understood that Larkin had actually used magic in a room full of luminite. Her stony face gave no indication.

"Very well." Melay rapped on the bars of Larkin's cell, and the lieutenant stepped forward, sliding his key into the lock of her cell.

Her plan had worked.

Larkin stepped out of her cell, and the lieutenant yanked her arms behind her back. She didn't know what the queen had in store for her. It didn't matter. She'd be the one to face the terrifying unknown, not Garran.

Her brother slammed his hands against the bars. "Larkin!"

She wanted to tell him to be brave, but the words remained lodged in her throat. All that mattered was that he knew how much she loved him.

Her heart swelled until she was certain he could sense her. *More than anything.*

Hathius fitted her with a luminite collar, the bone-deep sensation of Garran's grief snuffing out.

SIX

arkin stumbled between two guards as they shoved her forward, leaving Melay and the lieutenant Hathius behind. At the last set of cells before the exit, a man was slumped over, a river of blood curling into the hall.

Larkin's legs weakened at the sight, her guards hauling her upright. She comforted herself with the idea that if they wanted to kill her, they would have already done so.

"Where are you taking me?" she demanded, knowing they wouldn't answer. With the damned luminite collar around her neck, she couldn't even get a clear sense of their emotions.

The collar would normally be overkill for an Empath, but not her. Melay now knew that too. What if Melay assumed that Garran was also resistant? Surely she wouldn't allow him to stay in a place where he could siphon.

The consequences of Larkin's actions leached into her like acid as the guards hauled her up a spiral staircase at the tunnel's end.

You just chose not to think, Garran had said.

But her hasty action in the cell had meant that Garran was alive, and that was all that mattered. She couldn't get ahead of herself.

The stairs leveled to a platform. One guard opened a wooden door and pushed her into a hallway, and Larkin inhaled clean, thin air. They must have climbed all the way to the top of the peak.

Larkin was uncuffed and shoved into the nearest room with such force that she fell to the ground. The door slammed shut behind her.

The room was barren save for an excessively large tub and a wide, open window bordered with limestone. She stood, stunned by the sharp-sweet air and warm rays of afternoon sun. She'd been in the prison for over a day.

She didn't notice the three women in servantry garb at the far edge of the room until her eyes adjusted. They ushered her forward and wasted no time, stripping her and pushing her into the hot water.

Larkin hissed as a servant scrubbed her skin and scalp raw with buttery soap. A bath was a luxury she'd never experienced before, but it wasn't as enjoyable as she'd imagined.

"Do you know why I'm here?" she tried asking. The servants continued without response, as if they were washing a tub of dirty laundry.

Larkin calmed herself. Executions didn't require cleanliness. If she were to be killed, someone would have stuck a sword in her already. The bath had to mean that she was staying alive. For now.

They toweled her off, one of the servants combing through her hair and shearing away the rough ends. Another took Larkin's measurements, wrapping twine around her limbs and torso. She left the room and returned with an ensemble for Larkin to change into.

When the servants swept out of the room, Larkin clutched the towel to her body, too stunned to move.

It's a trap, she thought.

But with no way to escape, Larkin coaxed herself to pick up the clothing, tugging on undergarments, a tunic, and trousers that were plainly woven but finer than anything she'd ever owned.

As soon as she finished tying the laces of her new boots, the door creaked open behind her.

Larkin shot to her feet when she saw a young soldier standing at the entrance. The woman stepped into the room, her hand on the hilt of her sword. Larkin's mind leapt to a stealthy execution, imagining the soldier lunging forward to grab her hair, yanking her head back and slitting her throat. Larkin's hand shot to her neck.

The soldier arched a slim eyebrow. "I'm not here to take your collar off."

Larkin's hand slid down, finding her collar, and held on to it as she waited for the soldier to state her business. The soldier studied Larkin, her black, pin-straight hair swaying back and forth from where it was secured at the crown of her head. She was dressed in leather battle armor, metal plates embedded in the cuirass to protect the vital places of her body, light enough and leaving much of her tawny skin uncovered. The armor was designed for agility and war—movement—not just for shielding, like the clunky armor the city guards wore.

As the soldier made to move back toward the hall, luminite glinted from beneath her cuirass. A collar.

Larkin dropped her hand in shock. "You're an Empath." That wasn't possible—it was illegal for Empaths to join Melay's army or the city guard. "Who are you?"

She took a hesitant step back. The soldier couldn't possibly be working for Melay, yet Larkin wasn't sure that she was here to help her either.

"You're not really in a place to be asking questions, are you?"

The soldier gripped the pommel at her hip, sliding the top of her sword gently from its sheath and gesturing to the hall. A threat.

That settles it, thought Larkin. She was one of Melay's.

Still, soldiers killed Empaths. How could this woman be both? Larkin wanted to refuse to follow, but she didn't even know how to throw a decent punch, let alone fight against a sword unarmed.

With no choice, she followed the soldier out of the room.

A boy with a slight frame waited for them in the hallway, dressed in the periwinkle robe of a scholar. He was pale, though not pallid like the miners, and lacked a collar. *Healthy, and not an Empath,* thought Larkin. He had a round, nervous face and was surrounded by his own entourage of guards.

"Larkin, my name is Tamsyn Arkwright." The boy gestured to the soldier. "This is Jacque, and we're—"

Jacque cut him off. "Late. The queen is waiting."

Larkin faltered as Jacque marched down the hall, Tamsyn hurrying after her. Melay was waiting for *them*? A scholar, an Empath soldier, and Larkin? She wiped the sweat running down the back of her neck and followed the soldier and the scholar at a distance, the boots of the guards behind her heavy on the stone floor.

Larkin couldn't let her own bewilderment distract her. She owed Garran nothing less than constant vigilance. She couldn't afford to miss a clue or a hint at how she might free him or, at the very least, keep him safe for as long as possible.

She'd told him she would fix this. It was a promise she'd die by.

Tamsyn and Jacque led her through a labyrinth of torchlit hallways, the surrounding ornamentation growing more opulent the farther they walked. Gems and minerals were embedded in the ceiling in swirling patterns, sparkling in the light.

Larkin pulled her eyes away, repulsed at the queen's hoard, and caught Tamsyn sneaking curious glances at her before Jacque grabbed his shoulder and pushed him ahead.

The hall opened to a massive chamber.

Guards were stationed along the rich tapestries at the edges of the room. A bronze table atop the polished marble floor stretched from one end of the room to the other, vacant except for a handful of occupants at the very end. Perched in the head seat was Queen Melay.

Jacque straightened and Tamsyn smoothed down the front of his robe as they approached the queen, but Larkin's feet felt like they were soldered to the ground. Every muscle in her body was rigid with fury, but more than angry, Larkin was terrified. Terrified that none of this made sense. Terrified that Melay was staring at her. Larkin could sense nothing, but the queen looked pleased. And that was the most frightening thing of all.

Tamsyn glanced back at her and jerked his head forward, motioning for Larkin to follow. She complied.

When Larkin was close enough, she spotted the queen's bony hand on the table, the gold band of her ring winking in the light. The empty setting should have felt like a trophy, but it was only a reminder that the queen knew of her luminite resistance.

A few collar-bound Empaths dressed like Larkin occupied the seats on the side of the table opposite her. She immediately recognized Elfina. The dancer wasn't beaming or staring wide-eyed as she had done in the cells, but something was still bright about her. Not like the sun Larkin had seen from the limestone window, but subtle, like a torch.

The corner of Elfina's mouth perked up in a smile when she saw Larkin, and Larkin clung to the familiar sight, smiling back.

Larkin sat between Jacque and Tamsyn, thankful the soldier provided some distance between her and Melay. Hathius took his place on the other side of the scholar, and he was the first to shake out his napkin and place it on his lap. He had a shock of white through his hair, and a scar split his brow like he'd lived through a few battles. *Or a few drunken scuffles,* thought Larkin as she studied his smirk.

She pulled her gaze away and turned it to the boys who sat on either side of Elfina. The one closest to the queen had an unruly mop of hair, amber skin, and hazel eyes. He was familiar, but Larkin couldn't place him.

The other boy was clearly a miner, wan and barrel-chested, with a purple welt forming on his forehead. If he was the one the guards had wrestled from the cells, then this was Devon. He glowered at Melay, looking damn near ready to strike. The lieutenant seemed to think so too, his eyes trained on the miner.

Larkin's mind flashed to the blood curling into the cracks of the cellblock floor. The dead prisoner had done nothing to deserve his fate, while Devon had cursed the queen to Kyran's hell but was a guest in the palace, just like her. She knew she shouldn't feel fortunate, or relieved. She wondered if Devon knew more than she did.

A small, ashen girl sat farthest from the queen, her watery eyes darting frantically to each of the guests. She couldn't have been older than fourteen, and when Larkin caught her eye, the girl winced and stared at her lap, visibly shaking.

Elfina seemed to notice too, the light inside of her dimming as she watched the girl. The little one had reason to be afraid. They all did. *Vigilance*. Larkin couldn't let this charade—whatever it was—distract her.

Melay snapped her fingers. The aroma was instant, and Larkin's mouth flooded traitorously. Servants distributed silver plates to everyone but the queen and quietly left.

An entire roasted pigeon sat perched on Larkin's plate, surrounded by tiny potatoes in thick butter gravy. Candied cabbage was delicately piled next to the garnish.

But as irresistible as the sight was, no one at the table reached for their fork.

"Eat," Melay demanded. "This is the last decent meal you'll have in a while."

What in hells does that mean? thought Larkin.

"And the first, Your Majesty," said the boy closest to the queen. His hazel eyes sparkled, his tone mock serious. Elfina elbowed him.

So Larkin wasn't the only one to notice the hypocrisy. Years of starving them, and now the queen was commanding them to eat.

The queen smiled, as though the boy had said something flattering. "Then you will enjoy this, Casseem."

Casseem pushed around the potatoes on his plate with his

finger and beamed at the queen, as if to challenge her. He was either fearless or stupid. Maybe both.

He was also more patient than Larkin. Ignoring her utensils, she ripped off a piece of the pigeon's breast with her fingers, stuffing the meat into her mouth. It nearly melted at the touch of her tongue, and when she finished swallowing, she crammed in one potato after another.

Others began to eat, and Larkin watched them between bites. Some were more reluctant, like Jacque. Surprisingly, once Casseem picked up his fork, he ate as ravenously as Larkin. He caught her watching him, smirked, and gestured to his face. Larkin wiped food from her chin with the back of her hand, and he nodded in approval before elbowing Elfina, as if paying her back for earlier. A regular comic.

Larkin felt a flash of irritation. Didn't Casseem see the trembling girl at the end, the one who hardly picked at her food? Wasn't he worried? Maybe he wasn't. He hadn't witnessed Melay kill an Empath just to make more room in the cells.

Larkin dropped her fork, suddenly without appetite. She gulped water from her glass, her stomach rolling with nausea when she caught the queen's simpering expression.

"Aren't you going to eat, Devon?" The queen's voice took on a teasing lilt.

The surly miner hadn't touched his food. He kept his arms crossed, staring back at Melay. The others stopped chewing as they waited for him to answer, Casseem taking one last heaping forkful before sitting back.

"No," said Devon. The lieutenant looked to Melay, hand on his hilt.

The queen appeared amused. "As you wish." She snapped her fingers, and the servants returned to clear the plates.

Larkin was impressed by Devon's simple defiance. She thought of the riot, and the hairs on her arms stood on end. Melay had done everything in her power to break the spirit of Empaths. She was someone to be feared.

Vigilance, she reminded herself. Garran was more important than protesting the queen. But vigilance was difficult when she couldn't guess the intentions of Queen Melay. She knew little of the dynasty in general, only that Melay's parents had been Queen Cassia and King Mellum. The throne had been promised to Melay at birth, her parents now nothing more than ghosts. She'd owned Demura the moment she left the womb. Blessed by the goddess, indeed.

"I've been told that your arrest only took place yesterday, so you are aware of the realm's current state, are you not?" asked Melay. She had turned away from Devon and was looking at Larkin.

Larkin scanned the room. Everyone—the prisoners, Tamsyn, Jacque, and even the lieutenant—waited for Larkin to say something. Had she become the realm's expert on the capital's current affairs?

Or perhaps Melay meant something more than just the damage. "Destruction magic." Her voice echoed through the dining hall. "And disappearances."

Melay seemed disappointed with her response. "Yes, yes, I'm

afraid the disappearances have been happening for a while now. Months, in fact. Demurans in the hills pulled into the earth, disappearing forever." Melay waited, as though fishing for a reaction.

Larkin clenched her jaw in an attempt to remain stoic as her head spun.

The rumors Garran had overheard in the prison were true.

"Hundreds have vanished. Ones that some of us hold dear." The queen's gaze shifted to the mousy girl across from the lieutenant. "Isn't that right, Brielle?"

Brielle's hand darted to her cheek, brushing a tear away.

"Such a dreadful thing, your sister slipping from your grasp."

Stop it, Larkin wanted to yell, unable to tear her eyes away from Brielle, whose face had paled even further. The girl shrank in her seat. Larkin couldn't imagine the guilt Brielle was racked with, and the queen was purposefully making it worse.

"But it isn't your fault, Brielle," Melay continued. "It isn't the fault of anyone on the Surface, because this evil is coming from the Reach."

There it was again: the Reach. Larkin should have known the queen wouldn't be willing to find the true source of the horrors. She was going to blame it on a myth.

Garran had told the story to Vania yesterday. *People tell it to keep naughty children like you from doing anything bad.* That wasn't the whole truth. They told it to remind Empaths that their roots were grounded in evil. Melay pawning the destruction off on Kyran was just that.

Casseem burst out laughing, startling Larkin. "Your Majesty, you can't be serious."

On the other side of Tamsyn, Hathius shifted. "Watch your tongue," he threatened.

"I thought this would be enjoyable for you, Casseem, considering your flippancy toward the goddess and the gift of luminite."

The queen's cool demeanor worried Larkin; Melay wasn't one to take Empath defiance lightly. So why didn't she care? *She knows something we don't*, thought Larkin. Didn't Casseem realize this?

As Larkin considered kicking him under the table, she suddenly remembered where she recognized him from. He was the Empath who used to peddle fake luminite trinkets in the market. She wondered what other chicanery had landed him in jail.

Casseem placed his elbows on the table, resting his chin on his folded hands. "I have no stake in your plights, my queen. How could I? You've had me locked away for . . ." He shrugged dramatically. "I'm not quite sure how old I am anymore."

Melay flashed him a contrived smile. "A year isn't too long to lose track of time, is it? Your theatrics will bore your peers quickly, Casseem."

"Eighteen, then." Casseem grinned. "A merry birthday to me indeed."

"Where'd they go?"

Brielle's voice was barely audible, but something about it demanded the attention of the table. Hope. She was still hopeful she'd find her sister.

Brielle blushed and self-corrected. "Where did they go, Your M-majesty?"

Melay's shoulders relaxed, but Larkin didn't dare believe that she actually held any sympathy for Brielle. "I don't know what happened to the harvesters." The queen toyed with the empty setting of her ring, spinning it around her thin finger. "In fact, the only clue of the disappearances lies with the soldiers. Jacque?"

The corner of Melay's mouth twitched as Jacque hooked a finger beneath her own luminite collar and tugged at it, as if trying to give herself some space to breathe.

"Would you care to explain exactly what has happened to half my army?" Melay continued.

Jacque quickly dropped her hand. She held her shoulders back and head high as if she were in rank. "I did not witness what happened to them, my queen."

"Answer the question, soldier," said the lieutenant.

"I didn't—" Jacque's sharp jaw rippled, but her eyes and mouth were soft as she stared beyond the table at nothing, removed.

Jacque may not have seen what happened to the soldiers, but she'd experienced something horrible. Larkin was certain of it.

Something *had* happened to them. Maybe they were swallowed by the earth too. Going by what she knew, Larkin tried to calculate the size of half of Melay's army. Hundreds. Thousands?

Jacque continued. "We received word of destruction magic in the hills, and all of us were pulled from our stations. By the time we'd gathered soldiers and traversed the vale, three farms had crumbled to nothing, the farmers nowhere to be found. We followed the destruction east, to the edge of the hold, and ultimately into the mouth of the Reach. Just as you suspected, my queen."

Melay looked pleased with this answer, or perhaps with

how obviously rattled Jacque was. *She's toying with her,* Larkin thought.

"How many soldiers were sent into the Reach, Jacque?"

"Over ten thousand, my queen."

Larkin could hardly comprehend the number. Ten thousand was a third of the entire capital of Demura.

"And how many returned?"

Jacque hesitated. "I know the lieutenants of the battalions did not realize the journey in store. There are only twenty documented miles of the Reach, my queen. But that is not the true expanse of the underworld."

"How *many*, Jacque?" Melay repeated.

"One, my queen."

How many endless, snaking tunnels would it take to lose ten thousand soldiers? Larkin felt the room close in on her and fought the urge to try to loosen her own collar.

"And what happened to the last soldier?" asked Melay.

Jacque's throat bobbed as she swallowed. "I killed him mercifully, my queen."

"Destruction magic?" Casseem smirked.

"It's not funny," Elfina said, her wide eyes glued to Jacque.

Jacque blinked, focusing on Casseem as her lip pulled up in a sneer. "With a sword."

"And with that," Melay seethed, "you decimated my one chance at learning what happened to my army."

"The soldier had lost his mind. My commanding officer gave the orders to—"

Melay interrupted her. "What did the soldier say before he died?"

Larkin scooted to the edge of her seat.

"What did he repeat over and over until the moment you slaughtered him?" The bronze of the table was reflected in Melay's wild eyes.

Larkin understood now. Melay wasn't simply satisfied by Jacque's discomfort. She wanted the soldier to suffer. Payback for disobeying orders.

"*Answer her,*" demanded Hathius.

Jacque flinched. She wilted in her seat, as though finally surrendering to the last of the memory. The soldier took a deep breath, then uttered a saying Larkin was all too familiar with:

"'Though I have fallen, darkness will rise.'"

SEVEN

Otheil Kyran's words before he was thrown into the Reach, regurgitated by the one soldier who'd returned from its depths.

Larkin wanted to laugh.

"The god of the underworld has awoken from his slumber." The queen sat back in her chair, seemingly satisfied.

It made little sense. If Melay truly believed that Otheil Kyran was raining havoc on her kingdom, then why did she appear so content?

"Let me understand this." Casseem rested his elbows on the table and pressed the steeple of his fingers to his lips. "You want us to believe that Otheil Kyran has truly been immortalized *somehow*—that he is indeed a god and has killed thousands of Demurans?"

"I didn't ask you to believe anything," said Melay.

"She doesn't care if you believe it." Devon hadn't budged, his arms still crossed over his chest. "Not if the rest of Demura does."

Again, the lieutenant Hathius looked to Melay, as if waiting for permission to cut down the insolent boy.

Melay remained calm. "It doesn't matter what you believe. For generations, you Empaths have atoned for your sins and paid homage to the goddess, but it seems it hasn't been enough. Kyran has followed up on his word. Darkness has risen."

Casseem sank back in his chair, silent, his smug demeanor gone. But Larkin wouldn't give up so easily. Deifying the woman who banned magic and shaming the man who challenged her was nothing more than a way to put Empaths in their place.

"Everyone knows the tale of Kyran," Larkin said. "The soldier had clearly gone mad and was rambling off something he'd heard as a child."

To Larkin's surprise, the queen nodded. "Then what are *your* theories, Larkin?"

"Rebels," Larkin said. "There are thousands on this isle who are punished because they have magic. You've forced them to work the fields and the mines." Her voice grew stronger. "Empath rebels could have found their way into the Reach. They could be using the caverns as an outpost and a way to travel beneath the isle."

The light glimmering within Melay's eyes burned brightly— furiously. *Wrath.* "If such powerful Empath rebels existed, my soldiers would have defeated them by now and returned home."

"It doesn't matter," Larkin spat, feeling emboldened. "Why are you wasting *our* time when *your* people are disappearing and half your army's lost to the Reach? What does this have to do with us?" Larkin asked, realizing a moment too late that she had been stupid enough to ask the question that the queen was waiting for.

"Who better to understand Kyran's hell than his own kind?"

A lock clicked inside Larkin, cold metallic pieces opening a trapdoor. Her insides plummeted into ice.

"You're sending us in," Larkin said.

Melay's response was quick. "Why ever else would you be here?"

"Ilona's teeth," whispered Elfina, her face wild with fear.

But Larkin felt maniacal. Laughter bubbled from her mouth. "And what exactly do you expect us to use? *Magic?* The same magic you outlawed? The reason why we're here in the first place?"

"Silence, Larkin," Jacque hissed.

Larkin wasn't about to play to the whims of the queen like the soldier did. She wasn't a pawn. "If you wanted our help, then you should have let us use magic instead of treating us like abominations!"

The lieutenant stood, and so did Larkin, her chair scraping backward. Tamsyn cowered between them as Hathius placed his palm on the hilt of his sword.

Larkin knew the lieutenant had the upper hand. She was moments away from being gutted by his sword. But though she was blinded by luminite, she didn't miss the flicker of apprehension behind his eyes.

Larkin leaned in. "You've never been in a room with so many of us when we weren't on the other side of bars."

"That's what the collars are for," the lieutenant snarled, drawing his sword. "But if the collar isn't enough, maybe this will silence you."

Melay held up her hand. "Hathius . . ."

Hathius slowly sheathed his sword and sat down.

"That's enough," Melay said.

Larkin settled back in her seat, her body buzzing with adrenaline, just like when she'd shattered Melay's ring. She felt like she'd won something.

Both Casseem and Elfina looked at Larkin with a glint that might have been admiration, but she didn't care what they thought of her. In a matter of days, they'd be lost in the darkness of the Reach like the thousands of soldiers before them.

"So you're just sending us off to fend for ourselves?" Casseem asked.

"You won't be alone. There are eight of you, including my prized scholar. Jacque and Tamsyn will serve as your guides. Tamsyn Arkwright knows more than any living soul about the Reach's contents, and he has sacrificed himself to aid you."

Casseem glared coldly at Tamsyn. "Lucky us."

The scholar sniffed and held his head up, pretending he hadn't heard.

"*They're* going to lead us?" Elfina's eyes flickered back and forth between Jacque and Tamsyn. She had a point. An Empath soldier and a scholar? Countless trained lieutenants had already died!

"And if we refuse?" Devon remained calm, but his voice was liquid ore. Larkin wondered if he was regretting not eating.

Melay hailed a guard, who approached and eased the queen's chair from beneath her as she stood. "You are welcome to find out. You are all aware of the other prisoners in my possession. Prisoners dear to you."

"You—" Larkin started forward, then bit back every vile thing that fought to spill from her mouth. Garran wasn't being held captive because of her crime.

He was Melay's leverage. Her way of making sure that Larkin remained obedient.

"You will find Otheil Kyran and you will kill him. The fight will be for neither gold nor honor. You fight for your lives . . . and the lives of those you love. You cannot expect them to live if you do not return victorious. And there will be one among you who will be my eyes, reminding you of your duty to the queen."

Melay was hinting at a spy. Larkin watched Jacque's and Tamsyn's faces for any flicker of emotion, but she deciphered nothing. *Damn this collar!*

Then again, it didn't matter if there was a spy among them. Ten thousand soldiers had failed at an impossible task, just like they would. And Garran would die.

We do know what always happens, he had told her. *The worst possible outcome, every time.*

Even with the luminite against her flesh, Larkin still searched for emotion. Anything she could use against Melay. She wanted the queen to suffer at her hand; she wanted to crush her heart and watch the life drain from her eyes.

"Seven." Casseem's voice cracked. "You said eight of us. Even with your soldier and your scholar, we're only seven. Do you plan on accompanying us, my queen?"

Melay nodded toward her lieutenant. "Hathius, I'm sure you can take this from here."

Hathius led them single file down a narrow dungeon stairwell, past the cellblock where Garran was still imprisoned. They spiraled deeper and deeper into the mountain.

As their surroundings darkened, panic ricocheted around Larkin's rib cage.

Her eyes stung as the group stepped into a dim tunnel. They spread out, and Elfina and Larkin fell to the back of the group.

"This is where they keep the worst of us criminals," whispered Elfina. "When luminite alone isn't enough."

"What *is* enough?" asked Larkin.

"Isolation." Elfina's voice trembled. "Worse than death."

Hells, thought Larkin. If Melay thought Garran had a luminite resistance, she could move him down here. A life alone, in the dark . . . just like the soldiers sent into the Reach, if they were alive. And if she lost track of her party, the strangers she was supposed to depend on, she'd be alone. If they starved and she was the last to die, she'd be alone. If they found what was causing the destruction on the Surface but couldn't make their way back up . . .

She braced herself against Elfina's shoulder, suddenly light-headed, and was grateful when Elfina didn't shrug her hand away.

They reached a reinforced door at the tunnel's end, protected by two guards. One opened the door with an iron key, and they all filed in. Larkin clung to the handrail in front of her for balance; beyond her, nothing but a curtain of darkness. They were standing at the edge of a black pit.

Hathius took a torch from the wall and threw it into the deep. It hit the stone floor and sparked, illuminating a filthy boy with a shaved head. The boy didn't flinch, remaining in the center of the floor with his knees pulled to his chest. Larkin couldn't see his face in the dim glow, but he looked around her age.

"Amias! Ready to be brought to the light of day?" Hathius laughed. "Well, I guess I shouldn't be making that promise."

Jacque dropped to her knees to peer beneath the bars of the railing. "*Gods*. Amias?"

"You know him?" Larkin asked.

In the dim light, Larkin could see the muscles of her face twitch. "We grew up together. In Eversown."

Larkin started before crouching down beside Jacque. Amias of Eversown Farm? That meant the boy below was the infamous Empath who had decimated the entirety of Eversown at the age of twelve—a village turned to dust from his power of destruction, a fleet of soldiers murdered in the process.

"Melay made a declaration after what he did," Jacque explained. "She said that he had been executed. I don't understand."

"The queen is merciful," Hathius said. "She chose to keep him alive."

Amias lifted his head. Dead eyes stared up at them from hollow sockets.

A shell in the dark.

Larkin remembered hearing rumors about this boy—around half a decade ago. Had he been in this prison since his arrest? She couldn't fathom being alone for that length of time.

If Garran shared Amias's fate . . . *No.*

Even as Larkin watched Amias warily, hope blossomed inside her. If something sinister truly was lurking within the Reach, they wouldn't be sent in defenseless. Amias had been locked away because of his power. Because he was a weapon.

Now he would be *their* weapon.

* * *

The next morning, Larkin watched the cold dawn break through the barred window in her palace room.

The small hearth kept the room warm, and her plush bed was the nicest thing she'd ever rested on, yet sleep had evaded her all night.

When the sky was washed with light, a servant entered her room with a meal of bread and hard cheese. She set the tray on an end table and propped open the room's wardrobe, leaving Larkin without a word.

Larkin got up and walked to the wardrobe. Armor clung to the stand within, similar to the set Jacque wore. How kind of Melay to outfit them for the Reach. As if it would make a difference.

This is punishment, thought Larkin. That's all the mission was. Melay was sending them into the Reach like Ilona had exiled Kyran and his disciples. The queen's prisons were predictable. Awful, but predictable. Even a swift execution was predictable.

But this . . .

Numbly, Larkin undressed and tugged on fresh undergarments, a tunic, and trousers.

She studied her armor. Metal plates were sewn into the leather of the cuirass to protect her shoulders. Her greaves and bracers were fashioned the same way, with plates for her knees and wrists.

She slid on her cuirass, buckling a dozen different straps.

"I'm doing this wrong," Larkin muttered to herself, unbuckling and rebuckling all of them. Still wrong, but her hands were trembling too much to attempt again.

After fitting her utility belt, Larkin tied back her umber curls and turned to the room's mirror. She gritted her teeth as the luminite around her neck sparkled.

She was used to her murky reflection in the kitchen basin, but here, with such clarity, Larkin looked just like her mother, sharp-boned and strong-jawed—handsome, her father once called her. And in a way, she did look ready for battle.

When her mother had broken her leg, all those years ago, and Larkin was getting ready for her first day in the mines, her mother had sensed Larkin's nerves.

If you ever begin to panic in the caves, remember to sense those around you. There will be despair and anger, yes, but you will also find those lost in the thoughts of their families waiting at home.

Siphon from them, Larkin. Let the joy they cling to fill you up, and it will feel just like the sun.

She wished she could hear her mother speak those words aloud one more time. Her mother . . . If she only knew what Larkin was up against. Would she ever know, if Larkin never returned?

Larkin let out a sob, clapping a hand over her mouth, as if she could catch the fear and swallow it back down.

But fear, she knew, didn't like being told what to do.

Sinking to the floor, she let it seize her.

EIGHT

Melay's emeralds dimmed in comparison to the vale that stretched for miles.

Larkin and her companions rode on horseback down the trading route and toward the highland, each of them accompanied by a palace guard. Larkin never had the chance to speak to the others. *Plenty of time to bond in the Reach,* she thought grimly.

The wind rippled across the high grass and coaxed Larkin's curls free from her tie. She was used to seeing the vale at a distance when leaving the mines, but trotting through it was something different. Patches of creamy wildflowers swirled through the grass, the scent intoxicating, so much so that she didn't immediately notice the sinkholes pocketing the plains.

If the rumors were to be believed, Demurans had disappeared into those holes . . . Edric. Was he still alive? Were any of them?

Garran and the rest of her family weren't safe from this strange destruction either. If they were—if *all* Empaths were—perhaps she'd be excited that magic had finally overpowered Melay. But it seemed the source of the destruction had no intention of sparing her kind.

And the granite-and-luminite city was as vulnerable to the destruction as everywhere else. If Empath rebels were causing the destruction, maybe the caverns were offering a way around the Surface's luminite. Or the rebels were resistant, like her.

Even to Larkin it seemed far-fetched, but it didn't matter. She had to trust that she and her companions would uncover the reason behind the magic. It was her family's only chance at survival. Larkin clung to the thought as the group rode forward, narrowly avoiding a sinkhole in the middle of the road.

Occasionally, they'd pass farm villages brimming with thatched-roof cabins, but as they traveled farther east, villages transformed into heaps of rubble and splinters. Farmers shoveling away the destruction looked up as they passed, shielding their eyes.

They're hoping we're aid, thought Larkin, heartsick. To her left, Brielle curled over her saddle, squeezing her eyes shut. Larkin wanted to ask if this had been her farm but knew Brielle wouldn't hear her over the drumbeat of hooves.

When they reached the cragged and pine-laced eastern hills, the sun was midway across the sky. The horses slowed, swallowed by a cloud of dust as they ascended the switchbacks, and Larkin looked back to an infinite sea of gold and muted green. The city's peak was but a jutting outline against the backdrop of the sun.

Home. Already she missed the small, quiet box of the family kitchen, the smell of grease, and her mother's bread. She'd give this entire world for one more day near the hearth. But as soon as her horse rounded a bend in the trail, all thoughts of home disappeared.

A narrow path emerged between two feldspar boulders, and Hathius, who took the lead with Jacque, guided them through. The ground leveled to a trodden, bustling outpost in front of a glittering recess in the mountain.

Blue flags rippled above erect tents, embellished with Demura's seal: two swords crossed beneath a cut gemstone. Soldiers sparred and sharpened weapons, pausing as they rode up.

The horses circled and halted. Larkin's guard hopped off the horse and helped her down, and she gritted her teeth as her feet hit the ground, her thigh muscles screaming in pain. The only one of them who wasn't limping around and clutching their hips was Jacque. Amias squinted as he bent over and rubbed his legs, obviously spent by both the ride and the sun. If he'd experienced only darkness for years, she was impressed that he wasn't completely blinded.

He caught her looking and stared back at her, blinking. When Larkin waved, he didn't wave back. Maybe he *was* blinded.

Larkin was distracted when her guard handed her a pack. She quickly rifled through it, spotting a waterskin, a bedroll, and a week's worth of food.

"They're optimistic, aren't they?" Devon asked. He sauntered over to her, as fearless as he'd been in the palace.

It was the first thing he'd said to her. Larkin raised an eyebrow. She noted his muscles, which meant that he hadn't been wasting away in Melay's prison long.

Devon peered into her open bag. "How long do you think we'd last with this much food?"

Larkin shrugged. "We wouldn't die from starvation for at least a month after our supply ran out."

"And you know that from experience?"

Didn't *he* know from experience?

"Which mine did you work in?" she asked.

"The Vault." He gripped his bag shut in one hand, his knuckles bone-white.

It was the mine her father worked in, the most lucrative one of all. With a little luck and skill, perhaps Devon truly didn't know how long it took to starve, especially if he didn't have a family relying on him.

"Little food means little hope," he said. "If Melay isn't expecting us to get far, why send us in at all?"

Without giving her time to answer, Devon trudged off to join the rest of the group.

She couldn't shake the fact that Devon was right. If Melay wanted them to succeed, why not outfit them with more gear and reinforcements? Why not send in an army of Empaths, or at least a few guards for backup?

Slinging her pack over her shoulder, Larkin turned to see her party converging near the center of the outpost.

Beyond them, a wall of silky, iridescent luminite loomed over the camp, split in the center by a cleft in the mountain. The dark entrance was sealed by a portcullis.

The surrounding outpost soldiers ceased their sparring as they began hooting and whistling at the newcomers. Brielle flinched in surprise, but Elfina watched with mild curiously.

"Feed them to the beast!" hollered one, and the others cheered.

If we fail, you're as good as dead, Larkin wanted to scream back, but the vengeful thought was little comfort as they kept moving forward.

"Traitor!" another shouted. Larkin realized the soldier was screaming at Jacque and wondered if she was from Jacque's battalion. Casseem appeared amused as he watched for Jacque's reaction, but the soldier remained indifferent. Larkin wondered how Jacque had gotten herself into such a mess. She seemed to be a traitor to everyone, Empaths and soldiers alike.

Jacque turned and spoke with Amias, her hand resting on his shoulder. From the looks of it, they'd been more than just village acquaintances. Perhaps they'd been friends, or childhood sweethearts. Larkin felt a stab of jealousy, wishing there was someone here who was more than just a stranger. She had never needed the companionship of anyone other than her family, not until now.

Amias's dark, watering eyes found Larkin's. His fawn-colored skin was sallow but not pallid or sickly. Something about his vacant face told her it used to be softer. She could see the ghost of that boy in the edges of his full lips and the apples of his cheeks, places his smile had once clung to.

Something that had once been there was gone.

Larkin studied him, as though she could unearth the darkness lurking within using only her mind. Years ago, he had siphoned enough rage or terror or grief to destroy an entire farm. Did the destruction change him? Did he feel guilt, or was the emptiness she saw within him an absence of all emotion? It chilled her to think of what violence he was capable of.

But she needed him.

She needed to learn what all her companions were capable of the moment they were free of the luminite, but Amias was the most important. She could only hope that isolation hadn't made him even more unstable, especially when confronted by whatever lurked below.

Larkin flinched when Hathius hollered, "Open the gate!"

Soldiers hurried to a massive iron turnstile beyond the tents, taking to the spokes and working together to crank the wheel to the right. The iron screeched as the wheel began to rotate, and the portcullis lifted.

The jaws of the Reach opened to nothing but a glittering darkness. Above her, the sun shone brightly, the warmth deep and rich. Larkin always associated the feeling of love with sunshine. She closed her eyes and could feel Vania's hair gliding through her fingers, the relief that flooded her when her father came home late from the Vault. Larkin tried blinking her memories away, her eyes darting around to her seven other party members as they watched the raising portcullis. They were statues, so still and yielding to what was happening.

A scream built inside her.

Before Larkin could release it, she noticed Tamsyn squirming out of the corner of her eye, breaking her spell of panic. He tugged compulsively on his cuirass, his gear flopping about as he did.

Tamsyn wouldn't be able to sense her underground, but the other Empaths would.

Her companions would be relying on her as much as Garran did. Emotions were infectious, spreading from person to person like fire. If she wanted to sense courage from them, she needed to provide it in return.

Jacque squared her shoulders and walked to a nearby weapons rack. The others followed, including Larkin, and Jacque began passing around swords and throwing knives.

"You won't need those." Tamsyn fumbled with his twisted pack strap. "Luminite's a Surface mineral. You'll have full range of your magic once we enter the Reach."

"I'm trained in swordplay, not magic." Jacque tossed a sheathed blade to Larkin, and Larkin caught it ungracefully.

"Magic is the reason we have an advantage over the battalions. You need to trust your abilities," argued Tamsyn.

"I'd think before informing us of our own abilities, if I were you," said Larkin, resisting the sudden urge to push him over. His pack would probably send him tumbling headfirst.

"Save it, Arkwright." Casseem held a sword up, examining it.

"*Tamsyn* is just fine," the scholar muttered.

"Nonsense. Be proud of your surname. A privilege your queen deprived us of." Casseem pulled his sword from its sheath. "And anyways, none of us have any advantage over the soldiers. Unless you've all been brushing up on your destruction magic."

"Didn't fancy getting cut down by a soldier," Elfina said.

Brielle shook her head as she chewed her fingernail.

Casseem looked to Amias.

Amias tilted his head to the side and Larkin saw the slightest glint of anticipation behind his eyes, like he was waiting for Casseem to mention his past.

The moment passed in silence.

"That's what I thought," said Casseem.

Gods, she wanted inside their heads. Or their emotions, at the very least. Larkin tugged at her luminite collar. These people didn't feel real to her yet. And they wouldn't, not until she could sense.

Larkin was distracted as Hathius approached the party with

two torches, handing one to Brielle, who stared at it, her expression horrified. Her eyes darted around to the others, as if she hoped one of them would take the torch from her.

No one volunteered.

Hathius led them forward. Reaching the cavern entrance, he stepped aside and pulled a small key from his pocket.

Casseem was the first, approaching Hathius to have his collar removed before entering the cavern, followed by Jacque. Brielle and her torch went next, then Elfina, Amias, and Tamsyn.

Larkin looked over her shoulder. Devon hadn't budged. He seemed different now, angry, like a pot about to boil over.

A guard approached Devon from behind and gave him a shove. "Move it."

Devon stumbled forward, then swung his fist around. The guard caught it and punched him in the gut.

Fool. So much for a heroic protest. He was the one who mentioned the lack of food, and yet he seemed dead set on wasting energy.

Larkin glared at Devon as two guards towed him toward the cavern entrance and tossed him through. *Get in the damn mine,* she thought anxiously.

Devon scrambled to his feet, but Jacque and Casseem grabbed his arms, preventing him from trying to run back out.

"You're making it worse," Jacque hissed.

The miner thrashed but failed to shake them off.

Larkin turned away from Devon's struggles and walked to Hathius. She exhaled as her collar was unlocked, ready for the familiar rush of emotions to come flooding back, but her senses remained dulled. The solid luminite mouth of the Reach was still suppressing her, even at a distance. Larkin's resistance was no match against this much of the mineral.

"I do feel sorry for you." Hathius's voice rang flat against the luminite wall as he passed her the remaining torch. "Quite a burden to fall on such naïve shoulders."

Larkin whirled on Hathius. She had nothing to lose.

"And what do you think happens if we fail? You better pray to your damned Ilona that we return, or everything you love will crumble around you." Larkin cocked her head. "And if Kyran has a sense of humor, you'll be one of the last standing."

The lieutenant's smile fell. She had power over him after all.

His fault for being stupid enough to think Kyran was an immortal god.

Larkin walked through the cavern entrance. The gate descended behind her. She watched it lock them in.

Hathius glared at her from the other side of the bars.

"I'll have soldiers posted for the next one hundred and fifty days. That's well into autumn," Hathius said. "If the destruction ceases and you return to the Surface soon after, then we'll release you. Despite our differences, I do hope you succeed, Larkin. For Demura."

She wanted to laugh in his face. *One hundred and fifty days.* Just given the amount of resources they had, they'd last less than a third of that with the best of luck.

Larkin thought of the destruction magic and her task of finding its source. Hathius wanted her to succeed because magic had mysteriously found a way to defy the queen. Melay's army had failed to return with an answer. Did Hathius believe it was Kyran, or was he simply following Melay's whims? Perhaps, as

Devon suspected, he was just happy to enact their punishment by sending them into the Reach.

She knew she was wasting time wondering about the lieutenant. *Stop it,* Larkin ordered herself. *Save Garran.*

Nothing else mattered.

Larkin turned from Hathius and stepped into the shadows.

NINE

A n onyx world waited beneath Larkin.

Down below, the light from Brielle's distant torch licked along the walls of the shimmering tunnel. Pins and needles swept over Larkin's skin as she followed the rest of the group into darkness. She pressed her hand to her cuirass and tried to breathe, but her lungs couldn't expand enough.

Don't panic, she thought.

Larkin realized that the sound of heavy breathing wasn't coming from her. Footsteps echoed along the tunnel walls.

Someone was hiking back up.

The person collided with Larkin, and Larkin fumbled to steady them.

"Is the gate closed?" Elfina glanced behind Larkin, wide eyes glinting in the torchlight. "Sweet Ilona." She bent over to balance herself on her knees. "I can't do this."

"We don't really have another option, Elfina."

"It's Elf."

"Elf," Larkin repeated. "We should get moving." She spoke more confidently than she felt, worried they'd fall behind if they lingered.

Elf stood straight, wiping the hair from her forehead as she stared down at the path ahead. "I'm used to the vale, the wide-open spaces. I'd die if I were a miner. No offense."

You get used to it, Larkin wanted to say, but that would be a lie. Instead, she gently guided Elf in front of her. "My mum taught me some tricks to deal with the tight spaces, and the darkness. I can share them with you."

"I'd like that," said Elf.

"The first is to focus on ways to distract yourself. You're a storyteller, right? You promised me a story of Kyran's revenge, after all."

"That'll set the mood, all right." Elf grimaced, bracing herself against the tunnel wall as she began her descent.

At least she's walking, thought Larkin, following her. The slick wall rushed past her fingers; the narrow passage that led downward into the caverns was solid luminite. No wonder Kyran and his disciples couldn't escape. It was the perfect prison.

As Elfina continued, she regained her grace, floating from step to step. "I don't usually tell stories like this. I'm used to an audience and a stage."

"I can applaud? Gasp? Jeer at the villain?" Larkin suggested.

"I'll have to start at the beginning. The dry stuff. I can't drop you into the middle of a battle scene where Elesandre must conjure new limbs for her injured compatriot."

"Who's Elesandre?" Larkin asked. Already, Elf's breathing was growing calmer. The distraction was working.

"Proving my point already. You don't even know Kyran's disciples by name." The tremble in Elf's voice was dissipating. "Bianca Elesandre was Kyran's right hand. She was skilled as a medic, and conjured new flesh to heal wounds during the Uprising."

"Conjured new flesh from what?"

"Dead bodies."

Larkin wrinkled her nose. "That's unsettling."

"Oh, it's just wonderful, Larkin. Think of being able to heal whomever you wish! She was the most fun to tell stories about. Thaos Leander too. He was trying to find a way to overpower luminite. The tales are endless."

This caught Larkin's attention. "Was he ever successful?" she asked, thinking of her own resistance.

"Not sure. I'm just a storyteller, remember? I work with seeds of legends and make things grow. We made up tales of Leander stuck in the Reach, learning to defeat the luminite barrier and escaping." Elf's voice grew louder and more melodic as she skated around a shadowy dip in the path.

"And no one knows what happened to him once he was imprisoned?" Larkin pried as she clumsily followed in Elf's footsteps. Outside of her family's immunity, Leander was the first she'd ever heard of another Empath being able to resist, or attempting to resist, the mineral.

"No one knows what happened to any of them."

But Larkin did know what *should* have happened to them. Kyran and his disciples were condemned a thousand years ago. They should have lived their short lives in darkness.

Not should, she reminded herself. *Did.*

The air thickened with the scent of ancient water and the sharpness of the ore. They'd caught up to the others, their voices occasionally echoing against mineral.

Natural cavern openings weren't as linear as this. Larkin knew the difference between an earth-made cavern and one that had been scooped out by miners, and this path was made by men. Hundreds of years ago, the Reach was brimming with workers—miners, just like her.

She was used to mines. Maybe there was nothing frightening at all about the Reach. Maybe the soldiers were still alive below, searching for the source of the destruction.

But she wouldn't waste time with false hope. Real hope lay in what Tamsyn had told them back at the outpost: luminite was a Surface mineral. She'd be able to sense again soon. It was like waiting for a blindfold to be lifted. She couldn't imagine the magic unbridled, no threat of imprisonment. Freedom was close enough to taste. And once they all were free, she would know what they had to work with. Soldiers had swords, but seven of them could crush bone at the sense of fear.

Larkin would bank her hope in magic.

Ahead, Tamsyn had stopped, his manicured hand sliding along the wall. "Have you ever seen so much luminite in your life?"

"You can't imagine," Larkin responded brusquely. "When's the tunnel supposed to end?"

"A few miles, I think. I need to refer to my texts before we go deeper. They're important, you know. The texts will tell us precisely what we need to know to get us through the Reach."

"*I need to refer to my texts,*" Elf mocked, flawlessly mimicking Tamsyn's posh baritone. "*He's* the most educated person on the Reach?"

Larkin hid a laugh.

"I could have escaped if it weren't for the luminite," Devon's voice boomed in front of them.

Casseem chuckled wryly. "Any of us could have escaped

without the luminite. Melay coats the entire damned city with it so we don't go around melting off the guards' faces."

"You think the luminite would stop me from slitting a throat or two?" Devon's steps grew heavier, as if he was trying to make as much noise as possible. Larkin missed when he was quiet. "Why do you think I was imprisoned in the first place? The guards had it coming."

"Sucks all the air out of the room, that one," Elf muttered.

"He wants us angry," Larkin whispered in response, thinking about her conversation with Devon at the Reach's entrance. He'd fished for Larkin's reaction at the food supply then, and he'd rejected his meal in the palace in the hopes of riling up Melay.

Devon was bent on creating anger for the sake of it.

Casseem scoffed. "Are you *bragging* about murdering guards?"

"All I'm saying is that I've had the opportunity," said Devon.

"Please shut up," Jacque ordered from the front of the line.

Please, thought Larkin.

Casseem agreed. "We need to be able to hear what's up ahead."

"And make sure that whatever's up ahead doesn't hear us. We don't know what happened to the other soldiers," Jacque reminded them as the shimmering ring of light from their torches grew.

The tunnel was widening, the glimmer of luminite subsiding. One by one, the eight of them spilled from the tunnel, their light doing little to illuminate the dome of the chamber. The air was stale and sharp with mineral. Larkin looked up. The light reflected in a crescent along the ceiling, the sheet of luminite cresting before it fanned into veins at the farthest side of the small room. The opening that led deeper wasn't much wider than the tunnel they'd come from.

At the chamber's center, Casseem shrugged off his pack. "How many miles was that?" He swiped the damp hair from his forehead, stole Larkin's torch, and scrutinized the ceiling's dwindling luminite.

"From my knowledge, two miles," said Tamsyn. "But let me refer to my texts."

My texts, Elf mouthed dramatically, and Larkin bit back her grin.

Tamsyn removed his scroll case from his shoulder. He uncapped the case and tilted it until a roll of parchment slid into his open palm.

Brielle lit a sconce on the wall, cupping her hands around the flame and expertly coaxing it to life. She smiled briefly at the fire before she began to pick at the handle of her torch.

Casseem paced the floor, and Larkin watched his fingers flex at his sides. She sensed the tremor of something faint. Her resistance granted her the ability to sense, but surely Casseem couldn't. Not yet.

They locked eyes.

The corner of Casseem's mouth perked up. "Five hundred paces and I'll know exactly who's terrified of the dark."

So Casseem was still hindered by the luminite, which meant the rest of them likely were too. Larkin skirted the group until she was as far away from the mineral as possible, the emotions of her party clinging to her in bits and pieces.

Devon sulked to the edge of the chamber and threw his pack down, pressing his back to the wall. Beneath her skin, Larkin sensed a steady tremor stemming from him.

So his angry demeanor was a lie. He was terrified, perhaps more than anyone else. That explained the mood swings.

As for the others . . . It was hard to distinguish them within the sea of discomfort. As they waited for Tamsyn to read the map, Elf glided along the edges of the chamber as though attempting to distance herself from the group. Brielle set her torch on the ground and remained crouched, folding into her body as she observed the mineral ceiling. Jacque, on the other hand, acted indifferent toward the luminite, leaning against the wall with her hand on her sword.

The only disrupting wave was the curiosity that stemmed from Amias. He knelt near Tamsyn and rifled through the stacked documents near the scroll case. If he cared that the luminite was almost gone, he was doing a good job at hiding it.

"Careful," Tamsyn hissed as Amias pulled a scroll from beneath the pile.

"What is it?"

It was the first time Larkin heard him speak, his voice almost musical. For a boy who'd been locked up for half a decade, she'd expected something rougher.

"A taxonomy of cave edibles. We'll die without it," said Tamsyn impatiently, as though it was the dumbest thing he'd ever been asked.

Amias unraveled the scroll and studied it, his eyes flitting back and forth across the parchment.

Casseem cocked his head to the side as he watched Amias. "I didn't think Empaths could read."

"I'm full of secrets." Amias's attention didn't waver from the scroll.

"You sure are. You'd think that from sitting in a hole in the ground, you'd be a ghostly, shriveled little thing—"

Amias cut him off. "I've never been ghostly. Or shriveled."

"True, your arms are almost as big as Larkin's." Casseem glanced at Larkin and grinned.

Larkin crossed her arms over her chest. "The hells is that supposed to mean?"

"Miners are an intimidating lot. Take it as a compliment."

At Casseem's mention of her arms, Larkin realized how tense every part of her body was. The flitting emotions of her companions were teasing her. "We shouldn't wait here long, not when there's still luminite."

"Because our magic will protect us?" Devon drawled.

Larkin paced the edge of the chamber. Devon's eyes followed her, intent. "I don't know what's below," she said. "But I've never used a sword in my life. So yes, magic is my only defense. And that's the same for most of us."

"Can't imagine your destruction magic is much better than your swordsmanship, Larkin." Devon settled against the wall. "Have you ever been outside the capital until now?"

She gave him nothing, refusing to be baited even as her anger flared. Larkin knew his surliness was just an act, a cloak for his vulnerability. Soon, everyone else would realize it, too.

Tamsyn tapped his finger on the map. "I was correct," he declared. We've traveled about two miles. About eighteen more to go before the known Reach ends."

Jacque tugged at her leather glove, watching Devon and Larkin like a prison guard monitoring unruly inmates. "Let's move."

"You've been trying to foil this mission from the start." Larkin took a step toward Devon. "Why?"

The other miner pushed himself from the wall, his fear twisting cruelly. He'd been waiting for this question.

"Because even if Melay truly does believe in Kyran, this isn't a mission to kill him. The queen wants to take out her anger on us because she can. She threatened our families because she can. And once we die, which will happen, she'll send another group of Empaths down, and another." He shrugged. "Maybe until all of us are gone. Because *she can*. I won't play along."

Larkin gritted her teeth. So that was why he'd fought the guards. Why he'd mentioned the food. He didn't just believe that their mission was hopeless; he was making sure it was impossible. He was fighting for someone, just like she was fighting for her parents and Vania and Garran. Why wasn't he willing to fight for them?

Perhaps he only cared about himself. The thought infuriated her.

"Even if you don't think we have a fighting chance, you still need to try. Just like the rest of us," she said, pointing up. "People are relying on us. Family."

Devon stopped a mere foot from Larkin, towering over her. She sensed the swell of annoyance from the others. Beneath his glee, Devon's fear was still there. Fear she began to siphon.

"You mean Melay's hostages? Who is it for you, Larkin . . .

A sister? Brother?" Devon rolled his shoulders back. Although his voice softened, his eyes remained sharp with malice. "Even if, by some miracle, we discover that Kyran isn't a myth and we kill him, the ones you care about are still going to die." He shrugged. "Perhaps they're already dead."

Larkin grabbed him by the throat. She dug her fingernails in as she projected.

Devon screamed and ripped her off, stumbling backward.

Casseem lunged toward Larkin, dragging her away. She pushed him off as Jacque charged toward her, sword halfway pulled from her scabbard. "The hells did you just do?" Jacque yelled.

Larkin backed away from the both of them, watching Devon as he gasped for air. He dropped his hands, bloody fingerprints imprinted into his neck.

Larkin's fingerprints.

The shock from the others stormed inside her, charging every nerve, every muscle, every inch of her skin. She rubbed her fingers together, knowing she wouldn't have stopped if Casseem hadn't pulled her away.

"Did you just—" Casseem began.

Tamsyn cut him off. "Impossible. We're too close to the luminite."

"Larkin?" Elf asked quietly. She wanted an answer, just like the rest of them. But there was something powerful about this secret of Larkin's resistance. It felt like an advantage, something she wasn't ready to give up just yet.

"Miners are an intimidating lot, especially those of us with big arms and sharp fingernails," Larkin said. *Let them wonder.*

Casseem snapped his mouth shut, both satisfied and disturbed by her answer.

Larkin glowered at Devon as he clutched his neck. He'd felt the burning of his flesh. He knew she'd used destruction magic on him, and he could out her luminite resistance to the others. Larkin was relying on his pride alone to keep her secret.

Devon coughed, inhaling a ragged breath. "Fine!" he rasped, sliding to the ground. Perhaps the others believed he was trembling out of rage, but Larkin knew the truth.

"You want to play this game?" His voice grew steady again. "Here's what's going to happen. I am going to stay here while the rest of you go traipsing off into the dark. That's one less person you get to siphon from."

"Let me try to understand." Casseem made a show of rubbing his temples. "You're getting back at Larkin by threatening to stay behind?"

"He's getting back at all of us. Punishing us for trying," Larkin corrected Casseem.

Devon ignored Casseem, his eyes trained on Larkin. "In a week, I'll run out of food, and I'll slit my own wrists before I begin to starve. If the surviving soldier gave us any inkling of what's to come, the lot of you will already have been tortured into insanity below."

Larkin walked toward Devon and squatted next to him, her eyes locked on his. He glared back. If he wanted to, he could take one of his meaty fists and knock her out in one fell swoop. But he didn't. Perhaps he was afraid of what she might do. She flexed her hand at her side to taunt him, enjoying the way he flinched.

He could poison himself with his own nihilism. But he

wouldn't hurt the rest of her companions. Larkin could protect them.

She stood. "Let's go."

"Let's." Jacque fitted her pack. "The queen would want us to leave him anyway."

"We're leaving him because it's best for *us*," Larkin said. If Jacque was going to play the role of Melay's lapdog, Larkin didn't know how much she'd be able to take. *She's the spy,* thought Larkin. It was so obvious. The annoyance and suspicion she sensed from the others meant they knew as well.

"Call it what you want." The soldier motioned for everyone to follow, and the others shuffled around, picking up their packs. Casseem gave Larkin the torch back and followed Jacque down the new tunnel.

Amias watched Larkin from beneath the shadows of the chamber. She sensed a shiver of distrust; his hackles were raised.

Larkin returned his gaze. The most powerful Empath in the group was intimidated by *her*, even though he'd done much worse. If she found out why, she could exploit it.

The rest of her party filed into the next passage, and Amias pushed himself from the wall and picked up his pack. He swung it over his shoulder and walked toward her.

"I need you to be on guard," she told him. "There's a reason you're here, after all."

Larkin sensed Amias wrestle down his apprehension, and it dissolved into a strange mask of tranquility. He studied her indifferently, the softness of his face startling her. He was wary, but his serenity was genuine. She couldn't fathom how he could be both anxious and calm.

"And if I don't, are you going to hurt me too?"

He pushed past her and entered the tunnel.

Across the chamber, Devon smiled at her, as if Amias's rejection had meant that she'd lost.

She smiled back before entering the tunnel, leaving him alone.

She knew that she should be concerned by what she'd done to Devon, and how she'd demonstrated it in front of the others. She was reminded of a line from her mother's folklore tome about the Uprising: *One does not win battles when one thinks one will lose.*

As she walked, Larkin's torch illuminated soft patches stamped with muddled layers of boot prints. Soldiers.

Where did you go?

She almost toppled over Amias, who had stopped to adjust his boot. Annoyed, she stepped around him and continued walking. When she sensed his unsettling tranquility behind her, she knew he had caught up.

"He's wrong," said Amias.

"Who?"

"Devon. Melay isn't feeding us to this place because she wants us to suffer. She wants to spark Kyran's curiosity. We're Empaths, after all. She's hoping he'll let us get close."

Larkin didn't understand Amias's confidence. He had been imprisoned for half a decade in the palace, but he certainly didn't know the queen. He probably hadn't even met her.

Larkin decided to play along. "So you really think that Melay believes Kyran is alive, then?"

"I *know* she believes he's alive."

Larkin whirled on him, and Amias halted inches from her. Shadows pooled beneath his eyes and the hollows of his cheeks. He tilted his head to one side, watching Larkin with a coil of intrigue.

"How could you possibly know what Melay really thinks?" Larkin asked. "You—"

An eruption of terror sucked the air from her lungs.

She stumbled sideways into the tunnel's wall, dropping her torch and clawing at the slippery rock. Her rib cage felt like it was collapsing inward, crushing like gravel.

Amias plucked her torch from the ground. He was speaking, asking her a question she couldn't comprehend. When she regained her breath, she used it to scream an order.

"Wait!"

In front of her and Amias, Brielle's flame wavered as she started at Larkin's command. The party halted.

"What, Larkin?" Amias held the torch up toward her face.

"Did you sense that?" she asked, her eyes watering at the light.

"I sense *you*." He was confused. They all were.

Larkin hadn't imagined it. She shrugged her bag off her shoulders and pushed Amias out of the way.

Casseem called her name, his voice fading behind her. She hurtled across the jagged rock of the tunnel floor, climbing back the way they'd come, toward the terror.

Toward Devon.

TEN

As the light of the torches fell dim behind her, the pinprick of the chamber's sconce began to grow. The terror she had sensed died as quickly as it had come, startling her. The tang of iron filled her nose as she approached the tunnel's end.

Wetness spread over the dusty ground in thick ribbons. One of them must have spilled their water.

No, not water. The liquid was too dark. There was too much of it. She reached down and touched it, surprised to find that it was warm.

Larkin followed the ribbons to their source and pressed herself against the tunnel wall, clapping both hands over her mouth.

On the other side of the chamber, Devon lay sprawled on the ground where they'd left him, his head angled sharply against the wall, propped up.

His eyes were gone.

Blood trickled from wet sockets. His mouth was open, frozen in the terror she'd sensed earlier. Torn muscle dangled like rags from broken ribs.

Mere feet from her, something crouched over Devon's body, clutching Devon's dripping heart with a taloned hand. A fleshy crimson vine crawled along the wall near the figure, glittering oddly in the light of the sconce.

Eyes.

Dozens of eyes were embedded into the strange growth. The figure opened its other hand and pressed Devon's eyes into the mass, adding to the collection.

Larkin tasted bile, and her heart beat wildly. *Gods.* If she didn't get out of here, she'd be next.

She held her breath and slid against the wall, stepping backward into the tunnel's curtain of shadow. As she lifted her other foot, rock loosened and skittered out from beneath it, bouncing down the sloped path.

The creature went rigid. Its white talons squeezed the heart, blood coursing in rivulets down its wrist. Slowly, it craned its neck in her direction.

It had no face, only imprints where its eyes and mouth should have been. Two slits pierced its head, flapping outward as it breathed. Its skin was the color of raw meat.

What in Ilona's bloody name . . .

Its talons peeled away, and Devon's heart fell to the ground with a wet *thud*.

Larkin ran.

She plummeted down the tunnel and around a bend, blinded. Her toe collided with a rock and she careened forward, tumbling down the path.

Talons scraped against stone, the screech crescendoing as it neared. Light bloomed behind her, and she spotted the monster's silhouette as it rounded the corner.

Kill me quickly. The thought raced through her head as she kicked away a dropped torch. Not her eyes first. She couldn't suffer through it.

The moment she pulled herself to her feet, her body collided with something firm. Arms snaked around her waist and pulled her backward so swiftly her feet lost traction.

She and her rescuer stumbled away from the tunnel's exit.

A violent tremor shook the ground. All remaining light was extinguished as the mouth of the tunnel collapsed.

Larkin's scream was muted beneath the thunderous avalanche. She shielded her face as her rescuer fell. Clinging to the other person's cuirass, she coughed to clear the dust from her throat.

Larkin registered Amias's voice. "Are you hurt?" His calm was a constant within the erupting chaos.

As he released her, terror from the others roared through her body. She dug her numb fingers into the leather of Amias's armor. "I don't know," she mumbled, shaking.

"The torches!" someone cried. Was it Jacque?

"Brielle had one." The sharp voice was distinctly Casseem's.

"Brielle!"

Someone tripped over Larkin. She lost her grip on the leather, clawed at the empty space in front of her until she found Amias again, clutching his bracer.

"Can I check?" Amias asked.

Larkin nodded before realizing he couldn't see her. "All right."

The fear threatened to control Larkin's attention, so she honed her focus on Amias's fingers sliding across her scalp, her jaw, her neck.

"No blood," he said.

"BRIELLE! Oh gods, we're trapped." Larkin recognized the octave of Elf's voice.

"Stop moving!" Casseem yelled. "And stop panicking! The more one of us panics, the more everyone else panics. Vicious cycle."

The last of the loose rock rolled to a stop, and then there was silence.

"I'm here." At the sound of Brielle's meek voice, Larkin sagged with relief.

"Are you all right?" Cassem asked.

"There's so much fear, I can't think . . . I lost my torch."

Larkin swore beneath her breath, realizing Amias had dropped the other torch in the scramble. They were Empaths, for Ilona's sakes. Were they truly going to be thwarted by losing a couple of scraps of wood? She tried to think but could only see Devon's mangled corpse and the glittering vine of eyes.

"Tamsyn?" called Casseem.

"Everyone remain calm," Tamsyn announced from somewhere off to Larkin's right. "We're far enough away from the luminite that all of you can sense, and I'm sure it's overwhelming."

"Thank you, Arkwright. Just what we need to hear from the one person who *can't* sense," said Casseem.

"Quiet!" Jacque ordered. "Amias and Larkin? Alive? All right?"

"We're fine," Larkin responded, though she wanted to vomit.

She sensed Jacque's relief. "That's all of us. There's flint in our bags."

Larkin felt the ground before she remembered that she'd dropped her bag when leaving to check on Devon. "My bag."

"The other side of the rubble." Amias squeezed her arm and released her. "Sorry, Larkin."

She swore, but she couldn't despair over a lost bag. There were worse things to worry about.

Shuffling filled the cavern as the others began to dig through their bags. After much fumbling, a flame erupted to the left of Larkin, and Casseem held a piece of burning fabric.

Larkin retreated to the flame, the entire party scrambling into the tight orb of light. Their faces and armor were white with limestone dust. Elf shook out her hair, and a plume of powder erupted from it. Blood trickled from Tamsyn's forehead, cutting through the grime on his face. "Ilona have mercy," he said as he dabbed at the blood, but the wound didn't look serious.

"Behind you." Amias pointed to a spent torch jutting from the stone wall nearby.

Casseem slid the torch from its sconce. "Think happy thoughts so I can fix this thing."

"Nice attempt at setting the mood," Jacque muttered.

Casseem grumbled something incoherent as he and Jacque attempted to doctor the torch by hand, losing their flame at one point. With a liberal amount of oil from their bags and a clean garment, they managed to revive the torch.

The flickering light did little to illuminate the chamber beyond the dust-covered party. They stared at Larkin, waiting for her to speak, to make sense of the chaos. But she couldn't simply tell them. She'd sound insane, and surely they were already skeptical of her after she'd hurt Devon.

Larkin turned to Amias. "Tell me you saw it."

He nodded hesitantly. "I saw it, but I don't understand what it was."

Jacque leaned toward her, intent. "Tell us, Larkin." It wasn't a request.

"Devon is gone." *Gone.* She could not bring herself to say the word *dead.* They weren't more than a few miles deep, and one of them had been gutted by a monster.

She tried describing what she'd seen, fighting through the panic emerging from them. Tamsyn urged her to re-explain the excruciating details several times as he rifled through his papers in search of clarifying information. The creature's face. What it sounded like. What *did* it sound like? Was she sure she saw an eye-covered vine? How was that even possible?

"I don't know!" Tears sprang to her eyes as she clapped her hands over her ears, but Larkin couldn't mute the screeching sound of talons. It was in her head.

Ethera. Larkin glanced up at the mountain of rubble. A passage had collapsed in the mines a few years ago. She thought Garran had been beneath the rock slide, but he'd been mining with Adina. She'd yelled at him when she found him. Yelled until she sobbed.

That fear was real.

This monster was a nightmare.

"I don't want to believe what I saw either, but I'm not lying." The creature had harvested Devon's heart and eyes. She knew it wasn't eating the organs, but collecting them. It had an agenda, which made it intelligent. And that was the most terrifying thing of all.

Tamsyn rolled up his scrolls, shoving them back into the case. "If there were such creatures within the Reach, I would have known about them. There would have been some documentation."

"That history is a thousand years old, Tamsyn." Elf patted around for her bag, propping it up and leaning against it. "We don't know what's down here. That's why we make up stories on the Surface."

"Do you think that thing is what killed the soldiers?" Casseem scratched his head, loosening rock dust from his hair.

"No," said Larkin. The creature alone couldn't have killed thousands of soldiers, which meant either there were more of them or something deadlier was lurking below. "There was only one path between the portcullis and this cavern. We should have passed it. It's like it appeared out of thin air."

"It's a good thing you went back," said Amias. "If you hadn't, it could have followed us and we wouldn't have known better."

Larkin shuddered. "And it's a good thing you thought to do this." She studied the mountain of rubble. Amias's destruction magic was already proving to be lifesaving.

"You could have killed all of us with that avalanche, you know." Jacque frowned at Amias.

"Jacque, I—"

Casseem piped up. "Amias, you foolhardy little prison boy. How dare you create such a mess and almost kill us?"

Amias's mouth snapped shut, and he glared at Casseem.

The corners of Casseem's lips twitched. "You're welcome for that, Larkin."

Larkin realized what Casseem was implying. "Wait, *you* caused the avalanche?"

Casseem walked around the mountainous rockslide. "Your first assumption was a good one. Amias should have thought to use magic. But he dragged you away instead of trying to destroy the thing. I didn't even see it, but I knew you were running from something."

Larkin sensed the spitting flame of Amias's irritation.

"You knew Larkin was running from something, so you caused an avalanche." Jacque gaped at him. "Your logic astounds me."

"We're all alive, aren't we?" Casseem kicked a loose rock that bounced off Amias's knee. "And you. I hope you prove to be quicker on your feet. You're our key to escaping this place alive, especially now that we know what's down here."

"You'd best find another key." Amias calmly stood. "I don't plan on destroying anything. I haven't in years."

"Very funny," said Larkin. The boy had a dry sense of humor.

A fierceness solidified behind Amias's eyes.

"You're serious. What, your morals finally caught up with you and you've decided that you want to pursue a life of peace?" Larkin pointed at the ground. "Right now, when we could be in a den of monsters that want to claw our eyes from their sockets?"

"We have a competent soldier, and Casseem has already proven more than skilled in destruction. Jacque can teach me to use a sword, if that's what you want." Amias recited his argument like he'd been practicing it. He had clearly been expecting this.

Larkin jumped to her feet. "Ilona's teeth, Amias! There are thousands of trained soldiers who've likely died in this place."

He stared at her, silently holding his ground. Larkin clenched her fists. He did not get to abandon the mission. Not like Devon.

"Some of us still have families," Larkin went on.

Amias winced, and Larkin sensed the brief flicker of his pain.

She'd hurt him. Good. He deserved to be hurt. She needed all the help she could get down here, or Garran would be executed.

"Calm down, Larkin," Jacque ordered as she eased into her pack, methodically tightening the straps. "We need to get as far away from that thing as possible, and you're making it more difficult."

Larkin's chest heaved as she glared at Amias. Her fingernails bit into her palms, reminding her that Devon's blood still coated her hands. Though she'd never admit it, maybe she did need to calm down.

That didn't mean this was over. Amias would use magic. She just needed to find out what made him tick.

Tamsyn took the torch from Jacque and walked toward the nearest chamber wall, illuminating faint glyphs along the smooth rock surface. The next tunnel entrance was close by.

"We've made it to the alchemical lab," said the scholar. Something about his fascination reminded Larkin of the way light caught on falling water.

Elf sashayed toward him, reaching out to touch the wall.

Tamsyn grabbed her hand. "Don't. These markings are over a thousand years old."

She yanked her hand away. "It's not like anyone's going to read them other than us."

"It doesn't matter. We should respect the artifacts." Tamsyn returned his attention to the glyphs. "I think they're formulas." He paced down the wall, reading as he went. "The Reach used to be self-operating. Mined ore would get crushed and separated within the miners' settlement." He pointed to the tunnel entrance next to him. "They would cart the ore up here, where the alchemists would practice metallurgy with the rare ores. The common ores would be taken up to the Reach's entrance, where the smelteries used to be."

"I wonder what Daria thought of these," said Elf in awe.

"Who's Daria?" Larkin asked.

"Daria Monarc, Kyran's metalworking disciple." Tamsyn pulled a handkerchief from his pocket and wiped the dirt from his face, dabbing the wound on his forehead once more. He glared at the cloth, disgusted, before pocketing it.

"The most curious of all the disciples," said Elf. "That's what the tales say."

"Glyphs like this were common back then. Why would she care about the physics of ore crushing when she could destroy whatever she wanted in the blink of an eye?" asked Tamsyn.

Larkin tried not to show her frustration. Daria was dead, and whether or not she cared about glyphs on the wall wouldn't help them now. The disciples were nothing but ghosts.

She glanced around, realizing that there were only six of them. Brielle was nowhere to be seen.

Turning away from the group and the rockslide, Larkin squinted to see beyond their light, her heart thudding a warning. The chamber was larger than she realized. Another monster could be with them. It could have taken Brielle.

"Brielle?" she whispered, afraid of no response as she sought out emotion.

"Here."

Relieved, Larkin ventured toward the voice, her eyes adjusting. Brielle sat on a boulder, fidgeting with the buckles of her cuirass.

"You can't wander off like that." As the words left her mouth,

Larkin almost laughed. She sounded like her mother. "It's dangerous to be alone. You won't be able to use magic."

"I'm sorry." Brielle tugged at a buckle. "I needed to search the rest of the chamber, to see if there were any bodies from the Surface."

Larkin sat next to her, hesitating. She didn't know how to tell Brielle that the Reach was massive, and they'd probably never find her sister in it, alive or not.

"I can sense you," said Brielle. "You don't have to tell me. I know it's stupid to want to find her."

"It's not stupid." Larkin would do the same if Vania had slipped through her fingers. She'd scour every tunnel, every dank recess. "Do you have other siblings?"

"A brother," said Brielle. "Melay has him in her prison."

Larkin's throat tightened. "Mine, too."

Brielle scrutinized Larkin, surprised. "You're sad. Not angry?"

"I . . ." Larkin paused, confused. "No, I'm not angry right now. I'm sorry about earlier, with Devon."

"I thought . . ." Brielle pressed her open palm to her forehead and squeezed her eyes shut. "I can't figure out anything for myself."

"What is it?" Larkin asked.

Brielle dropped her hand. When she opened her eyes, they were unfocused in the muted light. "I saw my sister disappear. Gone, something dragging her down into the ground. The moment she vanished, rage surrounded me, hot but distant, and I couldn't tell where it was coming from. I thought I was losing my mind." Brielle wrapped her fist around one of her buckles. "I sense that rage now. I thought it was you."

"Maybe one of the others?" Larkin homed in on their emotions but sensed only anxiety and irritation. Not the type of anger Brielle was describing.

"I think it's in front of us." Brielle hugged her arms around herself. "In the dark."

Larkin swallowed. "Are you sure?"

"You don't sense it?" asked Brielle, and Larkin was drenched by her insecurity. "I must be mad."

Larkin furrowed her brow. It was difficult to sense anything beyond the muddled mess of their party. But she'd been the one to recognize Devon's terror when no one else did. If the mysterious anger Brielle sensed was there, Larkin would feel it too.

"You're not mad." Larkin ushered Tamsyn to her, catching the attention of the others. She took his torch and crept deeper into the chamber.

Her light spilled over the barren stone floor, and the chamber's waxy ceiling arched. At the very edge of the room, barely visible, was an entrance to another tunnel. Something emerged from the stone above the opening.

A hand.

The rotting appendage jutted straight from the rock wall, as though the rest of the body was entombed in stone. The fingers were curled in toward the palm, all except the pointer finger, which was trained on the tunnel entrance.

"What in all hells," said Jacque.

A subtle, molten anger trickled into Larkin, the anger Brielle had sensed.

It emanated from the hand, beckoning them downward.

ELEVEN

They obeyed the hand, walking in the direction of its crooked finger into the steep passage beyond. It was wider than the one they'd come from, and they followed a rusted cart track in a group, Casseem and Jacque in the lead, and Larkin and Amias falling to the back.

Their new world smelled pungent, like soil and decay from an overflowing graveyard. The distant drip of water was almost thunderous. Every so often, Larkin would stretch out her right arm, her fingers grazing moss. It was a comforting reminder that life could flourish down here, and a distraction from Elf, who'd been panicking for the past quarter of a mile.

"How do you think it got in there? Do you think whoever it is died before or after they . . . The thought of being stuck in the walls . . ." Elf threw her head back and pushed against Brielle and Tamsyn. "Can you give me some space? We're not a herd of sheep, for Ilona's sakes."

"I'm sure they were dead before." Casseem's voice was steady and confident, but Larkin sensed how unsettled he was. They all were.

No one else had mentioned the anger, and Brielle was so quiet that Larkin didn't think she had confided in anyone other than her. A part of her believed that the anger was coming from one of them, which was why she said nothing. If she sensed it again, maybe she could pinpoint who and let Brielle know that it was only someone they knew, and not a strange presence from the dark. The girl had been so nervous that Larkin felt obligated to offer some relief.

Larkin noticed that Amias's pace began to slow. She followed along, drifting farther away from the sphere of torchlight in front of them.

He bent over to fix his boot. "You can go on."

"It's not safe for us to be alone."

"Suit yourself."

She sensed annoyance. He was probably mad at her for her anger earlier, but she had no plans to apologize, not when she was right. Still, she wanted his respect. Larkin attempted to lean against the tunnel wall and scrambled to find it, almost toppling over. Her hand caught the edge of the rock, and she steadied herself. "So, you know Jacque from Eversown Farm?"

Amias straightened and began to walk again. "We were friends when we were children. Before my father died."

Larkin followed him. "Is Eversown, er, large?"

"I'm not trying to thwart this mission, you know. Not like Devon was."

They'd lost the light, but as Larkin halted, the noise of Amias's footsteps was silenced, and she knew that he'd stopped too.

"That's why you waited for me, isn't it? To have words."

She turned toward where he stood, sensing his intrigue. He was neither frightened of her nor angry. He wanted to hear what she had to say.

"My brother is going to die if we fail."

"A lot of people will die if we fail."

"And we've been sent in to save them, because ten thousand people with swords couldn't."

He stepped toward her. She didn't realize how cold the tunnel was until she felt the heat of his body.

"If we were here because of magic, why send in only seven Empaths and a guide?" he asked. "Tell me you haven't wondered the same thing."

Larkin opened her mouth but fell silent. She had wondered. Right before they'd entered the Reach.

A commotion ahead distracted her. The rest of their party had stopped.

"Let's catch up," Larkin said.

"I'm on your side," said Amias as they hurried toward the group.

"Is that why you waited when I ran back for Devon?" she asked.

"Yes. I didn't understand why you went back for someone you hated."

Fair enough, she thought. "I didn't hate him. I hated that he was trying to sway us. Make us angry for no reason."

"But *you* are angry," Amias said.

Larkin stepped backward, surprised. She knew she was angry, but not the kind of angry Devon had wanted her to be. "I just want my brother back."

She began to walk again, Amias following her. "And if you're on my side, you need to prove it." She turned and caught him as he stumbled, her hand tangling in the straps of his bracer. "Start by being careful. You'd really be useless with a broken neck."

She sensed his mirth. At least he had a sense of humor.

The light brightened as they approached the rest of the

group, Casseem's torch illuminating an ancient mine cart half buried by rubble. "Cave-in," Casseem announced. "We'll have to destroy it."

"And risk the whole tunnel collapsing on us?" Larkin stepped forward to study the blocked passage. "You got lucky once, Casseem. I'm not convinced it will happen again."

Jacque agreed immediately. "Neither am I. We'll need to find a way around."

Brielle cautiously approached Tamsyn to help unroll the map while Elf attempted to mount the makeshift footholds in the walls, looking for a route up.

Larkin remembered losing purchase when she and Amias had stopped. She squirmed her way through the group and hiked back up the incline, guiding herself with her hands until the rock gave way. She reached out and touched the other side. The crevice was wide enough to be another passage.

Beneath the echo of chatter, Larkin heard something else. Voices—indecipherable but distinctly human. She held her breath and strained to hear, making sure it wasn't her imagination. Soldiers. *Survivors.* It had to be.

"Over here!" Larkin cried.

When the group caught up with her, Casseem shoved the torch down the passage opening. The tunnel was tight but big enough for them to fit through.

"I heard voices," Larkin said. "Coming from this tunnel."

Casseem returned the light to the scholar's map as the rest of them crowded around the tunnel entrance. After scanning it, Tamsyn said, "This isn't marked."

"That cave-in looks ancient. This must be the way the soldiers took. It sounds like some of them are alive—they're right below us!"

"Quiet," Jacque ordered. She held a finger to her lips and shut her eyes.

"There," whispered Amias as a male voice echoed against the passage walls.

Jacque's excitement built. "The soldiers! They aren't that far ahead!" She ducked into the passage. "Hello!" She paused, waiting, before emerging. "I don't think they can hear me. We'll have to go to them."

"But this isn't marked," Tamsyn stressed again.

"Nice find, Larkin. I'm impressed." Casseem clapped her on the back before taking the torch back. "Let's go."

"No, no, no." Elf shook her head violently. "It's not wide enough."

"It was wide enough for them." Jacque pushed the dancer forward, following her.

"But this isn't—"

Casseem held his finger up. "One more time, Arkwright, and I swear to Ilona you'll regret it."

Tamsyn huffed and filed into the passage, Casseem following him.

Brielle waited, clenching the straps of her bag. "What if they aren't soldiers? What if the farmers survived the fall from the Surface?"

Hells, survivors seemed almost as plausible as soldiers so close to the Surface.

"We'll find out," Larkin said gently. "Now go on. I'm right behind you."

Brielle scurried into the tunnel, but Larkin hesitated. "Jacque?" she called. "When was the last battalion sent in? How did we catch up to them so quickly?"

"A few weeks ago," Jacque yelled back. "Maybe they're coming back up?"

"Sweet Ilona." Casseem's voice boomed. "That would be quite the stroke of luck."

"This doesn't seem right," Amias muttered.

Larkin agreed, but it didn't matter. They needed to find out whom the voices belonged to, and they needed to go deeper. This was the only way forward.

Amias followed Larkin as she stepped into the passage. Larkin lifted her arms, her fingers grazing both walls. She followed the tunnel with her hands and pushed against the rock as the path tightened.

Garran would tell her to count her steps when the passages were this tight. He was the only one who'd ever been able to sense her anxiety in the luminite-laden tunnels of Ethera.

She never counted her steps when he told her to.

The walls crawled closer together, and she wiped away the cold sweat and grit from her forehead.

One, two, three.

Melay must have placed Garran in a prison like Amias's already. He was alone, in the dark, either certain Larkin was dead or still clinging to hope. Larkin wasn't sure what was worse.

Four, five, six.

Amias's hand fell against her shoulder, his concern brittle as broken quartz.

"I'm fine," she snapped, feeling vulnerable. She hated that he was searching for her emotions and that he cared, and she hated even more that she liked the way his hand steadied her. She didn't want to seem weak.

"Aren't you a—"

"Miner who hates tight spaces. A walking paradox. Didn't really have a choice." Larkin blew air from her mouth.

Beneath them, the unfamiliar voices echoed, growing louder. Larkin could almost make out individual tenors—four, five of them? The party was almost as big as theirs.

Elf's panic bubbled through her.

"We need to turn around!"

"We are absolutely not turning around," Jacque told her. "The voices are right below us. We're almost there."

"We're almost *where*? You don't even know where we're going!"

"Either you walk or we're all stuck here until we starve to death. Is that what you want?"

"Ilona's sake, Jacque. She's panicking!" Larkin cried.

"Yes, thank you, Larkin. We can all sense that," Jacque hissed.

They were at the front of the line, and Larkin was second to the back. If she could reach them, maybe she could help coax Elf to move forward. Jacque's military tactics were obviously not working. What if the soldiers heard the shrieking and thought they were the monsters? Brielle cried out in alarm and then apologized as Larkin squirmed around her, but Tamsyn and Casseem were bigger, protesting as she tried to pass them.

"You need to let me out. Let me out!" Larkin heard the sound of fists on metal. She stood on her toes and peered past the flame. Elf faced them, beating on Jacque's armor as she screamed.

Larkin gasped for air as Elf's terror roiled through her. Maybe Elf was right. All of them plunging into the dark unknown was a mistake. They didn't know what they would find. Sweat dripped down her neck, pooling by her collarbone. She was soaked beneath her armor, stifled by the leather. She needed out.

Larkin spun around. "We should have sent a scout," she told Amias. She could push past him, climb back up. The others would follow eventually. They'd regroup and send one person. Jacque would do it.

No, that wouldn't work. No one could be alone.

Amias said her name softly. Orange light washed over his face, catching in his dark eyes. They reminded her of garnets. Only once had she seen a cut and polished garnet in a market-place stall, sparkling in summer mountain sunlight. Hells, it was so beautiful that she almost stole it.

Amias was holding on to the sides of her cuirass; she couldn't remember when he began touching her. "Do you want me to let you go?"

"*No—gods—no.*" Larkin flinched in embarrassment.

To her surprise, Amias wasn't amused but rather worried, as though he didn't want her feeling vulnerable either. She felt his hands tighten against her armor, his garnet eyes trained over her shoulder at the others.

"We're moving," he finally said.

Elf was still sobbing, but the sound of struggling had been replaced with shuffling footsteps. Larkin took a step back, and then another, clutching the walls for balance. It wasn't easy to walk backward, but she couldn't bring herself to break from Amias. He watched her, his eerie calm silk-smooth and heavy, quieting her rapid heartbeat. Another step back and her foot fumbled along the rough path, and he held her up.

She broke from him only when she was certain that the rest of their party had made significant progress forward. As the passage began to widen, Larkin pressed her gloved hand to her heart as if to trap Amias's calm inside of her.

They were free.

Light permeated the chamber ahead, as cool as the glow of the moon. One by one, they staggered out of the tunnel. Larkin emerged just in time to see Elf wind her arm back and punch Jacque in the face.

The punch was sloppy, like either Elf didn't mean it or she had never thrown a punch in her life. But Jacque wasn't expecting it and stumbled backward. Elf released a sob and clutched her hand, turning away from the group and lurching into the dark.

Jacque straightened, rubbing her face. "That went well."

"You deserved it." Larkin wiped the sweat from the back of her neck. She caught Amias's eye and looked away.

"Don't be so smug." The soldier pressed her fingers into her jaw and wiggled it back and forth. "I got us out, didn't I?" She dropped her hand, squinting toward the ceiling. "Now, where in all hells are they?"

Larkin glanced around but only saw Elf at the very cusp of the shadows, her back to the group. She rubbed at her shoulders, her disquiet like a dull hum, an aching wound.

They would be going deeper, and that narrow passage certainly wouldn't be the last, but she didn't want to think about what was below them just yet. Instead, she looked up, awe leaving her breathless.

The cavern ceiling was nearly two hundred feet above them, crusted with glowing crystals that sent streaks of light across a village of dilapidated cabins. To the right of the outpost, a natural pillar connected the floor to the center of the ceiling. The ground then gave way to an abyss, the cliffside disappearing into a black void.

"Hello?" Larkin called.

Jacque hurried into the village with a hand on her sword, kicking up dust in her wake.

"Incredible," Tamsyn marveled. "Hundreds of years ago, miners used to call this place home. Can you imagine living down here?"

"No," Elf said curtly, returning to Tamsyn's side as she glared at Jacque from a distance.

Larkin couldn't imagine it either. There were no settlements or camps within the capital's shallow mines, not even the Vault. This was the first town she'd ever seen beneath the world.

Garran would hate it, she thought. He was like her. Their favorite part of the day was leaving the mines to greet the afternoon. She looked up, blinking at the glowing crystals. They were beautiful but no match for the sun.

"Hello!" she called again. Silence greeted her. Odd. The voices had been close. They couldn't have come from anywhere else but this chamber. She watched Jacque's shadow move between the cabins. The soldier would find the people they'd heard any moment now.

Casseem shrugged off his pack, uncapping his waterskin. "There was a mining settlement on the map, wasn't there?"

"Yes, close to where the known Reach ended." Tamsyn wrestled with his scroll case. "Only problem is . . ." He unrolled the map and scrutinized it. "This doesn't look like the settlement on the map."

"Then the map is wrong," Casseem concluded.

"The map is certainly not wrong," Tamsyn replied, horrified, as if Casseem's remark were a personal affront.

"The passage Larkin found wasn't on the map either, Arkwright. I thought you were here because you were smart."

"I'm smart because I've *studied*. Two hundred years pre-Uprising to a century after the dynasty was established. I know the most about Kyran, more than anyone on this entire isle."

Larkin turned toward him. "Yet you don't seem to know that Kyran is dead."

Casseem hid his smirk behind his waterskin as he drank. "Kyran is dead, the map is wrong. Care to prove your worth?"

"The queen knows my worth, and therefore I don't need to prove it to *you*."

Larkin lost interest, and their bickering faded as she crossed the shelf toward the settlement. The tiny cabins were lined in rows, the ones left standing windowless and crate-like.

It would be the perfect base for soldiers scouring the depths below for the source of the Surface's destruction.

Dust kicked up from beneath her feet, the print of her boots leaving a trail, almost as though she were walking through powdered snow. There were no fire rings, food crumbs, latrines—no evidence of life at all.

She sensed the weight of despair and looked up toward Brielle, who stood alone at the center of the settlement. The girl's arms were wrapped tightly around her body as she scoured the vacant chamber. Beyond, Jacque continued to weave through the cabins, searching. She approached one, kicking the remainder of the door apart.

Both of them searched for evidence of different people. Soldiers, farmers. Yet this place was more lifeless than a crypt.

The farm girl and the soldier converged in the middle of the camp. Jacque rested her hand on Brielle's shoulder, and Larkin sensed Jacque fighting back her frustration. "There's nothing here. I'm sorry."

Larkin bit back her surprise at the intimate moment. She didn't know that Brielle had told others about her sister, or that Jacque would be so sensitive.

Brielle nodded to the door Jacque had broken. "I don't think wood is supposed to last this long. On the farm, we patch up the cottages every summer. Am I wrong?"

"You aren't wrong," said Amias as he approached. "No elements. No rain or heat. It's been preserved."

"No people either," Larkin said, looking at him. "We heard those voices, Amias. All of us did."

"We did," said Amias, unsettled. "It's silent now. Quieter than a dream."

Quiet. Larkin shut her eyes, realizing Amias was wrong. It was silent, but not quiet. Heat glowed inside her like a morning forge, just hot enough to burn. Subtle, but violent. It surrounded her, desperate for her attention.

Brielle said her name. Larkin opened her eyes to see the worried girl staring at her, clutching her stomach.

"You feel it?" Brielle whispered.

The anger had returned.

TWELVE

Larkin kicked a pebble into the trench at the edge of the settlement, listening to it click against rock until the noise faded. The other side of the chasm was invisible, but there had to be a path beyond the shroud of shadow.

"Where did you go?" she asked the void, the weight of defeat creeping over her.

The void said nothing in response. Only the anger answered. It wasn't fire, but it smoldered like coals. Hateful delight, the same exact sensation as the one she'd felt miles before. It was as though someone was one step ahead of them, emitting anger from the chasm's far side.

Maybe the anger and the voices were coming from whatever they were supposed to be hunting all along.

If Garran were here, he'd tell her to sleep, then get up, and keep going. *Keep going.* He did that on the evenings when they came home from the mines hungry and empty-handed.

But this place wasn't Ethera. She wasn't searching for luminite, but grasping the edge of whatever evil was waking up.

Though I have fallen, darkness will rise.

"I don't believe in you," she told the void, her voice wavering. "You're dead."

Jacque startled her. "Larkin, quit talking to yourself and help us set up camp."

She turned around. Twenty paces in front of her, Brielle was stacking rocks to create a perfectly symmetrical fire ring.

Tamsyn spread his papers around him. Elf picked through the ones on top. "Boring, boring, boring . . ."

Amias and Casseem had combined the food near their pile of bags and armor and were working to make a meal.

Larkin pressed a hand to the front of her cuirass as her stomach rumbled. Losing her bag was a problem, given how little food they had to begin with.

Jacque sat cross-legged on the ground, taking a honing stone to the edge of her sword. She watched Larkin as she worked.

Larkin walked toward her. "Preparing the latest report for Melay?"

Jacque was unfazed by the jab. "Do you want to eat?"

"Do I." Larkin peeled off her cuirass and tossed it in the growing pile. "Maybe food will help us come up with a way to get across the chasm."

"Or you could just conjure a bridge," Tamsyn said absently as he scanned a sheet of parchment.

There was a long, awkward pause among the Empaths.

"Tamsyn's jokes are better than mine," Elf said in mock outrage.

"He isn't joking," Larkin responded, jumping when she heard a loud *crack*. She shielded her face as the nearest cabin crumbled into a pile of splinters, a plume of dust rising and disappearing into the crystals' light.

Brielle lowered her hands, standing. "We need firewood," she said bashfully.

"What did you just siphon?" Jacque's tone demanded an answer.

"My annoyance." Casseem glared at Tamsyn.

"See?" Tamsyn gestured toward the pile as he stood to remove his armor. "Magic."

"Because we're not talking about destruction magic," said Casseem with contempt. "It's not like this place is cheery. To conjure even a chain link in this hell would be impressive."

"And we need practice for conjuration. Lots of it," Larkin said. "Thanks to Melay, we haven't *had* practice."

"Good." Jacque had moved on to rebraiding her hair. "There's a reason for the luminite. Idiots get cocky, and soon the entire city is in shambles."

"Are you going to continue defending Melay the whole time we're down here?" Larkin asked bitterly. "I know your job is to keep an eye on us, but give it a rest."

"I'm not *keeping an eye on you*."

"Sure," Larkin spat.

"I didn't say it." Elf looked away innocently, lifting her waterskin to her lips.

"I didn't just mindlessly follow the queen's orders." Jacque's stone flew across her blade with a *zing*. "Melay hates me as much as she hates you. Maybe more."

"You're a better spy than actor," said Larkin.

Casseem choked on his water. Amias's eyes darted to Jacque, waiting for her reaction.

Jacque threw her head back and laughed. "Spy? You're right. Perhaps when we complete our mission, I will return to Queen Melay and ask for proper training in espionage."

Beneath Jacque's laughter, Larkin sensed the bitter edges of discomfort. She wasn't convinced, and neither were the others.

"There's no spy," Jacque said. "Melay only wants you scared into submission. She wants us to distrust one another. Isn't that right, Tamsyn?"

Tamsyn considered it. "Plausible. I don't see why Melay would need a spy. It's not like we have any choice but to do as she asks."

"Says the one who thinks we can snap our fingers and conjure a bridge," Casseem said wryly.

"Listen." Tamsyn fumbled with the buckles of his oversized cuirass. "The luminite is far off, and with enough prac—"

Casseem cut him off. "No, *you* listen." He hopped to his feet and strode up to Tamsyn, towering over the scholar. Tamsyn's fingers froze on his buckle.

"Whatever you think you've learned from reading your tomes between gallons of honey wine and fine cheeses, you don't know a thing about magic." Casseem jammed his finger into Tamsyn's shoulder. "So let those of us who do figure out a plan."

"But—"

"Tamsyn?" Larkin interrupted, arching an eyebrow. "Stay out of the Empath stuff."

"Thank you." Casseem dropped his hand, returning to the fire without giving the scholar a second glance.

Tamsyn huffed, his irritation blistering as he shimmied off his armor and sulked over his reading materials.

Brielle lit the fire and Amias divvied up a loaf of bread, three strips of dried meat, and a hunk of cheese. They sprawled out on the remaining six bedrolls and ate around the crackling ring.

With a shard of wood, Jacque drew a map in the dust of their path so far in an attempt to pinpoint where the voices had actually come from. Grumbling, she swiped at the dust with her boot and redrew it. "We had to have missed a pathway in that last tunnel."

"One of us would have seen it," Larkin assured her, tearing her piece of bread in half. "Caverns are unpredictable. When I worked, some days I could hear voices of miners miles away. Other days, it seemed like the sound of my axe died right in front of me. Maybe they are much deeper, but the important thing is that we all heard it. We'll track down the voices, Jacque." *And hope we're prepared for whatever we find,* she thought.

Jacque combed her fingers through the end of her braid and nodded reluctantly as Brielle passed Larkin her water. It was only half full, and they didn't know when they'd be able to find more. Larkin thanked her with a smile, and Brielle brightened, smiling back.

"Feeling sentimental, Larkin?"

She snapped to attention. Casseem smirked at her.

"I'm not used to anyone but my family sharing with me," she said honestly, drinking from the skin.

Casseem stood and walked to the pile of splinters. Elf leapt up to help, and they took three trips between the pile and the campfire, carrying armfuls.

Casseem knelt near his collection, his eyes glittering in the firelight. "I miss my family too. I left behind four brothers, all thieves. I am quite possibly the most inept thief in existence, which is why I got caught."

He flexed his hands over the splinters, which began to rearrange themselves, forming a sheet.

"Magic on the other hand—well, let's just say my brothers

and I found all of the capital's weak spots. Luminite has its limits, after all."

"I remember you now," said Jacque. "You used to conjure fake luminite trinkets and peddle them. Your name made it all the way up the ranks. You were like a roach."

"Infamy!" Casseem grinned. "How wonderful."

Tamsyn clucked his tongue. "Sounds like a regular Ralic to me."

Elf laughed. "I don't see how Kyran's paragon disciple relates to Casseem. Mitisan Ralic committed his life to the needy, conjuring for the city's poorest."

"Don't I seem charitable?" Casseem teased.

Tamsyn scoffed. "Please. Ralic was a crook. He sold his conjured goods cheaper than the mainland traders, who could then no longer do business."

Elf stuck out her tongue. "I like my version better."

"Me too," Brielle said quietly, and returned to chewing on her fingernail.

Elf waved her hand in a broad gesture. "The audience has spoken."

Tamsyn pursed his lips and raised an eyebrow.

The limp sheet of fiber pooled around Casseem. When he was finished, he scooped up his creation and handed it to Larkin. "Your blanket."

Larkin smiled in surprise, taking the blanket from him. "Thank you."

Casseem winked at her. "Don't go soft on me." He pointed at Larkin and looked to Tamsyn. "See here? A blanket. This is what we would call *impressive*, and it's about as impressive as I can get, so you can bid your bridge and your visions of grandeur farewell."

Elf raised her waterskin in the air. "To splinters and blankets."

The skins went up one by one.

"Excuses," Tamsyn grumbled.

They spent the evening conjuring torches from the cabin's wood, and when they turned in, Larkin volunteered to take the first watch.

The crackle of their fire echoed strangely off the cavern walls, the air cold but stagnant. The others drifted in and out of sleep, their dreams unearthing bolder emotions. They were vibrant and discordant. Even in this place, not all of them were having nightmares. Some of the party's emotions rolled through her like a thunderstorm, while others were moonlight on placid water. She'd never sensed so many dreams at once before, and it calmed her.

Larkin was fighting off sleep when fresh terror prickled her skin.

She jolted awake. It felt like someone was having a nightmare, yet the terror was coming from farther away.

She stood and turned from the fire, walking toward the chasm on the far end of the settlement. As she neared the cliff's edge, she shut her eyes, trying to sense the direction of the fear. It stemmed from beneath her, in the dark below.

She hugged her body, feeling the pressure in her rib cage, like her bones were going to be crushed into gravel. The emotion felt like Devon's. Like death.

She hurried to the fire and fished a piece of burning wood from the pit. Returning to the cliffside, she tossed it into the dark. The flame shrank to a pinprick and exploded in a burst of sparks, finding the bottom.

They didn't need to go across. They needed to go down. Down the cliffside, to the horror streaming from whatever was still alive in the dark.

She thought of the voices she'd heard. They had come not from the settlement, but from the chasm below.

Someone was alive. And they needed help.

Larkin turned away from the void and hurried toward the dilapidated cabin. If Casseem could conjure, so could she.

She knelt near the pile of splinters and shut her eyes, sifting through them, finding a blissful dream from someone she wasn't expecting. Warm, like dry grass in a late summer meadow.

Larkin lifted her hands, and the splinters of wood collected between her fingers and assembled, fibers winding to yarn, coiling to strands, and braiding themselves.

The rope fell in her hand. She felt giddy, such blatant conjuration still foreign to her. She continued to weave the fibers, sweat dripping from her forehead, and started when a heavy hand rested on her shoulder.

"What in hells are you doing?" said Jacque.

"I figured out how to get past the chasm. We're not going across. We're going down."

THIRTEEN

Though the others hadn't been sleeping for long, Larkin and Jacque woke them to relay the plan, and all of them hurried to pack up camp.

Elf fastened the rope around the cavern's pillar with a knot she swore would hold up. "Out on the road, my troupe once conjured the most beautiful scarves. We tied them to trees for outdoor shows. I learned to climb pretty quickly." She tugged on the rope, nervous.

Larkin forced a smile. "Not so different."

She counted the others. They were all here except for Tamsyn. She spotted his flame at the far end of the settlement and walked over.

"We're getting ready to descend." She halted when she saw that he had uncovered glyphs in copper paint along the cavern wall.

"This is ancient Demuran text." He waved the torch along the paint. "Centuries old."

"Can you read it?" she asked, both intrigued and disturbed. The color reminded her of dried blood.

He nodded. "After the Uprising, when Kyran had been defeated and Ilona banished him to the Reach forever, she sealed the only known entrance with the portcullis we passed through. These glyphs were written by the miners who were trapped down here."

Larkin frowned. She'd never heard this side of the story before. "I thought the Reach was empty when she banished him."

"So did I." Tamsyn stepped back, his frustration crackling inside her. "They all returned to the Surface but couldn't get past the portcullis. Ilona wouldn't let them out. Perhaps she thought Kyran would somehow escape with them."

"They died down here, then."

"Kyran and his disciples enticed some of them to go deeper," said Tamsyn. "The others died of starvation. They ate the corpses to stay alive longer, hoping Ilona would change her mind and release them."

Larkin blanched. "Wouldn't there be bones?"

"Perhaps animals dragged them off. Or that creature you saw . . ." He shuddered. "We should go."

Larkin glanced up at the glyphs, imagining the miner who painted them, leaving the story for the next person who came along. "They hadn't done anything wrong." A thousand years had passed and nothing had changed. The dynasty still dictated who was allowed freedom.

"They left this place for a deeper world," said Tamsyn. "Just like us."

Larkin rubbed at the gooseflesh on her arms. "Speaking of which." She turned back to the rest of the group. Beneath the dull light of the crystals, Amias was roping himself in.

"Ilona's sake." Larkin kicked up clouds of dust as she raced back through the village. "What are you doing?" she cried when she reached him.

"Getting ready to descend." He slipped on his glove.

"I'll descend first." It had never been a question in her mind that she would be the first one. "It's my rope, and if it doesn't hold up, I should be the one to fall."

"It could break on any one of us," Amias said calmly, watching her.

"I should be the one to test it."

"I'm not doing this just for you." He kept his eyes on her, fumbling absently with a knot on his belt. "I have the least to lose out of anyone here. My family already thinks I'm dead."

"That's not a good—"

"*And* just because I don't like using magic doesn't mean I'm deadweight." His full lips pulled into the languid smile of someone who knew he'd won. "If it breaks on me, I'll just blame you."

"If you live." She examined his belt. She had learned how to rappel in Ethera, when mining the vertical tunnels. "And if you fall, it will be because of these sloppy knots. Not because of my rope." She reached out and yanked on one until it loosened. "See?" She pulled on his belt again, and he stumbled closer, bumping into her. She thought he would back up, but he remained planted. Their belts caught on each other, and she held on to him as she lifted her hip to free herself. Larkin rethreaded his knots, running her fingers along his waist to find the right links.

"You were worried before we fell asleep," he said softly. He'd been paying attention to her closely enough to sense her unease. Larkin felt her cheeks warm.

"You're observant," she said.

"When I want to be."

Larkin looked over her shoulder. Brielle used their fire to

light the ends of cabin planks, and Elf flung the burning wood into the chasm to gauge the depth of the bottom. Tamsyn paced behind all of them as he scratched his chin, and Jacque and Casseem assessed Elf's knotwork. None of them were close enough to hear Larkin and Amias.

She leaned into Amias until her cuirass pressed against his. He'd felt threatened by her, and she'd been angry with him, yet he obviously wanted her trust. She'd told him to prove that he was on her side. Was this an attempt?

"Someone's following us. Or maybe they're waiting for us. I'm not sure. Brielle and I—" Larkin drifted off when she saw something click behind his eyes, like she'd said something he'd been waiting to hear.

"The rage," he said.

Larkin released the remainder of her breath. "You feel it too. Gods, Amias. If it weren't for Brielle, I would have thought I was going mad."

"Neither of you are mad." His eyes darted to the party and back to her. "We haven't seen another creature, and rage follows us as though we're being watched."

"You think the creature is stalking us?"

He frowned, his lips parting as his thoughts formed. Larkin knew he was choosing his words carefully.

"I don't know, but I do think that we have a lot more to worry about than finding where those voices went."

"When do we tell the others?" she asked. "I don't want them to panic."

"We tell them when we know where it's coming from. Panic

spreads. Panic is useless," His mouth twitched. "Unless you plan on destroying with it."

"Because you won't."

"Because I won't."

"Amias!" Casseem called. "If you're too scared to go first, I'm sure someone else is brave enough to take the reins."

"Like you?" Amias called back.

Larkin ran her hands along the knots of his belt, checking them one last time. "I made just enough rope to get to the bottom and back up. No room for mistakes. Cross your fingers and pray to Ilona that this goes as planned."

His shoulder glided along hers as he pushed past her. "I'm not religious."

A grin crept across Larkin's face. She quickly sobered and turned toward the group as Amias walked to the edge of the cliff and sat down. Anxiety, hope, and determination streamed from him. Amias was calm when the rest of them weren't, but that didn't make him fearless. There was no such thing as courage without fear, after all.

Amias glanced back at her, and Larkin, suddenly terrified, felt her stomach plummet.

"Jacque, with me." Casseem grabbed the rope, and Jacque followed suit.

Elf chimed in. "And me?"

"Don't get in the way." Casseem motioned for Larkin to move back, and Amias flipped onto his stomach, lowering himself down the cliff.

Casseem and Jacque let the rope out together. Elf, Brielle,

and Tamsyn kept watch over the edge, but Larkin couldn't. She paced behind them, rubbing at her temples.

If he fell because of her . . .

"He's down!" piped Elf.

"What?" Larkin joined the others at the cliffside, lying down and crawling on her belly to peer over the edge. "How did he make it so fast?"

"He trusted the rope." Jacque stretched out her hands. "And us. He let his body weight carry him down."

Casseem slapped Larkin on the back. "Nice conjuring."

She gave a nervous laugh. "You inspired me."

"I have that effect on people."

Before Larkin could respond, Amias shouted from below. "There's a path!"

Larkin exhaled her relief. They'd found their way. *Hold on, Garran.*

Fueled by the excitement, Jacque and Casseem quickly retied the rope so that Amias could belay from the bottom. Jacque descended without issue. Casseem was next, and then Brielle, who squeezed her eyes shut and clenched the rope as she was slowly lowered.

Tamsyn had trouble.

He tried stepping downward but slipped, twisting as his shoulder rammed against the rock wall. "Sweet Ilona!"

Beads of sweat formed on Tamsyn's forehead, glistening in the firelight. "Pull me back up. Pull me back up!"

"I'm guessing your texts never taught you how to rappel." Larkin steadied the rope, her hand burning from the friction.

Tamsyn swore as he finally found his footing and pushed off, dangling like a limp fish from a line as he disappeared into the dark. Casseem called up to her when he had reached the bottom.

Larkin was next.

Elf helped tie her in. Larkin climbed down the edge and kicked away from the cliff. Even when the darkness swallowed her, the descent was fun. She felt inverted, descending into the stars as she tilted her head back, her body weightless.

Deeper. She didn't think she'd enjoy dropping farther from the Surface so quickly. How would they climb back up when they returned?

They'd find a way. They had magic, after all, and she had hardly explored what she was capable of. A simple rope had brought such fortune. The thought exhilarated her.

At last, she approached the bottom. Amias was waiting to catch her and lower her to the ground. Holding her shoulders, he turned her toward him.

"Still don't like magic?" Larkin asked.

The corners of his mouth perked up. "Conjuration's different." He tugged at the rope. "May I?"

She nodded.

His hands drifted to her belt, loosening the knot on her waist. He was careful not to touch her.

He pulled the rope from her belt, and Larkin held on to his arms for balance.

When Amias was finished disentangling her, he rejoined the others. Larkin stood alone as a realization dawned on her. Amias's rebuke of destruction magic wasn't logical; destruction was a core skill for conjuring. Without material, there was no way to conjure from anything but existing dust and splinters.

It was personal.

He'd destroyed an entire village as a child and had been locked up for it. She'd been so bent on saving her brother that she didn't care about Amias's reasons, even though they should have been obvious. She didn't want him to have any leftover trauma. She just wanted his help.

Amias tilted his chin up to watch Elf, his usual calm returning. She felt drawn to it, entranced until she shook herself from her stupor and trained her focus on Elf.

Elf rappelled, gracefully hopping back and forth across the rock like a creature in flight. She descended quickly and was almost to the bottom when she cried out. Larkin watched in horror as the rope rapidly coiled in a heap, the broken end whipping through the air.

Elf fought to find purchase on the rock, but it was too late. She was falling.

Casseem began to sprint toward Elf in the hopes of catching her, but they were too far away . . .

Elf's feet hit the ground. She fell backward, landing on her pack.

Larkin's heart plummeted. Brielle clapped her hands over her eyes.

"Elf!" Jacque cried, racing toward her.

Elf held up the palm of her hand. She peeled her pack straps off and sat up. "Thank you, gracious audience. There's no need for alarm. I'll be here for the foreseeable future."

Jacque swore as she helped the girl stand.

Their relief was like snow to a burn, and Larkin exhaled, bending over and pressing her palms to her knees.

Elf pranced toward her, beaming. "Are you all right? Is everyone all right?"

Larkin pressed a thumb to her chest. "Am *I* all right? My conjuration nearly killed you!"

"Don't feel so guilty. That was great!" Elf patted the dust off her trousers. "It was like I was flying."

"Falling to your death isn't flying."

Elf touched her hand to her chest. "You were worried about me!"

Larkin almost rolled her eyes. "Don't break your neck, all right?"

"I'll do my best." The dancer looked around. "What's next?"

Larkin plucked the burning plank back up from the ground and walked down the path. A streamlet trickled from the rock wall, and beyond the runoff a tunnel entrance was encrusted with tiny glowing crystals. The air smelled different. Not dank, but coppery.

Crimson streaked the ground.

"What in Kyran's hell." The plank slipped from Larkin's hand. Sweat prickled the back of her neck.

"They did make it this far." Tamsyn leaned over and vomited.

Elf screamed, her fear vibrating through Larkin. Jacque pushed Larkin back and drew her sword.

They found the body of a soldier. His eyes were missing, his rib cage peeled open and heart gone. Just like Devon.

It was his terror that Larkin had sensed.

She'd felt him die beneath her.

FOURTEEN

Larkin's fingers tingled with the panic of her companions. She needed the panic as much as vigilance. If they came across the monster that had gutted the soldier, she wouldn't be able to run, not when the entire group was with her. She'd have to use magic.

"Let's go," Larkin ordered. There was no point in lingering in the gore; Larkin knew exactly what had killed the soldier, and she didn't want to sit around and wait for it to show up. As she led the group through the tunnel, crystals glittered before them and shadows danced in the wake of their flames.

Tamsyn's map confirmed a labyrinth, and the scholar was certain they were at the beginning of the coiled tunnels. At every turn, he directed Larkin where to go. The crystals disappeared and cavities emerged, giving the illusion of a forked path and confusing Tamsyn more than once. They passed cracks big enough to squeeze through, but the alcoves were filled only with dripping stone teeth.

Upon turning left, Larkin grabbed the back of Casseem's armor before he stepped right into a bottomless crevasse, and they had to retrace their steps.

Tamsyn attempted to reroute them back to the tunnels of crystal, but the glittering light had vanished. Instead, the passage narrowed, and panic bubbled from Elf. They turned around again, finding solace in a grotto harboring a streamlet.

They had water, but they were lost and the mysterious anger was getting stronger.

Larkin took it upon herself to fill up everyone's waterskins, saving Brielle's for last.

"I don't think the anger is following us," Larkin whispered when the two of them were alone at the streamlet, the others assembling farther down the tunnel. "I think we're getting closer to it."

"It's not anger," said Brielle. "It's rage."

Larkin capped the skin and handed it to Brielle. "Is there a difference?"

Brielle wrapped a lock of stringy hair around her finger as she thought. "Well, before I was assigned to the farm, I worked in the mines. Do you remember the riot?"

"I was there," said Larkin. The taste of blood flooded her mouth, her personal ghost.

"So was I." Brielle untwisted her finger from her hair, her hand falling. "My dad died that day."

"I'm . . ." Larkin couldn't imagine losing her father. "I'm so sorry."

"It's not your fault. Nor his. And I try to remind myself that it isn't my fault either. There was nothing we could have done. The soldiers weren't angry at us. They were rageful. It was like they were delighted by their violence."

Delight. The heat of the emotion pressed into the bottom of Larkin's heart as though desperate to float upward. She'd thought the same, standing at the edge of the void. A smoldering burn so subtle, it almost tickled her.

"It's been miles," said Brielle in frustration. "How could we feel rage for miles?"

Larkin tightened the buckles of her cuirass, trying not to think of the truth blatantly in front of her, one she'd been running from. There was only one omniscient thing in life and lore. If Melay was telling the truth, then this god had every right to be delighted by his own wrath, his revenge.

He'd been waiting for a thousand years.

Though I have fallen, darkness will rise.

"Are you all right?" Brielle asked. "I didn't mean to upset you."

Larkin glanced down, realizing she'd ripped the strap of her cuirass clean off. "I'll fix it when there are conjuring emotions," she muttered, pocketing the leather and standing. "Let's go."

Larkin let Tamsyn take the lead with a map the scholar refused to lose hope on, but as they spiraled blindly through the labyrinth, the trill of panic against her flesh grew. Elf's breathing shortened to tiny gasps, and Larkin wrapped her arm around the girl's shoulder, not sure if she was helping.

Every so often, the smoldering rage would melt through the nervous blanket of the party, searing her. Amias would touch her arm from behind, a silent signal that he felt it too.

The lichen-laced passages began to blur with the ones filled with crystals. Larkin didn't know how much time had passed, only that they were on their third torch. She felt delirious, her bleary eyes catching on what looked like dead hands emerging from cracks in the stone, and vines made of eyes creeping along the walls. She'd jerk back, blink, and they'd disappear.

Jacque stopped them. She held up the nub of their torch,

and tapped her fist against the shaft of a crystal. "We've passed this crystal three times, and we're almost out of water."

"Gods." Elf's voice trembled.

"We're just a little lost. We'll find our way." Larkin held on to Elf tightly, muffling her own despair.

"We should rest." Casseem slid off his pack. "Amias, Larkin, and Jacque will take the first watch. I'm exhausted."

Jacque pinched the glove from her hand and tossed it on the ground. "How kind of you."

Although she was on watch duty, Larkin helped the others arrange the bedrolls. The passage was tight, illuminated only by the shaft of crystal Jacque claimed they'd passed already.

As Tamsyn squirmed into his bedroll, Larkin crouched next to him. "Tamsyn . . . was Kyran considered rageful?"

Tamsyn wiped the dirt from his bracer with his bare hand and grimaced. As he gingerly felt the edges of his healing forehead wound, he said, "I thought you didn't believe in gods."

"Otheil Kyran, the man," Larkin corrected.

"Kyran was pleasant, actually. Charismatic. Though, toward the end, I imagine he was rageful. He spent his life nurturing his disciples, who dedicated themselves to magic. Just like his followers, he had children who would inherit his magic and be stronger than he was. Ilona destroyed years' worth of work in a matter of days. I think anyone would be furious."

"Wait." Larkin stopped him, bewildered. "What did you say about children inheriting magic?"

Tamsyn blinked at her, then looked around at the others,

who'd begun listening in. Larkin sensed confusion; at least she wasn't the only one who didn't understand.

"None of you know?" Tamsyn asked, both astounded and a bit smug.

"Know what?" Larkin pried.

"Our magic isn't just based on skill. That power is familial. Inherited."

Larkin turned to Amias in surprise as he sat on the boulder at the edge of their tunnel camp.

"Magic is like a sieve." Amias set his bag down next to him and clapped the dirt from his hands. "Skills trickle down to the descendants while the ancestors are alive. When the ancestor dies, the sieve bursts, and the descendants inherit a flood of magic." Amias looked to the scholar. "They wouldn't know, Tamsyn. No one outside the palace knows. The knowledge has been buried."

Tamsyn sighed, exasperated. "Tragic."

"Not just tragic," Casseem shot back. "Cruel. Who do you think kept us from that knowledge?"

"Hold on." Larkin pressed her hands to her temples, her head spinning with questions. "Skills?"

"A talent. Empath families used to focus on honing one thing," Tamsyn explained. He sat up straight when he realized everyone's attention was trained on him. "Think of it as focused training. A family may decide that they want to specialize in conjuring weapons from ore, like Daria Monarc's family."

"Or healing, like Bianca Elesandre's family!" Elf's panic dissipated as she shot up.

"Exactly. If every generation continued to focus on their talents, they'd be the greatest weaponsmiths or healers of all time."

"So Melay's blinded us." Larkin gritted her teeth. "She's stripped us of our surnames, broken up families between the mines and the farms. Taken away our books." She looked at the other Empaths, sensing their hearts grow heavy. "She doesn't want us to know our lineages because she doesn't want us to uncover the talent our ancestors were honing."

"But we could still find them, right?" Tucked in her bedroll, Brielle wiggled closer to Larkin and Tamsyn. "My family has always been good at sensing negative emotions. More than others, it seems. Useful for destruction magic and warding off danger."

That explained why Brielle was the first to notice the mysterious rage, even before Larkin.

Casseem hopped to his feet and paced the perimeter of Amias's boulder. "My brothers and I were always good at quick conjuration. Silly things, trinkets and odds and ends." He looked to the dirt at his feet and flexed his hand. The dirt rose like vapor, and Casseem flipped his hand as it settled in his palm. He closed his fist and tossed an object to Elf, who caught it and held it up, delighted. A stone blossom rested between her fingers.

"Amias?" Jacque called from the other side of the tunnel, where she planned to take watch. "You said no one outside the palace knew this. Certainly, the palace's prisoners weren't informed, so why were you?"

"I . . . read," Amias said flatly.

"Why yes, we all got a nice glimpse of your prison library, didn't we?" Casseem said. "Polished cherry oak shelves and a cozy chair by the hearth. Did a lot to brighten up that hole in the ground."

"I had a tutor," said Amias.

"A tutor," Larkin said slowly. "Who visited you in your cell?"

"It doesn't matter," he said sharply. He was hiding something, but she wouldn't press him, not in front of everyone. She had her own secrets to keep.

Casseem paused in his pacing. "Rumor has it that Melay has a registry of Empath lineages. That's how she decides who to send to the farms."

"She can't use her registry anymore." Tamsyn cleared his throat. "I, er, burned it."

"You did *what*?" Larkin asked.

Elf clapped her hands together. "You lit her *registry* on fire?"

"Someone had to." Tamsyn examined his fingernails, his pride swelling. "Did you honestly believe I volunteered to come down here? No, no, no. I'm being punished, just like you."

Larkin didn't know what to say. She and Casseem exchanged glances, and he actually looked impressed. As was Larkin. She'd never heard of a non-Empath taking a risk for their sake.

"Tamsyn the Great." Elf spread her arms, creating an imaginary picture. "They'll be telling tales about the martyr sacrificing his life for us filthy Empaths."

"It'll be a boring story," Tamsyn said, but although he ducked his head modestly, delight fluttered through him at the attention. "First you'd have to begin with my parents. They own a shop on the north side of the capital. Their days are most dull, which is why they gave me up to the palace. They want to live vicariously through me, you know." Tamsyn glanced around and shrugged. "Not very exciting, unless the story ends with me getting eaten by an eyeless monster."

"We'll have to see, won't we?" Elf chirped as she slid to the ground.

"As intriguing as this lesson has been, we need to sleep," Jacque reminded them. "We shouldn't camp for longer than we have to."

Larkin rested against the tunnel wall as the others eased into their bedrolls, glad once again to keep watch. She could sense their excitement. Larkin wouldn't be able to sleep if she tried.

The revelation of the inherited magic granted her enough emotion from the others to conjure her strap back onto her cuirass. She patted it down, her mind whirling around her luminite resistance.

It had come from her mother's side. She'd always assumed it was some bit of fortune, when in reality an ancestor of hers had honed the skill. A gift that had somehow survived generations.

She felt like a stranger in her own body. There could be other things her ancestors had mastered, skills she didn't know she had.

And like unearthing a glittering vein in the darkest part of the mine, Larkin would dig them out.

FIFTEEN

When Larkin woke, Jacque and Amias were whispering urgently to each other from their bedrolls.

"You have to understand," the soldier was telling Amias. "I'm not home often."

"You must have heard something."

"They're all right," she said. "Skye's making sure your mother stays busy. They're making do."

"Good," said Amias, his cool relief blanketing Larkin.

"And they miss you. Which is why we need to survive this, so you can go home."

"We all need to survive this," he said. "Or there won't be a home."

Larkin's eyes fluttered open as Amias stood up and stepped over her, leaving camp.

She didn't know Amias still had family. She imagined what it would be like for them when he came home, after believing he was dead for so long, the surprise and joy. *Magic,* thought Larkin. *Magic in its purest form.*

Larkin sat up and stood, stumbling past Tamsyn, who was scrubbing his face clean with his sleeve as he kept watch. After visiting their makeshift latrine, she passed an inlet and sensed a flicker of wonderment from inside.

Larkin batted away glowing strings draped across the tunnel. A luminous insect landed on her. *Life.* It reminded her of the night sky in the canyon, with stars close enough to touch.

Amias was there. He sat on a boulder in the center of it all, gazing up. The wonder inside him was pure wilderness, fragrant and rich and thriving. Uncharted. *He's been in the dark for so long,* she thought. *He's been alone.*

As she silently joined him, he kept his eyes glued to the sweeping strings above, peaceful. His eyes glittered in the glow as though they were faceted.

"You stole my dream," Amias said softly. "The other night, when you conjured the rope."

She grinned, having known all along it was his. A vision warm and languid, like a nap by the hearth. It had been beautiful.

He added wryly, "You're welcome. It was one of my better ones."

"What was it about?" she dared to ask.

"One of the hot days up in the hills. We used to have them in the weeks of summer. My sister and I would go into the fields and lie around all afternoon instead of doing chores. We'd fall asleep and bake like bread."

"Skye," Larkin blurted.

"You were eavesdropping?" Amias's amusement trickled through her.

"The tunnels echo," Larkin protested. "It's hard not to." Reaching up, she siphoned his amusement, the nearest empty web catching around her fingers and braiding itself into a delicate bracelet.

Amias spoke as he watched her. "My father would get so mad at us. Skye especially though—she was the bad influence." He laughed softly.

Larkin concentrated on the bracelet as he spoke. She had been so angry with him after the avalanche. She had lashed out, certain he was being selfish because he had no one to lose. But now she knew differently.

Still, she needed to know. "How did your father die?" She sensed the stone-cold weight of his loss.

"Soldiers."

Larkin's fingers closed around the bracelet. First Brielle's father, and now Amias's. How could Amias bear to even speak with Jacque? Larkin's hands would have been around the Empath soldier's throat at once.

"And your mother? Is she still in Eversown?"

"Melay's leverage."

His mother in the dungeons like Garran. And from the distress that mingled with his grief, Larkin knew he was afraid of the queen. Beyond an Empath's justified fear of the queen. It was deep. Personal.

Larkin didn't understand it, but she loathed it. "Give me your arm."

Amias lifted his arm, palm facing up. Larkin tied the bracelet around his wrist, and without quite knowing why, she dragged her finger down the center of his palm. A strange spark ignited in her abdomen as they touched.

"Wait," he said, his palm still open.

She returned her hand to him, and he wrapped his fingers around hers. As he curiously examined the bracelet, she sensed his anguish ebb, and she realized he was using the distraction as a means of control.

"I know it hurts, but I want you to think about your family every time you look at it," said Larkin. "Especially your mother, who dreams about you as the little boy on the farm, and waits for you."

Even within the darkness of the chamber, she could see his eyes well. The vibrant love he emitted ripped through her so painfully, she thought her heart would break. Amias wasn't ashamed of her sensing it. He was offering it to her.

"You deserve home as much as the rest of us," Larkin whispered. "No matter what you've done."

When his eyes found hers, the spark in her abdomen swirled into a whirlpool. Larkin craved it, as if she'd hungered for the sensation her entire life.

"Thank you," Amias said simply.

Above them, the insects spun their glowing webs.

As they packed up camp, Larkin noticed Brielle was missing. She wandered downstream of where they'd slept, calling Brielle's name, waiting for her to say *here*, like she always did. But no response came.

She found Brielle tucked away within a recess, her knees curled to her chest. Her expression was as blank as the rock wall she was staring at. She'd left her armor back at camp, wearing only her trousers and sleeveless tunic.

"How long have you been here?" Larkin pressed her hand to Brielle's shoulder. "You're freezing. I told you, you can't be alone."

The skin near Brielle's elbow was mottled. "Did you hurt yourself?"

Larkin coaxed the girl's arm away from her knee and gasped.

Brielle's skin was peeled off from her wrist to the crook of her arm, the wound a spectrum of colors: red bleeding into black and yellow.

"Who did this to you?" Larkin lifted Brielle's chin with her hand.

The girl made a strong effort to look away, but Larkin clutched her chin.

Brielle blinked once, her voice flat. "He followed us."

Larkin jumped as rock grated against rock within the dark tunnel. She yanked Brielle up, rushing her back to camp.

"We need to go." Larkin grabbed Brielle's pack and heaved it over her own back. "There's something behind us."

Jacque hopped up when she saw them. "What in Ilona's name happened to her?"

"I don't know." Larkin pushed past Jacque. "Which is why we need to get out of here."

No one asked questions as they grabbed the rest of their things and continued deeper into the labyrinth, but as the passage tightened, Amias stopped and waited for Larkin and Brielle to catch up.

Amias studied Brielle's arm, and Larkin sensed the cracks in his calm veneer. "Did she do that to herself?"

"I don't know. She mentioned someone. She said that *he* followed us."

The ceiling declined farther, and Amias ducked as he fell in line with Brielle. "Who is *he*, Brielle?"

Brielle shrank into Larkin's shoulder, and Larkin clutched her.

"This isn't good." Amias pressed his hand to the low ceiling. "If she won't talk, we need to tell the others about the rage. It has to be connected somehow."

Larkin nodded.

In front of them, Elf's panic spiked. "Oh *no*."

Larkin let go of Brielle and pushed her way to the front of the group. Up ahead, the ceiling of the passage took a steep dive. The floor sloped up, and the remaining crawl space was barely large enough for a body to wiggle through.

"We should turn around." Elf was already inching backward.

Jacque looked to Larkin and squared her shoulders, as if waiting for instructions.

"Something back there hurt Brielle," said Larkin. "So badly she can't talk about it. Forward is our only choice."

"It's too small," Elf squeaked.

"You can always use destruction magic to make it larger," offered Tamsyn.

Casseem dropped his pack. "Destruction magic, says the only one in the group who isn't an Empath."

Tamsyn huffed. "With precision, you can—"

"None of us are precise. Remember the cave-in? That was me being *precise*. Perhaps our ancestors were all bumbling morons." He crouched down into a squat and walked forward, pushing his torch into the small opening. "Not even ten feet until it opens again."

Jacque pressed her gloved hands to the rough cavern ceiling. "Not partial to tight spaces, Larkin?"

"Not particularly," Larkin admitted. "But I'm not the one you have to worry about."

Elf flattened herself against the tunnel wall, sweat on her forehead glistening in the light. Panic trilled beneath Larkin's skin.

Casseem handed the torch to Jacque and shrugged off his pack, unbuckling his cuirass. "We'll test it. If the largest one of us can fit, the others will too. Who's biggest?"

"I think I am," said Amias.

Casseem frowned and sized him up. "No, no. I'm definitely bigger."

"This isn't a pissing match." Jacque pointed to the crawl space. "You seem eager enough, Casseem. Why don't you go first?"

Casseem yanked off his bracers and threw them on the ground. "Gladly." He took the torch back from Jacque.

"Don't burn yourself," Jacque muttered.

"And hurry up," Larkin ordered. Her attempt to remain calm wasn't working too well. She dug in Brielle's pack for an extra tunic and tied it around the girl's injured arm before sparing a glance at the empty passage behind them.

Casseem bent down, pushing his torch and upper body into the crawl space. The tunnel darkened tremendously. He wiggled his hips and kicked his legs, his swearing muffled by the rock.

When his legs disappeared, the rest of them crowded around to see into the passage. Casseem rocked and grunted his way through the hole, until he fell out the other end. The warm glow of his flame illuminated the chamber beyond.

"What do you see?" Jacque called.

Casseem crouched down to peer back at them. "Options."

The rest of them began stripping off their armor and packs, passing them through the hole to Casseem. When their gear was on the other side, Amias went next.

"I don't know if I can do this," Elf whispered as Jacque readied for the crawl.

"Casseem's a lot bigger than you. You'll be fine," Larkin said soothingly. She thought of what Casseem said—they had options now. But waiting for her turn made her anxious. The tight crawl space was the only choice; they couldn't stay here.

When she and Elf were the only ones left, Elf volunteered to go last. "You know, to keep watch and make sure you get through safely."

"I'll be fine. I'm a miner, remember? You should go next." *In case you need a push,* Larkin thought. Hopefully, she wouldn't get slugged in the face like Jacque.

Elf scraped her teeth across her bottom lip. "Fine."

She whimpered, kicked, and screamed through the entire crawl. Larkin bounced on her toes, her attention caught between Elf and the darkness behind her as she searched for movement.

When Larkin sensed Elf's relief, she dipped her head into the passage, her elbows pinned to her sides. She fell fully onto her belly when she was waist-deep, rocking on her hips to inch her way forward.

Jacque bent down and shot Larkin an uncharacteristic smile. "Not so bad, right, Larkin?"

It wasn't, at least not as bad as she had anticipated. She

pushed herself forward on her elbows, gritting her teeth as shards of rock dug into her arms. A few inches forward, her back rubbed against the top of the passage. She turned her head sideways when her neck began to ache, her gloved hands clawing at the rock wall, and inched herself forward again, and again. Her breath shortened, with her rib cage no longer able to fully expand, and her back scraped painfully against the top of the crawl space.

When Casseem was gauging the size of the passage, he apparently hadn't taken breasts into account.

Jacque reached out toward her, blocking the light. Larkin scooted her elbows forward and fumbled for Jacque's hands, grabbing on to her.

Suddenly, rage seared her abdomen so intensely that Larkin gasped. Brielle's terror crashed through the heat, and the girl screamed.

"HE'S HERE!"

Larkin cried out as claws sank into her ankle, yanking her backward.

"NO!" Jacque yelled, gripping her hands.

Panic seized Larkin as she frantically kicked at her attacker. "Don't let me go!" The nails cut deeper and deeper until Larkin thought her leg might be wrenched off.

Her head swam from lack of air, shallow breaths catching up to her. *Please, Ilona.* She couldn't die like this. Not trapped and helpless. Muffled shouts came from the chamber in front of her. Grating sounds from behind her.

Jacque's fingers dug into her wrists. "I won't let you go!"

"Hang on, Larkin!" shouted Amias. He and Casseem planted themselves around Jacque and anchored her.

"DESTROY IT!" Larkin's shin slammed into the bottom of the passage as she kicked. She was going to break her own legs.

"I can't see it!" Jacque dove deeper into the passage, grabbing Larkin's shoulder.

Larkin kicked free. Jacque yanked her through the passage and Larkin tumbled out, her shoulder slamming into the ground. She rolled onto her back and gasped for air.

"Get back, everyone." Casseem thrust his torch into the crawl space, searching frantically.

"Do you see it?" cried Larkin.

Casseem shook his head, a bead of sweat rolling down his cheek. "Too dark. Whatever it was, it's gone now."

Amias knelt next to Larkin. "Let me see."

She held her shaking arms out to him, her flesh decorated with cuts. Her tunic was spotted with crimson, and her trousers were torn from whatever had latched on to her. She lifted her shredded pant leg, her skin marred by long gashes. She couldn't tell if the wounds were from talons or fingernails.

"They're shallow," said Amias.

"They hurt like all hells," she gasped, noticing the alarm that still thrummed inside him.

"But you're alive. They'll heal," he said soothingly, his calm returning. She latched on to it, her body still trembling with adrenaline.

"We need to run. If that thing finds another way to get to us . . ." Jacque spun toward Brielle, panting. "Who's *he*?"

Tears streaked down Brielle's face. Her lips parted, but words did not escape her.

Casseem held the torch up to Brielle's face. "You can scream louder than any of us, but now you won't talk?"

Brielle flinched, and Larkin dizzied with the venom of her shame.

"Leave her alone, Casseem." Larkin shook away the sensation. "And it doesn't matter. I know who he is."

The queen had sent them down here for a reason, and as much as Larkin resisted the thought of a god ruling this underworld, the searing rage had settled in her bones. He'd been watching them. He had done so from the very beginning.

"Kyran," said Larkin. "*He* is Kyran."

SIXTEEN

arkin's torch did little to illuminate the forks as she stumbled through them. She listened to Jacque's footsteps close at her side, and glanced over her shoulder to make sure the others were catching up.

Jacque caught the back of her cuirass. "Careful!"

Larkin stopped short, her foot hovering over a treacherous vertical shaft. "Sweet Ilona." She stumbled away, wiping the sweat from her upper lip. "Thank you."

"For saving your hide?" Jacque bent over, catching her breath.

"Twice now," Larkin uttered. The soldier had fought for Larkin's life in the crawl space as if Larkin had been her sister. Perhaps Jacque was used to banding with her battalion to stay alive, but Larkin was grateful.

She counted the others as they rounded the corner, searching for Brielle. Amias had her under his arm.

Brielle's eyes found Larkin. "I'm here," she said quietly.

"I think we're safe," Amias said. "I don't hear anything behind us."

"How in Ilona's bloody name could Kyran be here?" Casseem panted between breaths, wiping locks of hair from his forehead. "Don't tell me you believe Melay's lies. Do you realize how ridiculous you sound?"

"Do I?" Of course Larkin realized how ridiculous she sounded. If Garran could only hear her now. Gods, or her mother.

Tamsyn yanked on his cuirass, setting it straight after their run. His face was bright red. "You said you weren't religious."

"I'm not," Larkin snapped. She sagged against the wall. Their constant anxiety was exhausting her. "But I don't know what else to think. We're being followed. I sensed rage that didn't belong to one of us. So did Brielle and Amias."

"Oh." Elf paused in tying her hair up, her eyes widening. "I sensed it, too. I just thought one of us was mad. I thought it was you."

"Me?" Hells, was she really that angry all the time? "It's coming from something surrounding us. Someone who is everywhere."

"If it's Kyran, then what are the creatures?" Casseem paced to the edge of the light. He turned back toward them. "Tamsyn?"

The scholar clutched his scroll case, his face crumpled as he thought. A bead of sweat dripped past his eyebrow. "We've seen only one creature so far. The soldier's corpse was evidence of another, but we still don't know what attacked Larkin."

Larkin lifted up her pant leg. The red gashes looked too shallow for talons, but then again, she'd never been attacked by something with talons before.

"There could be many creatures. And all of them could be angry." Casseem walked toward Larkin and plucked the torch from her hand.

"No." Amias glanced up, frowning as he waited. Larkin knew that he was trying to sift the rage's smolder from the rest of their emotions. "I know the difference between a mob and a person."

"Do you know the difference between a god and a person?" asked Larkin. "A god you don't believe in?"

"I'm not religious," Amias corrected. "But that doesn't mean I don't believe in the possibility of gods."

"You said Melay sent us down here because she believed Kyran wouldn't hurt his own kind. We could get closer to him," Larkin said.

Amias finished her thought. "He's watching us."

Brielle's agony suddenly began suffocating Larkin like blackdamp. Larkin turned to her and gasped as blood bloomed through the sleeve of Brielle's tunic. No, not just one sleeve. Both of them.

"Brielle, what . . ." Larkin charged forward as Brielle stumbled away from Amias, catching her hand. Larkin pulled up one of her sleeves as Amias raised the other. The skin had peeled from both of Brielle's arms, leaving raw, seeping gashes. "How did this happen?"

"She has been with me the entire time," said Amias, horrified. "I promise you."

Elf called for clean linen.

"He wants my flesh," Brielle whimpered, her eyes glassy and distant. "He told me he knows where my sister is." Even through the agony, her blossom of hope caught Larkin off guard. Brielle extended her arms, as though she were offering them. "All I need to do is give him what he wants."

Larkin knew it was nonsense. But she also had a strong feeling that Brielle was lucid, which made her words that much more frightening.

"What in all hells." Casseem tossed Elf a tunic. Elf glided her finger down the center, splitting it in two.

"Who?" Larkin took the pieces from Elf and began to hastily wrap them around Brielle's arms. "I need you to tell us, Brielle!"

"Kyran," she finally cried.

Larkin swore. She didn't know if Brielle was just regurgitating Larkin's theories, or if Kyran was communicating with her, but someone was hurting her. Right in front of them.

Larkin took Brielle beneath her arm, guiding her toward the group. "We need time to figure out what we're going to do."

Jacque tossed a new torch to Casseem. "And we need water. We need to get out of this labyrinth."

Casseem lit the new torch, tossing the stub of the old one to the ground. "Tamsyn?"

Tamsyn tightened his fist around the map, crumpling it. "This has been useless from the beginning."

Larkin pushed Brielle in front of her, hovering over her protectively. "Then we keep walking."

The winding gut of the labyrinth remained the same—coiled tunnels broken by even darker recesses. At every fork, Casseem would hold his torch before both paths in search of a draft. If his flame wavered, they would choose that path, though Larkin was never certain whether it was simply their imagination playing tricks on them.

Larkin kept talking to Brielle, asking her questions and trying to understand how Kyran could have been speaking to her. Brielle said nothing in return, the numbness that Larkin had sensed from her before returning. She steadily bled through her bandages, black circles blossoming beneath her eyes.

Just keep moving, thought Larkin, but as the dehydration cramps set in, she'd never felt so hopeless.

Their hiking had slowed to a crawl, but they didn't stop until Casseem collapsed.

He rolled onto his back, pressing his hand to his chest. Larkin picked up his torch, the light catching the sheen of Casseem's skin. He was shaking. "I feel like I'm dying."

"If we don't find water—"

"We're done, Larkin." Jacque sank to her knees, pulling off her cuirass as she panted. "Maybe after some rest we'll be able to keep going, but not now." She ran a shaking palm over her face. "We're done."

Larkin's heart raced, but she gave in, helping Brielle sit and using the last of her energy to search Amias's bag for her blanket. She wrapped herself in it and slid down the tunnel wall next to Brielle.

The weight of hopelessness was dismal. Amias lowered himself down to her other side, his breathing labored. At Larkin's feet, Elf curled into a ball within her bedroll.

"There's no escape." The words left Elf in a whisper, but Larkin knew she'd be sobbing if she had the energy.

"What did I tell you, Elf?" Larkin licked her chapped lips. Her tongue felt like sand. "When the walls close in, you need to distract yourself."

Elf peered out from her bedroll. "I don't have any stories."

"What about a riddle?" Jacque croaked. The soldier was propped between Casseem and Tamsyn, who both had their eyes shut.

Elf fell silent for such a long time that Larkin thought she'd fallen asleep. Finally, she asked, "What do you call someone who isn't an Empath?"

Casseem released a groan, his eyes fluttering open. "I don't know, what?"

Elf paused for drama. "Nonsense."

Amias choked on his laughter, spiraling into a coughing fit. Jacque's cracked lips peeled apart in a grin. "That was the worst joke I've ever heard."

"Utterly brilliant," Tamsyn said, his eyes remaining shut. *"Nonsense."*

Brielle hummed in mirth, settling against Larkin's side. Larkin took Brielle's hand, hoping the emotion was a good sign, but the girl said nothing. Larkin took a deep breath, then searched for the rage. She exhaled in relief when she couldn't find it. Another good sign, she hoped.

When the ember of their torch grew dim, Casseem's coarse voice cracked through the looming darkness. "Soldier . . ."

Jacque sighed. "Yes?"

"What's waiting for you when we get home?"

He was trying to lift their spirits by talking as if they would survive this. Larkin wasn't sure it was going to work.

A few moments passed before Jacque responded. "My betrothed."

Larkin's head snapped up in surprise. It had been Jacque in Melay's dungeons. Jacque who had screamed and sobbed. She'd been so composed since the dungeons, with her orders and rule-following.

Even at a distance, Larkin sensed the deep pang of Jacque's remorse, and knew that composure meant little. Jacque may have been good at burying her pain, but it wasn't gone.

If Jacque wasn't a soldier, Larkin reminded herself, she wouldn't be in this mess in the first place. Still, Larkin couldn't help but imagine her own mother and father. She'd sensed their love for each other, envying it at times. Jacque had someone waiting for her. If she never came home, her betrothed would never learn the truth of her sacrifices. It wasn't fair.

"He's a lucky man," said Casseem.

"*She* is."

This caught Amias's attention. "Who?"

"Risa."

"I knew it." Delight burst from Amias. "You've been enamored with her since we were five."

"I was enamored with *you* when I was five. With Risa, I was closer to eight."

Amias chuckled, and Larkin savored his brief and fleeting joy before a small sob escaped Jacque's throat.

"Everything I've done has been for her. Every decision I've made . . . I don't want the magic I inherited. I don't want children to pass it down to. I never wanted to take orders from—" Her breath hitched, and she sobbed again. "I've only ever wanted her."

"I'm sorry, Jacque." Larkin wanted to cry, but it was like she had no water left inside her. *I'm sorry, Garran.*

Larkin wanted to rebel against her fatigue, but her body was succumbing to the dehydration. She drifted to sleep.

At one point, she woke to Brielle snoring softly against her shoulder. Their second-to-last torch lay burning on the ground near Elf.

Larkin tilted her head back, and beyond the dim light a network of eyes glittered along the ceiling. Hands of the dead twisted along the tops of the tunnel walls, sinew braided together.

She was losing her mind.

Larkin rolled her head to the side. Amias was awake, watching the ceiling along with her. "He's here."

Here?

Larkin shot up as terror prickled down her spine. The torch was half burned; the others were slumped over, asleep.

She patted the vacant wall next to her. Brielle was gone.

Terror struck again, more violent, demanding her attention.

Larkin stood and almost lost her balance; she stepped over Elf and picked up the torch, rekindling it.

"Larkin?"

She'd woken Casseem.

"Brielle's gone, but I sense her. She's in trouble." She'd let them decide to follow her or not, but she wouldn't waste any more time.

Larkin's legs cramped as she rounded a bend in the tunnel, but she pushed forward, reaching another fork. Brielle's emotion was consistent now, like nails against slate. She quickened her pace, weaving through portals and crystals as large as she was. She batted away a glowing string of larvae as Brielle's terror crescendoed into an emotional shriek.

The tunnel mouth opened to darkness. As Larkin stepped into the abyss, her torch snuffed out.

So did Brielle.

Larkin screamed Brielle's name, holding her breath and waiting for a response. *Tell me you're here*, Larkin silently pleaded. *Please, tell me you're here.*

When she was met with silence, Larkin swore and searched

her pockets for flint and a knife. The air reeked of something rotting, and she gagged. Kneeling, she scraped her flint over the torch head until it lit again. She picked it up, finding nothing before the flame extinguished again.

Her only hope was the group she'd left behind.

"Help!" she screamed.

She lit it a third and a fourth time. The same luck followed her. Pressing her hand to the torch's crown, Larkin found it cold. She tossed it to the ground and struck her flint over and over again.

A figure holding a torch emerged from the tunnel's mouth. Amias. His flame choked and died. She cried out to him, and they found each other in the darkness.

"This room." She tightened her grip on his arms. "I can't keep my torch lit."

"Where is Brielle?"

"I lost her."

"That stench . . ."

Footsteps beat against stone as the others arrived. Larkin counted four; they were all here. As Casseem reached Larkin and Amias, he tried lighting Amias's torch. The flame erupted, and Larkin spotted a rope on the ground in front of them before the light died. She hurried to it and dropped to her knees.

"This is destruction magic," cried Tamsyn. "Something is eating away the tops of the torches."

There was someone in the room with them, putting out their flame.

"We need to turn back, now," Jacque commanded, drawing her sword.

"We can't leave Brielle." Larkin found the end of the rope, as thick around as her fist. Beneath the stench of the room, she smelled sulfur. She held her flint over the rope and struck it with her knife. Flame erupted, traveling down the wound fiber.

Larkin followed the rope, unable to keep up as the flame roared across the ground, forking and illuminating enormous basalt pillars. At the back of the hall, the fire climbed, zigzagging over a strange formation of rock before plummeting back toward the ground, creating an arch.

As Larkin neared, the rock grew more defined until she realized it wasn't rock at all.

Rock didn't have skin that peeled from bones, nor bent and broken limbs. Hundreds of figures, swords threading their rib cages, pinning them together. Shields with the crest of Demura garnished the arch of corpses.

Vibrations of terror grated her flesh.

"The missing soldiers," Jacque said. "*Gods*, no."

Something was different about the lower left side of the arch: an imprint of blood and open wounds. Larkin released a scream and sank to her knees.

Brielle's eye sockets were empty, her ribs flared open to reveal her stolen heart.

Jacque yanked Larkin up by the back of her armor and spun her around. "Don't look at her."

Larkin, clinging to the soldier, met Jacque's frightened eyes. They were both crying.

"We have to go." Jacque led Larkin toward the tunnel entrance, and Larkin obliged because she didn't know what else to do. Brielle was dead. Larkin had *felt* her die, just as she had with Devon.

"Stop," Tamsyn called out.

"We should have turned back when our light went out," cried Casseem.

"I said *stop*!" Tamsyn shouted.

Larkin froze. Jacque shivered against her.

"Why the orchestration of something so horrific?" asked Tamsyn. Though he was as terrified as the rest of them, he studied the arch in morbid fascination. "This is disgusting, but it's strategic. There must be a reason."

"Whoever did this is a monster." Casseem pressed his hands to the sides of his head. "One that's going to come after the rest of us." He spun around to the group. "That's reason enough!"

"No, Tamsyn's right." Elf wiped the tears from her cheeks. "This is a performance."

"Whose performance?" Jacque shouted. "Kyran's? This could have been me. I was part of one of the first battalions, and they switched me out at the last minute. I'm supposed to be pinned to that wall!"

"The performance has been going on for some time. It didn't begin here." Tamsyn pointed to the tunnel entrance, his finger trembling. "It started back there. At the beginning with Devon. The soldier at the bottom of the chasm. Now Brielle." Tamsyn turned to Amias. "Larkin said you told her what Melay's intentions were. Well, Amias?"

"Melay thinks Kyran will let us get close." Amias's knuckles whitened as he clenched the dead torch. His tranquility had vanished, and he was as wild with horror as the rest of them.

"He's not only letting us get close. We've been escorted this entire time," the scholar declared. "Kyran *is* with us."

Larkin knew Tamsyn was right, and she hated him for it. Who knew how long it would have taken them to find the entrance to the labyrinth if it weren't for the dead soldier? They would have wasted their time attempting to find a way across the chasm instead of down. And Brielle—Brielle had been a sacrifice to guide them here. Larkin bit down on her bottom lip to keep from sobbing out loud.

She should have watched Brielle more closely. She should have fought against the fatigue.

Tamsyn shook his head back and forth, as though alarmed by his own discovery. "The only thing that I don't understand is why. What are we being shown?"

Shown. They had been guided here and instilled with fear for a reason. Because they could do something that these soldiers could not.

Kyran wanted them to be afraid, and he wanted them to use their magic.

"It's a gateway," cried Larkin. "We need to destroy this wall." She turned to Tamsyn for affirmation, but he was doubtful.

"If this was set up by Kyran, why should we follow him?" Casseem asked in a frenzy. "How do we know it's not a trap?"

"Where would we go if it is?" Larkin licked her chapped bottom lip. "We go back into that labyrinth and we die. You know that."

Elf sidled up next to Larkin. "I'll be damned if I go back there."

Casseem and Jacque shared a glance, and the soldier buried her face in her hands. "Ilona's breath."

Amias threw down his dead torch and stepped forward. "We don't have another option."

Casseem grunted in disapproval and trudged up to the wall. "This is insanity."

Larkin followed him to the smoldering bodies, avoiding the place where Brielle hung. She walked to the center of the arch and pressed her hand to the stone face. Shutting her eyes, she sensed the intensity of the others. Terror collected at the base of her spine, gaining tension as she siphoned it.

A deafening crack filled the chamber. The wall shook, stone crumbling beneath her hands. It was too late to worry about a cave-in, but it didn't matter. Larkin was getting stronger. She had more control over her magic than she thought.

Beams of cool light shot from veinlike fractures, hovering, and for a desperate moment Larkin wondered if they'd broken through to the Surface.

The rest of the rock dissolved into dust. Larkin stepped through the curtain and into the bright void, squinting as her eyes watered.

She started to laugh, a raw hack that sounded as delirious as she felt. "Tamsyn."

"What?"

"It's time to revise your map."

SEVENTEEN

*I*mpossible.

Larkin marveled at the cerulean patchwork of lichen, larvae, and crystal that glowed like a sea of stars, emulating the soft blue of dusk.

Miles in front of her, mammoth stalagmites peaked like mountains. A waterfall broke through the cliffside to the left of them and plummeted into a lake hundreds of feet below.

The vast body of water stretched from the cliffside to the subterranean mountains beyond, the surface reflecting the brilliant color from the makeshift sky. The lake's only shore was dotted by a web of fiery light. Flames. Flames dotting roads, stringing together a cluster of huts.

"We go down?" Jacque croaked. The blue light from the lichen-crusted ceiling accentuated the hollows of her cheeks and the white cracks of her lips. The others looked just as gaunt as they crowded around Larkin. They needed water, and below them, an entire pool of it waited.

"It's a little world," gasped Elf. "It's so big . . . so open."

Larkin sensed a breeze of ethereal hope from her. But hope meant vulnerability. "Look out," she warned before descending. "We can't let our guard down."

The switchbacks before them were lit with the blue glow, guiding her. As she maneuvered downward, the others followed.

Jacque hissed to be careful as they neared the bottom. Larkin's toe hit a stone at the last moment, and she stumbled onto the flat earth, catching herself with her hands. Grit ate at her palms, but she only cared about one thing.

Water.

They had spilled into a small cove on the cusp of the lake. Larkin stumbled across the silky shore and collapsed, immersing her face in the water. She drank and drank. It was the most wonderful thing she'd ever tasted.

She emerged, gasping for breath. "It's clean!" she called, realizing she was the only one at the edge of the water. Where were the others?

"Larkin!" Elf shouted.

Larkin jumped to her feet, whirling to the path that cut through rock. A man in black stood before them. She staggered back in alarm.

His pale flesh reminded her of a skinned fish, like he'd been birthed and left in the dark. Larkin couldn't guess his age if she tried. But he was also frighteningly beautiful. And he wasn't alone. More people lingered behind him, with the same black cloaks and haunting faces. Larkin scoured for their emotions but found very little—too little.

"Casseem?" Jacque said.

"Hold your ground." Casseem's voice was stern. "Who are they? Arkwright?"

"I—I . . . ," Tamsyn stuttered, his bewilderment a buzzing pulse inside of Larkin. "I don't know."

The man lifted his hand and beckoned them closer.

When Larkin took a hesitant step forward, the people surrounding the man grew maniacally gleeful. This was not a gesture of goodwill.

Before she could scream an order to run, the sand at the man's feet began funneling upward, as if trapped in a windstorm. Casseem swore as a ghost of a sword appeared in the man's hand, grains of sand swarming and strengthening it.

Conjuration. They were Empaths.

They watched in stunned silence as sand whipped through the air, spiraling around the hands of the other Empaths. When their swords were formed, the Empaths crouched in battle stances.

"What do we do?" Elf whispered.

"Draw your weapons," Casseem replied.

"What weapons?" Larkin nearly screamed at him. She had one knife on her. The rest of their gear was back in the labyrinth. They should have been completely capable of conjuring weapons, but Larkin had had enough difficulty with just a rope.

"I'm the only one who kept my sword," Jacque said. "And if you think I would be foolish enough to draw my weapon on them, you're damned mad."

The group drew closer as the man began to conjure again, this time creating a chain of mottled shackles. Six pairs in all. He threw them at Larkin's feet.

"He wants us to *shackle* ourselves," said Casseem, a note of hysteria in his voice.

"We have to. I don't think the swords are for show." Larkin wasn't ready to die. Kneeling, she picked up a set of shackles and clumsily bound her own wrists with the cuffs.

Amias was by her side, following her lead. "I hope you know what you're doing."

"I don't." Larkin locked the cuff on her right wrist.

Elf glided forward, followed by Tamsyn, who was more intrigued than afraid. Jacque marched ahead, picking up the chain. "I don't surrender. I'm not surrendering."

Only Casseem remained. The leader of the strange Empaths strode toward Casseem, his sword raised and aimed at his throat.

"Casseem!" Larkin hissed.

Slowly, Casseem bent down and picked up the final set of shackles. "This is a mistake." As he locked himself in, the man in black scrutinized each of them before grabbing the end of the chain and yanking them forward.

Larkin stumbled but regained her balance quickly. The strangers surrounded them, walking the prisoners toward the village.

"Gods," Tamsyn breathed. "How long do you think they've been living down here?" He held out his fingers, counting, and then clenched his fist.

"Since the Reach was closed off," Larkin replied. "How else would they've gotten in?"

"The dynasty's opened the portcullis for the occasional adventurer. None of them reemerged, of course."

"Not Empaths," Larkin corrected. "Unless they were banished here." But she'd never heard of such a thing happening since Kyran was condemned.

Then where had these people come from?

The Empaths' conjured swords glistened in their hands like metal fresh from the forge. One of the Empaths glanced over her shoulder at them. Larkin noted her curiosity, like she couldn't understand the party's conversation. Despite the elaborate show of conjuring swords, the Empaths didn't seem threatened by them. But Larkin didn't know if that was necessarily good.

As they approached the village, the man in black yanked them forward by the shackles once more, the metal cutting into Larkin's scraped arms.

"Stay afraid," she told the others. The Empaths before them were hardly emitting any emotions. "In case we need to escape."

"Fear feeds them as much as us," said Amias.

Larkin swore beneath her breath.

Huts of marbled glass and smelted metal lined the pathway. The glass appeared onyx until she saw light from within one of them, and the color morphed into a striking violet. Other huts held different colors within the glass—bloodred and moss green. Blue the color of deepest midnight. Pale faces peered out from within, expressions warped behind the melted glass.

Larkin tried counting them, but there were too many. Hundreds of them.

The Empaths who led them stopped at one of the huts, their leader gesturing for Larkin's party to enter. There was nothing inside but a barren floor, and when Larkin turned around, the leader blocked the entrance.

He was not angry, but fierce. Confident. He gestured toward the floor, and when Larkin didn't move, he pushed her backward until she tripped, tangled by the chain that bound her to the others. Elf held her up.

The Empath gestured to the floor again. Simultaneously, the six of them sank to their knees.

"Say your final prayers to Ilona." Casseem was angry. They

hadn't fought when they had the chance, and now they were cornered.

"Shut up," ordered Jacque.

"They could have killed us by now if they wanted to," said Amias. Larkin focused on his calm to clear her head, and as she did, their captors parted, and a woman entered the hut.

The woman pulled off her hood, a sheet of white hair tumbling around her shoulders. Her beauty was surreal, her skin impossibly smooth and eyes ethereal as she gazed at the six prisoners. The bodice of her violet dress was adorned with silver shafts shaped like human ribs, and delicate silver bones were fused to the backs of her hands, mirroring the finger bones beneath. Larkin had never seen such conjuration magic. It was almost beautiful.

Larkin's stomach flipped as she sensed the woman's confusion. Concern emanated from the man in black. The woman spoke impatiently to him, but the language was harsh and nonsensical. A few words sounded familiar, but she could make no meaning of them.

Tamsyn clapped his hand over his mouth before dissolving into terror.

Blood thrummed in Larkin's ears. "Who is she?" she hissed.

"I think that's Bianca Elesandre," hissed Tamsyn. "Kyran's right hand."

A disciple.

"Bianca?" Elf gasped.

"Quiet!" Jacque hissed.

The shock of the party buzzed beneath Larkin's skin. A thousand-year-old outlaw stood before them.

"Maybe I'm wrong," Tamsyn said hesitantly. Then he violently shook his head. "No, no. I can't be wrong."

But if he was correct, Kyran's favorite disciple was standing before them. After all, they had suspected that Kyran had guided them here. This could be the moment they had come down here for, to confront Kyran *and* all of his disciples face-to-face, and here Larkin was, surrendering. Despair tugged her downward as she thought of Garran, and how far they'd come only to fail.

The woman flicked her silver-laden fingers back and forth. The rocky floor surrounding the party disintegrated and re-formed around their chain, shackling them to the ground. Another flick, and Larkin's cuffs dissolved.

Before Larkin could register her freedom, two of the Empaths lunged forward and grabbed her, dragging her to her feet.

"Wait!" Amias cried.

Larkin's heart hammered in her chest as the woman approached her, the beautiful Empath drenched in loathing. Her perfect lips pulled up in a sneer.

The panic of the party stole Larkin's attention. She needed to use it, break everything around her, make a distraction, fight for her life. If she tried, however, this woman would certainly kill her.

One of the men who held her gripped her wrist, his fingernails sinking into her wounds. She cried out, struggling against him as he forcefully straightened her arm.

"What does he want?" the woman asked Larkin in the common tongue, furious. She spoke their language!

"I don't—"

Pain tore through Larkin's arm, and she nearly buckled to the ground.

Everyone was yelling, their words and emotions confusing and vivid, the way dreams so often felt.

This is *a dream,* thought Larkin. It wasn't real. It *couldn't* be.

"Tell me what he wants," the woman repeated. "We had an arrangement. No more visits. No more puppets. Why is he breaking his promise?"

"Who?" The word scraped the back of Larkin's throat.

The woman lifted a finger, and silver bones dragged down Larkin's arm. The skin dissolved, and Larkin's vision clouded as her knees buckled. She tasted iron.

"*We don't know anything,*" Elf cried, or Larkin thought it was her. Beneath the ringing in her ears, Elf sounded so far away. Miles away.

Larkin tried siphoning, but the pain was too great.

The woman clutched Larkin's jaw and yanked her face upward. "I know he tortures you. It must be agonizing, but I promise you a quick death if you tell me . . ."

Larkin had been wrong. The woman wasn't beautiful. She was haunting—terrifying. And Larkin knew she'd kill each of them just like this.

After everything they'd already been through.

Through the black dots swarming her vision, Larkin saw the porcelain skin over the woman's cheekbone split open.

Startled, the woman released Larkin's jaw to catch the blood trickling down her face. She drew her fingers from the wound.

"Leave her alone." Amias's voice rang out.

The woman's eyes found Amias. "An Empath?"

Larkin tried to yank herself back, but the woman wasn't finished. Larkin cried out when her arm began burning, but when she looked down, she watched in wonder as her flesh knitted itself back together. By the time the man who held her released her, even the scratches from the labyrinth were gone.

Larkin's knees gave out. Elf and Amias were by her side, lifting her up and dragging her back to the rest of the group at the edge of the small hut. Amias's anger was a pulse of heat and brimstone. As quick as he'd caught her, he was gone, and Elf was the only one left clutching Larkin.

They were no longer shackled, their manacles having dissolved back to sand. The party swarmed around Larkin to protect her.

"Bianca," Larkin croaked.

Bianca's surprise confirmed that Larkin was right. "What sector are you from?"

"What does she mean, sector?" Elf murmured.

"I . . . I don't know." Tamsyn's dismay was a weight spiraling slowly through Larkin's body. "Gods, I should know this!"

Casseem shook his head. "Don't say anything."

But Larkin couldn't help herself. "We don't know what you mean by *sector*."

"Who is your disciple?" Bianca asked.

Larkin shook her head.

Bianca grew frustrated. "Where in the Reach did you come from?"

"Larkin . . . ," Casseem warned.

"We're not from the Reach," said Larkin. "We're from the Surface."

"Larkin!" Jacque snapped. Casseem swore under his breath.

Bianca took a step back. "The Surface? Has the dynasty begun exiling Empaths to the Reach once more?"

"Queen Melay has sent us into the Reach to find and kill Otheil Kyran," Larkin said desperately. There was no sense in lying. They had nothing to lose.

"I don't understand." Bianca narrowed her pale eyes, eyes that looked as though the color had been washed from them. They reminded Larkin of the river quartz lining the canal in the capital. "Why you? Why now?"

Larkin truly didn't know. Casseem's suspicions pulled at her, but Larkin batted them away. Bianca was confused, not distressed that they wanted to kill Kyran. Her allegiance with him had obviously been severed.

Had they stumbled across a death trap, or an ally?

Larkin was ready to find out. "We were forced. Demura faces destruction magic—something powerful stemming from the Reach. People are disappearing. Our queen believes that it is coming from Kyran, that he's acting out some sort of revenge."

And the queen is acting out her anger on us, thought Larkin. Bianca could be their only hope of getting out of this mess.

With this news, Bianca grew serious. "I no longer consort with Kyran, and have not for a very long time."

"You made a deal with him, didn't you?" asked Tamsyn, intrigued. "An arrangement, you said. You have territories within this place. Sectors, you called them. You stay away from each other."

"Our paths down here are delicate. You cannot simply go breaking through walls and expect not to damage a millennium's worth of fortification. None of us cross into other sectors."

Bianca pointed through the foggy glass, toward the cliffside they'd come from, her confusion overtaken by a fiery fury. "That passage was sealed off for a reason."

"We didn't know, I promise you. We were only trying to find our way deeper. We'll be on our way if you could provide aid to us," Larkin pleaded. "Terrible creatures hunt us. Two of us are dead. If we could find Kyran—"

Bianca cut her off. "If you're concerned about beasts, they are worse the deeper you go. Traversing there is up to you, but I will not guide you. You may rest at the edge of the village, and then you will leave this place and never return." She spoke rapidly to her Empaths in their strange language, and they fled the hut.

Jacque shifted. "What's happening? Tamsyn, what are they doing?"

"Refortifying where we broke through, I think." Tamsyn tapped his finger against his lips, thinking. "My grasp on the language of old isn't as strong as I thought."

"Otheil and I have an agreement." Bianca glared at Larkin. "My people have been safe here for hundreds of years, and I will not put them at risk for you, nor for your queen. Do you understand?"

Larkin had no choice but to nod, but Ilona be damned if she gave up as easily as Bianca wanted her to. Rage had followed them here, rage she had assumed belonged to Kyran. Somehow, he was watching them, creating the arch of dead soldiers to fill them with fear, providing a way to destroy the wall. Kyran had led them here, to his estranged disciple. A woman who was frightened of Kyran, and who knew where he was.

There was only one possible explanation: Otheil Kyran wanted to be found.

And Bianca Elesandre was the key.

EIGHTEEN

asseem paced back and forth through the sand at their camp. "We need to leave before Bianca changes her mind and decides to rip out our throats in our sleep. Hells, we shouldn't even stay to rest."

It was easy for Larkin to disagree with him. They'd been able to wash in the lake and had already foraged enough mushrooms for a feast. Elf assisted Larkin with conjuring a net, and Jacque and Amias were trying their luck with fishing in the shallow waters off the camp's shore.

In the distance the falls roared, and the lichen cast enough pale blue light that Larkin could see everything. She hadn't realized how much she'd missed *seeing* clearly. Bianca's universe had brought more hope than she'd felt in a long time.

"We need to eat and sleep," said Larkin. "You heard Bianca. Otheil Kyran is alive, which means we're on the right track. Brielle died because we weren't prepared, and I refuse to let that happen again." She looked to Tamsyn for affirmation, but the scholar was staring blankly at his hands, confused and unsettled. His hair was still wet from washing up, and with a clean face, Larkin could see the rosy hue of his boyish cheeks.

"You're young," Larkin stated. "You couldn't learn all of Demura's history in a lifetime, so don't beat yourself up."

Tamsyn pursed his lips, more annoyed with her response than encouraged.

Elf skirted the edge of the camp, staring in wonder at their makeshift sky and oblivious to the conversation. Larkin would have to reason this one out on her own.

"And Bianca is keeping something from us," Larkin continued, poking at the meager fire. "That much is obvious. I just need some time to convince her that we can be trusted."

"*Convince* her?" Casseem yelled, startling Larkin. "She *hurt* you. She's not helping us, Larkin. You heard what she said!"

"She only hurt me because she was terrified and angry. She thought Kyran had sent us." Larkin stood and brushed the sand from her pants. "Why?"

"Why?" Tamsyn repeated under his breath. He brushed the sand from the front of his tunic, sighing impatiently. "We have more questions than answers. We thought that Kyran was alive because he was a god, but Bianca is alive too. Is she a goddess? She asked us who our disciple was, and the sectors must be the territory of the other disciples, which means they must be alive too." He glanced back toward the village, a cluster of gemstone huts in the distance. "We need to understand how this happened if we want to defeat Kyran."

"Exactly," said Larkin. "And we have that chance, right now."

Casseem pivoted to stare at her. "And I'm assuming you think you can coax that information from Bianca without your skin melting off?"

"Whose skin is melting off?" Jacque trudged through the sand toward them, Amias close behind her. She carried the wadded net in her hands, three wriggling, bone-white fish trapped within. Kneeling, she set the net on a stone slab.

"Larkin's, if she thinks she has a chance at pressing Bianca for more information." Casseem picked apart the lichen, throwing pieces into the fire one by one. He watched Larkin from across the flame, irritated. No, something more complex than irritation. The heat ignited her nerves and upset her stomach. He distrusted her.

Amias knelt and focused on detangling the fish from the net. "Bianca's dangerous."

"She was defending her people," Larkin argued. "She didn't know who we were. Wouldn't you do the same thing?"

Amias said nothing, but his guilt stirred inside her. Larkin almost felt ashamed for not having realized sooner.

He'd used destruction magic when he swore he wouldn't. Amias had wounded Bianca to save Larkin.

"I'm not making light of what you did, Amias. I'm grateful, truly."

"I'm still with Casseem." He avoided eye contact with her, sliding a knife from his pocket to clean the fish. "I'm sorry, Larkin, we should leave."

Larkin stepped back, stunned. "That's it? You had to use magic, so now you want to go? We don't even know what direction to travel. The Reach stretches beneath the entire isle! Are we just supposed to wander until we stumble upon Kyran? I don't have the luxury of that kind of time, Amias. If Melay thinks I'm dead, then my brother dies too."

"Everyone dies, Larkin." Amias glared at her. "Not just your brother, but every single person on the Surface. They will die if we don't find Kyran. They will die if we run out of water. And they will die if Bianca changes her mind and decides that we're too big of a liability."

"So what?" Larkin's eyes stung. "You're saying that's more

terrifying than being lost forever? Or are you saying that no matter what we do, everyone will end up dying anyway?"

Amias's eyes softened. "Larkin—"

"You've made your point." Larkin wiped at her eyes.

"Larkin's right. Wandering aimlessly would be asinine." Tamsyn stood, clapping sand from his palms. "We may be a liability, but I can't leave, not now. You must be curious to learn what Bianca has seen. She's been alive for centuries."

Casseem's anger intensified, heating like iron in a bloomery. "We don't have the luxury of being curious, or have you forgotten why we are here?" He snapped off a lichen branch and hurled it into the fire. "You never cared, Arkwright. You say you're being punished like the rest of us, but I have a hard time believing this is more than a junket for you."

"Oh yes, a junket!" Tamsyn exclaimed. "What better way to marvel at the Reach's wonders than to go on a life-threatening mission with a party of hostile Empaths while the entire isle is in jeopardy."

"Hostile?" cried Casseem.

Jacque speared the sand with a knife. "Stop it." Her eyes found Larkin. "All of you."

Larkin noticed the rage simmering inside herself, rage she hadn't noticed until now. Her own rage. Casseem was making decisions too quickly, not considering what was best for the party in the long run. By either happenstance or Kyran's will, they had stumbled across one of his disciples. They couldn't throw away their greatest chance of finding Kyran and getting out of the Reach alive.

She thought of Garran in his cell, her mother's face when

the guards came and took them away. This was bigger than her or her family, but the grief would be enough to drive her. She had to make the right choice, even if Casseem wasn't willing to do so.

"Listening to Casseem means listening to what Bianca wants." Jacque sliced down the belly of one of their slimy fish. "Regardless of what she can teach us, she wants us gone, and I personally don't know how to defend myself or any of you against her magic."

"If Bianca is afraid of what you're capable of, she may not risk hurting you," Tamsyn offered. "She knows we'll use magic on her." He looked to Amias.

"That will *not* happen again," Amias said darkly. Larkin was certain that if he wasn't consumed by the guilt of using destruction magic, he'd be on her side. He had been ever since the mining settlement.

"We leave when we wake." Jacque shimmied the stone slab into the fire, the fish flesh sizzling. "End of discussion."

Casseem nodded, satisfied. Elf was worried, surely thinking about leaving the spacious cavern for another tight passage. And Jacque's decision only kindled Tamsyn's irritation. Amias avoided Larkin as they ate and cleaned up, and Larkin knew that she needed something bigger than her words to convince them.

As they lay down to rest in the sand by the dying fire, Elf sidled next to her. "I think you're right. I think we should stay."

Larkin turned toward her. "Are you only saying that because you're afraid of the tunnels?"

"No," Elf said too quickly. "I mean, that's a part of it. If the

Reach is truly as big as the isle? I can't wander without direction. I won't."

"You should tell them!" Larkin pushed herself up on her elbows, resting her chin in her palm. "That's three against three."

Elf chewed on her lip, and Larkin sensed her battling doubt. "It doesn't matter what I think. I'm not like Casseem and Jacque."

Larkin reached out and took her hand. "Who is Melay hanging over your head?"

Elf's anguish weighed against Larkin's chest. "My troupe," she said. "All of them."

"All of them," Larkin repeated. "You have every right to make decisions with the rest of us."

Elf smiled sadly.

"I mean it," said Larkin. And she did.

Of course Elf didn't want to speak up. Every time she had, they'd shoved her into a tight passageway. But she mattered—her brightness, her enthusiasm. They had so little else down here to begin with. "I'm going to try my hardest to make sure we don't go wandering into the dark again. I promise you."

Elf sniffed, squeezing her hand. "Thank you, Larkin."

Larkin rolled onto her back, thinking of ways they could stay, if only for a little longer. Casseem was too stubborn to listen.

She'd have to go against his orders.

NINETEEN

She dreamt of bandaging Brielle's wounds.

He wants my flesh.

As Larkin rolled the bandage over her arm, the fabric bled through, soaking crimson until she had no choice but to start over. Brielle's skin began to tear, the wounds crawling up her arms like veins.

He's here.

Larkin woke with a start. Everyone within her party was still asleep, but the air echoed with commotion from the village. Larkin pushed herself from the sand and crept away from camp, brushing off her clothing as she walked.

As she passed through clusters of huts, emotion bled into her, intensifying as she neared the village center. Larkin's head pounded. The assortment of love and joy and worry was overwhelming. She focused on the contentment she sensed—the calm—until her head cleared.

She passed by villagers, some carting mushrooms to huts, while others toted baskets of laundry to the lake. It was almost like she was back at the capital, except the emotions weren't suppressed by luminite. They were vivid, stealing Larkin's breath away, as though she were seeing color for the first time. The Empaths weren't ashamed of how exposed their feelings were.

This was what her world was supposed to be like. This was what had been stolen from her.

A man stepped onto the path before Larkin and stood in

her way. He was the same man who had found her party at the bottom of the switchbacks, the one who'd brought them to Bianca.

This time, he did not need to conjure a sword. He pulled back his cloak to show her the weapon.

Furious, he jabbed his finger toward the camp she'd come from. The message was clear. *Leave.*

I'm a threat, she thought. She held her hands up, thankful she had no weapons.

"Elesandre," she said, hoping he would understand. "Take me to Bianca. Please."

Larkin tensed as the man drew his sword. Maybe Casseem was right after all.

No. She needed answers now. They needed a direction, or they would die. And she believed that Bianca would help them.

The man lowered his sword, turned away from her, and began to walk. Larkin sighed in relief and followed him.

He led her to an onyx hut, a rancid stench wafting from the open door. Larkin covered her nose with her hand as she entered, then halted in shock.

Bianca stood over a bed occupied by a corpse. The dead man's chest was ripped open. Blood pooled within the cavity as though he'd been very recently killed.

Bianca must have sensed Larkin's horror, because she glanced up and scowled, saying something in the harsh language of old. Larkin recognized some of the words: *leave, distraction, fear.* She was breaking Bianca's concentration, though she didn't know what the disciple was focusing on.

"I believe I told you to leave as soon as you woke," Bianca said in the common tongue. *Surface tongue,* thought Larkin. *But how did she learn it?*

"I need to speak with you," said Larkin. "And then I promise we will leave, as soon as the others wake."

Larkin faltered as she caught sight of a pile of bones at Bianca's feet, dried skin and tendons clinging to them. She spotted the seal of Demura on shredded armor. These were the remains of several soldiers from Kyran's arch. Bianca's people must have hiked up the switchbacks to collect them.

The corpse on the table released a groan, and agony left Larkin breathless. It wasn't a corpse at all.

"He's still alive!" she cried.

"Silence." Bianca shut her eyes. "Of course he's still alive." The disciple lifted her hands, blood beading on the delicate silver bones and dripping from her fingers. She flicked her wrist, and one of the skeletons at her feet disintegrated. Bianca flipped her palm upward, a cloud of flesh and bone hovering before she guided it into the open cavity.

"Come here." Bianca beckoned Larkin forward.

Slowly, Larkin approached until she could see within the man's chest. His slick heart pulsed, quivering as Bianca destroyed parts of it and conjured them anew with matter from the skeleton. Within moments, Bianca had destroyed and reconjured the man's entire heart, mending his rib cage and resealing his chest.

Larkin was shaking. She had never seen magic like this before.

The disciple turned away, washing her hands in a stone

basin. "Speak, but do not waste my time. I have much to get done."

Larkin remembered Bianca's specialty from Elf's stories. *She was skilled as a medic, and conjured new flesh from the dead bodies to heal wounds during the Uprising.*

"You used the dead to mend his heart," Larkin stated.

Bianca wet a cloth and began cleaning the blood from the man. His chest rose and fell as he breathed, asleep.

"He needed a new heart," Bianca said. "Every hundred years or so, we all do. Sometimes we are lucky enough to come across life matter to use. Other times, we are not so fortunate." She looked to Larkin. "The corpses of your soldiers are a gift, and we would not have found them if you had not come this way. For that I thank you."

Death was a strange thing to be thanked for. "We didn't gather the bodies. We thought Kyran had done it."

"I too think he did so," said Bianca, "which concerns me for many reasons. Most importantly, that he would not claim the corpses for his own. Kyran needs them as much as we do."

Kyran and his disciples were not naturally immortal. They must have been doing what Bianca did—using the dead to reconjure the living. She couldn't wait to tell Tamsyn, picturing the wonder on the scholar's face.

"He isn't a god," Larkin breathed.

To Larkin's surprise, Bianca chuckled. "God? Otheil? The dynasty has not changed much over a millennium after all." Bianca wiped her bloody hands on the towel. "Those who've controlled Demura have always created gods when it suited them."

"You don't believe in the gods?" said Larkin.

Bianca laughed again. Larkin's curiosity seemed to have calmed the disciple. Or at least amused her.

"I don't know, child. But I do know Otheil isn't a god, though he wants to be one. And he thinks the way to do so is by living forever."

"But he left the corpses behind. Is it because he's killed enough?" Larkin thought of the thousands of soldiers, and all of those who had disappeared from the farms in the vale. "How has he survived for centuries?"

"You are not the first Surfacers to wander into my home since the Reach was sealed off." Bianca walked to one of the glass walls and stared out into the village. The glass blurred the cavern beyond, but Bianca watched carefully, as though she could see everything happening within her universe from the hut. "The Surface's dynasty has permitted adventurers to enter over the centuries, perhaps hoping for them to return with tales of the Reach. It is how I've learned the change of language." Noxious guilt brewed within the disciple. "And how we survived."

Bianca was estranged from Kyran, but she was not innocent of his crimes. Larkin tried to keep her fear at bay, hoping the disciple would not sense it.

"I do not plan on killing you." Bianca's gaze remained transfixed by the glass. "You are an Empath, and I want you to succeed in finding Kyran as much as you do."

Larkin had made the right decision after all. She hoped Casseem would think twice about listening to her once he found out. Still, Bianca's well wishes weren't exactly what she'd hoped for. "Then why won't you tell us where he is?"

"We have an arrangement. If I do not interfere with him, he will leave me and my people alone." Bianca brushed her fingers on the glass as if she were touching the village itself. "When I was banished, my child remained on the Surface. I never want to feel that loss again. These people who live here are my children now. My descendants. Some, the descendants of other disciples who have chosen me to take care of their followers. They know they are safe here."

"But how would Kyran know you helped us?" Larkin asked.

"He knows you are here, doesn't he?" Bianca left the hut, and Larkin followed her outside. The disciple looked upward, toward the cliff, the switchbacks, and the yawning hole within the cavern wall. "He led you here. He's testing me."

Bianca did not try to stifle her own dread, and Larkin felt a strange urge to comfort the disciple. Bianca was trapped, powerless. If Larkin were in her position, she would do anything to protect her people. Her family.

"I laid to rest any hope of being a good person a long time ago, but Otheil . . . he has fallen to an evil that I will not plummet to. I've had many centuries to ruminate on Queen Ilona's decision. We were right to be condemned, but she should have killed Otheil, at the very least." Bianca paused. "This angers you. Why?"

Larkin noticed her own anger, just like the anger she carried in her heart back at the camp. She thought for a moment. "I don't want to believe our queen has been right all these years. I believed Kyran's exile was only a story to justify our punishment."

"I see," said Bianca, saddened. "Ilona has been immortalized, yes? Your queen worships her?"

"Most Demurans do, as the Goddess of Light."

"Well, she is not right." Bianca reached toward her with pale fingers. As she touched Larkin's cheek, a shiver raced through Larkin, the graze familiar. Bianca's hand was cool and soft, like her mother's.

"There is no such thing as Light, child. There is only Darkness. You will be fighting it with every step you take toward Kyran. And you will either succumb to it or claim it as your own." Bianca's eyebrows furrowed as she thought. "How many of you did you say have died within this place?"

Larkin winced as she thought of Brielle and Devon, and their horrible fates. "Two."

"So there were eight . . . All of you are Empaths?"

"All but one. Tamsyn is a scholar. He was supposed to know enough about the Reach to guide us."

Bianca dropped her hand with a spiral of curiosity. "There were seven of us. Your queen knew that her soldiers had died. And she knew you were underprepared and didn't have the skill to conquer Kyran, and yet she sent you anyway."

"We assumed that she was hoping to entice him."

"No random band of Empaths would intrigue Otheil. You would have been dead days ago." Bianca lifted the cold silver of her finger to Larkin's chin, awestruck, and it was as though every muscle inside of Larkin was charged with light.

"All of us had children before the Uprising. All of us practiced our magic, hoping our children would one day inherit it. And they were left on the Surface as we were cast into the dark." Bianca brushed the pad of her thumb across Larkin's cheek, wiping away a tear. "You were not blindly chosen for this task. Your queen knows exactly who you are."

Larkin stared in disbelief at Bianca, shaking her head. "That's impossible."

She was only a thief from the canyon. Not a descendant of Kyran's disciples.

TWENTY

escendants.

Larkin stormed away from the village and across the beach, kicking up sand in her wake. One of them had to have known.

Melay had hundreds of Empaths to choose from. She could have sent in an Empath army to find Kyran, or those more seasoned in magic from the depths of her prison. Instead, she chose them. Children who either knew little of magic or refused to use it.

At camp, the others were just waking up. Elf and Casseem were attempting to conjure new bags and torches from a pile of shredded lichen. They must have been using Amias's emotions; Larkin gleaned a tender ache from him. Love, she realized. He was speaking with Jacque, their heads bowed in intimate conversation. Perhaps they were discussing the farm.

Casseem hopped up when he saw her, hot with anger. "Where in hells have you been?"

She ignored him, spotting Tamsyn, who knelt in the sand, scratching something in charcoal on one of his scrolls.

She halted at the edge of camp. "Why did you burn the registry?"

Tamsyn glanced up at her, confused.

"The registry," Larkin repeated. "Why did you decide to burn it? What did you find out?"

"Find out?" Tamsyn rolled up the parchment. "I told you why I burned it. Melay had taken a sudden interest in lineage, and I wanted to stop her from doing anything—"

Larkin interrupted him. "Did you know? About us?"

Tamsyn scoffed, impatient. "Larkin, I—"

"We're descendants of the original seven." She turned and faced the rest of the stunned group. "We're the descendants of Kyran and his six disciples."

She waited for Tamsyn to feel guilty, ashamed he'd kept such a secret from them. Perhaps horrified that she had discovered the truth.

She wasn't expecting genuine astonishment.

"I didn't read the registry, Larkin. I wouldn't have known what to look for. How in Ilona's name did you find this out?" The scholar began to rifle through his parchment, as if truth of their ancestry had been within his papers all along and he'd simply missed it the first ten times.

Larkin was relieved to sense the astonishment from everyone. That meant Melay had kept every one of them in the dark. They would absorb this together.

Casseem was more outraged than she'd ever sensed before. "Did Elesandre tell you this? You went to see her, after everything?" He wasn't angry at Melay. He was angry at Larkin.

"What do you mean, *after everything*?"

"We decided to leave, not berate the woman for information she wasn't willing to give!" Casseem turned to Jacque. "That's what we agreed on, right, Jacque?"

The soldier was still reeling. "Descendants?" She smoothed

down her long ponytail and sank back into the sand. "I can't even siphon properly. Are you certain?"

"No, she's not," said Casseem. "She's just taking Elesandre's word for it."

"Bianca was as surprised as I was!" Larkin didn't want to admit that Casseem had a point. Even though the discovery made sense, there was no evidence. *And why would Melay send only seven Empaths?* Larkin had wondered this from the very start of their mission.

"It doesn't matter what you think, Casseem. This has merit," said Tamsyn. He began scribbling on one of his parchment sheets, his fascination gliding through Larkin. "The queen's interest in the registry was sudden, and the arrests of many of you were quite random, were they not?"

"I was arrested right before the temple was destroyed," said Larkin. "When I should have been the least of Melay's worries."

"The guards were always patrolling our farm, always looking out for something amiss." Elf's eyes were wide. "Maybe they were waiting for me to step out of line."

"And Jacque was arrested even though she followed orders," Larkin said.

"And where did that get me?" Jacque glowered at the ground, knuckles white as she clenched her fists. "I should have known something was wrong." Her eyes filled. "Risa likely thinks I'm dead, and I'm sure she's received word that I'm a traitor too. All for what? My bloodline?"

"I suppose that would make one of us Kyran's descendant,

then!" Casseem gasped mockingly. "One of us fits that narrative, after all. What do you say, Amias? Crushing villages, following in the footsteps of your dear old ancestor, god of the underworld himself. After all, the queen threw you into a Reach of your own, didn't she?"

The warmth drained from Larkin's body so quickly, she thought her heart would stop, like she'd been tossed in the capital's canal in midwinter. She could see the cold in Amias's eyes, the film of ice as clear as glass. On the outside, he was stoic—so expressionless, it was like he wasn't alive at all.

He stood from his boulder, turned from camp, and walked away.

Larkin snapped from her spell of cold. "Amias?"

Jacque hopped to her feet, turning to Casseem with venom. "Idiot. Do you have any idea what he's been through?"

Casseem crossed his arms as though he could hide his guilt. "I was proving a point."

"Ilona's sake, Casseem! I watched Amias's father get slaughtered by Melay's soldiers the same day Amias was condemned to the dark, and you thought to make a joke of it to *prove a point?*" Jacque brushed a clenched fist beneath her eye.

Gods. Larkin watched Amias as he strode between two boulders, disappearing. She knew his father had died, but she didn't know it happened the same day as his arrest.

Casseem opened his mouth.

"Shut up," said Larkin, storming past a slack-jawed Elf and hurrying after Amias.

She followed him through a sandy field of boulders, still

thawing from the darkest dread she'd ever felt. She wanted to steal the dread away, lock it up so he would never be haunted again. It terrified her that she didn't know how.

But she could make sure that he wasn't alone in his despair.

At the edge of the cavern, Larkin climbed the steps carved into the rock wall. The vast lichen sky sprawled out above her, a chaotic swirl of light and color. The cliffside path was dotted with beautiful, variegated moss, reminding her of the rainbows over the capital when the spring storms broke. The beauty granted her courage as the path widened, and she stepped out onto a vista point.

Amias stood at the edge, watching the false stars. His fists were clenched so tightly that she could see every one of the veins that threaded his arms. She knew he could sense her, like she could sense the corrosion of grief in him. But there was also the wonder she'd grown familiar with in the glowing grotto. She sensed him fighting to cling to it as he stared out at Bianca's world, desperately attempting to bury his anguish.

"When we were closer to the Surface, you asked a question." She approached him, hesitant. "Why send down only seven Empaths and a guide? I'm just trying to make meaning of that question. The numbers could be a coincidence."

"And if they're not?" Amias turned away from the ledge. His eyes were rimmed red. "I didn't have to hurt Bianca, Larkin. I could have stopped her some other way, but I couldn't control myself. I've been a monster all along."

"Melay's the monster, Amias. She's the reason your father's dead."

He winced, tears rolling down his cheeks before he furiously brushed them away. "They were reassigning him to the mines. All he did was pull away when a patrol grabbed him, and the soldier gutted him with a sword. It was every nightmare I'd ever had, but real."

Larkin pressed a hand to her mouth, her bottom lip trembling against her fingers. The soldiers could have done the same thing to her family when they broke into her home.

"I don't remember it happening. I don't remember destroying the barns, the wagons . . . I remember dust."

"You were a child."

"I lost control."

"She took what you loved, and then she punished you for it!" Larkin's voice was full of fury. "To Kyran's hell with Melay, Amias. This whole damned realm *should* be nothing but dust."

Again, Amias winced at the mention of the queen. The quiet, cold thunder of his dread rolled inside her.

Five years alone. Larkin couldn't imagine five years without falling asleep against her mother, or pressing her lips to Vania's hair. Five years without jumping into her father's embrace when he came home late from the mines. Without Garran's hand in hers, comforting her when they'd left Ethera with nothing to show for it.

Larkin crossed the shelf, wrapping her arms around Amias's neck. He tensed, but she didn't let go. She wanted him to sense the darkest corners of her grief and rage, hoping he could take comfort in her.

Maybe he would. Or maybe he'd pull away.

She waited—*waited*—her eyes shut and face buried in the crook of his shoulder, the pulse in his throat thrumming against her cheek. Finally, he relaxed and embraced her back, starved, elbows pinning her sides, the tips of his fingers pressing against her spine.

They were so close that Larkin's lips were now flush against his neck. She didn't dare move, unsure if she'd ever breathe again.

She didn't care.

Larkin at last released Amias, confused when she sensed remorse, but then realized it wasn't from him. His eyes flitted back and forth as he searched hers, and she cursed herself for being distracted so easily before noticing movement below.

Amias took her hand, the bracelet she'd given him pressing against her wrist, and they peered over the edge of the cliff as Bianca emerged from a crevice in the cavern wall, walking back toward the village. When the disciple was directly beneath them, she paused and looked up, finding Larkin.

It was Bianca's remorse Larkin had sensed, but over what?

"I think she wants us to go into that cave." Larkin looked up at Amias, her head light and face flushed. Perhaps this was a good distraction.

"I think you're right," said Amias. "Should we tell the others?"

Bianca's eyes bored into Larkin, communicating with her. Whatever was in the cave was dire, something she was entrusting Larkin with.

"No," said Larkin. "She only wants us to go."

"How do you know?" Amias asked.

Because I'm hers, thought Larkin. She couldn't explain how she knew, only that Bianca's emotions spoke to her. It was intuition. But Amias wouldn't understand until she had proof. "I just do."

They hurried back down the cliffside and followed the path that Bianca had taken. The crevice entrance was small but not tight, and Larkin easily scooted inside.

Three lit torches rested in sconces along the wall of the circular chamber, illuminating charcoal markings. At first, Larkin thought they were glyphs, and wondered if Tamsyn would need to translate, but then she began to recognize a pattern. There were some glyphs, written tightly within a swirl of curving lines and sharp edges, and waves indicating water. Other lines pointed upward, petal shaped. Fire.

Larkin stepped backward until she recognized the image in its entirety.

"Holy hells," Larkin breathed.

A map.

TWENTY-ONE

Tamsyn stood in front of the map, pressing his hands to his chest as if protecting his emotion from the group. He wasn't only bewildered, but distraught. Almost comically so.

Larkin didn't understand what was wrong. She thought he would be overjoyed to see the map. He'd fawned over the luminite tunnels and the glyphs on the walls, after all.

"I know nothing," he cried. "I'm . . . utterly useless here."

"You can read the glyphs," Casseem said brusquely. "That's more than most of us can do."

Larkin wasn't sure what he meant by that, but it irritated her. Still no thanks, no apology. Not after she was right about staying to see if Bianca would help them. Without her, they would be blind, with no idea where Kyran was.

But Larkin had found this map because Bianca trusted her. Bianca had placed her entire village at risk to help them kill Kyran, and to help Larkin get home.

"I know all of you think my obsession with this place is foolish." Tamsyn ran his hand gently across the map. "My mother and father gave me up to the queen at a young age—*seven*. Can you believe I've been accruing utterly useless knowledge for half my life?"

"You've been studying texts over a thousand years old," said Amias. "My tutor always told me to question the tomes Melay held."

"Well, apparently your tutor was better than mine," Tamsyn said jealously.

Casseem snorted.

Larkin wasn't so ready to brush off Amias's statement. "But your tutor worked for Melay."

Amias was quick to respond. "She was an Empath, and cunning."

"You were imprisoned," Larkin pressed.

Amias's intrigue danced through her. He enjoyed her interest. "So was she."

"Melay has many Empaths working for her," said Tamsyn. "She often attempts to school the children within her prisons to seem forgiving. And to indoctrinate them." He returned to studying the map. "I can't get into that now. We need to focus." He tapped his finger against the map, the rind of his nail blackened by charcoal. "The names of all the disciples are scribbled in glyphs, so the map is split into their sectors, as Bianca called them. The language down here in the Reach must have morphed over time. Very difficult to read. But . . ." He pointed at the center of the western portion of the map. "Kyran." He drew a line upward, northeast. "And Bianca. This, here, is where we are. A short hike to the west, and we'll reach a river."

"A river." Jacque joined Tamsyn, studying the map. "That's the river? That leads right to him."

"Then we're lucky," Tamsyn replied, scratching his chin. "Incredibly lucky."

Larkin and Elf shared a grin. There was no labyrinth to get lost in. The direction was clear.

Casseem mumbled to himself as he paced the floor, and Larkin studied the map from behind Jacque and Tamsyn. It was barely more than a sketch, very few land markers distinguishing paths and areas, but the map was cut by thick charcoal lines into clear territories. Smeared text skated across the line closest to her. "What does this say?"

"*The agreement.* It must be the treaty Bianca mentioned."

"They all stay out of each other's way." Bianca must have drawn this map ages ago to serve as a reminder of the depths that belonged to her, and what did not. Kyran's sector was between hers and that of the disciple named Brendis Pellager. She counted the sections of the map. "There are only six sectors."

"Rahele Ekko doesn't have one of her own," Tamsyn announced. "Perhaps she's with one of the others. Surely, some of them must get along. I mean, they had children, for Ilona's sake."

"Or magic eventually made it impossible for them to be civil to one another," Jacque said crossly.

"Maybe we should ask Bianca." Larkin reached out and traced the village, her fingers gliding over Bianca's surname. *Elesandre.* She'd never had a surname of her own. It was beautiful.

She had many questions she wanted to ask Bianca, but the most important was about the agreement. If the disciples did not venture into one another's territories, then how could Larkin and the others be certain that Kyran had been following and guiding them?

"It's too easy," said Larkin.

Casseem pivoted, facing Larkin. "So now that we actually have a plan and we're doing what you say, it's too easy?"

"Back off, Casseem," said Jacque, taking Larkin by surprise. Jacque looked to Larkin. "What do you want to do?"

"Follow the map." Elf's eyes found Larkin. "Right, Larkin?"

"Yes," said Larkin. "I think it's too easy, but it's our only lead. We must follow the map. We'll pack up as soon as we get some sleep."

Jacque nodded. "A sound plan."

As Tamsyn unrolled his scrolls and began to sketch the map, Larkin turned around, realizing Amias had left the cavern.

She found him right outside, leaning against the rock wall. Crossing his arms, he watched her, waiting for her.

"I should have listened to you about Bianca."

She paused in her tracks.

He continued. "But I was afraid."

His shame dizzied her, the tips of her fingers and toes going numb. She didn't understand.

"Come here," he said.

She was nervous, though she couldn't place why. Walking to him, she joined him against the rock wall, waiting for him to speak.

"I didn't choose to side with Casseem because I thought he was right. I chose to because Bianca terrified me. She still does. When she hurt you, my first instinct was to destroy. It was like I had no other choice. I never want to feel that way again."

"Maybe you would have never felt that way again, but we would have been wandering in the dark for a very long time." Larkin rolled her head to the side to see him mirroring her pose, looking back at her. He was at peace, relieved of the secret's burden. She had the urge to run her thumb along the edge of his phantom smile, right where it pulled down at the very edges.

The path was clear before them, yet worry still unsettled her.

"Kyran wants us to get close to him, just like Melay wished for. I just hope we don't . . ." She drifted off.

Amias could sense her. "You think this is a trap?"

"I think this is a game." Her heart sped, not with thrill, but with panic.

Amias turned from the wall, his hands on her shoulders. "You can't overthink it."

Of course she couldn't overthink it. It was likely that some of them—if not all of them—were going to end up dead, wasn't it? All of her pain, their work. The horror they'd faced. It would be for nothing. Everyone on the Surface would be gone, Demura nothing but pockmarked wasteland.

Even with Amias standing in front of her, and the majority of the party still being alive—even their recent fortune—she felt incredibly alone.

"I'm scared."

"I know." Patiently, he added, "It's all right to be afraid."

She searched him, finding a new flurry of emotions. Weightless, like feathers, but fiery and bright, like embers.

Courage. Larkin had never matched an image to it before. She hadn't realized how cold the cavern was until his courage warmed every part of her. The courage didn't douse her panic, but made room for it. For the first time in miles and miles, she felt safe.

Courage was the only thing that could drive them deeper.

They made camp within the map chamber's dry walls, light licking up the edges of the map as Tamsyn sketched out every last detail. The rest of them were too exhausted to stay up with him. Elf and Casseem conjured one large blanket made of lichen, and Larkin huddled among the other four as she tried to sleep.

When she did drift off, she dreamt of the riot. She and Garran leaving the mines, and the tumultuous rage from both the miners and the soldiers who descended upon them. Larkin lost Garran to the violent crowd. She screamed his name, fear crushing her.

Larkin woke, clutching her chest. She rolled onto her stomach and gasped for breath.

The fear was here, now.

"Larkin?" Elf rubbed the sleep from her eyes.

Larkin lifted her head, shuddering. "Something's wrong."

Tamsyn blinked at her, a nub of charcoal pinched in his hand.

"Where's the threat?" Jacque murmured.

Here. Larkin stood, darting to the cave's exit.

The air was still within the village, and yet she heard the wind, just like back home. There weren't many trees in the capital, but the ash in the market square had leaves that would silver and brittle at summer's end, clicking with the wind.

Click, click, click.

The memory of summer faded, and she sensed the deepest winter. Tremors seized her. She spotted movement and looked up as shadows crawled across the ceiling.

Click, click, click.

They skittered into the cracks within the glowing lichen sky. Larkin blinked, and they were gone. A shiver gripped her spine, and she stumbled into the nearest boulder. Her bones were ice, the force inside her like a chisel to the cleft of her ribs, sucking the breath from her lungs.

Bianca.

The village huts in the distance were dark silhouettes in the blue glow. She could smell death already. She pushed herself up and ran when the cold snuffed out, warmth flooding her.

The dread was gone.

Please, no.

Larkin broke through the village. Rivulets of blood dripped into the cracks of the trodden rock. She slipped on gore and caught herself.

Some huts were left open, others smashed in like eggshells. The villagers lay in open doorways or beds soaked warm and red. They were propped against glass walls and sprawled across the village streets. Their eye sockets were empty. Their hearts were gone.

Wet glass crunched beneath her feet. Every hut and alley was a tomb.

Jacque screamed her name from a distance, the soldier's footsteps muffled as Larkin's ears rang. A churning tumbled through her, and her stomach lurched. She pressed her hands to her knees and vomited, spitting the last of the bile from her mouth.

As Larkin lifted her head, she spotted a man watching her from the edge of the village. A survivor. He began moving toward her. As he grew closer, she saw a web of purple veins spidered across his chest, his body dewy and skinless.

He'd been flayed. How in Ilona's name was he still alive?

He continued sulking toward her, his bowlegged movements disjointed. She assumed he saw her approach before realizing that he didn't have a face.

Her scream was silent.

The creature hurled toward her, sprinting like a rabid dog, its hands clicking when they hit stone. *Talons.* It clawed the ground. Larkin ducked and rolled as it launched in her direction. She siphoned Jacque's terror, flexed her hands upward, and projected.

Above her, the creature dissolved into an arc of blood and sinew. Her magic tore through its face, and the howl that had been curdling inside him found release through the new mouth.

The creature hit the ground with a wet thud, dead.

Larkin shot up.

Click, click, clickclickclickclick.

Jacque shoved her out of the way and lunged forward, and as Larkin fell again, she caught the flash of polished iron, and the spurt of blood as Jacque's sword sliced into the neck of a second creature. The monster collapsed, its head rolling off the path and behind a hut.

Jacque held out her hand. Larkin grasped it, and the soldier yanked her up.

"First Devon," Larkin gasped. "Now the village." There wasn't just one creature. There must be hundreds. Thousands.

"We need to focus, Larkin. I'll search the perimeter. Find the survivors. The others must still be asleep. Tamsyn—"

"Come with me," Larkin pleaded. "I'll need either your fear or your sword if I'm attacked."

Jacque hesitated, scouring the village. "All right," she said, following as Larkin took off.

There were more creatures, but they were dead. She stepped over a thread of entrails. Bone flecked the ground. A broken jaw yawned at her.

Within the courtyard of gore, the agony was suffocating.

She followed it to the medical hut and a familiar figure sprawled across the ground. Larkin dropped to her knees, slid her fingers under the silver ribs of Bianca's bodice, and flipped the woman over.

Bianca's gown was gashed open at her abdomen, the wound beneath dark and glistening. She still had her eyes, red stars bursting in the whites of them. And her heart.

"They made you watch," Larkin cried. "*He* made you watch." She'd been wondering for miles what these creatures were, and now she knew. They were minions. Kyran's minions.

Bianca's lips moved. What escaped her mouth was more blood than sound.

"I can save you." Larkin's hand slid through a mound of warm viscera near her feet. She gathered it in her fist. "I can heal because I'm yours. I just have to try."

A tear trailed down Bianca's cheek.

"Jacque." Larkin refused to peel her eyes from Bianca. "Jacque, I need to conjure. Think of Risa—of home."

Bianca's agony began to fade.

"That's it," Larkin whispered, knowing her ancestor was trying to help her, fighting to feel hope or love even when her descendants lay slaughtered around them.

Larkin waited, searching Bianca for the first bright spark she could siphon. She waited as the viscera grew cold in her palm. She waited as Amias called her name from within the village.

She waited even as Jacque knelt and brushed Bianca's eyelids shut.

TWENTY-TWO

We need to run."

Larkin heard Casseem's voice as though he were on the other end of the cavern, but she knew he stood with Jacque and Amias on the beach behind her. She knelt in the water at the edge of the lake, Bianca's blood soaking her tunic.

A thousand years' worth of generations, gone. Bianca had initially refused to help them because of this possibility.

He knows you are here, doesn't he?

Yet she'd done it anyway. She'd allowed hundreds of her descendants to be killed in order to help one. Larkin could only think of one reason Bianca would make such a sacrifice: She believed her risk was worth it if it meant freeing the world of such an evil as Kyran. And she believed in Larkin.

One day, Larkin would tell Garran of the ancestor who'd given her the key to saving him.

Her eyes burned. Amias had said that the sieve of magic burst when an ancestor died, flowing to the descendant, but Larkin didn't feel any different. Would she? Or did she have to somehow find a way to tap into Bianca's magic within herself?

Beyond Larkin, Elf sat on a boulder half submerged in the water, watching the falls. She'd said nothing since she saw Bianca's body, but her grief had been fierce. It still was. Every so often, Elf would extend her hand and spread her fingers wide before balling them into a fist. *Magic?* thought Larkin. She wasn't sure.

"Get your things." Casseem cast about, organizing items as Tamsyn and Amias brought them to the beach in armfuls. "Whatever we have. Search the huts. Take any food you can find. Tamsyn, you'll set us on our course. Larkin, Elf!"

Larkin stood, pinkish water streaming from her clothes into the lake. She spotted Tamsyn hurrying toward them with an armful of items, and Amias near their cave with two packs slung over his back.

Tamsyn's hands trembled as he fumbled with his scroll case. He was missing part of his armor.

"Forget the scroll, Tamsyn. You were staring at that map all night." Larkin needed to pull them together. Casseem was right, for once. "You know the way. Where do we go?"

Tamsyn wiped the sweat from his forehead, panicked. "The falls, I think." He glanced back at the village. "Are we just going to leave them like this?"

"Larkin." Jacque pointed her sword toward a small dark shape in the sand. "You'll want to take a look at that."

Without answering the scholar, Larkin stooped down next to the bloody shape. A severed hand from one of the creatures. The flayed stump had five bony, hooklike shapes protruding from it.

"They don't have fingers, only talons. It's the strangest thing I've ever seen."

Larkin touched the edge of the talon, running her finger along its curve, a small bump at the apex. A knuckle. The talon wasn't nail, but bone. "These *are* its fingers."

Jacque shuddered. Larkin siphoned and projected, easily

separating talon from palm. She pinched it between her fingers, holding it up to the lichen light.

Minions of Kyran, harvesting eyes and hearts.

"Click, click," she whispered, and tucked the talon in her pocket.

Larkin stood as Amias approached, carrying her armor. He dropped the pile of gear into the sand and helped her crawl into her cuirass. She tugged on one greave and, when she couldn't find the other, took it off. Armor seemed so pointless when hundreds of Empaths had been slaughtered by talons as sharp as the one in her pocket.

Larkin sensed Amias struggling to find his calm. His gaze fluttered back and forth between the others, distracted, and she noticed the swift and steady beat of dread inside of him. He fought it—no, he *battled* it. Silently Larkin felt him wrestle back control.

She took Amias's hand, and he blinked, focusing back on her. Within a breath, Amias had buried the dread so deeply inside himself that she could no longer sense it.

"Elf!" Casseem barked, and Larkin started, turning toward the water.

The back of Elf's shoulders sagged. She slid from the boulder and trudged toward them. Her face was placid. Still, Larkin wished she had something comforting to say.

Nothing would be comforting, she thought. They were headed back into the dark.

Tamsyn led them around the shore of the lake. With the sand, there was no path, but as they neared the waterfall, the ground hardened, and water grooves threaded the rock.

Tamsyn lit a torch, and the falls caught on the light, the crashing water beating up a mist. They passed beneath the arc of water and hurried through a narrow fissure, the walls of the new corridor like melted candle wax. They paused to gather themselves.

"What in hells are they?" Casseem's voice was etched with agitation. "And how did Kyran learn to control them?"

"Bianca said that there are more beasts the deeper we go," Tamsyn replied. "But we don't know if they're native to the Reach, or whether Kyran controls them all."

"Bianca never mentioned Kyran controlling monsters," said Larkin.

"Maybe the village was attacked after we saw the map. That's no coincidence." Tamsyn violently shook out the map, almost tearing it in half. "All the secrets Bianca carried with her of this place, the invaluable knowledge. A thousand years' worth, gone, just like that."

"She'd be alive if it weren't for Larkin." Casseem watched her behind the glow of his torch.

His face was neutral, but Larkin sensed the slurry of his disgust. She didn't want to give him the pleasure of sensing her react. But the rage within her carried a life of its own, uncontrollable.

"It's not her fault." Amias squeezed her hand.

Her finger caught on his bracelet as she pulled away. She didn't need him standing up for her. "The villagers are dead because of Kyran, not me."

"If we find Kyran at all, it will be because of Larkin." Jacque's hand rested on the pommel of her sword. "We'd know nothing about the Reach past the village if she had listened to us. Apologize."

"I don't want his apology." Larkin's gaze remained locked on Casseem's. "I don't want to hear a lie."

"Stop squabbling. Our goal is to find Kyran." Tamsyn held up their new map, and the party crowded around except for Casseem and Larkin, who held back, hovering outside of the group. Tamsyn had a point, but Larkin knew this argument wasn't her fault. Casseem was dead set on being livid with her, and she had done nothing wrong.

She needed to focus. Larkin squinted at the scroll that Tamsyn had transcribed. A recess was circled in fresh charcoal, accompanied by ancient Demuran text.

"Passage of the Damned," Tamsyn translated. "It's within the portion of the Reach that Bianca marked as Kyran's sector."

Larkin peered closer. The Passage of the Damned, at least fifty miles north of their location, was most traversable by a swiftly flowing river.

"How heartening," said Elf.

"At least we have a path forward." Jacque adjusted the sheath at her waist. The soldier had yet to misplace a piece of her armor, unlike the rest of them.

"I'll lead." Larkin took the torch from Tamsyn and walked ahead. She needed a distraction. No, not a distraction. She needed assurance. She could still smell Bianca's blood on her clothes.

"Tamsyn," Larkin called out, "tell us about the disciples. If it's true that we're their descendants, then one of us now has Bianca's magic."

"We could always test it," said Casseem. "Cut someone open and have everyone try to heal them."

"That tops the list of your stupid ideas," Jacque replied. "No one is getting cut open."

Amid the bickering, Larkin sensed Tamsyn's surprise at her request, followed by pride. But then Tamsyn said something that she wasn't expecting.

"Elf can name them."

Larkin paused when Elf said nothing in response, turning around. She spotted Elf's shadow at the very back of the group, sensing the girl's discomfort.

"Are you sure you want me to do that?" Elf asked quietly.

"You know the stories well enough," said Tamsyn.

"All right." Elf glided deeper into the passage as she thought. "You already know Otheil Kyran and Bianca Elesandre, mender of flesh and bone. Thaos Leander and Daria Monarc were both alchemists, Monarc's interest being in conjuring weaponry for those without magic, and Leander's in thwarting luminite. Rahele Ekko . . . she actually advised Ilona herself before the division of Empaths and the dynasty."

"Really?" asked Larkin. She couldn't imagine an Empath willingly working for Ilona, and especially not one of Kyran's disciples.

"Elf's actually right with this one," said Tamsyn. "Ilona said she wanted Ekko to educate her on Empath culture, but historians believe that it was really to cull secrets from her."

"Mitisan Ralic, the giver . . . ," Elf continued.

"*No*," Tamsyn corrected sharply. "He was a charlatan."

"I told you, I like my version better." Elf's tone was honey sweet. "And finally, Brendis Pellager. He, well—"

"Pellager liked to kill people," Tamsyn said quickly. "A corpse collector. Some say he was even more diabolical than Kyran, but less intelligent."

Elf agreed. "Even in my fables, Pellager was the most awful of them all."

"So can we assume that Devon was Pellager's," Casseem concluded. "They both were nasty pieces of work."

The group quieted. "Don't speak ill of the dead," Jacque murmured.

"Let's focus on evidence and what we know," said Tamsyn. "Larkin . . ."

Larkin's heart sped in her chest. Did Tamsyn also see her connection to Bianca?

"I'm almost certain you are Leander's."

Larkin's stomach fell heavy with disappointment.

"Who did you think you came from?" Casseem asked her with a smirk.

"Why do you think she's Thaos's?" asked Elf, intrigued.

"Because of her luminite resistance," Tamsyn stated.

Larkin halted in her tracks, stunned, and spun around.

"Was that supposed to be a secret?" Tamsyn asked dubiously. "You demonstrated your ability for us. It was the very first thing you did when we entered the Reach."

Larkin opened her mouth, but nothing came out. No shock emitted from Amias. Did he already know?

"My family is resistant." Larkin turned and continued to walk. "My mother, specifically. I've been that way my whole life."

Casseem scoffed. "You didn't think to tell us this sooner?"

"What difference would it have made?" Anger built within her again. *Let him feel it burn,* she thought.

"So Larkin is Leander's, which means Jacque is Monarc's," Tamsyn declared.

"I don't make weapons," said Jacque.

"She was good at wielding them too."

"If I'm Monarc's, then Casseem must be Ralic's," said Jacque. "We can all see the similarities."

"That's the nicest thing you've ever said to me," said Casseem.

Elf piped up. "And me? I don't really feel like I fit with any of them."

"This is stupid." Larkin kicked a rock down the channel. "We can't uncover our ancestors by mulling over how we act. It's our abilities, not personality traits."

Amias's hand grazed hers, and she sensed the brush of high grass and the warmth of the sun. His tranquility. But she pulled away. He wasn't making anything better. Amias was simply another layer of emotions she had to sift through, a bright reminder of calm on top of her own frustration.

She sensed heat in her abdomen, wondering if he was frustrated with her. But that didn't seem like Amias. The heat intensified as if coals smoldered inside her, and she pressed a hand to her stomach, discomforted.

Larkin halted. "Tell me you feel it, too."

"The rage," Amias announced with dread.

Kyran was here.

Larkin stepped forward, blinking through her haze. Her skin buzzed, her pulse quickened. *Show yourself, you coward.*

Larkin lifted her torch, surprised when it shone on unearthed roots.

"Trees? How is that possible? We're too deep underground," Jacque hurried to inspect the roots, and Larkin lunged forward, catching the soldier by the buckle of her cuirass.

Not trees.

"Careful," Larkin breathed, releasing Jacque and creeping deeper. The tendrils swelled and threaded together. Light spilled along glistening crimson. Spiked bones punched through the webbed veins, dripping with blood.

Casseem walked past Larkin. "What in Kyran's bloody name is that?"

They weren't roots. They were sinews.

A current of rot wafted around her, and Larkin clapped a hand over her nose and mouth. Sweat prickled the back of her neck as she drowned beneath the sludge of her companions' disgust.

As if Kyran knew she wasn't paying enough attention to him, the rage intensified. The coals inside Larkin caught fire.

Elf plucked the torch from her, and Larkin gripped her stomach with her free hands, almost buckling over.

"Careful, Elf. He's here," Larkin cried. Her eyes darted around. *Where are you?*

Elf ignored her, dancing along the edge of the web and dipping the torch toward a thread of tendrils, the light catching on a glittering mass of eyes.

A mosaic—a patchwork of thousands of bodies. Bits of bone, appendages, entire mangled corpses. Eyes glinted off the light, hundreds adorning the corpses like gemstones, hands and arms and legs.

"What is it? Tamsyn!" Jacque drew her sword.

"I don't . . ." The scholar choked, and retched.

"It burns," Amias gasped.

Larkin reached out toward him, clawing the air when Amias didn't grab on. His attention was caught on the thatched grate of rib cages stretching along the ceiling, jaw slack in horror.

Larkin.

The hairs along her spine stood on end. She whirled to the right, and saw a corpse sunken into the rock. It had no legs, no ribs, its spine a twisted, gore-laced tail. One hand dangled from a limp wrist, pointing at her.

LARKIN.

The corpse's mouth hung open, its eyes still in its skull, bright and wet and glistening.

I can show you your mother. The corpse's wrist twitched. *She is waiting for your father to come home. Thickening the stew with flour. Don't you want to see her?*

Her will crushed like parchment in a fist. "Yes."

The corpse stretched a finger toward her, cartilage popping.

As Larkin reached out to touch it, someone grabbed her shoulder.

"Don't," Casseem warned.

He was on the ground before Larkin knew what had happened, her hand screaming in pain. Casseem sat up, shocked, clutching his face where she'd hit him.

Jacque dragged her backward. "What in Ilona's name is wrong with you? And why in all hells were you about to touch that thing?" Amias helped Casseem to his feet. He gaped at Larkin, appalled.

"Don't touch me."

Larkin shook Jacque off and hurried toward the silhouette of Elf ahead of her. Her head swam, the voice of the corpse echoing inside her.

She was going mad.

"We can't leave!" cried Tamsyn. "We need to understand what this is."

Larkin approached Elf, who had halted. A bloody mass unfurled like a spider's web and barricaded the pathway.

"It's so angry." Elf wasn't so much horrified as she was enthralled. Gripping a femur bone of a rotting skeleton, she twisted until it popped from the cartilage. Then she yanked it free, holding the bone like a sword. Larkin's stomach lurched, but Elf just calmly held her hand up.

She clenched her fist.

Veins and muscles seethed and dripped away, the brittle bone beneath snapping. Larkin cowered as it fell in chunks, narrowly dodging the falling masses.

When the rumbling stopped, Larkin peered out from under her arms.

Elf wiped a bloody chunk from her forehead, looking at Larkin expectantly. "You going to help, or what?"

TWENTY-THREE

A passage lay hidden behind Elf's destruction, the path beyond untouched by the lace of the dead. Light glimmered at its end.

Casseem shoved a protesting Tamsyn forward. "Just because you find the aroma of corpses refreshing, doesn't mean the rest of us do."

"But the clues to Kyran—"

"We saw everything there was to see, Tamsyn." Larkin brushed past Casseem to take the lead, not wanting to spend another moment with the bodies.

I can show you your mother. The corpse hadn't spoken to her. Kyran had. Or she was losing her mind.

Larkin shook her head back and forth, clearing it. Far in front of them, she heard the rumble of water. It wasn't possible that they'd already made it to the river. According to Tamsyn, they had a ten-mile hike before reaching the bank.

Light grew as their tunnel fanned into the wide expanse of a glowing forest. The trees were strange and polyped, branches covered with new growth that gleamed a soft pink and blue. Their light softly illuminated jets of water spouting from crevices in the walls.

Someone touched Larkin's shoulder. She tensed, thinking it was Casseem.

She turned to find Amias, his attention caught above, wonder flourishing. She sensed it bloom in her heart, fortifying every muscle inside her. A smile crept over his lips, and she followed his gaze upward.

The trees illuminated the dome ceiling and a menagerie of ancient sea creatures frozen in stone. At least, Larkin thought they were from the sea. She'd overheard fishermen's tales of ocean monsters enough times, tales that miners had probably picked up from sailors at the docks. Docks Larkin had never seen.

Above her was a patchwork fleet of fins and flippers and barnacled bellies, barred, bony mouths agape and hungry. Ruffled tentacles coiled behind pillowy masses. The cavern smelled like the fish carts in the market square. She held her hand out, mist from the jets collecting on her skin, and then licked her palm. Salt.

"We're beneath the ocean," Tamsyn said as he emerged from the tunnel opening.

"I've never been to the ocean," Larkin whispered.

The jets were so loud, she almost didn't hear Amias.

"It's beautiful. Someday, I'll take you there."

She wondered when he'd seen it himself. The surreal beauty made her ache. She wanted to be above, in the water and the sun.

"How many people have seen something like this before, do you think?" Tamsyn asked, mesmerized.

Elf pointed. "At least two others."

At the cusp of a shadow, Larkin spotted a pair of corpses propped against a tree and shuddered. She took the torch from Elf and walked toward them, and as she neared, she smelled the rot. They couldn't have been dead for long. Their flesh was shriveled but hadn't peeled from the bone. Their eyes were missing, and she knew they'd been plucked and placed within the amalgamation back down the path. Just like Devon's. And Brielle's. And those of the villagers. *Gods.*

"Their armor," Jacque said, stricken. "These are our soldiers. They made it this far!"

Larkin paused in surprise at the sight of the seal of Demura on armor similarly plated to her own. That couldn't be. Bianca had said that she hadn't seen any soldiers pass through her village. Was it possible that they found another way down through the labyrinth?

Something snapped beneath her foot.

"Watch out!" Elf screamed.

Larkin looked up to see a rope holding a large boulder give way. The rock tumbled toward her. Her heart lurched in panic before Elf yanked Larkin back and punched her hand into the air as the boulder loomed over them.

The rock exploded. Larkin ducked to avoid the shards. She could hear the others rushing forward, but by that time there was nothing but rubble and dust.

"Booby trap," Elf concluded.

Jacque sheathed her sword. "That was incredible."

"Where did you learn *that*?" Casseem studied the rubble. "You've been holding back."

"No one blinked an eye when you caused a cave-in." Elf crossed her arms, defensive.

Larkin peered into the shadows. "The soldiers knew about the monsters, then. They were trying to protect themselves." She didn't want to think of how many of their own they'd witnessed torn apart before their own demise.

"Over here!" Tamsyn cried. Halfway across the misty cavern, he stood in front of a recess lit with lichen. Larkin joined him, followed by the rest of the party, and peered into the opening.

The hollow was filled with bones and rotting fish carcasses, and also familiar items—swords and maces, bedrolls, scraps of Demuran armor. Jacque rummaged through the blades while the others dug in the knapsacks that were lined along the far wall. There was a healthy supply of oil, and new flint. They stuffed their pockets with the useful treasures, and Tamsyn exclaimed in surprise, holding up a thin, leather-bound book.

A journal.

"Camp twenty-nine. The river is swift and unchanging. We argue constantly about the current we aren't taking advantage of, though none of us can figure out a way to make a raft. My own feet are bloody and raw and every step is agony."

"They made it to the river." Jacque ran her fingers through her ponytail compulsively. "But how is that possible?"

They had quickly cleared out the recess and huddled together. Their fire was smoldering, the air too damp for a proper flame, and no one had the energy to liven it.

"I don't know." Tamsyn flipped through the book. "The next several pages are too waterlogged to read. There's mention of soldiers disappearing: at camps, sleeping, and while treading down the river. The journal writer gets more frantic, the entries shorter . . ." He turned another page and began reading again.

"The channel has widened to a reservoir, and we have stumbled

upon what I can only describe as a channel made from the insides of a carcass."

Larkin recalled the language on their new map. "The Passage of the Damned."

Tamsyn continued.

"The walls are constructed of the dead . . . woven bone and flesh . . ."

The dread of the party permeated Larkin as the soldier's tale unfolded before them. She had thought they'd already made it deep into the bowels of this nightmare. They'd hardly begun.

Tamsyn flipped a page.

"We will not survive this."

Another page.

". . . a terrible mistake . . ."

And another, and another.

"Beasts live within this place. They hunt us as though their only wish is to drive us to madness. We cannot sleep. If we sleep, they will come to feed. Our quartermaster has been swallowed by insanity, feeding his own flesh to the monsters."

Tamsyn's fingers trembled as he flipped through the remaining pages. "There's one last entry."

"Read it," said Jacque, although her voice held a quaver.

Larkin pressed a hand to her chest, ordering her heart to quiet. Whatever the final entry relayed would reveal what they had to overcome. Being frightened was a luxury she couldn't afford, especially when the party could sense it.

She needed to be brave for them. For Garran.

Tamsyn swallowed, flipped the page, and began to read.

"Our quartermaster's wounds have sprouted new limbs. Hands grow from his chest. He tried to slit his own neck to kill himself, but the wound simply transformed into another mouth. I don't know if I will die, but I will not leave this place as myself. My only hope is that the battalions who follow us do not take this path, or there is no hope for us at all."

Tamsyn shut the book.

"*No hope for us at all*," repeated Larkin, amazed. "They were right in Kyran's lair!"

The scholar clutched the book in his hands, his eyes glazed. He said nothing, though his terror spoke more than words could.

"Tamsyn." Larkin waited until the scholar looked at her. "They had swords. We have magic."

"Bianca had magic too, Larkin." Casseem picked at his thumb, staring at the crevice of their small cavern. "What *happened* to them?"

"The same thing that happened to Brielle." Amias bowed his head, and Larkin sensed the poisoned weight of his guilt.

Brielle. Larkin wrapped her arms around her body, pieces of their labyrinth journey clicking into place. Kyran had been torturing Brielle right in front of them. "Something was destroying parts of her, something she couldn't see, driving her to insanity."

"But what happened to these soldiers wasn't just destruction magic," Amias said slowly as he furrowed his brow in thought.

"The mouth," said Larkin. The quartermaster couldn't stop the torture, so he tried to kill himself, but his tormenter had refused him even that.

"We know what happened to them. What might happen to us." Elf bit her lip, her fingers fidgeting at her sides. "So what do we do?"

Larkin sagged with defeat. There was nothing honorable about continuing when death was inevitable. It was just stupid.

"We follow Tamsyn's map and keep going." Jacque slid a blade from her pocket and polished it on a scrap of linen she had found. "We have no other option, and the queen would want us to continue."

Larkin's eyes darted to Amias. As stoic as he was, his emotion grew violent at the mention of Melay. He forced it back.

Larkin wasn't as easily forgiving. "Melay isn't here. You can spare us the performance."

"She's doing her best to keep the people of Demura alive." Jacque's doubt was a pang in Larkin's side.

"How long have you been telling yourself that lie, Jacque?"

Jacque parted her lips.

"Larkin," Amias said softly. "You don't—"

"Let Jacque speak for herself." Larkin waited for Amias to retort, but he only pressed his lips together. *He knows I'm right,* she thought, her eyes grazing the group. *They all do.*

To Larkin's surprise, Jacque's will collapsed, and she said, "A long time."

Larkin sat back. At least she admitted it. "Why?"

"Survival." Jacque observed the others cautiously, hesitant. "I was in the ranks to become a lieutenant, Larkin. I joined the army to funnel money home. Somehow managed to sneak in under the name Jacqueline, my mother's name, and the common surname of Harper. I defied the queen then, but once I was in the army, I knew how much I could lose if I defied her again. I have three sisters. And Risa." She reached up to find the end of her ponytail, but then dropped her hand. "If I broke any more rules, I could lose them."

Larkin swallowed, glancing away in embarrassment. She was so focused on the betrayal of an Empath employed by the queen that she had never thought to ask why the soldier enlisted.

"My battalion found out I was an Empath," said Jacque. "I thought I was done for, but my lieutenant brought me to this outpost up north, near the sea. She sat me down in barracks full of soldiers and told me that everyone within the room supported me and was ready for Melay's strictures against Empaths to change. They all believed we had a chance to do good things with our magic."

"Rebel soldiers?" Larkin asked with surprise. Soldiers who wanted to help set Empaths free from Melay's rule?

"Just because you didn't know about them doesn't mean they don't exist," said Jacque.

"What happened then?" Elf scooted closer to Jacque, still clutching the femur.

"I said no." Shame fell from her. "I had too much at stake. I couldn't be their emblem. I couldn't afford to be part of a rebellion. I needed to keep sending money back home. But maybe if I had rebelled, we would have dethroned Melay and none of this would have happened."

"No," Larkin said. "Kyran would still be terrorizing the Surface. People would still have died. You . . ." Larkin paused, her anger leaving her as quickly as it had taken hold. "You were looking out for your family. You did what I would have done."

Casseem interrupted them, watching Larkin as he spoke. "What we did in the past, who we were on the Surface, that doesn't matter here. The only way we can survive and save those we love is to keep moving and hope we don't die along the way."

A purple welt was forming on Casseem's cheek. Was this his way of making amends with Larkin? She was tired of all the anger and frustration she felt from fighting Casseem.

"We move forward?" asked Elf.

"We move forward," Larkin repeated. "We're not going to fall to the same fate as the soldiers. We have magic, after all." Even though Kyran had murdered an entire village of Empaths, she had to believe that their magic was enough.

"I don't." Tamsyn threw his scroll case across the cavern floor. "I am completely useless. I've studied for years, but I can't make sense of anything that's happened so far. You might as well leave me behind."

"You're not staying back, Arkwright," Casseem said.

Larkin agreed. "We need you. Plus, we need your flair for the dramatic. Fuel for our magic." She winked at Tamsyn.

Tamsyn groaned and lay down. "Happy to hear you're making use of my terror and anger and general insecurities."

Casseem nudged Tamsyn with his toe. "Thank you for your service."

Truce, Larkin thought. She hoped it would last.

TWENTY-FOUR

When Larkin woke, Elf was gone.

Her mind immediately went to Brielle and she shot up, sensing the surrounding space for any jarring emotion, but the vivid dreams of the others were distracting.

Elf couldn't be alone. None of them could be alone.

As Larkin stumbled to her feet and hurried through the narrow exit of the sleeping chamber, a shudder gripped her. Elf's emotions were like a lute out of tune, but she was somewhere close.

Larkin found Elf near the polyped trees and bit back a scream.

Elf crouched in front of the soldiers' corpses, examining what she'd dismembered. A filthy blade lay on the ground near Elf, discarded. She had flayed the remaining skin and sinew from the bones and broken up the skeletons, arranging everything in front of her as if she were organizing the mundane, like clothing or food.

Elf wore nothing but her sleeveless tunic, parts of the shirt destroyed so that her back was mostly bare.

Larkin clapped a hand over her mouth when she saw Elf's back. Bony growths jutted from between her shoulder blades. Blood trickled from her broken skin. Shaking, Larkin searched for Kyran's rage but found nothing.

Elf turned around. She must have sensed Larkin's horror.

"You're awake!" she exclaimed. "You should go back to sleep.

Your dreams are so lovely to work with." Her face puckered, and she rolled her eyes. "Tamsyn and Amias are awake too."

"What are you doing?" Larkin cried.

Elf frowned. "It's none of your business, really."

"Like hells it isn't!" Larkin hissed, then paused as she heard the footsteps of the others approaching.

Amias was the first to reach her. "Kyran's doing?"

"No, I don't sense him," said Larkin, her mind veering to the tangle of corpses behind them. Brielle, losing her mind in the labyrinth as her skin was slowly peeled away by an unseen tormentor. Bianca's everlasting life, and her ability to mend her villagers. The quartermaster.

Destruction and conjuration of flesh and bone.

"She's doing this to herself," Larkin whispered.

"How did you make these?" Tamsyn's voice was measured, but Larkin sensed a curling thread of morbid intrigue.

He walked to Elf and knelt, reaching out as though to touch the strange growths.

Elf tilted her head toward the dismembered carcasses. Tamsyn jerked back his hand. His curiosity flared. "What does it feel like? Can you move them?"

"Not yet." Elf hopped to her feet with grace, turning back to Larkin. "Are we ready to go?"

Larkin knew that her stiff smile wasn't fooling Elf, though the girl seemed oblivious to her and Amias's panic. "Amias and I will go wake the others." She looked to Tamsyn. "Watch her?"

Tamsyn's eyes widened as he attempted to inconspicuously shake his head.

Elf distracted herself with rearranging the bones, and Larkin mouthed *Watch her!* She grabbed Amias's arm and dragged him back to their camp, waking Jacque and Casseem and quickly relaying what had happened.

"She's going insane!" hissed Larkin as Jacque scrambled for her sword.

"Wait, wait, what are you going to do with that?" Larkin pointed to the weapon.

"What do you think?" Jacque yanked the sword from its sheath. "I'm going to cut those damn things off!"

"You'll hurt her," Larkin protested. At least, Larkin thought she would. She didn't really know, never having seen anyone use magic this way before.

"We need to be calm about this." Casseem threw a pack over his shoulder. "We can't panic Elf. Not if we want her to explain why she's doing this."

"Be calm?" Jacque gripped her sword.

"Wait until you see her," Larkin muttered.

"Well, I believe in you," Casseem said coolly, swiping up another bag from the ground.

He strode from the cave, Larkin close behind him. When Elf came into view, he halted. A strangled choking noise escaped his mouth.

"Told you," said Larkin.

"It's fine," he squeaked. "Fine!"

"Like Kyran's hell it's fine," Jacque grumbled, flipping her sword in her hand. "Larkin's right; only a mad person would do that to themselves. And if she's mad, who's to say she won't be giving us bony little additions in our sleep? Mad and magical is a dangerous combination. Too dangerous. If we don't stifle this behavior right now, we might have to kill her ourselves."

"Ilona's breath, Jacque, you're not killing anyone. And put your sword away!" Larkin ordered through gritted teeth.

Jacque begrudgingly obliged.

Elf waved at them. "I hope someone grabbed my bag!"

Casseem held it up, grimacing. "Right here."

Elf studied them, her face brightening with understanding. "Oh, don't worry about me." She reached back, touching one of the bones jutting from her shoulders. "Just an enhancement."

"Enhancement," Jacque growled, trudging forward.

As they began their hike through the forest, Larkin kept a close eye on Elf, noting that she wasn't acting deranged. Elf led the group, stepping lightly even as blood leaked from the wounds in her back.

The forest seemed to stretch on forever, pure wilderness within the Reach's depths. The luminescent fuzz that had fallen off the trees floated in a sheet of low-hanging fog. The beauty was coaxing Larkin to let her guard down, but she had to remain vigilant.

Tamsyn let out a string of swears to Ilona.

Larkin spun around, scanning the immediate area for any signs of stalking creatures.

But Tamsyn's eyes were glued to his new map.

"Holy. Hells." He knelt in the middle of the path.

Larkin dropped her bag and hurried to him. "What is it?"

"I may be onto something," he said.

As the rest of the party crowded around Tamsyn, he slowly

spun their new map of the Reach on top of the old, as if trying to align them a certain way. No . . . He wasn't trying to align their new map with their old map.

He was aligning it to a map of the Surface.

"My dimensions for the new map are off, so it may be hard to imagine." He traced his finger around the outer edge of the Reach, and then lifted the parchment, doing the same to the Surface map. "See the shape of the isle? It's roughly the same on both maps. Right now we're at the very outskirts of the Reach, which is beneath the west bay."

On the Reach map, Tamsyn dragged his finger down the underground river. "We're about to head inland, to Kyran's sector." Tamsyn pressed his finger atop the Passage of the Damned, and then lifted the Reach map to show the Surface map beneath.

Casseem swore.

Kyran's sector was right beneath the capital.

"This entire time he's been below us?" The question left Larkin in a whisper. "But the capital mines . . ."

"Kyran's sector must be below the mines," said Tamsyn.

"That's not possible," said Jacque.

Larkin felt like weeping. They'd traveled for miles, witnessed so much death. Devon. Brielle. Bianca and her villagers. And Kyran had been right beneath Larkin's feet from the start of the destruction.

Amias's hand rested on her shoulder. "We couldn't have known."

Larkin leaned her head against his arm, exhausted.

Elf hovered over the rest of them. "This is good news, isn't it? It means when we find him, the journey home won't be so long."

"If we can find a way up," said Larkin.

"We have magic." Elf shifted one of her bony growths.

"First we have to kill him." Tamsyn rolled up the map, pointing the parchment forward. "River's close."

As they neared the edge of the forest, Casseem and Elf each lit a torch, dousing the tops with oil to keep them lit. A curtain of mist washed over them as they entered a corridor of sweating walls. Larkin's curls fell limp around her cheeks, and condensation dripped into her eyes. She squinted, making out a decline in the path and the shape of a trickling riverbed ahead of them. While the walls sluiced, the bed was only a dribbling creek.

"This is the river that's supposed to lead us to Kyran, right?" Larkin asked. "The one on the map."

"Yes," said Tamsyn, disappointed.

"I thought that we would be able to, well, float down it." Casseem wiped the moisture from his face.

Tamsyn made to grab the journal from his pack, and then stopped, clearly realizing that moisture and paper did not go well together. "Maybe the tides of the ocean affect the water level."

"So we'll have to walk. At least we're on the right path." Jacque looked to their left and right. "Which way?"

Tamsyn pointed to the left, and they began their trek.

Camping in this will be a nightmare, thought Larkin. Fifty miles, Tamsyn had said. They'd traveled ten. Forty miles was three days' worth of walking with the very best of luck.

It was obvious that the others were thinking the same thing, gloom hanging over the party like the ever-present mist. Even Elf's spirits seemed dampened.

"There's something up ahead." Casseem hurried forward, Larkin following closely behind him.

A large crag three times Larkin's height jutted from the center of the water. As they neared, the shape softened to a woman carved of stone, and Larkin halted.

The woman was robed and hooded, her face solemn, eyes shut. A chain wound over her shoulders and down her kneeling body, pinning her arms to her torso. Larkin shivered at the thought of an artist creating something so purposeful in a place so desolate. The rock wasn't stained, and no lichen grew upon it.

Larkin sensed Tamsyn's awe as he approached. "She hasn't been here long," he murmured.

"Who is it?" Amias asked.

"The robes indicate a disciple," said Tamsyn. "But I don't know which one."

The woman didn't resemble Bianca, though Bianca's appearance may have shifted over the years. Larkin had no way of knowing. There were more statues beyond, lining the side of the tunnel, only shapes in the absence of light.

Larkin took Casseem's torch from him. She stepped around the kneeling woman and walked farther down the tunnel. The creek diverged into even shallower streamlets and disappeared into crevices in the rock face. Her sodden boots crunched against wet gravel, her light rolling along the figures of two more women and three men, all robed and hooded. These disciples stood, and they weren't wrapped in chains.

Larkin smelled iron.

Don't be stupid, she thought. She'd grown far too familiar with the stench of blood. The statue of the final woman was covered in it, fresh enough to glisten.

"Whose blood is that?" Casseem asked as he approached.

"We passed through a tunnel made of corpses. Take your pick." Larkin reached out and touched the statue, the crimson sticky against her fingers. It didn't matter whose blood it was. It was meant to send a message.

"Bianca," said Tamsyn.

He was right. Beneath the blood, Larkin could see the stark resemblance. The meaning was clear.

One disciple down.

"Is this part of the river within a sector?" Larkin asked.

"Not from what I remember," said Tamsyn. "Do you think Kyran's sending a message to the other disciples, warning them?"

"Maybe." Larkin wiped her hand on her pants. "Or it's a message to us."

"He's warning the other disciples—or us—that they'll die if they help us." Amias rubbed his arms, shivering.

Larkin was certain he was right. The other disciples wouldn't pass through the river often, if at all. Not if they were devoted to remaining within their sectors like Bianca.

She glanced back at the kneeling stone woman. "Rahele Ekko didn't have a sector of her own. Does this mean she's chained to one of the other disciples?"

"Or Kyran," said Tamsyn.

Larkin shuddered.

"We should set up camp here." Elf pranced through the aisle, spinning on her toes. "These statues have stories to tell. We need more time with them to know their secrets."

"Statues don't speak," Jacque said bluntly. "And I don't want to be around them any longer than we have to."

"I want to take some time to search the area at the very least, make sure we don't miss something." Tamsyn pointed, plucking the torch from Larkin's hand. "Like that."

Larkin followed his finger, spotting glyphs written upon the wall past the statues.

"Careful," Larkin warned. "If Kyran wrote them—"

"I don't think he did." Tamsyn hurried toward the glyphs. "Remember the ones back at the mining settlement?"

"I'll see if I can find lichen for a fire," said Amias.

"It's too wet to light anything." Jacque followed him down the channel. Elf trailed along without the slightest bit of concern for her blood-soaked back.

Larkin's shoulders sagged as she rubbed her forehead. They could be walking right into a trap. The tunnel of corpses, the statues. She'd once seen a child throwing stale crumbs at a pigeon in the market square, giggling with glee when the pigeon followed the trail. The girl was thrilled by how easily she could control the bird.

Was Kyran gleeful? She didn't know. She sensed nothing here. Perhaps that was a good sign.

They could defy his wishes and run to a different sector in the hopes another disciple would help them. Maybe the others were stronger than Bianca and her villagers. Maybe they were waiting for the right moment to rise up.

Or they'd steal Larkin's flesh and bones for themselves. The other disciples were content with being immortal, weren't they? If not, they would have let themselves die already.

Larkin dropped her hand, her eyes focusing on a fiery orb in the darkness. *Kyran's doing?*

"Casseem?" she called. She couldn't remember if he had a torch with him. Larkin slipped between the statues and walked deeper into the offshoot passage, the ground hardening to solid rock beneath her feet. The orb grew brighter and larger.

She halted at the sight of a figure, her heart stuttering.

A mirrored wall sliced through the width of the tunnel, preventing her from walking any farther.

Larkin reached out and touched it, her fingers leaving greasy stains along the glass. Iridescence swirled along the mirror's surface. She stared at her reflection. How long had she been down here? Her cheeks sharpened outward at an unnatural angle, the skin under her eyes bruised. She looked chewed up and spit out. Her reflection told her weeks, but it hadn't seemed that long. They must have gone for days at a time without sleeping.

This mirror was here for a reason. Her stomach clenched. *What do you want?* She searched the surrounding space for rage but only caught hints of Tamsyn's intrigue behind her. He was still reading the glyphs.

Larkin followed her bloody, worn reflection down to her untied laces. "Hells." She bent down to tie her boot. When she stood up, she saw Amias in the mirror behind her.

No, not Amias. The man had Amias's complexion and his dark eyes. But the similarities ended there.

She didn't know this man.

As Larkin tried to spin around, the man lashed out and caught her shoulder, forcing her to stare straight ahead at her reflection.

He clapped a hand over her mouth, impossibly strong, holding her as she thrashed. Larkin wrenched at his hand, scouring the air for any emotions to siphon. *Gods, Tamsyn! Come on!*

The man waited until she ceased to struggle. His robes were like those of the statues, and there was something frightening about his ethereal beauty. Just like Bianca's.

He slowly released his hand from her mouth. "Scream and I will crush your heart."

"Disciple," she coughed.

His dark eyes met hers in the mirror, the corners of his smooth lips perking up, though Larkin sensed no delight.

She sensed nothing at all.

"Do I resemble a statue, Larkin?" His voice was satin. "You should have listened to Casseem. You chose to stay with Bianca. You *chose* to seek her help, and because of that, she made a mistake that cost her the life of everyone she cared about, including her own."

Gods, no. It couldn't be him.

Larkin watched, paralyzed, as his hand glided to her belt, fingers wrapping around the hilt of her remaining knife and pulling it from its sheath. She knew she should scream, even if he did crush her heart.

At least she'd be able to warn the others that Kyran was here.

They could kill him if she gave them enough warning.

"Choice." His eyes didn't leave hers. "People only look up to decision makers, isn't that right? You've been challenging Casseem because you want to make the choices."

"I don't," she said.

"All you have is your family. Your brother." Kyran clucked his tongue at her. "If you don't make the right choices to save him, no one will. He is why you fight to lead."

"You don't know what I want." Her voice trembled.

His eyes smoldered with rage, yet she couldn't sense it now. She could only see it. A warm, solid body, but an apparition.

This man wasn't really Kyran. He was a messenger.

"I control elements, command armies. I am everywhere within this world, and I live forever. I know what you want, Larkin."

A howl sounded in the distance. "Tamsyn," she cried, thrashing once more. "Don't hurt him!"

"Leading means making choices. You won't survive without making one."

Tamsyn's fear erupted inside her. Larkin threw her arm and siphoned, her palm connecting with the man's face.

In the mirror, she watched his flesh melt away as she projected. He did not scream; he only smiled. His lips curled like burning parchment. His teeth gnashed at her.

Larkin threw the man off her. He slumped to the ground, dead, and Larkin took off into the darkness.

She burst from between the statues and stumbled into the shallow riverbed. Monstrous shrieks and scraping talons reverberated in her ears. Shadows swarmed along the walls, dropping into the channel.

She had to warn the rest of the party.

Tamsyn cried out for her, his terror starkly familiar. Like what she had sensed in Bianca's village. Brielle. Devon.

He was dying.

The black curtain subsided as light shone from behind

her. As if pouring from a hive, creatures swarmed around the scholar—blistered skin, mouths veiled by flesh. Talons tore him apart.

A creature detached from the ceiling and landed in front of her. Larkin siphoned and projected, carnage showering her, before someone shoved her out of the way.

"RUN!" Casseem barreled forward with a torch, swiping the air as he siphoned. The creatures surrounding him burst.

"Run, Larkin!" As he swung his torch, the light caught on beasts skittering downward from cracks in the ceiling.

"Casseem!" Larkin screamed.

He looked up as a beast descended on him, knocking him into the water. Larkin siphoned and projected, blood spurting from the creature's neck as her magic devoured its flesh.

"Get up!" she sobbed.

Casseem pushed the dead beast off him, flipping over and crawling toward her. Larkin ran to him, one of the creatures launching itself at her. She rolled through the water, landing on her back.

Casseem.

Larkin reached up toward him, grasping his fingers. For a bright moment, she sensed his cool relief before his hand was ripped from hers.

She watched as he was dragged away, talons threading his hair and yanking his head back.

Fingers of sharpened bone ripped across his throat.

Every breath was a scream.

Larkin dragged herself to her feet, racing down the tunnel

and away from the swarm, the wet noise of ripped flesh, grating bones, clicking talons. She cried for help until her lungs were spent, falling to her knees even when she knew the creatures were still close.

The roar of water answered her.

I control elements.

The river. Kyran had destroyed the river, disintegrated it into the mist that hung in the air, and now he was reconjuring it.

Water barreled toward her, the current scooping up the sides of the tunnel as it flooded the passageway.

Tamsyn's agony stole her breath. *Gods*, he was still alive.

Hold on, Tamsyn. Larkin siphoned his horror as it weakened to a trickle.

The river crashed on top of her. Larkin projected, and while the current whipped around her, she knelt, safe in an eye of vapor.

Then the roiling of Tamsyn's terror died with him, and the river tore Larkin from her knees.

TWENTY-FIVE

She let the river take her.

Larkin's father had insisted on teaching her how to swim, but the capital canals had never been so fierce. He would have jumped in to save Larkin if her head had gone beneath the water. He would have saved her now, when her lungs threatened to burst.

By fortune, Larkin's boots scraped against the riverbed. She launched herself upward and broke through the surface, barreling into a boulder that knocked the breath from her lungs. She scrambled to gain purchase on the slippery rock and failed. Blinking the water from her eyes, Larkin spotted glowing patches of crystal above. She could see.

She could see!

In front of her, water cascaded in a sheet of silver, broken only by a crag near the bank. Larkin took a deep breath, and then another, kicking her legs in front of her when her body was buoyant. Her boots slammed into the crag, toes wedging into a crack in the stone. The current whipped her toward the bank, and she grasped the ledge.

Her cuirass was pulling her under. With one hand, she somehow managed to unbuckle it, shifting her body and grip until the current pulled the armor from her torso. She watched it float away.

The roar of water swallowed her cry for help. She tried imagining where the others had been when the hoard had attacked.

Amias, Jacque, and Elf had gone off in search of lichen. Had they searched beyond the statues, or back the way they'd come?

It didn't matter, she realized. Not if the current had sucked them under. Not if they didn't know how to swim.

Larkin clawed at the gritty bank, mustering the strength to pull herself from the current's grasp. She rolled to her stomach and spit up water. Her eyes darted to the corpses bobbing along the glittering silk. Monsters.

Tamsyn. Casseem.

A sob ripped through her. She couldn't succumb to grief, though, not yet.

The current was the same as the direction they'd been walking, which meant the others were downstream. Larkin picked herself up and began to run.

She'd never been alone before, not in her entire life. Alone meant no comfort, no solidarity.

It meant no magic. She would be defenseless.

Larkin hurdled over plumes of glowing lichen in her path. If she didn't save them, Jacque wouldn't get home to her fiancée. What if she never saw Elf again? And Amias . . .

Casseem. Tamsyn.

Larkin tripped, grit from the bank skinning her hands as she fell. She curled her knees to her chest and held on to them.

A heavy weight crushed her. She fumbled in an attempt to find the buckles on her cuirass, to strip them open so she could breathe, and then remembered she wasn't even wearing it. Larkin gasped, coaxing air into her lungs.

She'd felt this way before.

It was soon after her mother's accident. Her family hadn't

eaten in days. Vania wouldn't stop crying. Her mother's and father's misery and guilt bled into Larkin from downstairs as they tried to pacify the toddler with warm water.

She lay curled beneath the quilt atop her bed, clutching her stomach. If death came for her, her family would lose her as a worker.

But she'd be one less mouth to feed.

Larkin felt the weight of the hay mattress shift. Garran took her frozen hands in his, warming them.

"What are we going to do, Larkin? When the morning comes, and we're too miserable to leave our beds. What are we going to do?"

She began to cry.

"Tell me. *Promise* me."

"We're going to get up," she promised. "And we're going to work."

Get up.

Off in the distance, she heard her name, just like the skeleton had spoken to her in the tunnel of corpses. Luring her, the promise of seeing her mother held between its rotting teeth.

This was another trick, a world of nightmares crafted just for her, taunting her around every corner. But this time, Casseem was not here to pull her back.

Larkin tore at the ground. She squinted, blinking until she saw a shadow against the glow of lichen in the distance.

She remembered the cave-in, when Casseem had used

destruction magic to sever the passageway. The darkness had been tangible, and she barely recognized the voices of her party.

She knew better now. She knew the sound of her name on Amias's tongue, the way he held onto the *r* just a moment too long. How his voice rang sharp when he was desperately worried.

Pulling herself to her feet, Larkin began to run.

She ran until she could no longer feel the ground, hurdling over a cluster of crystals along the bank. She could barely make out the shape of his body, but the relief he emitted—the way he called her name like it was the only word he knew—was a beacon in the darkness.

He gathered her into his arms, bright, warm, weightless. She'd been certain she'd never sense comfort or relief again.

Amias wound his fingers through her curls and pressed his lips to her cheek. He held her up when her knees gave out, his emotions flooding her like a tonic. He was without armor, and she felt the rapid beat of his heart through his tunic.

"I was alone." The thought of it haunted her. "Casseem . . ."

"We're here," he said.

We.

A bright and airy voice echoed against the channel walls, followed by the clamor of footsteps. Larkin regained her strength and broke from Amias, spotting two figures easing toward them, limping and haggard.

The crystal glow illuminated Elf's blood-slicked forehead. Jacque's hair fell in strings over her face, her skin drained of color. But they were all right.

"We were at a bend in the channel when the water came,"

said Amias. "We clung to the rock and avoided the worst of the water."

"I can't believe it! I thought . . ." Jacque fell silent when she sensed Larkin.

"Larkin," Elf said softly, the light leaving her eyes. "Both of them?"

Larkin heard Casseem scream at her to run. She felt the ghost of his fingers rip away from hers. She sank to the ground in her own despair. Jacque held on to her, and Larkin melted into the soldier's armor.

Their grief seized her, corroding her bones like swords in the rain. Her blood rusted. A patina bloomed across her flesh. She couldn't breathe, but she could scream—welcoming grief—because it was theirs, and she wasn't alone.

Elf rested her head against Larkin's arm. Amias held her hand. And Larkin cried until her body couldn't bear another sob.

When Larkin told them of the ambush, she left out the visit from Kyran's messenger.

Larkin had no evidence other than her memory, and she wasn't foolish enough to believe Kyran himself dead. No magic could have given him the power to present himself to her like he had, and Bianca had confirmed that he wasn't a god.

She'd imagined him. Casseem and Tamsyn were dead, and she wouldn't burden the others with her delusions.

As they sat around the fire on the bank of the river, Tamsyn's scream rang cacophonous against the clicking talons. She couldn't shake the echo of it away.

If she and Casseem hadn't fought so often, would she have stayed by his side? Would he and Tamsyn still be alive?

If she was truly Bianca's, would she have been able to save them? The creatures had spilled Bianca's blood just like Casseem's and Tamsyn's. Still, her hope that she was the disciple's descendant was fading.

She would have felt Bianca's power inside her by now. She would have known.

Their acrid fire smoked, and Larkin lacked the will to rekindle it. Her face was stiff and swollen from crying.

Across the embers, Jacque took a honing stone to her blade. The soldier had managed to hold on to her weapon this whole time.

They'd lost all but one bag, and Amias sliced up their two remaining smoked fish. Larkin wasn't hungry, but he made her take some anyway, avoiding her eyes when he pushed the portion into her hands. He carried grief in the lines of his face.

Elf sat at the far edge of the bank, dipping her toes in the water that pooled into a glowing inlet. She destroyed tufts of lichen, gathering the splinters near her in a luminescent pile.

Larkin stood and walked to her as Elf began to conjure, the splinters drifting through her hands. Elf molded them to a wide plank floating in the pool. Her creation began to lengthen and take form, the edges curling up.

A boat.

The growths protruding from Elf's shoulders had stopped bleeding, but the skin surrounding them was still raw and tender.

"What is this for?" asked Larkin.

Elf frowned. "I thought it would be obvious."

"I don't mean the boat." Larkin reached out and ran a finger along Elf's shoulder.

The girl flinched away, glaring. "They aren't finished."

Larkin opened her mouth, then sensed the embarrassment that Elf fought to bury deep.

"I'm not mad," Elf said.

"What are you using to conjure?" Jacque joined them, interrupting the conversation. The soldier's sword had returned to its sheath, pressing to her thigh as she knelt between Larkin and Elf.

Elf massaged the splinters into the boat's stern. "Our memories and dreams find new life this deep down. Love hides within them, sometimes—often—buried beneath sadness. I find it."

"You mine it out." Larkin's throat tightened.

"You don't have to mine." Jacque took a handful of splinters and pressed them into Elf's waiting palm. "The last time I saw Risa, we spent one night on the farm before I was assigned to the docks for watch. You know the Demuran wedding ceremony?"

"Yes," said Larkin. "Empaths aren't allowed—"

"Risa didn't care." Jacque grinned, lost in the memory. "Rings forged by fire in front of our guests. The ritual would take place near the stables." Pain flashed across Jacque's face, but as Larkin sensed the layers of warmth beneath it, she understood.

"She'd planned the flower crowns for the autumn bloom." Jacque released Elf's hand. "I have relived that night over and over again since the moment we lost the sun."

Elf smoothed the splinters along the boat's edge. "That's a beautiful memory."

Jacque winced, rubbing her stomach.

"What's wrong?" Larkin asked.

"It's nothing," Jacque said, then grunted. With a swift motion, Larkin yanked up Jacque's tunic, hissing as she caught sight of her abdomen. A mottled knot bulged from Jacque's stomach.

"That doesn't look like nothing, Jacque!" Larkin said.

Jacque smacked the back of Larkin's hand away. "Piss off!" she yelled, unable to suppress her tingling worry. "I slammed up against a rock during the flood." Jacque pressed a hand against the bottom of her rib cage. "You have much larger things to concern yourself with." She nodded toward the conjured boat. "Like not drowning."

The boat didn't sink.

They floated down the river with nothing but a deflated bag and two torches, the wood of Elf's craft glittering subtly from the luminescent lichen.

The scenery shifted as the channel narrowed, and they drifted through alcoves and lagoons of glowing fungus and lichen, the tang of rich earth filling the once-stale air. Threaded silk spun by insects gleamed in the soft light. It seemed like the closer they got to Kyran, the more vibrant and enchanting the Reach became.

When the current slowed, they meandered through the river. Jacque sat pinched within the boat's bow, Elf on top of the stern as if it were a throne. Larkin and Amias balanced the craft in the middle.

Black water splashed the side of the boat, the sound of it all that held the silence at bay. Larkin's memory held her hostage. The orb of her torch in the distance, the grease of her fingers smeared across the mirror.

Kyran, his message.

Tell them.

She shook her head, but the memory continued. Tamsyn's scream, Casseem's fingers, the click of talons.

Amias slid next to her, facing her, their legs touching. Larkin ached to let him hold her, but it would invite questions she couldn't bear to answer yet.

They had been six strong since Bianca's village, the deaths so abrupt that Larkin's face was still damp from crying. Kyran could as easily claim her life, or Amias's. She'd grown close to the others only to be corroded by grief.

His calloused knuckle pushed up against the bottom of her chin. Clusters of crystals above gleamed traitorously, exposing her stained and swollen face.

Amias moved his hand, and the pad of his thumb brushed the bridge of her nose, the curve of her cheek. His face tilted toward hers as he caught a snaking tear.

A delicate scar split the edge of his lower lip. If they had been anywhere else, Larkin would have closed the distance. Parted her mouth, blindly learned the shape of the scar with her tongue.

The scar would only be the beginning. Her eyes drifted to the cusp of his ear, trailing his jaw to the slope of his neck. *Kiss me,* she wanted to say. *Kiss me before it's too late.*

She could surrender to her every craving for him. She could surrender, and he could die.

Larkin's skin buzzed as Amias dropped his hand and pulled

back, the mask of his calm still strong but not impenetrable. He hadn't stifled his fear quickly enough.

Larkin wondered if he feared her longing like she feared his comfort. There was too much to lose.

"Once," Elf began, "when humanity was new to Demura, magic was free."

"A story," Jacque said, intrigued.

Larkin's shoulders relaxed. She couldn't take comfort in Amias, but she could in Elf. She closed her eyes and let Elf's words sweep her away.

"The ports held ships with sails of vibrant reds and blues and golds. Markets dotted the trading routes. Strangers built homes in the fields of the vale. Some built with pine and iron; others conjured." Beneath the faded crystal light, Elf's brow furrowed. "Empaths were indistinguishable from those who did not possess magic. Magic was born everywhere. Magic was governed, until a miner discovered a beautiful glimmering mineral within the hills, and magic—the ability to wield or subdue it—became power. Fear grew alongside the power, and the dynasty closed the docks and built up an army, defending the isle from Empaths and outsiders alike." Elf arched her back until her shoulders grazed the water, hooking her feet beneath the lip of the boat. She began to speak again, her voice measured. "Maybe those who can't wield it are right to be so terrified. Without the mineral, we are limitless if we are not alone."

"We haven't been given a chance to govern ourselves in a very long time," said Larkin before Jacque hushed her.

Elf hung off the boat for a long while. When the lagoon ended, she pushed herself back up, settling back into the boat.

One by one, delicate bones peeled away from her shoulders.

Larkin had seen the pattern before, on the skeleton of a bird. Her jaw went slack.

"Sweet Ilona," breathed Jacque. "What have you done to yourself?"

They aren't finished, Elf had told Larkin.

Wings. Elf fanned her wings, the bones threaded by sinew and cartilage. She released a breath as though she'd been holding it for miles.

A strangled noise escaped Amias. "It's . . ."

"Beautiful," Larkin finished, her eyes welling again. The wings, the boat, the way Elf so easily mined love from their memories. How strange she'd been acting after the village. "Elf . . . is Bianca's."

She wanted to weep, knowing Bianca's guess had been right. They were the descendants of Kyran and his disciples.

And Larkin did not belong to Bianca.

"I didn't say anything because I knew you wanted to be hers." Elf slid down to Larkin and touched her shoulder. "I didn't want to hurt you."

Guilt curled poisonously within Larkin's gut. "You don't have to protect me."

"I want to," Elf said brightly, but her expression fell, her alarm sharp and vibrant. "There's—" She broke off, a gasp escaping her.

As Larkin watched, Elf's face crumpled. Her eyes slid out of focus.

"There's something terrible ahead."

A chill crawled up Larkin's spine. She turned to the expanding river, straining her eyes until they ached.

Far off into the distance, an orange dot floated in the blackness, the shadows before it splotchy and shapeless, but something was there.

Amias grabbed her hand. "I smell death."

Larkin inhaled; the stench was metallic and sickly sweet. The *hush* of Jacque's sword leaving its sheath broke through the river's quiet trickle. The soldier climbed over the boat and dipped her leg into the water, surprised. She hopped out of the boat with a splash. The water only came up to her knees.

Larkin lit a torch and sank into the water. She waded cautiously out to the nebulous shadows. Flame licked along dark, red ripples. Pink foam clung to her legs.

Blood.

TWENTY-SIX

As the shape in the water sharpened, Larkin retreated to the memory of Melay's banquet.

Before them, crimson water engulfed a marble table, its shadowy dinner guests unmoving. *Dead,* she thought, bridging the distance. Jacque and Amias flanked her sides, Elf behind them.

Her light pooled over intricate floral patterns carved along the marble's edge. Delicate dishes lay empty and gleaming. The illusion evaporated as they inched closer, and Larkin caught sight of the cartilage crushed between the marble tabletop.

Not marble. The entire table was bone.

Her breath rattled. Another step, and the light cast over slumped bodies. They hadn't been dead long. Their skin still carried color, their hair rich and lively. The eyes of one were gouged out. Another was missing its lower jaw, tongue flopping limply.

Jacque screamed, her terror shattering through Larkin.

Larkin caught Jacque's elbow as the soldier sank into the blood.

"Jacque!" Larkin fought to find balance. Even with the worst of the mutilated bodies, the soldier hadn't reacted like this. "What is it?"

"*Gods,*" Amias cried, his dread beating through her. "Risa."

Larkin released Jacque and followed Amias's stare to the

woman with no eyes. Her golden hair was matted and stained pink at the ends, her lips scaled.

"Bastard." Larkin waded toward the bodies, heart pounding in rage. *Sadistic monster.*

"He's taken her from the Surface," Jacque wailed. "No, no, no . . ."

Larkin's skin flushed with sweat. She inched around Risa, the table's length infinite, torchlight rolling across each guest.

"I can't—" Amias jerked back violently, his horror threatening to drag Larkin downward. Her flame passed over a pretty girl across the table with her throat torn out. She looked just like Amias.

Skye.

Larkin wanted to comfort him, but her body felt cast in iron. The ringing in her ears muted Jacque's screaming, grief dulling her senses. If Risa and Skye were here . . .

Mum.

An arm's length away, Larkin's mother was slumped over her plate. Her mouth was slack, and blood dripped from her blank eyes.

Black dots prickled Larkin's vision. A scream bubbled inside her.

Mum. The ground fell out from beneath her feet. Larkin bit through her tongue, blood flooding her mouth. Her torch fell from her hand and rolled to the center of the table.

Mum. He'd murdered her. *Mum . . . Mum . . .* She had a birthmark on her neck in the shape of a berry. Her mother had a bump on her nose. Her mother had a scar near her temple.

This wasn't her mother.

"It's not real," Larkin whispered. She whipped around and searched for the rest of her party. "It's not real! It's a conjuration!"

The ringing in Larkin's head had died, and her ears once again roared with sound: the *whoosh* of the current, Jacque's tired sobs . . . Amid the grief, she sensed Elf, calm and collected.

The winged girl knelt and pulled Jacque up. "It's not Risa." She pointed to the table. "There's my troupe mate Oggy, the one missing his arms. But he's safe, just like Risa. I promise you."

Jacque clung to Elf, burying her face between the girl's boned wings and her shoulder.

Larkin spotted Amias near the boat, his arms folded close to his chest, and went to him. The color had drained from him, his shallow breaths rising in a vapor. She stood on her toes, her lips pressing against his cheekbone.

Pulling away, she whispered, "I will kill him for this."

It had been Larkin's mission all along. Kyran had stolen hundreds from the Surface, claimed thousands of soldiers within the Reach. He'd slaughtered Bianca and her descendants, and Devon and Brielle and Casseem and Tamsyn.

But this. He was threatening them, showing them what he planned to do.

Larkin left Amias, thrashing back through the water. She gripped the false Risa and threw her into the water. She yanked on Skye's chair until it toppled backward, and then Oggy's.

As Larkin hovered over the lie pretending to be her mother, she noticed one more shadow looming at the edge of the ring of light. She felt the table, her trembling fingers wrapping around her torch.

The final dinner guest was wearing nothing other than a

pair of ratty, bloodstained trousers. Grub-white skin draped his bones. His arms rested on either side of his plate, and his wrists tapered into hands layered on top of hands, bony and blood crusted.

Larkin let out a cry when he peeled open milky eyes.

"Larkin?" Amias called out, wading toward her.

Larkin stood frozen. Though his face was slashed with new red wounds, he was clearly a man. Or had once been.

Words hissed horribly from an opening in his neck.

"Make yourself at home." His voice was a raw gurgle. "Our lord has collected your friends." He gestured to her mother. A terrible laugh escaped the slit in his threat.

She tasted bile. "Where is Kyran?"

"I am here to speak for our lord Otheil. He has created me in his own image. Everyone from my battalion is dead, but I have been chosen. I am his."

She sensed Amias's revulsion. "Larkin, his mouth. His hands . . ."

At first, Larkin thought that Amias was pointing out the deformities, and then it struck her.

Our quartermaster's wounds have sprouted new limbs.

The journal. The story of the soldier's battalion, and the first to go insane.

This was the quartermaster.

The quartermaster grinned from both mouths, blood trickling from behind pink-stained teeth. He cocked his head to the side, the bones in his neck cracking. "This is where everything ends."

"He's been tortured," Elf said, more awestruck than afraid.

Was it possible? Had Kyran destroyed bits and pieces of this man until he could do nothing but submit? The flesh stripped from Brielle's arms . . . If Kyran hadn't killed her, perhaps this would have been her fate.

The quartermaster's milky eyes seemed eager, but Larkin sensed nothing from him. He was alive without his humanity. Did he have free will? *Obviously not,* she thought. He'd referred to Kyran as *our lord.*

She played along. "What does he want from us?"

"What does he *want?*" The quartermaster pressed his lips shut, humming. "This isn't about what he wants; it's about what you do."

Larkin darted her eyes around, checking to make sure she wasn't being purposefully distracted.

"It's about how you prove yourself to him," the quartermaster insisted. "The choices you make."

Larkin tensed.

Leading means making choices. You won't survive without making one. Kyran's words, spoken to her in the mirror. If she had to choose, then her choice was to put this creature out of his misery.

Larkin siphoned and projected before she could think about the consequences. She crushed his head, blood and slime slipping down his chest before the body fell sideways and into the water.

"Why did you do that?" Jacque yelled. "Now we'll never find where Kyran is!"

Larkin looked back at the three other remaining party members, resolute.

Amias's frustration slid across her skin. "You killed him because you were impatient?"

Her anger flared. "I made a choice, per his request. I wasn't going to play his game of riddles."

Why didn't Amias understand?

Elf grabbed Larkin, her fingernails digging into Larkin's wrist. "That terrible thing I told you about on the boat—the one I sensed—the quartermaster wasn't it."

Larkin followed Elf's eyes to the darkness past the table. The passage was silent except for the slosh of water at her feet.

"Larkin, I can't do this," Jacque whimpered. "I feel ill."

It was unlike Jacque. She probably hadn't recovered from seeing Risa dead, but Larkin couldn't stop. Kyran wasn't done with them. But she was done with him. This needed to end.

"Then stay back."

Emotion struck Larkin hard in the gut. She stumbled, the sensation nothing she'd ever felt before. She was being boiled atop a raging fire, crushed within an ore mill.

She felt like dying.

"No," Amias groaned. He staggered away from her side and fell into the water, his eyes darting across the darkness. His shoulders rose and fell in short, shallow breaths.

Larkin hurried to him. She could barely sense his panic beneath whatever lay ahead, but she knew it was strong. "Amias, what's wrong?"

"This is death." His eyes fogged over.

He couldn't succumb to whatever this was. She needed him.

"Amias, look at me." Sweat poured from his face. *Gods,* she thought. *He's sensed this level of anguish before.*

"Stay with him." Elf skated into the darkness, the skeletal fingers of her wings swaying. The light caught on a giant mound in the water up ahead.

"Elf, wait." Larkin laced her fingers with Amias's, dragging him upward. Jacque wasn't far behind them, clutching her stomach.

Hells. The two of them were falling apart.

As Larkin neared Elf, the shape in the water took form, and she realized what had been piled to the ceiling of the channel.

Armor.

Clutching Amias's hand, Larkin followed Elf around the pile. There wasn't just one. There were dozens—rotted leather and rusted steel. A monument of every soldier Kyran had consumed.

Jacque retched. "I'm going to be sick."

Fighting her own nausea, Larkin climbed out of the water and onto solid ground. The piles of armor ended. Carnage sheeted the ground; the gore glistened against the light of her flame.

They moved. Breathed.

Before her, a sea of bodies stretched before her endlessly, their limbs intertwined like a knit cloth. Their breaths rose and fell rapidly in unison. Long claws grew from crooked fingers. Fleshy tubes punctured their abdomens and wound around the bodies, disappearing into the walls. They were being kept alive.

Skin had grown over some of their faces, as with the Reach creatures she'd seen, while others still looked human.

The lost soldiers—they were Kyran's monsters in the making. He'd stolen them.

"He's tortured them." Amias's voice broke. "Not just the quartermaster. All of them."

"Larkin," Elf whispered.

Larkin glanced down and realized that at some point she had released Amias and was already wading through the bodies, possessed by her horror to get closer. Up ahead, one of the bodies did not breathe in sync along with the other silent ones, its wretched scream locked in her throat.

Larkin looked back at Elf, the winged girl struggling to hold Amias up.

"Prepare yourself for what it will say," said Elf.

A shudder seized Larkin's shoulders. Elf knew what she was about to do.

Larkin maneuvered around limbs and knelt near the woman who tried to speak. Her teeth rippled beneath her mask of flesh—open, close, open.

Larkin lifted a trembling finger and projected. The mouth yawned wide as the mask ripped apart.

The woman's teeth were stained with blood, her tongue chalk-white. "Seaside Port," she babbled. "Second in rank, right of the lieutenant."

What in all hells. Larkin stood, turning back to her party, and repeated the woman's words.

"That's my rank," Jacque gasped. And then she released a bloodcurdling scream.

TWENTY-SEVEN

Jacque's shriek tore through the air, deafening. She stripped off her cuirass and threw it into the water.

The front of her tunic was doused in blood.

Jacque lifted up the hem of her shirt. The open sore across her abdomen grew before Larkin's eyes. Her skin was dissolving.

"No!" Jacque shrieked, stumbling backward. "You can't let him take me!"

Elf launched herself at Jacque, grabbing the soldier by the arm.

Larkin whirled and raised her torch. Kyran was here. He was in the room with them.

"Where are you?" Larkin yelled into the darkness. She hurried deeper, trampling over bodies. She spotted a viney mass creeping along the wall, the corpses hardened into a form of their own.

The beckoning hand protruding through the Reach wall. The twisted arms she had seen in the labyrinth. The mass that Elf had broken through.

The rage.

The vine of corpses spidered across the ceiling before disappearing into the cracks.

Otheil Kyran had threaded himself throughout the Reach. These limbs were connected to him.

"We need to get her out of here, now!" Larkin cried.

Amias shook himself out of his stupor, grabbing Jacque's other arm. The three of them stumbled forward, and Larkin led them around the breathing sea, explaining that Kyran was con-juring and destroying through the twisted masses above. "The tangled corpses above are a part of him. He's transforming the soldiers slowly enough to torture them. If we don't get out of here—"

"You can't let him take me!" Jacque groaned in agony.

Seaside Port. Jacque's station. *Second in rank, right of the lieu-tenant.* Her status. Kyran knew it. He'd been listening in with ears and eyes that once belonged to others, using stolen limbs to sense and siphon and project, just like he was projecting onto Jacque. He was going to kill her, and Larkin didn't know if she could stop it from happening.

But she would put up a fight.

Larkin pressed forward. "Amias, Elf, keep up with me!"

Unlike before, there were no crystals, and no glowing lichen. Her torch did next to nothing to illuminate the passage, but as they hiked, Larkin spotted the creeping shadows above that indicated Kyran's presence.

They couldn't backtrack. Jacque wouldn't survive, and Larkin couldn't remember seeing any other passage branching off the river.

Larkin siphoned their agony into herself and projected, gore raining down on them. If she had to destroy every single one of his limbs, she would.

Silently, Kyran reacted, and Jacque screamed again.

Larkin spun around, the others several feet behind her. She was close enough to see the material of Jacque's tunic shift on its own.

Amias dragged Jacque to a vacant part of the floor and laid

her down, and as Larkin reached her, Jacque lifted her shirt to reveal the shape of a hand pressing against her stomach from the inside, as if something was trying to claw its way out of her.

The quartermaster, the mutations. The thousands of bodies surrounding them, all soldiers, all turning into monsters.

Kyran wasn't trying to kill Jacque. He was claiming her as his own.

Jacque grabbed Larkin's collar, pulling her close. "You have to kill me, Larkin. You can't let me become a monster like them."

The soldier's eyes rolled back as fingers pushed through the muscle of her abdomen and stretched toward Larkin.

"You can't kill her," Amias pleaded.

"Like hells I will," Larkin growled. Her eyes stung in anger. "I wouldn't do that to Risa. You'll be at your wedding even if I have to carry you to the Surface myself, Jacque. Jacque!" Larkin slapped the soldier's cheek; Jacque's skin felt cold and clammy.

What would Jacque do if Larkin had been the one writhing in agony? She'd do the same thing she'd done all along.

Move forward.

A burst of energy filled Larkin, and she flung the soldier's arm over her shoulder. "Wake up, Jacque!" Larkin cried as Amias took Jacque's other arm. The soldier groaned once, but nothing more. She was deadweight.

Larkin clambered to her feet, heaving Jacque with her. Elf guided them over the piled bodies, Larkin and Amias stumbling after her as quickly as they could. *Forward, forward, forward,* she chanted to herself. She felt Jacque's body convulse.

"There is an opening up ahead!" Elf cried.

"Come on." Larkin tugged on the soldier. "We can make it."

Jacque whispered Larkin's name, a quiet moan. Elf reached the tunnel entrance and stopped.

No.

Larkin handed Jacque off to Amias and ran to Elf, skidding to a halt when she realized why the girl had stopped.

They stood at the edge of a cliff, their torch a pinprick of light at the mouth of a yawning abyss.

Larkin scoured the surrounding space for another path, then panicked. She couldn't see in the dark.

Jacque sank to the ground, agony escaping her in small gasps. Amias knelt next to her, nervously lifting Jacque's tunic.

"Gods," he breathed.

Larkin hurried to them, spotting an arch of rotting hands twisting along the ledge above them. Jacque wasn't safe.

"Go find another route," she ordered Amias.

Amias hesitated, his dread flaring.

"Do this," Larkin whispered. "For Jacque. For Risa."

Amias gritted his teeth and stood, and Larkin sensed the swirling embers of courage. He ran toward the breathing sea.

Please let him find a way, Larkin thought, turning back to Jacque. Elf knelt next to her. The soldier's skin was gray and slicked with sweat. The hand was no longer amorphous, each of its digits visible, with its broken nails and bulging knuckles.

"*Gods*, let me die," Jacque whimpered. "Please."

"We could buy ourselves time and destroy it," Larkin suggested. It would hurt Jacque, but she couldn't think of another way to fight Kyran.

"She'll bleed out unless I heal her." Elf hovered her hands over Jacque's abdomen. Her face crumpled. "I can't conjure here."

Without warning, Jacque heaved herself up and pushed Elf out of the way. Elf skidded backward, and Jacque drew her sword, the edge hovering at Larkin's throat.

Slowly, Larkin lifted her hands. Terror flashed across Jacque's eyes and through Larkin before Jacque buried it.

"I'll do it myself," Jacque hissed.

Larkin made a fist, and the sword disintegrated.

Jacque was quick to react, rolling over to her stomach. The invading hand scrambled against the ground to find purchase, the chilling sight distracting Larkin for a moment too long.

Larkin lunged, grabbing on to Jacque's foot. Jacque kicked her in the chest and Larkin fell back, gasping for air.

Jacque dragged herself up and hobbled toward the cliffside.

"Elf!" Where in the hells was she?

Larkin launched herself at Jacque, knocking the soldier over. Then she rolled across the ground and back to her feet.

Jacque released a piercing shriek, falling limp. The growing hand was debilitating her, buying Larkin more time. She made to lunge for the soldier again, but Elf held her back.

Larkin whirled around. "We need to get her away from that ledge, or she's going to kill herself!" A sob escaped her. Kyran had killed the others so quickly; this grief was different. Her companion was going to die, and Larkin had no choice but to watch it happen.

"Look at me, Larkin." Elf's skeletal wings fanned outward, tears streaking her cheeks. "I think I can save her, but I need to conjure. I need you to help me."

Behind Larkin, Jacque groaned. The soldier would come to at any moment now.

"Please," Elf pleaded.

How? How could Larkin give Elf what she needed to conjure when it felt like she would never feel happiness again? "I can't."

"You *have* to."

Larkin shut her eyes, and Elf wrapped her arms around Larkin, holding her.

"You have to," she repeated.

Larkin nodded and closed her eyes tightly, concentrating. She rested her head on Elf's shoulder. At first, dread was all that filled her. But love . . .

Jacque had pressed the splinters into Elf's hands, telling them about Risa and their forbidden ceremony. The rings, the flowers in their hair.

The farther they fell from the Surface, the more their hearts ached for home, and those left there.

The day Larkin's mother came home from the mines with a broken leg, her father set the bones in their bedroom.

Her mother's misery did not stem from the pain.

"We won't be able to feed them, Jallus," she wept. "Not if I can't work."

Outside the room, Larkin sat against the wall with Garran's head in her lap. She combed her fingers through his hair, listening. Larkin wasn't worried for herself. She only wanted her mother to know that this wasn't her fault.

Her father had trudged from the room, haggard and drained

of hope. He didn't notice them as he walked down the narrow stairs. Garran had fallen asleep in Larkin's lap. She eased him off and stood, sneaking into her parents' room. As Larkin scooted onto the bed, her mother winced and opened her eyes. Her mother's leg was wrapped in a makeshift cast of blankets. Her waxy face shone with sweat, her anguish deeper than Larkin had ever felt.

Her mother whispered her name.

Larkin took her face in her hands. "I'm going to take care of you."

Larkin opened her eyes as Elf began to destroy, harvesting material for the conjurations. Above, the arch of limbs disintegrated, the matter drifting to the ground like ash.

Elf's wings splayed wide. Muscles and ligaments painted the bones, and when they were coated, Elf forged veins and tissue and flesh. The ash layered onto her skin in dove-white feathers.

Elf's grip on her loosened, and Larkin pulled away, sensing the tremor of Elf's fear. But the fear, she realized, was only a part of her courage.

"He will not win." Elf stood, and began to run.

Larkin scrambled for the torch and lifted it above her head just in time to see Elf race toward Jacque, grab hold of her, and launch into the abyss.

TWENTY-EIGHT

Larkin sprinted to the edge, screaming Elf's name until she tasted blood. As she slammed her fist into the ground, someone grabbed her shoulder and yanked her backward.

Larkin took a swing at Amias, missing. He pulled her close and held her as she fought back. They slid to the ground and she clutched him, every part of her shaking.

He waited, silent, and she sensed his compassion.

But she didn't want his compassion. She wanted her companions. Her family.

"They're gone." Larkin's voice was hollow. "Elf took Jacque off the edge. They're . . . they're dead."

"You don't know that." He stroked her hair, and she pressed against the weight of his hand.

"She doesn't know how to fly, Amias. She was desperate." *Stupid,* thought Larkin. How could Elf be so stupid?

Larkin's grief was overpowered by hate. Hate for Melay, hate for Kyran and his twisted games. Hate for herself for letting Elf coax emotion out of her.

For not finding a way to save Jacque.

Kyran had made sure that there was no hope this deep within the Reach. They could wait here until Kyran decided to claim them as he'd tried to claim Jacque, or they could press on without their party, without hope.

Choice.

Just like they could choose to continue, she could choose to be honest with Amias.

"I'm afraid of losing you."

He pulled back, and she found comfort in the fact that he wasn't surprised. She reached up and touched his cheek, tracing upward and through his short hair. His determination solidified inside her.

"Then we need to keep going," he said.

Larkin nodded. It was time to share with Amias what she had seen. They needed every advantage now to survive. Which meant she could no longer keep her secret.

"I have to tell you something. Before Tamsyn and Casseem died, Kyran visited me."

Amias furrowed his brow. "What are you—"

"He came to me. Appeared out of nowhere. He told me that I wouldn't survive without making choices. I killed him, Amias, but he isn't dead. Whoever it was looked like him, and carried a message from him, but it wasn't actually Kyran."

"Choices," Amias repeated. His eyes flickered back and forth as he thought. "What does that mean?"

"It means that I choose to keep going," Larkin said firmly. "Did you find another path?"

"No." Amias looked over, his eyes widening in surprise. "But it looks like we can continue forward after all."

Confused, Larkin stood, turning back toward the abyss. Beyond their light, a stone path jutted from the cliff they stood on and arced into the void.

"This wasn't here when we arrived," Amias said.

Larkin shivered, looking up. She couldn't see Kyran, but a piece of him was there, lurking beyond the blackness. He'd created this path for them when they were distracted.

Did she have a choice? Or was Kyran in control of everything she did and everywhere she went?

Larkin patted her trousers. Her waterskin was half empty, a remaining torch hanging from her belt. She carried a few drops of oil in the vial within her pocket.

It had to be enough.

Larkin walked toward the path's edge.

"I'm right behind you," said Amias.

Larkin stepped onto the bridge, wondering if it would disintegrate under her feet. Kyran had that power. Her pulse sped. He was the one with a choice, not her. He could choose to let her fall or let her find him.

When she looked down, her stomach dropped.

It was like Elf and Jacque had fallen to the center of the world. She couldn't let what happened to them distract her, not now.

Her flame illuminated the far side of the chasm. As Larkin stepped onto the platform, she halted, struck with awe.

A portcullis sat within stone, the gate half open and baring its teeth. The surrounding rock face curved outward, smooth, etched like limestone brick. Striking purple flags cascaded over the stonework, swords clashing beneath a gemstone. Demura's seal.

"Kyran has created a palace for himself," Larkin breathed. "Just like Melay's."

Amias took her hand. "It's identical."

A mirror world, she thought in awe. Kyran hadn't simply created a lair beneath the capital. He had created a second palace, for himself.

They had arrived.

I will kill him, she had sworn to Amias. But all the anger propelling her forward vanished as she stared into the portcullis's hinged mouth.

"I'm scared too," Amias whispered.

She squeezed his hand, and they continued through the open gate.

Their torchlight flooded the palace's empty courtyard, the fountain dry, the gardens barren. *An omen,* she thought. Kyran was showing her the Demura he wanted.

They crossed a mock bridge made of stone, the large double doors left ajar. As they entered, their world burst into color.

The palace's parlor was made of crystal. Two staircases spun up the walls, gleaming bright rainbow rays against the torchlight. Stunned, Larkin wondered what this meant. Did Kyran mean to keep all this for himself while the outside world remained desolate? What use did he have for such beauty?

Maybe this was only a distraction. She had to focus. "We need to find the throne room."

Amias pointed to the door between the staircases. "There."

His confidence surprised her, but she didn't question him. Larkin stepped forward, and she saw her haggard face reflected a thousand times within the crystals' facets. It reminded her of the mirrored tunnel where she had seen Kyran's messenger.

Releasing Amias's hand, Larkin approached the throne room and stepped through the doors.

Death hung acrid in the stagnant air, the space before her dark and vast. Larkin saw nothing, heard nothing but the rattle of her own breath. To find Kyran—to know what lay ahead—she'd have to go deeper.

Larkin walked forward, wetness squelching beneath her boot. She looked down, and her torch snuffed out.

She let out a cry and spun around, slamming face-first into a wall that hadn't been there before. Larkin frantically patted down the wall to find where she'd entered from, but there was nothing. No crevice, no path.

"AMIAS!" Her voice echoed around the ancient space, the utter darkness. A resounding exhale rushed through the chamber, the noise of breath leaving a thousand sets of lungs. The sound made the hairs on the back of her neck stand on end. The chamber fell to silence again, and she stood still, listening.

Amias screamed.

Larkin yelled out his name and began sprinting through the chamber, searching for his emotions, but felt nothing.

The same thing had happened with Brielle. With Tamsyn.

"*No,*" she cried. "*No, no, no . . .*"

A damp breath curtained her neck, and every part of her body tensed.

Welcome home.

Pain sliced into Larkin's left shoulder. She clutched her arm as warm blood began trickling down. Then her other shoulder split apart.

Destruction magic. Kyran was going to tear her limb from limb.

She clamped down on the slickness of blood and torn flesh,

and took off running into the dark. At the break in the rock, she turned right and down the new passageway.

Larkin tripped and fell, her arms skating across hot, sticky ground. She heard the voice again, but it was only a rumble—indecipherable at first. Vibrations of terror struck her heart.

I can taste your fear.

She scrambled backward, tucking herself within a corner. She clapped her palms over her mouth to quiet her breathing, then yelped when the back of her hands began to burn. She felt the skin beginning to peel back.

"What do you want?" she yelled.

The darkness didn't respond.

She tried again, louder, but her voice hoarsened quickly. She grew dizzy as the blood drained from her. Larkin's head dipped, and she yanked it up again, conscious of every one of her muscles—the way they clenched, how they submitted to the loss of blood. It wouldn't take her long to die this way.

Is this how Otheil Kyran wanted her to die? After all this?

He could have made her bleed out during her first hours within the Reach. Unless the sole purpose of this entire journey was so that he could see her suffer.

Do you want to see me? Kyran asked.

Her heart clenched in fear. "Yes," she whispered, weakening. She was going to pass out soon.

Then Larkin let out a hiss. Her skin burned with conjuration magic; Kyran was closing her wounds.

Dull light blanketed the room. She looked up to a spattering of crystals just bright enough to make out her surroundings.

Larkin rose to her feet, lurching as the ground swayed. She'd found herself in the bowels of a pulsing, beating being, one that had swallowed thousands of bodies before her. They were embedded in the walls—thousands of faces with eyeless sockets and gaping mouths.

She could hear its heart, the pulse steady and strong. The beat thrummed in her ears, as though it lived inside her.

Tendrils of sinew swept downward from the chandelier, twisting together into a mass in the center of the room mere feet away from her.

Kyran.

Larkin approached him. He was immobile, withered, and fused within a throne of the flesh and blood he'd stolen from his victims. Melay had been both wrong and right.

Kyran wasn't a god. But he was a wicked, vile man. He was evil.

Petrified, Larkin swept her eyes over him. Thin threads of sinew shot forward from Kyran's limbs, piercing into a body that sat huddled between Larkin and the throne.

Larkin screamed when she recognized Kyran's prey.

Kneeling before the throne, punctured by a web of gore, was Amias.

TWENTY-NINE

Amias's head hung limp, and Larkin was smothered by his agony. He was alive, not even ten paces away from where she stood.

An inexplicable calm washed over her. Miles of terror and death had brought her here, but she'd made it. Kyran was bleeding Amias, trying to distract her, weaken her. If she succumbed, Amias would die, and so would she.

Amias's body was ruptured by the tendrils of sinew. She counted six wounds: one in Amias's shoulder, one in his hip. His hands and knees were both punctured, the sinew anchoring him to the ground. Nowhere fatal, not yet. Larkin had time to figure out how to save him.

Limbs peeled away from the edges of Kyran and his throne and wove into the rock face surrounding him. Larkin thought of the vine of eyes near Devon's corpse, the hand they'd found in the alchemical lab. The lace of carnage had grown thicker the deeper they went. A thousand years, and he'd used the bodies of others to grow and grow, threading himself through the Reach to see and control all that happened within. He knew Bianca had helped Larkin. He'd destroyed the river for them to nearly drown in because he'd been there. He'd killed her torch near the arch because he'd been there, watching her. Watching all of them, *ragefully*.

And Demura . . .

He was there too. The ends of these tendrils, rooting upward from the ground. All of the missing villagers he'd grabbed with his limbs were now a part of him, their bodies only a way to sustain himself.

Their emotions nothing but fuel.

This realization cut into her, but she refused to let it swallow her. She had to focus.

When Kyran finally spoke, the mouth of the withered man did not open or move. Instead, the faces he decorated himself with—the corpses he'd gleaned that fortified his throne and the walls surrounding her—opened their mouths, their voices like tearing parchment.

I am glad to see you. I have been wanting to see my own within the flesh for a while.

The blood in her veins ran cold.

He was wrong. He knew nothing of his descendants. He was lying to her, playing with her now as he had the entire time she'd been in the Reach.

"I'm not yours."

To Larkin's right, one of the tendrils peeled apart, revealing a row of crusted, beady eyes that blinked at her.

The chorus of heads sang to her again. *Do you think that I cannot see what is happening on the Surface? Do you think I am unaware of my descendants?*

Amias cried out in pain. Larkin lunged toward him, but a tendril laced with bone thorns lashed at her. She dodged it, rolling to the right of Amias.

Larkin crouched, siphoning his pain and projecting it onto the tendril. As it melted, Amias screamed. "Let him go," she snarled.

Don't act foolishly, Larkin.

"Larkin," Amias croaked. A warning.

Larkin shouted as another tendril ripped through the center of Amias's torso. He let out a scream and fell limp.

I won't kill him.

"You've killed the others!" she shouted.

They were all appendages. But Amias is more. He is not my heir, but he is powerful. And you care for him. This is important to me. I understand the pain you've suffered. This place was never meant for you. For any of us. Look what it has done to me. Only one person is to blame.

"You." She felt weak and accusatory. "You chose this form. Bianca . . ."

Bianca was beautiful, but her heart and mind were ravaged by this life of darkness. Physicality means little, my child.

She flinched. "I am not your child."

You refuse me because of my form? You are an Empath. You've seen for yourself how forms can change. The winged one showed you.

The threads of corpses that held Kyran in place squelched with tension. As Kyran reached out a shriveled hand, flesh melted from his bones. Wrinkled skin dripped away from his skull, his arms, his torso, until he was nothing but muscle fused to his throne.

He was conjuring a new form, although not from any emotions she could sense.

It dawned on her that Kyran was not siphoning emotions from just this space. He was threaded throughout the entirety of the Reach, and his limbs had now breached the Surface. He could siphon from anywhere.

Muscle and tissue stretched over Kyran's face, and rich, dark curls grew over his scalp. At last, his flesh recoated him, and he lifted his head.

She recognized the man from the mirror. Right before he killed Casseem and Tamsyn.

Kyran's lips pulled into a wicked grin, and then he was pulled backward into the tangle, swallowed by the corpses of his throne.

He was gone.

No.

She jumped to her feet, the breath rattling in her lungs. "KYRAN!"

Larkin lifted her hand to destroy, but there was nothing to siphon. Amias was unconscious, and Kyran was gone, his rage suppressed.

Amias.

She hurried to him, gathering his blanched face in her hands. His wounds seeped blood, but the one in the center of his body would kill him soon. Her hand clenched as the urge to use destruction magic flashed through her.

The faces within the throne parted their lips again. *Do not hurt me again if you want him to live. Patience, child. There is still a performance to witness.*

Larkin stood as the corpses near the center of Kyran's throne untangled themselves, separating from one another, and revealing an opening.

Come, Kyran ordered. *Leave Amias where he is. I will not harm him.*

The tendrils squelched, and Larkin flinched, stepping forward until the sinew threading Amias ceased to move.

Closer.

Larkin shielded her eyes, stepping through the bright hole and into Melay's palace.

THIRTY

arkin had never visited the throne room of the palace before, but she knew this was it. The walls glittered with embedded gemstones and were hung with tapestries with Demura's seal.

There was something off about all of it. Demura's seal looked different from how she remembered it, the design thinner and rougher, the colors paler.

She glanced upward at the bright cavern crystals that clung to the ceiling. She was still in the Reach—of course she was.

Shadows loomed within the chamber's edges. At first, Larkin thought she'd been lured into a room full of Kyran's creatures, but she realized they were people, watching her from the shadows. She sensed no emotion from them.

A dark-haired man stood facing the throne, his hands clasped behind him. His green robes clung to his strong frame.

As Larkin approached the man, he glanced back, and Larkin recognized Otheil Kyran. Kyran in his first form. Before the Uprising.

From the darkness behind the throne, a woman stepped forward and into the light.

Melay, Larkin thought immediately, but there were small differences. Her nose was longer, as was her hair. She looked older than she did now. Although she appeared to be flesh and blood, Larkin knew it was more of Kyran's magic.

This was not Melay; it was someone rendered to look like her and forced to assume her mannerisms.

Bianca's word returned to her. *We had an arrangement. No more visits. No more puppets.*

Puppets like Kyran's creatures. Like his performers. They were humans, the emotion and will tortured right out of them. Larkin's lips parted, every inch of her trembling uncontrollably.

"Otheil." The woman's voice was husky and rich. She glided down the platform steps to the young Kyran.

"She's beautiful, isn't she?" Kyran's deep voice projected, clinging to the corners of the chamber, ringing in Larkin's ears. She looked around, unable to find him.

"Just like how I remember. Before she deceived me. Before this Uprising began."

Larkin walked forward toward the woman and realized her mistake. She wasn't supposed to be Melay.

This was Ilona.

The puppet of Kyran smiled, bending forward and kissing Ilona on the mouth.

Before she deceived me. Were Ilona and Kyran together? In love? She'd never heard this part of the history before, and neither Tamsyn nor Elf had ever said anything.

Rock grew over the crystal that lit the chamber, and Larkin was plummeted into darkness, but not for long. The stone was destroyed within moments, crumbling away from the crystal, and the room illuminated again.

A scene change.

Seven people were on their knees in front of the throne,

facing Larkin, their hands bound behind their backs. Kyran was in the center, handsome and brooding.

Larkin recognized Bianca Elesandre at Kyran's right side, but her skin was marred from war, and her hair was dark, draped in a braid over one shoulder. While she couldn't put names to faces for the others, she knew they were the remaining disciples: Leander, Monarc, Ekko, Pellager, and Ralic.

Larkin walked behind them, absorbing the moment the seven were brought before Ilona for sentencing.

"You've taken my men," said Ilona. "And you've destroyed my city."

"You will believe what you want to," said Kyran. "I've done nothing but attempt to protect my people from your injustices."

Ilona scoffed, pacing the floor in front of the seven. "Injustices! Is it injustice to protect the hearts and minds of vulnerable Demurans? You are finished pillaging emotion from my people, Otheil. You are finished using their pain and sadness to cause destruction within my hold."

"Don't hide your envy with false heroism, Leliana. I know the truth."

"The truth?" Ilona stopped in front of Kyran, lifting his chin with the tips of her fingers. "The truth is, when evil is defeated in my hold, it is banished."

Kyran's piercing eyes left the queen's and found Larkin's.

Larkin stumbled back, surprised, catching herself at the edge of the room. Again, darkness fell.

"Why are you showing me this?" Larkin's impatience echoed through the black chamber.

Kyran's smooth, deep voice answered. "I must show you the past in order for you to understand the present."

The light returned once more, and Ilona stood in front of her throne, her hands clasped in front of her, chin raised high.

From either side of the chamber, children began to flood the hall. They were dressed in the same kind of tunic and trousers that Larkin was given before the palace dinner, and they all wore a simple mineral collar around their necks.

Empaths.

As the children filed in, Vania entered the room from her right.

The sight brought Larkin to her knees, and her eyes burned. She knew this wasn't Vania, not really, but at the same time she couldn't help herself from holding out her arms to beckon her little sister forward.

Vania grinned and broke into a run. Larkin swung herself around to see Garran. Vania leapt into her brother's arms and began to weep.

Larkin pressed her hand to her heart. Kyran was playing toward her weakness. This wasn't a representation of the past. How could it be, with her brother and sister at the forefront of the scene?

With Vania in his arms, Garran turned and joined the other Empaths.

"My children." Ilona smiled sympathetically. "With so much evil outside the palace walls, I hope you will come to appreciate your new home in the palace. I will do my best to offer you the protection you deserve until this reign of terror ends."

Reign of terror . . . Was Ilona speaking of the Uprising?

The chamber plummeted to darkness once more, except this time, the light returned within a heartbeat, and it wasn't Ilona in front of the throne. Chestnut curls spilled over delicate shoulders, and upon the queen's youthful face, there was a malicious smile.

"Melay," breathed Larkin.

No, sang the chorus of heads within the chamber behind her. *Ilona.*

"No." This was impossible. It had been a thousand years.

Your doubt intrigues me, sang the chorus from behind her. *You see me in the flesh. And Bianca. Why would Ilona be any different?*

A cry escaped Larkin.

Melay hadn't stripped Empaths of their surnames. Melay hadn't broken families apart between the farms and the mines. Melay hadn't forced Larkin to traverse the depths of the Reach by holding her brother hostage.

Queen Karsyn Melay didn't exist. It had been Leliana Ilona all along.

"How can she still be alive? Ilona isn't an Empath," Larkin said. "She hates Empaths!"

And yet she uses them. She's used their magic to keep herself youthful. She used you to get to me. My own kin.

"Vania and Garran." Melay—no, Ilona—held her hand out as the crowd of children parted, and her brother and sister stepped forward, climbing the steps to the queen. The *goddess.*

A war between two powers that should have died centuries ago was still thriving because of immortality and magic. Magic that ran through Larkin's own veins.

And she wasn't just a bystander. She was at the center of it. Kyran's assassin.

Kyran's descendant.

"Both of you will play a great role in the war to come," said Ilona.

She doesn't want us. Only our power. And only if she can use it. We are but props to her.

Ilona bent down to the same height as Vania. She pressed her thin hands into Vania's face, cupping the girl's cheeks. "Your sister would be so proud of you."

"No!" shrieked Larkin.

And when she is finished with them . . .

Ilona yanked Vania's head to the right. A loud crack echoed within the chamber, and the girl slumped to the ground.

Larkin charged forward, siphoning to project destruction upon the goddess. She didn't care if this goddess was only a puppet—a figment. Larkin needed her to suffer.

The room went black. Kyran's searing rage returned.

Hands grabbed at Larkin—her neck, shoulders, waist—throwing her backward, pinning her arms behind her. The stench of rot and iron sank into her as the hands covered her mouth.

She couldn't breathe. Fingers clawed into her mouth and broke off in her hair. She gagged and swallowed her bile, searching for rage, fear, anything to destroy the animated death that tore at her.

Finally, the hands released her and she was spit back out into Kyran's lair. Larkin rolled onto her belly, lifted her body up with shaking arms, and vomited.

She gasped for air, wiping her mouth with the back of her

hand. When she glanced up, Amias was still unconscious, and Kyran was gone.

Again, the mouths of the chorus fell open.

She will wield us as weapons. She has already begun.

Ilona had oppressed Empaths for centuries because she was envious of their magic. She'd made Larkin's life a living hell through the illusion of her descendant, Queen Melay.

Kyran wouldn't be relaying any of this to her if he didn't have an agenda. There was something else he hadn't told her.

"What do you want?" she asked.

"Larkin, no." Amias coughed, spitting blood from his mouth. He was awake. Barely.

"Hold on, Amias," she whispered.

It is not what I want, it is what you need. Ask me, child. Ask me what you need.

Amias let out a scream.

"No," Larkin sobbed. She was supposed to be strong enough for this. For Garran. Kyran was supposed to die by her hand. But Ilona had her brother, and Kyran had Amias, and she was about to lose everything.

Look at me.

Larkin looked up and blinked through her tears. The curtain of death had parted, and Kyran—the young Kyran—stood in the center of his creation. He wore greaves made of bone, tendrils of flesh fused to his bare torso. Blood dripped down his chest. Again, he suppressed his agony. He must have been used to conjuring himself.

This time, he spoke to her directly. "Ask me what you need."

Larkin parted her chapped lips. "What do I need?"

"You need the boy to live." Kyran spoke softly. "And your family. That is all you need, isn't it? I've been following you, child. Listening to you. Sensing you."

A sob tore from her mouth. Yes, this was all she needed.

"Magic is supposed to strengthen over generations, but Ilona has taken this from us. I'm old, Larkin. And there are things about the mind and body that cannot be renewed with conjuration. But you have overcome much in a short time. You are capable of defeating the queen. I have even forged you a path right to her throne."

Kyran held out his hand, and bone dust crumbled from the ceiling and hovered before him, reshaping into a dagger.

"My death will make you the most powerful Empath on this isle," he said, handing her the dagger.

All this time, it had been her mission to kill him.

And Kyran had been waiting for her to complete it.

THIRTY-ONE

t was too simple.

You already sense the rage within yourself, she thought. *All that rage, waiting to break free.*

Kyran had been the most powerful Empath in Demura for centuries. Had he been evil all along, or had the power corrupted him? Would it corrupt her, too?

"What do you think will happen to Garran if you return to the Surface without my power?" Kyran asked when she hesitated. "Do you think the queen will release him? That she will release *you*? The moment you return, Ilona's luminite-gilded blade will be at your throat. Your mother will die. Vania will die. Garran . . . Perhaps she will keep him alive."

"Please," Larkin begged through gritted teeth.

"Ilona has a taste for the young and vulnerable. And with such power . . . what a weapon Garran could become. A replacement for Amias, perhaps."

"What does Amias have to do with this?"

"You can ask him yourself, when you heal him."

When she healed him. She would only have the power to heal Amias after Kyran died.

Larkin had no choice. It did not matter if Kyran's power corrupted her, or if she was brave enough to take on Ilona herself. If she did not do this, her brother and her family would die. Amias would bleed out in this very room.

Killing Kyran was exactly what she wanted, and yet she felt robbed of the victory. It wouldn't be by her hand. She wasn't in control.

"Let me see him, please," she pleaded. "Let me be with Amias."

Larkin stood, approaching the boy and the tangled mass that impaled him. She couldn't bear to look at his body, choosing instead to focus on his face.

She lifted his chin and wiped the crimson from his lips. His garnet eyes found her, vacant and bloodshot, a small glimmer of life left within them.

They had been so close to succeeding, but Ilona had deceived them—used them. She was as much of a poison to Demura as Kyran was.

Larkin's eyes fluttered shut as she sensed shards of glass slicing through her in a whirlwind, and gasped at the painful emotion.

It was Kyran.

She dug deeper, sifting through the glass, unearthing him, until the shards caught fire within her, turning molten like the rage she was all too familiar with. She understood.

He hated her.

No, he hated everything. Everyone. He did not want Ilona defeated for his people. He wanted Ilona dead because of what she had done to him. And all of the lives Kyran had consumed. The corpses and bodies he'd claimed as his own to breach the Surface. Casseem, Tamsyn, Brielle, Devon—Kyran hadn't thought twice about killing them.

This power—this rage—would consume her. What would happen to her? Would she be able to control herself? Power corrupted. Power transformed.

Larkin kissed Amias's forehead. She imagined a world where they escaped, families safe and well, living beyond the city's boundaries. A farm at the base of the eastern hills; summertime; warm breezes laced with pine; meadows of tall, dry grass rippling beautifully. She would walk through them barefoot, her hand caught in his. When he laughed, she would no longer find it surprising. She would have already memorized the sound of it.

He would feel nothing but bliss and peace, and just like his laughter, it would be expected, the sense of it like breath in her lungs.

She tucked the thought of it away in her heart, the only place such a life could ever exist.

Larkin didn't know what she expected Kyran to be like when she first entered the Reach. Part of her imagined a beautiful, young, and malicious version of himself, like Bianca. Another part of her thought she would find some terrible creature like the quartermaster.

Kyran was both. He was huge, and constantly consuming. Immortal, connected to so many bodies, yet utterly alone.

She approached Kyran, touching the smooth skin of his face. Blood rushed in rivers from the punctures in his body, though he didn't care, watching her with eager eyes. Her fingers drifted downward to ribs and muscle, and she pressed her palm to his heart, feeling the thrum of it as it pumped his blood—blood he shared with his monstrous creation. She could still hear it echo through the chamber. *Incredible.* After all this time. Just like with Bianca, she couldn't even imagine the kind of conjuration it took to keep his heart beating for a thousand years, his mind as sharp and capable of evil as it always had been.

And she would be the one to end it, but not with his blade. She would not make this easy on him.

Larkin siphoned and projected his rage, flesh and bone melting away as she sank her hand into his chest.

He screamed, his hate bolting through her as she wrapped her fingers around his heart. Blood spurted, the beat of the organ quaking through her palm.

She heard the squelch of a tendril near her ear. It lashed out, punching into the back of her neck, wrapping around her head.

His blinding rage was no longer just coursing through her body.

It was a part of her.

In his dying moments, Kyran had fused himself to her.

Not only himself. His creation.

She saw the Reach.

The Passage of the Damned, the languid river, the ocean menagerie. She saw Bianca's empty cavern and the coils of the labyrinth.

And then the unfamiliar. Rivers of molten metal and chambers filled with hot bubbling water, crawling with strange reptiles and glowing flowers. Underground cities of stone spires, stretching for miles. Honeycombed cliffs and chasms of fire. He was showing her the other sectors.

Then, he showed her the Surface: Demuran fields studded

with sinkholes, collapsed farms, and ruined caravans. The city in shambles, a pile of rubble on the mountain, the only standing structure: the peak of the palace.

Every emotion known to man poured into her: collisions of fire and ice, bright sparks and dark waters, roiling and raging and bursting through her.

Her body hitched as she released a scream she couldn't hear. The sensations were tearing her apart.

Destroy it.

She became a sieve, latching on to those emotions most dark: the roiling, the weight, the fire.

Siphoning, projecting. The world was only pain and an endless void.

THIRTY-TWO

Larkin's eyes blinked open to the cold light of crystals.

She lay on her back. All around her, dust drifted downward, catching in her eyelashes, coating her skin. It gathered on the ground in front of her, picking up and swirling back through the air when she released a breath.

Warmth swallowed her body, liquid filling her ears.

She sat up, pain tearing through her. By the dim light, she made out a figure slumped over in the blood.

She crawled to Amias. His body was lanced by the tendrils, his clothing crimson and sticking to his flesh. He was alive, but an empty shell, his breath hollow and fading.

She eased him onto his back. His eyes were glazed. She didn't know if he could see her, so she leaned over him, gently touching his face and taking his hand. His trembling, bloodstained fingers twitched as his agony resurfaced.

She needed to end his suffering. But there was no light from him. No joy, no tranquility. She had no way to mend him, not even with her new power.

Her new power . . . Kyran lived inside her.

His blood had always been hers. Deep down, had she known this? Had she wanted so desperately to be Bianca's because she had secretly known what dark potential ran in her veins?

"I can't save you." Tears of frustration spilled from her eyes.

Amias wasn't supposed to leave her like this. They'd done the impossible, killing Demura's god of the underworld. She should have been thinking of returning to Garran, and his release, of home. She'd entered the Reach wanting only her family's safety.

Amias was supposed to mean nothing to her.

"I told you I would bring you home," she whispered. "Don't make me break my promise."

Amias's eyelids fluttered, but his breathing continued to slow.

"We aren't finished." She touched his cheek, the pad of her thumb grazing his colorless lips. "We are supposed to survive this. I'm supposed to meet Skye, and your mother. My father will love you, and so will Vania. My mother will be suspicious of you." Something caught between a sob and laughter bubbled from her. "Garran will sense how much I think of you and never stop teasing me for it. And somehow—*somehow*—we will escape the queen. Live quietly in the hills. Bake like bread beneath the sun. You'll take me to see the ocean. And . . ."

Larkin shut her eyes, pain silencing her. *And someday I will love you.*

And at the very last, she felt something stir within him.

A spark.

Bright.

Furious.

Ribbon and rope were simple objects woven from thread and hemp. A sword was nothing more than honed iron. But this . . .

Amias's screams echoed off the cavern walls as she worked. His agony should have doused anything else he emitted, but she clawed through it, finding his bravery, the spark in darkness.

"You're going to live," she kept telling him, her voice soft. She had to make him believe that he would.

She could not fathom the time that had passed, nor how he stayed alive. The magic seemed impossible, against the rules of what she knew, but it was working. She knew to destroy the blood in him that pooled the wrong way. She knew which organs inside him needed mending, and how. She knew how to open his veins and fill them again.

She knew, she knew, she knew all of these things that she had never learned.

When his wounds were closed, she sagged with exhaustion. Larkin hauled Amias away from Kyran's tomb and to the edge of the room, where she collapsed with him in her arms.

One of her hands remained pressed to his chest, rising and falling with his breath.

It was the most beautiful thing she'd ever felt. Larkin let out a sob.

Amias's hand twitched against hers. "What did you do?" he asked hoarsely.

Larkin ran her finger across the little white scar near his lip. The crystal light caught in his garnet eyes. The color had returned to his cheeks.

"You don't have to worry." She wiped blood from his forehead. "You aren't Kyran's descendant. I am."

She watched his face and sensed his awe as her words resonated inside of him. "Larkin . . ."

"It's all right." She forced a smile. "It's just magic. I'm his."

He lifted his hand to tuck a curl behind her ear. "You're his descendant, but you aren't him."

Hearing the words from Amias gave Larkin strength. She pressed her cheek into his open palm. His skin was cold. Turning her head, Larkin breathed on his fingers, warming them.

"My mother will be suspicious of you too," Amias said.

Larkin grinned against his hand. Amias had heard her. No, he had done more than hear her. He'd fought to stay alive for her. For their future.

"Let's go home," she said.

THIRTY-THREE

As Larkin and Amias sat at the threshold of Kyran's throne room, Larkin studied their surroundings. "We're beneath the palace." Before her, the two crystal staircases wound upward. "He told me that he'd conjured a way for us to return to the Surface."

"Through Melay's palace?" Amias asked, groaning as he sat up. He was in pain. Too much pain.

Larkin nodded.

"She'll kill you." Amias's cold terror shattered though her, terror greater than when Kyran held him in his clutches, on the verge of death.

"What did she do to you?" Larkin whispered.

He clenched his jaw, shaking his head so gently it was almost a shiver.

"I won't let her hurt you," Larkin said. "I'll never let her hurt you again. But you have to trust me. The only way out is through Melay's palace."

Larkin had healed Amias to the best of her ability, but he was not well. With his arm around her shoulder, she dragged him upward, where she found a tunnel entrance to another set of stairs, the spiral steps lined with glowing crystals.

Kyran had made this passage for her. He'd granted her the

power to save Amias, and now she was doing what he wished of her.

First she was Ilona's pawn, and now she was Kyran's. Kyran was dead, and if she didn't kill Ilona too, Garran would still die. Maybe even the rest of her family.

Every fifty steps or so, Larkin would stop to let Amias rest. She was breathless herself, the air thinning as they climbed. But Amias was breathing much too hard.

Maybe she'd healed him wrong—missed an internal wound. She hadn't understood what she was doing when she was doing it, after all.

She couldn't let Amias sense her worry. "Everything will be all right when we get out of here." Larkin pulled her water skin off her belt and passed it to Amias. He sat up to drink, uneasy. In the light of the crystals, shadows sank into the hollows of his face.

"I need to tell you something about Melay." Amias wheezed as he spoke.

"Shh." Larkin ran her fingers through his hair. "You need to rest."

"It's important that you know before we reach the Surface. Before we face her." Amias shivered. "I wasn't just sitting in a hole in the ground for five years. You know that, right?"

"So the rumors weren't true?" Larkin asked with a small smile.

"I was only in confinement for a year." He chuckled and winced. "I suspect that if I had been living in a hole in the ground since I was twelve, I'd be even more reserved. Which is saying something. No, I had a room in the palace."

"You *did*?" All this time, everyone thought Amias had been executed.

"I rarely got to leave it, of course. Melay couldn't have anyone knowing that I was alive. She would visit me often though. Even have meals with me . . . just the two of us. She presented herself as a savior. She could teach me how to control myself, and maybe one day work for her."

"She wanted to use you." *Just like she is trying to use us now,* thought Larkin. "But how could she teach you? She's not an Empath."

"There are a few Empaths who secretly work for her," said Amias. "Melay hates Empaths, yes, but she's not an idiot. That's why she hasn't ordered all Empaths to be killed. She wants to keep the power alive to use the magic at her convenience. As long as it's under her terms."

"And what did she want to do with you?"

"She wanted me to hone my destruction."

"She wanted to make you into a weapon?" Larkin was unearthing so much darkness in him, breathtakingly silent darkness.

Amias's eyes glassed over.

"You don't have to tell me," Larkin said as she stroked his cheek, wishing there was a way she could make reliving this moment less painful for him.

"I need to tell you." Amias took a deep breath, pain etched into his face. "Because this secret is exhausting. It's poisoning me."

She stroked his hair again in encouragement, silently bracing herself.

"Melay wanted me to have the right tools to practice destruction. I needed emotion, and she provided it. She tortured people in front of me. The agony was both a threat and a fuel. Because if I didn't practice magic with their pain, it meant they had been hurt for nothing."

"*Gods*," Larkin whispered. How many innocent children like Amias had Ilona taken advantage of over a millennium?

"When I was younger, I'd cry after. She'd hold me like a mother. Wipe the tears from my face and tell me that I would understand someday, that this would only make me stronger. And I believed her for a long time. I did what she wanted, even. Performed her exercises. Destroyed."

Everything clicked into place: why Amias didn't want to destroy, why he panicked when they'd come across the tortured soldiers. The trill of fear Larkin sensed when she mentioned Melay. He wasn't stubborn, and he wasn't a rebel. He was simply trying to survive without spiraling down into the darkness of what the queen had done to him.

Ilona had taken advantage of a child. She'd nearly ruined him because of her greed. Anguish from the memories flooded him. She hated how he suffered.

"What changed?" she asked. "Why didn't you become her weapon?"

"My tutor," said Amias. "She told me more often than not that I had a choice. And I grew older and realized that she was right. So I began to refuse. Melay wasn't too happy, and the torturing became more frequent. Sometimes it was even people I knew. Empaths from my old farm. Every time the guards marched me down to the carving board, I expected to see my mother or sister pinned to it. That never happened."

"She needed to keep them alive for leverage," said Larkin.

"I taught myself how to remain calm in the midst of the worst emotions. If she couldn't threaten me by torturing others, she was powerless. And it worked. She finally grew tired and shoved me in a cell. I was certain I'd die there. I never expected this."

"To die in this hell instead?"

He snapped out of his daze, and his eyes found hers. "I'd rather die here with you than live without a single purpose, wasting away in the dark."

Here with you.

He relaxed, as though he'd found momentary peace. And she wished more than anything that she could let him relish it.

"Kyran told me something important, Amias," Larkin said hesitantly. "Something that terrifies me, something I don't understand yet. The queen—Karsyn Melay—she isn't who we think she is. Melay is Queen Ilona."

Larkin didn't sense any alarm from him.

"I'm not surprised," Amias said, breathing deeply. "I've been wondering about Melay myself since we met Bianca. I was in the palace for five years, and Melay—Ilona—didn't ever seem to fall ill or age."

"Who's been keeping her alive all this time? The Empaths in the palace?"

"Maybe." He bit on his lower lip, thinking. "My tutor knows more than I do." He managed something between a wince and a smile. "And luckily for us, she lives just above the palace dungeons."

Larkin hoped this was confirmation that they could enter the palace with an immediate ally. If Amias's tutor had coaxed him to reject Ilona's routine of torture and destruction magic, it meant she'd been working against Ilona for a while.

After Amias rested, they continued upward. Larkin dwelled on her task as they climbed. Killing Ilona seemed so much worse than killing Kyran. Kyran was evil. Ilona, on the other hand, was supposed to be a protector. The Goddess of Light. If Larkin succeeded, she'd change a thousand years of ingrained Demuran myth.

But was that her job?

The crystals began to dwindle until there were too few to light the way forward. Shadows were swallowed by darkness, and the ground leveled out. Larkin ran into a wall and, without thinking, siphoned Amias's agony to destroy it.

As the dust settled, Amias inhaled deeply. "I know where we are. Smell that?"

Larkin inhaled, the scent of blood all too familiar.

"If you walk along the wall, you'll find a sconce. Should be flint tucked behind it."

Larkin walked down the wall until her fingers brushed something cold and sharp. She reached around the sconce, finding the flint and a half-burnt torch. She lit it, illuminating the empty space.

"Where are we?" Her voice echoed.

"The palace catacombs, parallel with the prisons," said Amias. "You'll need to help me. I can barely move."

Larkin hurried to him, passing the torch. She tugged his arm over her shoulder, almost falling with his weight. *We're almost there*, she thought.

They passed stone tombs, some open, others sealed. To the right, the floor dipped into a giant pit.

"What's that?" she asked.

"Don't go over there," he gasped.

Larkin didn't question him further.

The place seemed uncared for, which she found strange. There was also no luminite. Things only grew stranger when they wove between the pyres and the torture racks. Now she understood where the scent of blood had come from, and why Amias was so familiar with this place.

This was where Ilona had brought him to practice destruction.

"Amias . . ."

"We're almost there. See that passage up ahead?"

Larkin squinted, spotting a small alcove that she would have walked right by if she hadn't known to look for it. When they reached it, Larkin groaned at the sight of more stairs.

"Leave me here." Amias pushed himself away from her. "It's a short flight. When you reach a trapdoor, knock four times rapidly. Pause only for a moment, and then do it again."

She could see the sheen of sweat on his forehead. He was falling apart faster than he could hold himself together.

"Are you sure we can trust her?"

"Please, Larkin," he grunted. "Just go."

Larkin left him, hurrying up the short flight of steps to an aged trapdoor. She took a deep breath, quickly knocked four times, paused a moment, and then knocked again.

She waited.

Larkin tried the door, but it was locked. Amias was wrong. Her stomach clenched in panic. Both of them were a mess, and surely by this point the queen knew Kyran was dead. Maybe the palace would be mostly vacated, all of the soldiers at the Reach's entrance, waiting for them to return.

Larkin jumped at the sound of a loud thud above her. The trapdoor swung upward, and she squeezed her eyes shut.

The light. *The pain.*

She tried to peel her eyelids open, but they refused to cooperate. She stood up straight, wobbling on the step and scrambling for the door's frame for support. Larkin blinked rapidly, hoping for her vision to adjust, but she only saw shapes.

Then the sharp edge of a blade grazed her throat.

THIRTY-FOUR

Who in hells are you?" a woman asked, her voice discordant. "And where did you come from?"

Larkin winced as tears poured from her eyes. "Please . . ."

"Hela!" Amias cried from below.

"Amias?" the woman cried. "Gods!"

Larkin felt the blade disappear and she blinked frantically as her vision came back in patches. She followed the woman—Hela—back down into the darkness and, with her help, was able to haul Amias up and into the palace.

"Cover your eyes," Larkin whispered to him as they entered the room.

"Have you been below all this time?" Footsteps sounded as the woman hurried across the room. Larkin heard the glide of chained curtains, and darkness fell across her eyelids. She blinked a few times—better, but not perfect. The blurred figure of the woman was hunched over a basin, squeezing out a cloth. She knelt next to Larkin.

"I can't believe you survived the Reach." Gently, the woman began cleaning Larkin's face. The water was warm and felt sublime. She would have cried if she wasn't weeping already.

"You know where we were?" Larkin focused on the dark eyes of the woman, and the splatter of freckles along her cheekbones. "Hela?"

Hela retreated back to the basin. "The queen maliciously told me where she sent Amias. Her way of toying with me."

She returned and knelt near Amias, but when Larkin reached for the cloth, Hela smiled and offered it to her.

Larkin gently lifted Amias's head and placed it on her lap. She passed the cloth over his face, wiping away the smears of blood. So much blood, not all of it his.

When she was finished, he remained still, watching her. His eyes were so tired, and she sensed the strangest mix of anguish and relief from him.

"We must be quiet. *Silent*," Hela emphasized, standing to bar the door. "Now, how did you get from the Reach to here?"

Larkin exchanged a glance with Amias. Where was she supposed to start? "The Reach is beneath the palace."

Hela frowned. "That can't be . . ."

"The Reach is everywhere," said Larkin. "Kyran had conjured his own throne room right beneath Melay's."

Hela's shoulders sagged. "Of course he did."

The tutor's reaction felt strange to Larkin. "Did you believe he was a god? Because he isn't."

Hela was quick to respond. "I believe that Kyran was the most powerful Empath to ever live." The corners of Hela's mouth perked up as she watched Larkin carefully. "And I'm not naïve to the powers of magic."

"What is happening, Hela?" Amias croaked.

Hela laughed, surprising Larkin. "Do you mean the state of this damned isle, or your chances of surviving the queen's wrath?"

"The queen knows that Kyran is dead, doesn't she?" Larkin asked.

Hela nodded. "She sent four battalions into the Reach to find you. Or any of you who were left. Are you the only two survivors?"

"Yes," said Larkin.

"And you're not Jacque, so you must be . . . Brielle? Elfina?"

"Larkin."

Hela paled, her disbelief striking Larkin.

"You know," Larkin said, suddenly unable to meet Hela's eyes. "You know I'm his."

"You knew all along, Hela?" Amias asked quietly. Larkin sensed something heavy stir within him. "Who we were?"

"Don't look so betrayed." Hela swiped the dirty cloth from Larkin's hand. "I didn't tell you because I was trying to protect you. A failed strategy, I know, but my intentions were good, I promise you." Hela watched Larkin carefully. "If he's dead, you're in a very dangerous place, Larkin."

"What of my brother, Garran?" Larkin asked. "Do you know where he is?"

"No," Hela said. "I don't know where Melay is holding him. But she's holding your entire family." She looked to Amias. "And yours."

Amias's dread roiled in Larkin, and Larkin felt her blood run hot. "I'll kill her."

Hela arched an eyebrow. "You do not mince words. You're lucky I am not aligned with the queen." The tutor glanced at the curtained window. "It may be best most of your family is locked within the prison. Safest. The remaining soldiers have been taking to the streets as of late. Many Empaths have died. I worry that Melay has decided she will no longer have mercy on any Empaths, now that Kyran has destroyed most of what she holds dear."

"I need to help them! I'm the only one who can." Kyran's powers ran through her veins, begging to be used.

"I agree," said Hela. "And I will keep you safe as we come up with a plan. Together."

Larkin knew that she and Amias needed all the help they could get, but Hela worked for Ilona. Amias trusted her because Hela had taught him and had been kind to him. Still, Larkin wasn't convinced of her desire to keep them safe.

"You have every right to be skeptical," said Hela, sensing her. "I will prove to you that you can trust me. But first, you must be starving." She walked to the door, simultaneously placing a finger to her lips. "Don't make a sound."

Hela brought back a sack of fruit, a loaf of bread, and a rind of cheese. Larkin ate ravenously, and Amias more slowly.

"I will heal," he promised Larkin. "You're trying to hide it, but I can sense your worry."

"How did you . . ." Larkin glanced up at the luminite molding around the room and then back at Amias.

He shot her a sheepish grin. "When Tamsyn mentioned your resistance, I didn't want to steal your glory. And I prefer to keep things close to the chest. But there was a reason Melay kept me in luminite chains in a dungeon by myself."

"You should have said something!" she cried, thinking of the disciples. "You must be Leander's descendant. He was trying to find luminite's weakness . . . Perhaps he taught it to Kyran."

Hela chuckled as she bit into an apple. "Leander? Of course not. Thaos Leander was a fool. He was in search of an alchemical remedy to luminite, not a magical one." The tutor smiled gently. "Amias is Rahele Ekko's."

Larkin thought of what Tamsyn had told them. "Rahele was the disciple aligned with Ilona, wasn't she?"

"She was," Hela said. "Ilona chose her because of her skills, and her caution. She was thoughtful with her power."

Something darkened within Amias. Larkin wondered if it was because Ilona had used him and his ancestor.

"I will tell you more about Ekko later," said Hela, scooting to the edge of her bed. "But for now, I must understand what happened within the Reach. How did you survive?"

Amias opened his mouth.

"Amias," Larkin said, cutting him off. Hela could turn around and tell Ilona everything.

"It's all right, Larkin." Amias turned to Hela and told their story. When he explained what had happened to Bianca, Hela was devastated. She was disturbed by what Kyran had done to the soldiers, and himself, but wasn't surprised.

"He let you kill him because he wants you to kill the queen?"

"Because he wants me to kill Ilona," said Larkin.

Hela visibly stiffened. She knew the truth about Melay, then.

"So you've helped keep her alive," said Amias, hurt. "Even after what she did to me?"

Larkin sensed Hela's shame. The tutor reached out and touched Amias's arm. "Many of us have, over the years. I'm sorry, Amias—truly—but Ilona forced me into a position that would have cost me the lives of my family if I had said no. You must understand, the war between Kyran and Ilona has been a fine balance for a thousand years. I have spent my life terrified of what Kyran would do if Ilona died."

"Kyran's dead now," Larkin said bitterly. "And Ilona . . ."

"Is still alive." Hela sighed. "Which is why this opportunity to overpower her is so important. I swear to you I will keep you both as safe as possible until it is time to do so." Hela stood. "Hide in the catacombs. I will have the servants pour me a bath while my room is vacant, and then you can wash up."

They did as she said. When the bath was poured, Amias let Larkin go first.

She pulled the curtain around the tub and began to undress. The only armor she had left was one bracer, which she peeled off. At last, she sank into the warm water. She worked feverishly to scrub off the grime and blood from the Reach. It was caked in her hair, beneath her fingernails, threatening to mark her forever.

Eventually she was clean enough, and Hela brought her a simple linen tunic and trousers to change into. "I conjured these from memory, so I do hope they fit. If not, I suppose you have the skill to fix them yourself." Hela glanced up at the room's luminite molding, and then said, "I must attend to the queen, but I will be back tonight. Remember what I said about silence." She then left them alone.

As Amias bathed, Larkin changed into the conjured clothes.

She studied her hands, calloused and cracked and bloodied. Even though she'd worked in the mines her entire life, she did not recognize these hands. These were worn hands.

A beam of light caught on her clothes. She followed it to the slit between the curtains.

The *sun*.

Larkin walked to the window and peeled back the curtain, blinded, the sun as hot as she remembered it. The light bathed her, drying the water from her hair, burning off the last droplets from her skin. She smelled the resin of pine, pungent and sugar-sweet.

Hela's window faced not the city, but the western edge of the isle. Larkin spotted the ribbon of blue ocean along the horizon. She lifted her hand, pointing one finger. So close, she could almost touch it.

What would happen to her if Ilona was overpowered? Would her family travel to a farm near the sea? Would she have the choice to never spend another moment in a mine again? There would be no edicts, no rules. She could have a surname, if she wanted one. Most of her lineage was burned up with the registry, but Larkin could create her own. Something that sounded nothing like *Kyran*.

And perhaps after Amias was reunited with his mother and Skye, would he come with her?

She heard him pull back the curtain, and turned around. He stood behind her wearing only his trousers, water speckling his chest.

The sight of him stunned her. Dark marks marred his body from where Kyran had punctured him, scars from the moment she thought she would lose him. Her eyes landed on one peeking out from over his hip bone, and she flushed.

Amias watched her with curiosity, and she knew that he was trying to sense her emotions. But what was she feeling, exactly? Her heart was racing, and her stomach had twisted itself into a knot.

She wasn't sure what the emotion was, but she liked the way she felt, and what she was beginning to sense from him. She wanted more of it.

The flecks of water on his shoulders glinted in the light, reminding her of the crystals that had guided them so often in the Reach. For the first time, the memory didn't bring her dread, or sadness, but hope.

Bianca had been wrong. There was light in this world. Larkin had found it in the darkest places, where she thought there could be none at all.

"I need to tell you something," Amias said as she stepped toward him. "Melay—Ilona—came to me before we were sent to the Reach. She told me that if I kept an eye on the group, and made sure we didn't stray, she would let me go free."

Larkin stopped, glancing up. Water trickled down the curve of his cheek, and she fought the urge to kiss it off his face.

Instead, she whispered, "So you're the spy."

His lip twitched, and she sensed his relief. Was he expecting that she would be mad at him? "It's not like you had a choice. None of us did. Not when she threatened our families."

"I didn't tell you because I wasn't ready to talk about Melay, or about the hold she had over me. The way she broke me."

"You don't have to explain." Larkin reached out and gently ran her finger down his chest. His breath hitched, and she sensed the same strange emotion she had sensed when they were in the Reach—a spark dissolving into a whirlpool.

She could name it now: desire. And she wasn't ready for it to leave her.

She held her breath as he dipped his head, his lips against her neck, teeth grazing her skin. Her body was flint against a blade. A shower of sparks when his lips found her jaw. Again, when they were against her own.

Larkin soaked up every warm, bright tendril he emitted, his light filling her with an understanding of what this was. More than parted lips and slick skin. More than her own desire and beating heart at the top of the world.

They broke away from each other, breathing heavily.

What if they left? What if she could find Garran and free him without Ilona ever finding out, and they escaped, leaving her to her damned city, her damned isle? They could gather their families and find safe passage to the mainland. A place where she knew no one and no one knew her. A place where they could start over.

Amias kissed her again, drawing her back to the moment. It was a fantasy, but this—this kiss, and everything she sensed pouring from him . . .

This was real.

"Is this all right?" he asked against her lips.

"*Please, gods,*" she breathed.

He gently tugged at the waistband of her trousers and dragged his calloused thumb along her stomach. His desire escalated into something brighter, faster, something strong enough to coax a moan from Larkin.

It wasn't her own ecstasy that threatened her control. It was his, and she wanted nothing more than to drown in it.

They spent the evening tangled between borrowed blankets. As Amias bent over Larkin, she touched him, memorizing the places that sparked the deepest desire as he kissed her shoulders, her collarbone, the space between the cleft of her ribs. The tips of her fingers and toes hummed with the brightness that poured from him, and the sensation of his lips against her skin.

She'd be damned if this was the last time she sensed Amias like this. As luxurious as this felt, Larkin knew that she needed him.

Over the next few days, Larkin and Amias anxiously waited in Hela's room as the tutor brought them food and news of the outside.

"You can't battle Ilona's armies by yourself, Larkin," Amias said as he paced the floor, wincing slightly as he walked.

Larkin sat on the edge of Hela's bed as the tutor pored over maps of the city at the room's small table.

"I can," said Larkin. "I just haven't before."

Hela looked up from her map. "Fighting an army single-handedly isn't something to attempt lightly. You'll need to kill. Are you comfortable with that?"

Larkin held the tutor's stare. "If it means saving the remaining Empaths in the city, then yes. I have no other choice."

Hela's gaze hardened. "Just be mindful that you don't grow too comfortable with the idea."

"If you're trying to imply that I won't be able to control the magic Kyran passed down to me . . ."

"Killing a person changes you, Larkin." Amias ceased his pacing, his hands clenched into fists. "It doesn't matter what side of the battle they're on."

Larkin stood, raking her fingers through her hair. "I can't just keep waiting, not when Ilona has my family." She thought. "What about Jacque's battalion? You heard what Jacque said, how they were prone to rebel. Maybe they'll help us."

"Do you know which battalion?" asked Hela.

"I know they're stationed at Seaside Port," said Larkin, remembering the sea of tortured soldiers, and the woman who spoke to her. *Gods*, she wished she could forget the moment.

"There are many battalions stationed there. Do you know the lieutenant's name?"

Larkin didn't. She knew nothing of Jacque's battalion other than the fact that Jacque was second in rank.

"I'll try to find out more about her battalion, but you need to lie low." Hela rolled up the maps. "If Ilona finds out that you are alive, your family will be in even greater danger."

Larkin cried out in frustration.

Hela flinched as a vase near her bed shattered, then glared at Larkin as Larkin unclenched her hand. "That was expensive."

"So make a new one, Empath," Larkin said sourly.

"Breaking things won't suddenly make Hela wrong." Amias chastised, as though she were a stubborn child fishing for attention.

She wasn't fishing for attention, but she sure as hells was stubborn.

That night, as she lay on the floor next to Amias, Larkin thought of the ability of destruction she'd acquired from Kyran. Other than saving Amias, she'd hardly tapped into the magic, but she didn't feel differently than she had before Kyran had died.

She was the one who wanted to fight Ilona and her armies, not Kyran. She was certain of it.

Hela reentered her room at the break of dawn, waking them.

"I have news," she said gravely, dropping a second sack of food at her feet.

Larkin shot up, rubbing the sleep from her eyes.

"Queen Melay—Ilona—is rounding up the remainder of their soldiers. They are up to something, and I'm deeply worried for the remaining Empaths on this isle."

"You think she's going to kill all of us?" Larkin asked, horrified. Amias sat up next to her, alert.

"Her power has been threatened, Larkin. The city is desecrated, and her army has been greatly weakened. The dynasty may not withstand another riot. We have no other option than to act now."

Larkin and Amias exchanged glances. To hells with a plan. They needed to get to the streets and warn the canyon.

"But that isn't all," said Hela. "You told me that your entire party died. Why did you lie?"

"What are you saying?" Larkin's heart leapt into a frenzy. "I watched them die, one by one."

"Are you sure about that? The queen's battalions just returned to the Surface, two girls in tow. They're believed to be the only survivors."

Larkin felt hope flare in her chest. Jacque and Elf . . . They were alive.

told you." Amias stood from their nest of blankets, his excitement fluttering across Larkin's skin.

"You said she'd conjured wings, did you not?" Hela asked.

She had been so quick to disregard Elf's wings, so scared to hope.

"I didn't think she could use them," Larkin said.

"You doubt our magic," said Hela. "I don't blame you. You've been stripped of what you are actually capable of." She studied Larkin closely. "Well, not anymore."

"Where are they?" asked Larkin. "What's going to happen to them?"

"The queen received word from a messenger only moments ago," said Hela. "I was with her. I came right here."

"So they are bringing them back to the palace?" Larkin's heart beat heavy in her chest.

"Yes, to be imprisoned and interrogated," said Hela grimly. "And then likely executed."

Of course. Larkin should have expected this. "We shouldn't have waited to do something."

"You will not act rationally with such anger," said Hela. "You are going to end up getting Jacque and Elf killed if you allow rage to lead you."

"*I'm* going to kill them?" she cried. "Ilona's armies are

organizing as we speak. I should have warned the canyon the second we resurfaced!"

Hela matched her fury. "Be quiet!"

Larkin siphoned the tutor's fiery anger, holding it like a breath. Her fingers flexed in anticipation. Hela shielded her face, and Amias winced.

They were both expecting this from her—this loss of control.

Larkin forced herself to relax, her fury losing charge and fizzling out. "When will they be here?"

"Likely after dark." Hela swept across the room and barred her door. "We have a few hours to devise a plan. *If* you can control your temper."

"Who has them?"

"Hathius."

Hells. Larkin dreaded the thought of seeing Melay's lieutenant again. "I'll meet them in the stables."

She waited for Amias to argue with her. To tell her that he was coming along.

But instead, he said, "You'll be able to use magic in places I can't. My resistance to luminite is weak in comparison to yours, now." He smiled sadly at her. "Hathius won't expect it."

She returned his smile. "I hope you're right."

Hela was silent as she thought. "You will need something to distract Hathius and the soldiers. The queen's alchemist has been creating small explosives to stanch the riots. I can set one off close to the palace."

"And I'll distract Ilona," said Amias.

"What?" Larkin stared at him. He couldn't be serious.

"Amias . . . ," Hela said quietly.

"Imagine what would happen if I arrived in the throne room. I would be the loyal spy returning to my commander. She'll want to know everything: how I managed to escape the Reach, how I entered the palace . . . how I destroyed the rest of you." Amias leveled his gaze at Larkin. "It will distract her long enough for you to save Jacque and Elf, at the very least."

"Absolutely not," said Larkin. "I've sensed how you fear the queen. I can't let you do this."

"It's not your choice," Amias told her. "It's mine."

Larkin hated that Hela was with them. She wished she could speak to Amias alone. "I promised you . . ."

"I know what you promised." He brushed her hand with his knuckles. "I'm not holding you to it."

He was trying to remain strong, forcing his unyielding calm to the surface. But Larkin knew better, and what she'd soaked up from Kyran was only aiding her. This emotion was different from anything she'd felt from him before. Cold and crushing, but painfully slow.

"She will hurt you." Larkin's voice shook. "After everything we've been through."

"Larkin is right. If she suspects anything, she will take you to the catacombs, Amias." Hela's dread was so heavy that Larkin could barely breathe beneath it. "Ilona will keep you there until she gleans from you everything she wants to hear."

"I know." Amias reached out, and his tutor took his hand.

"I don't know if I can bear to witness it, Amias."

"Why would she take him to the catacombs?" Larkin asked.

"It is surrounded by a reef of luminite," said Hela. "Magic can be performed within, but Amias won't be able to escape."

"She'll torture you!" cried Larkin, rising to her feet.

"Just as she's done before. And I've survived, Larkin. Every time." Amias stood, gathering her in his arms. Larkin clenched the back of his shirt, burying her face in his shoulder. She could do nothing to stop him from making this decision. If Ilona was distracted, her family would have a greater chance at living. She needed to believe that.

Amias kissed her forehead. "Get them back, Larkin. Get them back, or all of this will be for nothing."

Larkin pressed herself to the outdoor wall of the palace. She tilted her head up to examine her handiwork: twenty barely noticeable hand- and footholds made from destroyed bricks leading from Hela's window to the ground.

With the cover of twilight, Larkin crept between the wall and the mountain scrub. The stables were just down the hill, if she remembered correctly. She hadn't spotted any guards around the outside of the palace, yet. Then again, Queen Melay was running desperately low on guards.

Ilona, amended Larkin. There was no Melay. Larkin still struggled to accept it.

The isle had been beneath the same queen's rule for a thousand years. If Larkin and Amias didn't stop her, she would rule for another thousand.

Amias.

Had he entered the throne room yet? Knelt before the queen, surrendering himself to her?

Move faster, damn you, she thought, hurrying forward, ducking behind a luminite statue. She slid down the hill behind the stables, and then pressed her back to the stone structure and held her breath, listening and hearing nothing.

According to Hela, Hathius was due to arrive tonight, but what if the information Hela received was inaccurate? What if Jacque and Elf had already been escorted into the palace? No, she wouldn't think like that. Amias's sacrifice couldn't be for nothing.

Larkin looked around, spotting wooden barrels at the far end of the wall. She climbed between them, sinking until she was pinned between barrel and stone. The sky darkened to the periwinkle of Bianca's cavern, and then to a deeper blue. Finally, onyx.

She spotted only one person, a stable boy lighting torches along the walls and the nearby path that led to the palace's gates.

Hooves sounded from down the hill. Soldiers.

Larkin scrambled from her hiding place, scooting along the wall until she could peer around the corner. She counted twenty soldiers on their horses, Hathius among them. *Hells.*

Hela had said she would set off an explosive as a distraction. Larkin hoped that as soon as it went off, most of the soldiers would race off to investigate.

She listened intently, but instead of a loud *pop* or a crackle of sparks, the ground vibrated, reminding her of Casseem's cave-in.

Avalanche.

"What in Ilona's name!" Hathius roared.

One of the watchtowers at the city gates had crumbled. *Hela.* She'd used magic. She remembered Casseem telling her of the secret spots in the city out of reach of the luminite. Had Hela known about those places?

Larkin marveled at the kind of power she would have to possess to destroy something so large.

"You! Go figure out what in hells that was," Hathius snarled. "The rest of you, stay with me. Something's afoot."

Larkin swore beneath her breath as the single soldier took off toward the crumbling tower, leaving most of the soldiers still pacing in front of the stables.

Elf was close enough that Larkin could hear her whimper. *"Please."*

Larkin sensed her anguish; they had hurt her already.

"You're lucky the queen wants a word with you, or I'd kill you here myself," said Hathius.

Larkin was out of time. If Hathius wanted blood, she would give it to him. She stepped around the wall and into the clearing.

Larkin spotted Jacque and Elf before they saw her, Hathius himself holding the ends of their luminite shackles. The other soldiers were scattered across the clearing, unpacking from the ride, and she counted sixteen of them. Larkin sensed their alarm and confusion as they drew their swords.

Elf squeaked her name before Jacque clapped a shackled hand over her mouth.

"What are you doing?" hissed Jacque.

Larkin slowly approached. "I don't want to hurt you, Hathius."

She expected Hathius to laugh, but instead, he stared at her stone-faced, and she sensed a trill of nervousness. Larkin dared to look away from Hathius to find Jacque and Elf once more. They were covered in grime and blood, Elf's tunic bright red and plastered to her skin. *They cut off her wings.* No wonder she was in so much pain.

Hathius flung an arm out at his guards, ordering them to stay back.

Larkin continued forward. "Let my friends go, and tell your queen they escaped."

"The moment she finds out you are here, your brother will die," Hathius declared, his smile contrasting sharply with the emotions he emitted. "If he isn't dead already."

"Larkin!" Elf screamed.

From the corner of her eye, Larkin saw three soldiers running forward, swords raised. Within a breath, she siphoned and projected Elf's terror. Their swords disintegrated. One screamed and fell to his knees, clutching the spurting stump of his wrist. She'd taken his hand.

Larkin's fingers trembled at her sides as the remaining soldiers faltered. She'd terrified them.

"Seize her!" Hathius screamed.

Five more soldiers lunged toward her. This time, Larkin siphoned more deeply. The soldiers collapsed, screaming.

The wounds would heal. Eventually.

Her pulse thrummed in her ears as the remaining soldiers ran, abandoning their lieutenant. Hathius did not retreat. He grabbed Jacque by the hair and hauled her to him.

"I don't want to kill you, Hathius," Larkin said. And it was true. As much as she knew he deserved to die, she'd already spilled blood, the injured soldiers groaning as they crawled away.

Hathius grinned wildly and whipped out a dagger, making to slide it across Jacque's throat, but Larkin was quicker.

She crushed his head, his body falling forward limply onto Jacque. The soldier gave a yelp and leapt out of the way, sending Hathius's corpse tumbling to the ground.

Blood. It pooled around the fence posts the way it had the legs of the quartermaster's table. For a moment, panic seized Larkin before she turned to her friends, who stared at her in awe and horror.

She pointed to the stable. "In." They had little time before Ilona was notified of their presence.

Elf and Jacque quickly complied, entering the barn doors, where the three embraced at once.

"I thought you were dead," Larkin cried into Elf's hair.

"We almost died." Jacque pulled away. "Especially me. But Elf—"

"I flew, Larkin." Even exhausted, Elf's grin was bright. "Well, glided."

"Flew, glided . . . you saved our hides." Jacque lifted her tunic to show Larkin the starburst scar that marked her abdomen. "She fixed me up right too. Destroyed that thing coming out of me."

Elf frowned. "Ignore the scar. I was panicking. I'll fix it."

Jacque studied the mark before dropping her tunic. "I kind of like it."

Larkin quickly sensed the air for anyone approaching before whispering, "How did you get caught?"

"After we fell to the bottom of the chasm, we couldn't return to you," said Jacque. "The drop was long and there was no easy way up. But there was a passage beneath the river, one that looked"—she shared a glance with Elf—"well traveled."

"I think we passed into another disciple's sector," Elf said excitedly.

"Did you see anyone?" Larkin asked, remembering the vast landscapes of the Reach that Kyran had shown her.

Elf shook her head. "Luckily, no. If I remember Tamsyn's map correctly, we were on the outskirts of Brendis Pellager's territory."

The disciple who liked to kill for fun. "Thank gods for that."

"We hiked upward and crossed into the river," said Jacque. "We'd made it to Bianca's cavern when we were captured."

The soldiers had entered the Reach to seek them out. Ilona wasn't going to risk them getting away.

Jacque watched her carefully, and Larkin wondered if she was trying to read her emotions. "It's true, then. You killed Kyran. How in hells did *you* get back to the Surface without getting caught?"

Larkin quickly told them everything, leaving both Elf and Jacque in shock when Larkin relayed Melay's true identity.

"And you're obviously Kyran's." Jacque gazed out past the barn doors at the carnage Larkin had wrought.

"We'll discuss it later," said Larkin quickly, still shaken by what she'd done. "But, Jacque, I need to talk to you about your battalion lieutenant. If you found her, could she be convinced to fight alongside the Empaths?" She explained the situation with Ilona and Amias, and the planned slaughter.

"I don't know. I may have squelched any hope of her uprising when I refused to join them." Jacque frowned, the dread heavy in her heart. "They're stationed at a private outpost a few miles north of the city. I may be able to reach them before they're ordered to the capital." She scratched the back of her neck. "If they're still alive."

"I know you can convince them," said Larkin. "For Amias, and for Risa. Ilona has them both."

Jacque steeled herself. "I guess I can no longer pray to Ilona for sweet mercy, now, can I?"

"If we have the advantage, I can begin leading the Empaths to safety before any violence breaks out," Elf said. "But I'll need time to get them out."

"Good thinking," Larkin said.

"We'll need your help, Larkin," said Jacque. "Melay—Ilona—has lost a lot of soldiers, but there are still more than my battalion will be able to conquer."

Larkin thought of Garran. Her family. *The moment she finds out you are here, your brother will die.*

"I'll be the distraction," said Larkin. "I'll try to keep as many soldiers off both of your backs."

Jacque's eyes glittered. "I'm glad you're all right. You and Amias."

"Me too," Larkin said. She could be thankful she and Amias were still breathing, but it wasn't enough.

She wanted to storm the palace. She wanted to save their loved ones *now*—all of them. And yet she couldn't.

Larkin remembered Amias's words from when they were back in Bianca's village: *Everyone dies, Larkin. Not just your brother, but every single person on the Surface.*

She couldn't be selfish, not anymore. Not when so much was at stake.

THIRTY-SIX

Larkin watched the dusky sky turn pale lilac from her hiding place, tucked inside a cliffside crevice beyond the palace's outer gates.

She surveyed the city and the people within: the shops that opened, who left their homes to go to work, how many guards were patrolling around the rubble. The numbers were dismal. The path to the mines and the market square were both barren, and she caught sight of only one patrol. Surely Ilona knew by now that Larkin was in the capital, so what was she waiting for?

Maybe she doesn't have the numbers, thought Larkin. Even if that was true, she had to prepare for the worst possibility. She couldn't enter the canyon early; Elf was still trying to get Empaths out, and Larkin's presence would cause a disturbance. She had to be patient. It was the only way to save as many lives as possible.

The city was in shambles. Kyran had done more than wage a war against Demura. He'd won. Not a building she saw was standing whole. Even the gentry homes were missing walls and roofs.

Every second she waited was one that Amias spent with Ilona. *I'll . . . distract her long enough for you to save Jacque and Elf,* he had told her. And then what? Would he assume the role of her pet?

Or would Ilona kill him?

She swallowed and pushed away her anxiety. If she fell to her emotions now, Ilona would win.

Larkin heard the hooves above her, their vibrations rolling through her body. The palace guards were descending. She squinted to focus on the fields surrounding the city. Hordes of soldiers tore through the plains beyond the gates.

The attack on the canyon was beginning.

Larkin looked to the north and saw nothing. If Jacque couldn't find her battalion, or if they didn't feel obliged to rise up, then Larkin would have to fight this battle alone, to the very end. Even if Larkin left now, the soldiers would reach the canyon before she would. Every moment she waited, more would die.

She needed to move.

She brushed the dirt from the baggy trousers and tunic that Hela had conjured for her. They made her look like a little girl. She felt like one.

Larkin crawled down the side of the mountain, jumping from the cliffside and landing in the nearest alleyway. She'd never been allowed to enter it before given its closeness to the gentry's homes, now dilapidated and vacated. Where did they go? Perhaps they paid their way off the isle, smuggled in a vessel. Or perhaps they were all dead.

Most of those still trapped in the city were Empaths. She needed to hurry.

She tore out of the alley, running through a maze of houses and shops and counting the breaths she took. As she neared one hundred, she approached the vacant market square and caught sight of a shopkeeper cowering near the window of his shop.

No, *the* shopkeeper. The one she'd stolen from on her birthday.

Larkin drew closer and stopped to catch her breath, meeting the shopkeeper's eyes. There was no pinprick of recognition. She'd been consumed with hate for him, and yet he'd forgotten about her.

He pulled the curtain shut, and she turned away.

As Larkin descended into the canyon, the first plume of black smoke marred the sky. She'd smelled burning bodies the night after the riot. This smoke didn't carry the stench of charred flesh, not yet.

Down the slope of the ravine, barrels rolled down the street, alight with flame. The chaos was supposed to be a distraction.

Terror was rampant, easy to siphon. Larkin curled her fingers into a fist and took a deep breath. She picked up the scent of sulfur and the tang of blood. Death. There were too many doors kicked open, too many Empaths being dragged into the streets.

She was scouring the smoke and chaos for Elf when two guards spotted her, one of them charging toward Larkin. A flick of her fingers, and the woman's greaves melted. The soldier released a piercing wail and collapsed, her agony squeezing the air from Larkin's lungs.

But she needed it, the agony sustenance to her power. She splayed her fingers again, and the other soldier grabbed at his face as the flesh began to peel back.

Larkin left him behind, the echo of his scream haunting her. She descended, covering her nose and mouth with her hand. Smoke stung her eyes.

Elf was still nowhere to be found. Now was the time to be a distraction.

Groups of soldiers had finally taken notice of her. They poured from the buildings they were raiding, releasing any Empaths from their grasp as they charged toward her. Larkin siphoned and destroyed, disarming them—hurting them—their pain so intense that she could hardly think straight.

A horn sounded. She knew that noise, because she'd heard it before, during the riot. A battle call.

Soldiers flooded the streets, rushing toward her with bright, shining blades. Blades of luminite, Larkin realized. They were so naïve.

She crushed a jaw, a shoulder. *It's their fault,* Larkin chanted to herself. *Their fault, their fault.* If they weren't attacking her, she wouldn't have to hurt them.

The remaining soldiers retreated toward the palace. Another battle horn sounded, one she was unfamiliar with, more somber. Perhaps a cry to pull back.

Larkin licked her lips and tasted blood. It ran dark and thick through the cracks in the cobblestones.

Look away.

She ran deeper into the canyon. Smudged Empath faces stared out from windows, watching her. She sensed their terror. They were afraid. Of her.

A man left his home, stalking toward her with a miner's axe raised above his head.

"I'm protecting you!" Larkin shouted. "Stop!" Her eyes darted to the open shutters behind him, and the children peering at her. A little boy covered his eyes.

The man swung at her. Larkin siphoned, shattering the weapon. Stunned, the man glanced up, as if to make sure the luminite cables were still in place. He ran at her with his fists.

"I don't want to hurt you!" she cried. When he got too close, she broke his hand. He screamed, dropping to his knees. The children at the window began to cry.

"Hells, why don't you listen?" she yelled, running toward the Empath. She hurriedly tore a strip of fabric from her tunic and began to bind his hand as he stared at her, anguished and confused.

Larkin muttered an apology and took off deeper into the canyon, leaving her guilt behind. She passed Adina's home, the door flung open and the stoop smeared with blood. Larkin thought of Kyran's creations in the Reach, the bodies laced together on the floor of the cavern, flayed.

She couldn't stop. If panic brought her to a halt, she would never be able to continue.

The heavy crunch of iron greaves sounded behind her, and a high-pitched shriek ripped through the air. More soldiers had arrived. They were entering the canyon in waves.

Empath families careened past her, their children in tow, their terror feeding her. *Run,* she wanted to scream, but it was too difficult to form words as the dark emotions twisted through her body.

Kyran had made a life from this. He reveled in it. She felt it too, igniting her insides, the power radiating from her until she couldn't contain it. She spotted a soldier up ahead and crushed his arm when he raised his weapon. Larkin stumbled, catching herself on a near stoop. She forced her eyes shut, hacking from the fire.

Kyran was consuming her.

Her ears rang. She opened her eyes, realizing that she'd reached the bottom of the canyon, and the crevice of the exit that led toward the capital's southern gate. The area was vacant except for a girl who knelt in the center of the street, her face buried in her hands.

The power inside her ebbed, and she remembered the reason she was here. Not to inflict pain. Not to punish. If she allowed wrath to drive her, she'd be no better than Ilona or Kyran.

Larkin stood, walking toward the girl. "You have to get out of here," Larkin said as she reached for her shoulder, noticing the blood seeping through her tunic. The two gashes at her back.

Larkin dropped to her knees before her. "Elf."

"I started from the back," Elf said. "I was lucky at first; the southern gate was unguarded. Maybe seven or eight families made it to the hills, but I ran out of time. Look at the dead, Larkin." Her eyes were glassy and distant. "All of the ones I let down," she sobbed. "I deserve to die alongside them."

Larkin thought of the Empaths, the soldiers. Thousands upon thousands of lives. This type of destruction could not be undone. Not by any magic.

Larkin held her. "We didn't cause this death, but we can stop more from happening. You can't give up."

"What do I do?" whispered Elf.

Larkin pulled away from her. "What you've done ever since you grew wings."

Elf wiped her face with the back of her hand.

"You are the reason Jacque is alive. You are the reason there will be survivors today." Larkin pressed a kiss to Elf's cheek and helped her stand. "There are others hiding in their homes. Lead them out of here. This isn't over."

Larkin sensed the swirling embers of Elf's courage. They carried the heat of rage, the tremor of fear, the levity of hope. Elf's eyes hardened with determination.

"Keep the soldiers off my back," Elf yelled, hurrying into one of the nearby homes.

Larkin leapt up and turned back toward the canyon's mouth, racing up the slope when she heard another horn. Another battle call. But this one was different. Brighter, somehow.

Another battalion spilled into the canyon.

Not just any battalion. It was Jacque's.

THIRTY-SEVEN

L arkin skated along the edge of the canyon, back to the palace. Chaos still pulsed through the ravine, yet a breeze blew through the walls, the scent of pine cutting through the stench.

Jacque rode up to Larkin with her sword drawn, blood splashed over her new armor. Members of her battalion spilled around her and into the canyon. "Go!" she cried. "We'll take it from here."

Larkin nodded and ran up the hill, forming a plan as she reached the market district. She would make her way down into the prisons, destroy the brick and mortar of the cell walls, and release everyone from prison.

After I find them.

She shielded her eyes against the sun and squinted. The palace's first gate was left unguarded, but beyond, Larkin saw the glimmer of luminite armor near the portcullis. She would have to sneak back through Hela's room.

Larkin veered off the path. She crept to the stables, winding her way back through the mountain scrub and around the palace. She made to sneak around a stone courtyard, noticing the strange mounds of clothing that littered the ground between the granite.

Bodies, she realized blankly. Bodies in the queen's courtyard. They were positioned the same distance apart, faceup. Their clothes and hair were filthy, but the rot in the air wasn't overpowering. She hadn't passed them on her way to the stables. They'd died and been positioned like this recently.

A trap? she wondered. Did Ilona know she would come this way? Was she about to be ambushed?

She studied them, a numbing chill washing over her when her eyes rested on the corpse in the center of the courtyard. A boy.

Her mind was making a mistake. The ghost of Kyran lingered inside her, making her question her decision to save the Empaths in the canyon.

She should have stayed in the palace, where Ilona was. With her family.

Her brother.

Just leave it. Ilona still has Garran.

In a trance, Larkin stepped into the courtyard and walked toward the dead boy. He was the same build as Garran—the same height—but the boy's face was bruised and swollen by death. His nose was too big, his mouth too small. It wasn't him, it wasn't him, it wasn't him.

Why couldn't she walk away?

She thought of the body of her mother at the quartermaster's table. This boy was another conjuration made to look like Garran. This was a trick, a planted corpse to make her suffer.

Larkin smeared the tears from her eyes and knelt.

The real Garran had a scar on his arm from his mining accident.

She slowly rolled up his tattered sleeve, her thumb grazing a raised white line.

Darkness clouded her vision. She'd killed Kyran. She'd escaped the Reach. She'd done everything to get back to her family.

I fought for you.

I killed for you.

I came home to free you.

She threw herself over Garran's body, shaking uncontrollably. A thousand screams were lodged inside her. A thousand sobs. And yet they stayed put, festering, destroying her from the inside out.

She'd kept her promise to him. She'd told him that she would fix this. She'd crawled through the bowels of hell to *fix this*.

Garran wasn't allowed to die.

A breeze tossed Larkin's hair. From somewhere nearby, a wren sang. She used to hear them from the canyon, early in the morning . . .

What are we going to do, Larkin? When the morning comes, and we're too miserable to leave our beds.

What are we going to do?

Tell me. Promise me.

"I'm going to get up," she promised.

Vania is still alive. She heard the perfect tenor of her brother's voice as clearly as if he'd spoken. *Mum and Dad. They will die without you. She will kill them all.*

Get up.

Get up.

GET UP.

Larkin pulled herself from Garran's body. She kissed his forehead and folded his hands across his chest.

She would come back for him. Her mother, her father, Vania—they would all get to say goodbye. But Garran was right.

"You were always right," she whispered.

Larkin needed to get up. She had work to do.

THIRTY-EIGHT

L arkin snuck around the palace walls until she found the footholds leading to Hela's room. Grasping one after another, Larkin yanked herself up, tumbling into the room before she'd realized she'd climbed all the way to the window.

The bedroom was empty. Larkin spotted a shiny luminite panel on the floor that covered the passage to the catacombs. The lock mechanisms were unlatched.

Hela had left it open for her.

Larkin felt grief tug at her, threatening to chain her to this room. But if she collapsed—if she took the time to mourn for Garran—she'd be doing exactly what Ilona wanted. The *goddess* had already stolen too much from her.

Her family needed her. Amias needed her. Garran would want her to keep going.

Larkin dragged the panel from the trapdoor, slowly lifting it and slipping under the lip. She sat on the stairs, listening to the muffled voices below. They were close.

Larkin crept downward and into the nearest chamber. The sconces were alight with fire, and she saw the flicker of movement beyond.

The pit. She and Amias had passed it when they were making their way up from the Reach, but Amias had purposefully avoided it. She moved silently between the tombs as her heart thudded violently.

She stole her way to the edge of the balcony, terrified by what she was about to find.

For Garran, she thought.

Two staircases wrapped downward and into the pit below. Ilona stood at the center of the open room, her dress reflecting the torch light. Her scaled luminite gown flared out at the waist and spilled across the ground behind her.

Larkin flexed her hand, gritting her teeth. If she got closer, she'd be able to focus her aim on Ilona's bare neck.

Larkin scanned the rest of the pit. Hela was at Ilona's right side. Amias knelt before them, unbound.

He had succeeded in proving his loyalty. Just as they had planned. Yet to see Amias in front of the queen as he was, subservient and meek, made her want to scream. Larkin clenched her teeth, tasting bile.

She counted only five guards at the front of the chamber, blocking a barred door that must lead to the prisons. The rest of Ilona's soldiers must be defending the palace and fighting in the canyon.

Larkin hadn't been spotted. She still had the upper hand.

"We didn't return to the Surface together." Amias's voice echoed in an otherwise silent room. "As I said, we were all separated. I thought I was the only one alive."

"I want to believe you."

Larkin's stomach rolled at the cloying sound of Ilona's voice.

"After all I've done for you, I want nothing more than to believe you would never betray me, Amias." Ilona approached him and knelt, reaching out to caress Amias's cheek.

Blood bloomed in Larkin's hands as her fingernails sank into her palms. She felt Kyran's power stir inside her. *Let me out,* it seemed to beg her. *Let me out. Let me kill her.*

Ilona continued. "But with Kyran's kin alive and murdering my soldiers, I have my doubts."

"My queen . . ." Amias was more terrified than Larkin had ever sensed him before.

Use his fear.

"You've been so receptive to my methods, Amias."

KILL HER.

Larkin realized she'd already siphoned Amias's fear without thinking. She didn't know if she could kill Ilona from where she stood, or if she'd accidentally hurt someone else. Hela, or Amias.

She couldn't let Kyran's power rule her choices.

As the magic inside her waned, Ilona's soldiers parted, one opening the door to the prisons. A lieutenant emerged, dragging a girl with a wild mane of dark curls.

Larkin's blood ran cold, her heart thudding in panic. *No!*

Ilona glided to the back of the room, settling into a plain makeshift throne.

Amias couldn't hurt Ilona or any of the guards dressed in luminite, but there wasn't enough in the room to douse his ability to sense completely, not if he was resistant. When Larkin realized what was about to take place, she clapped a hand over her mouth, stifling her scream.

The lieutenant stopped before Amias, holding Vania tightly.

"Looks just like her, doesn't she? It would be a shame if something were to happen to Larkin's only living sibling, all because you didn't want to tell me the truth." Ilona cocked her head and thought for a moment. "I suppose something will happen to her regardless, or you wouldn't think me serious, now would you?" The queen's teeth flashed. "Cut off one of her fingers."

Over my dead, bloody body, thought Larkin.

She had to think quick. If she tried to use magic from up here, she'd be slower. Vania or Amias could die when Ilona realized she was here. If she jumped from the balcony, she might hurt herself, but she could kill the majority of those in the room before any of them knew what had happened.

"I told you I know nothing!" cried Amias.

Vania shrieked and twisted in the guard's grasp.

Larkin rushed to the edge of the balcony, ready to dive over. Ilona glanced up at Larkin, her grin victorious. "So predictable. Hela, now."

Larkin had been lured here.

Before she could think to move, Hela locked eyes with Larkin.

Traitor, thought Larkin. Hela had been in line with Ilona all this time.

The tutor's eyes left Larkin, falling on Amias. "I'm so sorry, Amias."

Hela raised her hand, flexed her fingers over her heart, and clenched her fist.

Fabric, flesh, and bone dissolved, and for a moment, Hela's heart was exposed, emitting its last few frantic, quivering beats before she collapsed.

"No!" Amias cried, diving toward Hela and scooping her body into his arms.

Ilona's horror and rage tore through Larkin as Larkin faltered, dazed. Had Hela believed this was the only way out of Ilona's control?

A victory horn echoed faintly through the layers of stone and luminite.

"The rebels, my queen!" cried a soldier.

The rebel battalion's footsteps were thunder as they stormed the bridge, even from deep within the catacombs. They were alive, and strong in number. Jacque had won.

"Kill them," Ilona ordered the lieutenant, seething, before fleeing toward the guards.

Larkin jumped from the balcony, landing on the stone below. Her leg popped, and she screamed in pain before launching herself at the lieutenant. She crushed his windpipe, leaving him gasping and wheezing on the floor. Vania backed away, terrified.

Larkin limped forward, collapsing as Vania fell into her arms. "You're all right." She held her sister as the child clung to her, sobbing into Larkin's hair.

Larkin glanced up. Ilona and her guards were no longer in the room.

Neither was Amias.

Move, she ordered herself. If she didn't move, something terrible was going to happen.

Holding Vania's hand, Larkin limped to the open prison door and pushed through the passageway, blades of fire shooting through her leg. She'd broken it—she was certain—but she had to find Amias.

A long tunnel stretched before her, lined with the same barred doors. Cellblocks. The bodies of the five soldiers littered the stretch of tunnel. Larkin bit back her pain and limped past them, clutching Vania's hand tighter.

Heat licked through her, tortuous, charring her bones. The rage was so unlike him, she was certain it couldn't be Amias's. It felt like Kyran's.

BOOM.

The ground shook, rock dust trickling from the ceiling. Larkin entered the next room to an array of hairline cracks decorating the walls. The pillars that once supported the ceiling were nothing but mounds of dust.

Amias.

Up ahead, two people were on the ground, one hovering over the other. Larkin pushed Vania behind her as the figures before her sharpened in the dim light.

Amias held Ilona to the floor by her throat. The queen clawed at his hand, his wrist marred and bloody, but his grip remained tight.

Not even a luminite dress could save Ilona now.

"Why?" cried Amias.

"Because you are hers, and Rahele loved you like a fool!"

Amias jolted back, his shock mingling with Larkin's.

Rahele Ekko—Kyran's disciple, and Amias's ancestor. Larkin's mind raced, trying to understand how Rahele had been in the palace all this time.

She was supposed to be in the Reach. *Hela.*

"She never went in." Ilona struggled against Amias's grip, coughing. "She pledged allegiance . . . remained in the palace. How do you think I've stayed alive all this time?"

Hela—Rahele—had lied after all. She'd said that many

Empaths had kept Leliana Ilona alive all of these years, but there had been only one. That's why Ilona never killed her. She needed the disciple, a woman who'd been honing magic for a millennium. Rahele's skill was valuable if the queen could use it for herself. Hells, it had saved her from a thousand years of darkness.

"You could take her place," the queen wheezed. Her hands left Amias's wrist. "You could be my right hand, Amias, as you were raised to become."

Amias flexed his hands, and Ilona screamed as the skin on her forehead split, blood pouring down her face.

"How about I leave you to bleed all over the floor instead?"

Larkin said his name softly.

Amias shut his eyes. His guilt leaked into her, his pain growing deeper and more subtle as he suppressed it. Even after every horrible thing Ilona had done, Larkin couldn't imagine Amias torturing her to death. If he did, he would leave this room a different person. He would be burdened by guilt for the rest of his life.

Larkin herself could handle such a burden, but she didn't want Amias to suffer too.

Ilona's widened eyes darted to Larkin, and her faced twisted in fury. "Her?" The queen tore her attention from Larkin and back to Amias with a snarl. "I have cared for you for years, Amias. I have given you everything you need to be the most powerful Empath in this realm."

Ilona's chest heaved, her breathing ragged. Ilona thought that Amias wanted power. All those years, and she didn't know him at all.

No, thought Larkin. Ilona only *hoped* Amias wanted power.

A last desperate hope that Amias would be her new Otheil. If Amias was the realm's most powerful Empath, and she had controlled him before, she could do it again.

"Rahele died for you." The words left Ilona in a hiss. "I have sacrificed . . ."

Amias dug his thumbs into the hollow of her throat. Ilona's voice faded as she writhed for breath.

Larkin felt Vania tremble behind her, her sister pressing her face beneath Larkin's shoulder blades. The back of Larkin's tunic was soaked in tears.

"Amias." His name left her lips boldly this time, demanding his attention.

Amias complied, his expression painted with anguish and hatred. She knew those feelings intimately.

From inside herself, Larkin summoned tranquility. The same tranquility she sensed so often from Amias. The calm that had grounded her in the Reach. His calm.

Amias showed her that this emotion was possible, even in the darkest moments. And she would remind him.

"She doesn't deserve this, Amias, and you know that," said Larkin.

It wasn't only that Ilona deserved a punishment worse than death. She also didn't deserve Amias's rage, and Larkin wouldn't let her claim what innocence Amias had left.

Ilona's reign would end, and with its ending, Amias would find peace. Larkin would make sure of it.

THIRTY-NINE

Most of Jacque's battalion had survived, but the soldiers fighting for the queen were not as fortunate.

Death stained the capital, the mountain swallowed by smoke. It would take the rest of summer to know how many Empaths were left alive, and maybe even longer. But there *was* life. Demura had survived both Kyran and Ilona.

Larkin wanted to see her parents, to collapse in her mother's arms. She wanted to help her father bury Garran in the vale. Somewhere beautiful. Somewhere he'd never had the chance to see.

But Larkin couldn't stay to witness the rebels releasing Ilona's prisoners from their cells. She still had a job to do.

Through the night, a few members of the rebel battalion escorted Larkin, the remainder of her party, and Ilona across the vale. Moonlight caught on the ruins of many of the farms they passed, but it was peaceful. The destruction had finally ceased. Rebuilding could begin.

At dawn, they arrived at the mouth of the Reach. The jaws of the portcullis were wide open.

Leliana Ilona had pieced together well enough how this was going to end. Holding her head high, she walked herself into the Reach and waited until the portcullis lowered behind her before turning back toward Larkin.

The queen was dressed simply, no longer wearing her luminite gown. Larkin made sure Ilona would have no defenses against the remaining four disciples who waited to greet her. If she survived long enough to meet them.

Wrapping her delicate hands around the bars, the queen smiled at Larkin as she approached. It was the closest Larkin had ever been to the queen, even closer than when Ilona had visited Larkin's cellblock. Maybe she was imagining it, but the queen looked so much older now, her body frail, her skin thinner than parchment.

She was mortal.

"You can't sense me now, can you?" Ilona glanced up at the shimmering luminite surrounding them. "But isn't that what you wanted all along? To sense me suffer?"

Ilona was right—the luminite was too thick for Larkin to sense her. But Larkin didn't need to sense to see the way Ilona's fingers trembled around the bars, or hear the inflection in her voice.

And her eyes—the terror in her eyes was what truly gave her away.

"You killed my brother." It was the first time Larkin had said the words out loud. She'd been forced to fight away her grief until now. Now her grief had returned, and she wouldn't combat it.

Garran lived through her grief. It was the only way he would ever visit her again.

"And you destroyed my army," Ilona said coolly. "Decisions are costly, Larkin."

Indeed they were, and Larkin was wondering if she was making the right one now. Maybe she should have let Amias kill Ilona. Maybe Larkin should have killed the queen herself.

But Ilona didn't deserve such an easy escape.

"If you make it back to the palace, you can keep your life," said Larkin. "You will likely come across many of Kyran's creations. There's even one who's made in your image."

Ilona's smile fell.

"Think the other disciples will be partial to befriending you, after you exiled them for a dozen lifetimes?" Larkin asked, then turned to go.

"You can't leave me defenseless." The demand left Ilona as a growl. "I gave you weapons!"

"You want a weapon?" Larkin gave the queen a cloying smile. "You sent me to kill Kyran for you. I *was* your weapon. You'll fight this one alone."

Beyond the outpost and remaining soldiers, Vania picked flowers in the meadow. A breeze whipped her dark hair into a tangled mass.

Suddenly, Larkin wasn't angry.

Jacque's lieutenant approached Larkin. Strands of the lieutenant's gray hair were coming undone in the wind. She was the same age as Larkin's mother, but her eagerness was youthful. "We need to talk." Wary, she asked, "Are you planning to seize the city as your own?"

Seize the city? Larkin couldn't begin to fathom what the lieutenant was asking her. "I don't want to rule." She wouldn't dare tempt herself, not when she knew what the darkness inside her was capable of. She wouldn't want people to follow her out of fear. "I'll leave that to you," said Larkin. "Choose a ruler, or take the throne for yourself. I won't interfere, as long as Empaths stay free."

The lieutenant's smile was hesitant. She held out her hand, and Larkin took it.

Larkin understood why the lieutenant didn't trust her, after everything. One battle couldn't undo a thousand years of distrust. Mending her relationships with those who did not share her magic would take time. And Larkin would have to be patient.

Larkin pulled away from the lieutenant and limped toward her sister. Larkin expected a grin, the same way Vania smiled when Larkin and Garran came home from the mines, sprinting to Larkin and jumping into her arms. But things were different now.

Vania waited, cautiously watching Larkin approach. She held her tiny bouquet of wildflowers in both hands. Her cheeks were stained red, but they were dry. She was perfect and beautiful and yet somehow looked much older than when Larkin had left.

Vania held the flowers out, and Larkin felt her composure uncoil. Larkin reached her little sister and fell to her knees, gathering Vania in her arms.

Larkin felt brave, and terrified, and relieved. She felt like collapsing in grief. For a fleeting moment, she even felt like laughing, as if there was no other way to release the emotion trapped inside her. She felt everything, an amalgamation, brimming over until Larkin worried she'd frighten or overwhelm her little sister. Especially when Larkin began to weep.

Vania wrapped her arms tightly around Larkin's neck. "I love you too."

EPILOGUE: AUTUMN

Within the farm's small and cramped forge, Jacque and Risa melted gold together, creating their rings.

They both wore white, with yellow flowers tumbling through their loose hair. Sunlight clung to Risa's golden hair as she and Jacque poured the liquid metal into the casts.

Larkin caught Amias's eye as he stood between Skye and his mother. The corner of his mouth twitched as he withheld a smile from her. A smile she craved.

Her mother's elbow jutted into her ribs. "Don't embarrass me," she murmured. Her father coughed to mask his laughter.

A few wandering eyes were staring at her, amused. Skye covered her mouth to hide her giggle, and Larkin flushed. This whole *desire* thing was much too new to her. She was almost beginning to miss the damned luminite.

At least she wasn't the only teenager in the village struggling to keep her emotions in check. She decided to avoid Amias's eyes for the remainder of the ceremony.

Larkin studied the other guests. Casseem's older brother, Teneil, whispered something into Risa's brother's ear, flirting. On the other side of the forge, Elf stood with her troupe, passing an azure handkerchief down the line of Jacque's sniffling sisters, until it reached Jacque's father, who wiped his eyes.

Elf winked at Larkin, and she grinned back.

When the rings were doused in water and cooled, the girls' faces glistened with sweat from the flame. Risa leaned in and kissed Jacque, both of them alight with joy, like an endless glitter of stars on the clearest night. Infinite. Hopeful.

The audience began to sing the hymn of bonding.

They were married. Not everything was lost, after all, and the fate of their love was in their hands alone.

So is mine, Larkin thought. She knew this was true, and yet it was still so hard to believe. They were free. All of them.

Jacque's commanding lieutenant was temporarily reigning over the demolished capital. The Empaths who had survived had conjured this village at the end of their world. Larkin was given the honor of naming it.

Aerie Farm. A nest in the sky. That's what it felt like.

She'd told the lieutenant that if she chose to toss the city's supply of luminite into the ocean, the Empaths would return to help her rebuild. Although she thanked Larkin for the proposal, Larkin knew it would never happen. The lieutenant respected Larkin, and had so far honored her agreement with the Empaths, but she did not trust them. Perhaps she never would.

She couldn't worry about that now. The capital was not hers.

But Aerie. She would fight to the death for this village, and those within it. And that was all that mattered. As long as the lieutenant, or whoever else came to power, left them alone, they could live peacefully for many years.

While villagers mingled around the forge and helped conjure tables for the celebration, Larkin approached Elf, who was dressed in a tunic of brightly colored fabrics and a traveler's cloak.

She beamed as Larkin approached.

"Leaving tonight?" Larkin asked.

"Yes, tonight. Just wanted to stay for the wedding and all."

Elf backed up, spreading her arms to show off the pattern of feathers on the inside of her cloak. "Conjured it myself. How do I look?"

"Lovely, but I miss your wings."

Larkin had only meant it as a joke, but Elf grew serious. "Yes, yes. Perhaps my wings will make a return. They are useful in these open skies, after all. But first, I need to uncover the mainlanders' feelings about Empaths."

"What if they outlawed magic ages ago, just like we did?" Larkin knew so little of the mainland, after all. "Will you come home?"

It was hard to imagine Elf and her troupe sailing to the mainland and all of its harbored mysteries. Larkin felt like a large hand was squeezing her heart.

Elf scratched her chin. "No, I believe we need to tell the mainland about us. They deserve to know."

Larkin nodded. She knew that sharing the tale with others granted Elf power over their story, their narrative. The truth had been buried beneath myth for so long.

Elf embraced Larkin. "I will miss you."

"And I will tell my children the story of your wings," said Larkin.

She sensed Elf's joy, and knew she'd granted the girl the only gift that mattered.

The ocean was the biggest thing she'd ever seen. It made the caverns that snaked beneath the isle seem minuscule.

From somewhere deep within her, Kyran spoke.

You can own it all, he told her. *Every land, any people you come across. It is yours.*

Is that what Kyran had hoped for? That she would hunger to seize the world?

Is that what had happened to him?

There was one thing that perhaps Kyran hadn't planned for. Larkin was stronger than he was.

Her feet sank into the wet sand as briny waves beckoned her outward. She found delight in the fact that she could pull herself back if she wanted.

But she didn't. Not now. She wanted nothing but sea spray and the crust of sunset melting into the horizon.

And Amias.

She sensed his hesitance long before he reached her, encouraging him by holding out her hand. He finally took it, standing next to her in the water.

"I hated watching you limp across the beach," Amias said. "Will you ever mend it?"

The breeze brushed across her smile. "It humbles me. Reminds me I'm mortal." She squeezed his hand. "Maybe when Elf returns from her tour, I'll let her mend it. She's a better healer, after all."

Amias said nothing in return, only watched the waves alongside her. Perhaps he knew that words pooled inside her, ones she so rarely spoke, afraid of her parents' grief.

"Garran would have loved this," said Larkin.

"It is hard not to love it."

He was right. She did love the ocean. The vastness of it. The possibility. It reminded her of Amias.

She pulled her feet from the sand and turned to face him. His cheeks were bitten red by the wind, dark eyes glinting with sunset-gold.

Larkin never thought she'd see the ocean. And she never thought she'd have the freedom to love someone like this. And that's what this was—love. It had culminated over the heat of summer, as they sweated in the fields together beneath the sun. As they washed off the sweat with ocean salt. As she grew to care for Skye and Amias's mother like she cared for her own family. It was love.

And Larkin was ready to feel it now.

ACKNOWLEDGMENTS

I have learned more about being an artist in the three years I worked on *Eight Will Fall* than in the eighteen years of writing that came before. This book has been a test of my resilience, and I'm so grateful that I didn't have to make the journey alone.

To Kathleen Rushall, the First of Her Name, Queen of Badassery, Agent Extraordinaire, Wielder of Negotiations, and Fierce Protector of Sanity: I am beyond privileged to be your client. Thank you dearly for these past seven years.

Levente Szabo and Katie Klimowicz, thank you for making *Eight Will Fall* absolutely stunning to look at. Thanks to Ilana Worrell, Jie Yang, Cynthia Lliguichuzhca, and the rest of the Holt team for your dedication to this project. To Tiff Liao, thank you so much for helping me mine Larkin's deepest desires and make her shine in the darkest parts of the Reach.

Thanks to Hayley Wagreich, Joelle Hobeika, Josh Bank, Sara Shandler, Les Morgenstein, and Romy Golan at Alloy Entertainment for giving me the opportunity to create this story.

To Kristin Briana Otts and Christine Autrand Mitchell, thank you for the notes, the coffee dates, and most importantly, your friendships when I needed them most.

Melanie Kramer, Rachael Allen, Dawn Miller, Janine Clayson, Shari Lambert, and all my LitBitches, thank you for the page reads, brainstorming help, and support along this wild decade-long journey we've shared together.

To my parents, Heidi and Mike, my siblings, Carli and Stefan, my grandparents, Shirley, Walter, Wendy, Nancy, and Armen, along with my wonderfully supportive extended family: thank you for your love, and for cultivating safe places where I could grow to become a dreamer and a storyteller.

Leah, thank you for the car rides of our late teens and all the writing that soon followed. I wouldn't be where I am if I hadn't finished that first manuscript by your side.

Thanks to the Fresno State MFA community for being so supportive of this alumna, even though she writes young adult horror. Your enthusiasm is refreshing and I am so grateful for it.

To all my friends who have supported and encouraged me over the years online, in group texts, and in pubs over too much whiskey, you know who you are. You have listened, made me laugh, inspired me, and defined who I am. Thank you for all of it.

Thomas Bergersen and Steve Jablonsky, thank you for creating the music that shapes my stories, and to the five Bs of gaming: Bethesda, Bioware, Black Isle, Blizzard, and Bungie, for developing and publishing the dungeons and worlds that inspired the Reach.

Thanks to all the early readers, bloggers, and Instagrammers who have taken the time to express their excitement for *Eight Will Fall*. Your posts and messages have made the past few months a joy.

And finally, to the boy who diligently read the terrible chapters I posted on my Myspace blog all those years ago, the man I fell in love with, who has held me as I cried after every hard rejection, read every bad draft, and believed in me when I couldn't believe in myself. Jesse, you are the reason why I have never given up. I love you.